LEARNING LOVE

By

Al James

To Barbara and Mushtaq,
Best wishes from
Al

RB
Rossendale Books

"We must love one another or die."

W.H. Auden
1st September 1939

Published by Rossendale Books
11 Mowgrain View, Bacup,
Rossendale, Lancashire
OL13 8EJ
England

Published in paperback 2012
Category: Fiction

ISBN : 978-1-291-17580-6

Dedication

To Jan, my wife and inspiration, who always encourages me and has taught me how to love.

Acknowledgements

The many scenes and characters in this novel inevitably derive from my experiences through life, but with one exception have been created entirely in my imagination. The exception is the scene at Auschwitz-Birkenau. The museum there exists as a permanent memorial to man's inhumanity to man. Much of what happens in that scene derives from my personal experiences during three visits there over the past decade. On 3rd September 1943 the fifth division of the eighth army crossed the Straits of Messina to Reggio Calabria in what is known as Operation Baytown. Tom's experience in chapter 3 is based on various accounts of the landing, but is otherwise entirely fictitious. Patrick offers his own interpretation of Harry Harlow's experiments in chapter 32, but the experiments really did take place during the 1950s and 1960s.

My wife Jan's encouragement also extended to reading the manuscript twice, to many valuable suggestions which would improve the novel, and to proof reading. Vincent Walsh at Rossendale Books has been patient in guiding me through the publishing process and I am more than grateful for that.

1

"Don't touch!" said the voice in his head. Little drops of water were falling out of the sky all around him, making his face wet. He wiped it with his hand and looked at the strange shaped object stretching out of the ground. 'Don't touch Marco!' said the voice again. Familiar all his life that voice, the woman's voice he loved. And yet, there was the temptation. He loved the feel of things, loved to feel them as well as look at them, stroke them gently in his hands to understand them. Just looking didn't make enough sense. And yet, mama, who he loved more than anyone, told him always not to touch.

The sunlight filtered through the trees onto the muddy patch of ground where he was standing, staring down at the strange hand shaped thing reaching out of the ground, inviting him to touch. Was it trying to touch him? Desperately he wanted just to reach out his hand to touch, just gently. He stretched out his right forefinger.

The touch was electric current. It threw him backwards onto the damp ground behind him. Was that his voice shouting out? There was another voice in his head now, telling him 'run, run away from this scary place, run home!' He picked up his large round body, turned and ran through the squelchy mud as fast as his legs could manage, struggling back up the slope and out of the steep river valley. By the time he reached the top and found the narrow street that led back to the town he was panting hard and breathless.

But the strange thing sticking out of the ground wouldn't leave his brain. He kept seeing it everywhere he went and the following morning he was drawn back down the steep slope, half running, half falling forwards, squinting against the slanting September sun. It had rained more heavily in the night, as it had through the late summer, heavier than usual for the time of year and when he got there, the little stream at the bottom of the valley was flowing faster. But the hand was in the ground beside the stream. He didn't have to get his feet wet to stand and gaze at it. He wasn't going to touch it again. Not after the last time, but he couldn't help looking at the strange object, and he didn't know why. Inside him was a new need. He wanted to tell. '*Mano*,' he tried to say over and again.

Mama, was what she heard repeatedly and out of context, and mama, mystified, went to see Father Leonardo. Young, and not long out of seminary, Leo had taken it on himself to 'take Marco in hand' as it were and had told Signora that he would help out where he could. She was after all more than eighty and now she really did need his help. So he found himself following Marco on one of his rambling walks through the narrow streets to the edge of the small town of Sottomonte.

It didn't take long for him to reach the row of three seats overlooking the sea below, and Leo expected him to rest there a moment, not least as a result of his age. But to his surprise, Marco didn't stop and sit and didn't turn back. Instead, in the heat of the overcast afternoon, he staggered over the point where the paved area ended and began scrambling down the steep side as if he was heading for the sea sparkling in the distance beyond. Leo looked down at the valley running parallel to the rough downward path Marco was taking, and realised that he was making his way towards the stream which drained the Aspromonte way above and beyond them. 'Must have rained a lot up there,' he thought to himself, gesturing mentally up to the mountains. In winter it could be full, foaming its way down the valley below to become a fierce river winding and twisting its way to the sea. By the end of summer it almost always dried up. Except this year he knew it would still be at least trickling along its bed.

"Marco, take care!" he called out, his desire for Marco's safety replacing his need to conceal himself. At first he didn't think he'd been heard as the shape of Marco below him continued scrambling down for a few more metres, unable to stop himself quickly. Then coming gradually to a halt, he turned and looked to find the source of the voice in the figure of the slim young priest standing above him. Surprised, he waved before turning and continuing down the last few metres to what was obviously occupying him.

"*Mama,*" he seemed to say again, several times, and obviously wanted to show him what was so absorbing his attention. The priest looked down, seeing at first only the muddy and eroded bank above the stream. But Marco was clearly not satisfied with his response. He looked more closely, until suddenly he spotted it. Astonished, Leo could see not *mama* but *mano*. Stretched out of the damp ground, still connected to whatever was in the soil beneath it, was what looked like part of a hand. He recoiled, instinctively crossing himself, before looking again. But there was no mistaking it. In the embankment in front of him were at least three skeletal fingers and the thumb of a left hand.

2

Anna's hands gripped the sides of the exit hatch. It was cold, despite her protective gear, and as she looked down at the patchwork of green fields and trees beneath her the panic welled. The noise of the engine was deafening, drowning all other sounds, even the voice of the instructor attached to her and waiting to jump. As he turned round towards her she lip read the word 'ready,' saw the raised thumb and knew the moment had arrived. With a deep breath she fell into space.

Immediately there was a rushing sensation of cold wind. Looking upwards she could see the plane rapidly disappearing ahead of her. She was amazed by the sense of free fall. Together with the instructor strapped to her she was quite literally diving and falling through space. It was both scary and exciting all at once and incredibly noisy. She wanted the experience to last, but the greenness below seemed to be rushing towards them at an alarming speed, and she knew he would soon pull the cord. She saw the movement of his arm underneath her, and there was a moment of panic when nothing at first seemed to happen. Then a whoosh followed by a sharp pulling back on her shoulders and under her legs told her the chute had opened. Their speed slowed rapidly, and now the sensation was of being some giant bird gliding on the air current. She pushed her arms out, winglike, to exaggerate the feeling.

"Gliding," she thought, "This is like gliding." Now it was quieter. The awful racket of the plane was gone and so was the sound of the freefall through the air. All the fear was gone, and she could enjoy the sensation of gradually, very gently, gliding down to earth. She couldn't remember when she last felt as calm as she did now. It was a moment of just being alive, simply existing in this one special moment of peace where her body felt completely at one with the vast universe around her. The tension of the last few weeks for those few minutes dissipated into the magical calmness of gliding through air supported by the parachute. The ground moving steadily towards them wasn't frightening and she really didn't want it to end.

*

"Does it have to end?"

Anna Rosenthal had planned her next appointment with Dr Patrick, her psychotherapist, to follow the jump. Anxious about how she would feel, she thought it would be a chance to process whatever she felt afterwards.

"How do you mean?"

"The wonderful feeling. You know now you can feel good again. You can recover."

"I can't do a parachute jump every day!"

"In your mind you can, so to speak."

"But . . . ."

"No buts . . . . that's what we agreed."

She smiled, remembering again how ready she usually was to offer an obstacle to the suggestions he made, and how she'd agreed with him not to.

"You know now that there are things in life – or at least one thing – that can make you feel good – and you didn't have to take anything to get there."

"Only jump out of a plane!"

"OK. What was the best part of the experience?"

"Gliding down afterwards. Definitely. The feeling of peace – absolute peace – being held – being held in the air. And the gentle landing – well not that gentle I suppose, it was a bit of a tumble, but you know what I mean."

"Being held."

The words, reflecting her own, triggered something inside and brought tears to her eyes. Patrick waited. The sound of distant traffic intruded into the silence.

"Are you crying?"

It felt like a challenge, sparking a response.

"You know I'm angry don't you. As much at myself as at Ben. For letting myself be so, well, taken in by him. I got rid of all the pictures of us together. Ripped them up and threw them away. And I made a resolution: I wasn't going to be taken in by a man, by anyone, ever again. Instead, I was going to find myself. To be myself – whatever that means. That's why I'm here really."

She stopped, but Patrick didn't say anything. The silence lengthened. Eventually she felt impelled to speak. "Do you know, sometimes I get behind the wheel of my car and just want to drive fast, really fast. On the motorway I can get to over 100 miles an hour. It's like I can't help myself. I don't want to hurt anyone else – that worries me – but it feels as if I don't care about me."

"Why not?"

"Because I don't matter. Because I'm not important."

"Are you angry?"

"Of course I'm angry. I'm so angry he treated me like that . . . and I let him do it!"

The tears flowed freely, uncontrollably. It took three tissues before she could speak again.

"I'm sorry. It's not your fault, I don't want to shout at you."

"Even though I'm a man?"

There was the flicker of a smile. "Even though . . . at least you're older."

It was Patrick's turn to smile. "Some benefits then."

Laughter eased the tension welled up in her, and she calmed down, rubbing her eyes. Then she lifted her left arm, palm upwards.

"Look."

He could see scratches on her wrist, not especially deep, but recent. The skin was scabbed, still healing. "Tried to cut myself. I wasn't very good. It hurt too much, and I'm a coward."

"Do you think you'll do that again?"

"Don't know. Doubt it. Not really my kind of thing."

"What if you do?"

"It will hurt again . . . . and I'll probably stop."

"Why punish yourself in the first place?"

"It's my thing – punishing myself. I've done it as long as I can remember. Maybe it's the Jewish thing too."

Patrick looked at her, unsure how to respond. He waited.

"The Jewish consciousness. Our destiny to always to be the persecuted race. I don't do religion, but being Jewish is part of me, I wouldn't want it to be different."

"Ben was Jewish?"

"Not properly practicing, but he was born into it, and it still had some hold over him."

"Did he self harm?"

The question shocked her and she reacted impulsively.

"Of course he bloody didn't. Why should he?"

The meaning of his question began to penetrate and the anger subsided as fast as it had risen.
"I've been stupid."
"Be patient with yourself. Allow yourself time to get over Ben and what the relationship meant for you. And what it means for you now."
She sighed, a deep outward breath.
"And to learn how to be myself."
He nodded. "That's harder than it sounds. You've got to give yourself time to get over what's happened."

*

In her own world as she eased off Patrick's drive and into the stream of traffic. Changing gear as she did so, she let the clutch out too fast and stalled the car. The jolt brought her back to herself. The car following up behind her stopped suddenly and blew its horn loudly. In the mirror she could see a young guy with a baseball cap gesticulating at her, his face contorted into a gurning rage. For a moment she thought he was going to get out of the car and attack her. Instead, he drove round her roaring his engine, mouthing obscenities and raising a finger in a hostile gesture as his car passed hers.

"Bastard!"
It unsettled her again. Starting the engine, she lurched the car forwards, raced through the gears and down the hill to the roundabout. In front of her a blue Peugeot was waiting for the roundabout to clear. Anna watched the cars from the right, spotted a space wide enough for both herself and the car in front, let the clutch out and moved forward. The Peugeot stayed still. With a crunch and a splintering of glass she drove into it, stopping her car once more with a jolt. There was a moment of disbelief before she registered what had happened.

"No!" she shouted, almost screamed, and for a second thought it was the same guy again, until she saw a different guy indicating to her that they should turn off the roundabout and park along the side of the first

turn off. She could feel the rage rising in her once more. In front of her a slim young guy, perhaps her age and wearing a jacket and tie was getting out of his car and looking at the damage to the rear of his vehicle. Quickly, she switched off her engine and got out to meet him, while he was still bent over the back bumper.
“Why the fuck didn’t you go? The road was clear ahead of you!”
He straightened up, looking surprised.
“Hold on, a minute, it was you who hit me!”
“But you just stayed there when it was clear!”
“Sorry. The law’s quite clear. Hit someone from behind and it’s your fault.”
“Oy oy! I don’t believe this!”
“I’ll need your insurance details. You’ve bent the bumper and smashed my rear light.”
“Oh my God! So like a man. So bloody self righteous aren’t you.”
He waited calmly, not responding while she stood there looking at him in some kind of amazement before she turned back to the car, got her handbag and scrabbled about and found what he’d asked for.
“How can you be so fucking calm?”
“Does it help to get so angry? Here. These are my details. You’ll need to contact your insurance company. They’ll sort it out.”
She looked at him incredulously.
“How can you be so pompous?”
He made a gesture with his arms as if to say what else can I do, before turning with half a smile, getting into his car and driving off, still calm, leaving Anna standing watching him.

Back in her car, she took a deep breath and tried to compose herself. Someone else was making a noise with their horn on the roundabout, unsettling her again, although it didn’t seem to have anything to do with her. Tears began to well in her eyes; everything was going wrong.

*

Patrick checked himself in the mirror. The greying, thinning hair and the paleness of his face made him look distinctly older, though older than what he couldn't really say. His appearance contributed to making him a kind of father figure for clients and patients, and probably in recent years more a grandfather. He didn't think he would be making love in the moonlight under a crumbling pier on a hot summer evening again, wondering not if they would be discovered but whether a part of the underside of the pier would fall, or maybe if they lingered too long, whether the tide would come in and soak them through.

When he thought about it, sex in unusual places seemed to have been a speciality. An estate agent had given one of his old girlfriends the keys to a house she wanted to buy at the time and he went with her to see it. 'Vacant possession' it was, so the place was empty for them to view. Half way round she pulled him into a cupboard, and not a particularly large one. Somehow or other it had happened in there too.

With Laura it had all changed. Then she walked out. For the past few years he'd been celibate as a priest. Not something he was proud of. In fact somewhere within was a sneaking shamefulness about it, as if somehow he wasn't fully a man. His job told him there were lots of men in their early sixties who were sexlessly married, but that didn't really change anything. The thought of being single and sexless for the rest of his life was hardly something he looked forward to, and somewhere not far from the surface of his consciousness, the thought filled him with dread.

He locked the outside door of his counselling room, and double checked it. One last thing remained before he could settle; a visit to be paid. She'll be waiting for me, he thought, and then mentally corrected himself. Not any longer; it will just be surprise. As he walked in the direction of her house, it was still something of a struggle to get used to his mother's deterioration.

Reaching the house with its faded yellow door, he checked that his key was in his pocket, but rang the bell, wanting to let her know he'd arrived, not wanting to startle her. Through the frosted glass he could see the tiny body moving into what she called the lobby. She seemed to be opening the door, but then stopped as if unsure what to do. He tapped on the glass to remind her. Almost instantly the door opened and a tiny head on top of a frail body peered out at him.
"Patrick? Is it Patrick? What a surprise!"
Hardly, he thought to himself. I was here yesterday. A few years ago he might have said it, but now it seemed an unnecessary gesture.
"Yes, it's me. Just calling in to see you."
"Well come in then." She lifted her arms up to to embrace him, as if she wanted to kiss him, but he avoided her with the gentle pressure of his hand on her shoulder, keeping the distance that felt safe for him, even now. She didn't seem to notice, and followed him as he moved past her into the living room beyond.

As usual, it felt like stepping back in time into the same small square of a living space he'd known all his life. The clutter of dancing figurines and odd ornaments had grown over the years, mostly bought by him for birthdays and Christmases. The TV had been upgraded several times from the initial black and white model from his childhood to the now neat silver model in the corner. And there was a new chair into which her ageing body slipped and slept for some of the day. Quite how much he didn't know, but guessed it was increasing. The kitchen was still the narrow scullery arrangement, with various piecemeal fixtures.

"Tea?"
"I'm always ready for tea. What day is it?"
"Tuesday, All day."
"Aren't you at work?"
"I'm finished for today. Last client went half an hour ago."
"Have you been to the hospital?"

"No. It's a private day today."
"What day is it?"
"Tuesday. Second Tuesday in September."
"September? It's my birthday isn't it?"
"Soon. End of the month. Do you remember when?"
"Twenty fifth isn't it?" she said, without having to think.
"You'll be eighty eight."

Patrick could feel himself slipping into the old pattern that had governed his life. She didn't have to do much to set it off. He could feel the discomfort like he always had, but it was easier now he could identify it and even allow himself to go along with it. She was his child. He was her parent.
"It feels very old."
He looked at her small frame and increasingly deep set eyes within the sharp features of her face, and the wrinkled, lined skin of advanced age.
"You're as old as you feel," he said, not quite taking in exactly what she'd said, but she missed the unintentional irony.
"I feel old."
The thought scared him. 'Live in the here and now,' he sometimes told his clients – 'What's happening in the here and now? How do you feel now?' At eighty eight, for his mother, here and now was it.

She had sat herself down and was staring into space, inside her own thoughts; if there were any thoughts at all.
"I'll get that tea."
She looked at him and smiled vacuously.
"Tea?"
"Oh . . . yes please."
He made the usual clattering of cups and saucers.
"Here's your tea."
"Has it got cream in it?"
"Of course."

"You know I like cream in my tea."
"How could I forget."
The vacant look returned. It was almost as if he didn't exist.

"So where is your wife then?" she said suddenly out of nowhere.
"Wife? I haven't got a wife"
"You did have."
"Long time ago."
"Where is she then?"
"I really don't know. Not for ages."
"Is she dead?"
"Not as far as I know. We divorced, she went her own way. I'm a free agent now."
She thought about that for a while.
"I didn't know you were divorced."
"You did – you always have done. You just forget."
She picked up the irritability in his voice and responded in kind.
"How could I forget that?"
"Well you have. Laura and me, we divorced years ago. I don't have anything to do with her now."

Suddenly out of nowhere Laura was in his mind again, in the kitchen they'd shared together, staring into space, avoiding looking at him. He didn't know what to say, or whether to do something, so he carried on with the washing up. The soap bubbles moved above his wrists when he plunged his hands into the hot water. Laura broke the silence.
"It's not working anymore."
He didn't reply.
"It isn't, is it."
"I don't know what to say."
"Be honest with yourself. You know it isn't."
"That's what you think." He didn't want to accept what she was saying. "I just don't know."

“We’ve grown apart. It isn’t just me – it’s you as well. What do we do together now?”
“Well . . .we . . . . lots of . . . .surely lots of couples do different things . . . . have different interests. . . .”
“All the time?”
“Well . . . .”
“All the time! You don’t really want to do things with me anymore.”
“That’s not true.”
“It is. You know it is. Look how we’re arguing now . . .”
“Arguing?”
“Yes, arguing! What else are we doing? We can’t agree on anything anymore. You just don’t want to face it Patrick.”
“That’s not . . . . .”
“It is true! You’re lying to yourself.”
He was standing in front of her on the other side of the kitchen table, drying his wet hands impotently on the sides of his trousers.
“Can’t we . . . . go to Relate or something.”
What for? What will that do?”
A black housefly, oblivious to the tension in the air, flew into the space between them. He swatted it ineffectually, and it doubled back on itself. He tried again, but the fly escaped in the direction of the sink with impudent ease. For a moment both of them followed its path.
“I just think we ought to try.”
Laura looked back at him and then on impulse came round the table and raised her right hand to take his still damp left hand in hers.
“Look at me Patrick.”
For a moment he resisted, before lifting his head and looking directly at her.
“You’re forty two. I’m thirty five. We don’t make each other happy any more. No . . . . . don’t protest. I know you know. We’ve got to face it. We have to separate. We can start new lives . . . find someone else in time perhaps. Find ourselves Patrick.”

And now she had. The card each Christmas told him. Even a late family for her; two smiling boys in school uniform. The elusive happiness found.

"I said do you want some more tea?"
"What? Oh yes, do you want me to make it?"
"You were miles away. Thinking about that hospital again?"
"Oh . . . er . . . . yes, I'll make the tea."
"Can't think why you get so wrapped up in it."

The strange idea of himself physically wrapped up in something called 'hospital' came into his mind. Like a large newspaper perhaps. He dismissed the absurd thought and put the kettle on. But he did get wrapped up in things; or in people, more particularly. Felt a great sense of responsibility for other people, especially his patients, and to her. It still hadn't changed, she was still dependent, to some extent physically as well now. Without realising it till he'd done it, he sighed, loudly, but she didn't notice. She was in her own world again, probably forgotten he was even in the house, standing by the kettle, waiting for it to boil. He collected the two cups and made the tea for them both, and had to speak to her to draw her out of another reverie.

"Have you got a girl friend then?"
He never ceased to be surprised with how her mind could wander and then come back to something, sometimes many minutes afterwards.
"No, not at the moment. Drink your tea."
"Are you going to?"
"Going to what?"
"Get a girl friend. Young man like you needs a girl friend."
"OK. Yes, I hope so."
He didn't want to get into the discussion, but she seemed to want to carry on talking.
"It's what your father would have wanted."

To his knowledge, there were just two black and white photos of his father. One was a wartime wedding photo, with his mother looking impossibly young and glamorous in a suitably utilitarian wedding outfit, and his father in his khaki uniform, his black hair slicked back brylcreem style, looking pleased with himself. The other photo, he thought taken a bit later, was with two army friends, all very merry with their arms draped round each other, looking as if they'd had a few beers. Then nothing. What happened to his father after that had been a mystery to him all his life. "Lost in action, presumed dead," was what his mother said the war office told her. Somewhere in all the papers was the official letter. Through his life, that was all he knew. No way of finding out what had happened.

"Do you know what I fancy?"
Now her voice interrupted his reverie.
"I could do with some fish and chips for tea."
"Do you want me to get you some?"
"From that nice Indian chippie down the road."
"I think they're Chinese actually."
"Yes that's the one."
"OK, I'll go for a walk down there. Mushy peas as well."
"Yes, why not?"

*

Something is different. He has no words to understand it, no way of working it out, but something has changed and he is part of it. It's a feeling in his body – it's how they look at him, 'it's alright Marco, not your fault, don't worry.' He can smell them differently – since *mano* – since then, things have changed. 'He's disturbed. He's not himself, what does he know? It's not his fault. *Poveretto*! Take care of poor Marco.'
'Give him time. He'll be all right. I know my son.'
Mother's voice, talking, words, strange words around him. Different. He wants to be comforted, wants to be reassured. She is taking his

hand, taking him home. A dog is walking towards him, he stretches out his hand to touch the dog.
"Don't touch Marco. It will bite you!"
He lifts his hand. The dog goes on its way, ignores him. 'Don't touch!' The words are inside his head. 'Don't touch!' He remembers the words. *Mano*. He touched the hand. Don't touch. But already his forefinger is touching a spider's web, on the doorframe, where he lives. He looks at it, notices the interconnected lines of the web, sees the spider within, wants to get hold of it in his large hand. He looks at his mother. 'Don't touch.' Inside his head or outside? He moves his hands and steps up the two steps into the tiny house and his mother follows him in.

3

(Southern Italy 1943)
Tom watched the sun disappearing over the horizon shielding his eyes against the brightness. Near him a small group of soldiers were gathered around one tattered newspaper. All around him on the headland were soldiers from his regiment. On the surface it was calm but he could feel an underlying tension. The next big push was coming. He wanted to get some sleep, aware they were bound to set off before dawn; that was always the pattern. Gradually the chatter died out leaving the crickets to fill the silence, sounding much louder than English crickets. Soldiers around him were falling asleep, and he hoped he would soon join them. Despite his anxiety, he lay back on the ground, and drifted off.

At some point in his sleep he must have begun to dream. He experienced himself trying to run away. He didn't know what he was running from, but could feel an inner anxiety, and his feet wouldn't move properly. They seemed stuck in some kind of dense mud, and the more he tried to move them, the more they seemed to stick. Two soldiers were approaching him. He wanted to turn and run away in the opposite direction, but still he couldn't move his feet. One of the soldiers threw something which flew way above his head. Then the other soldier was right in front of him, carrying a rifle. He waited for the soldier to lift the rifle and shoot at him, but instead he raised the rifle parallel with his body and thrust it into his chest. He woke, sweating all over.

The dream brought back an old childhood fear in the pit of his stomach, so that he felt he needed to relieve himself, even though he knew he didn't. He was on his bike, aged about eight. Two boys made him stop and started hitting him for no reason. He escaped, but they chased him, throwing stones, and one stone crashed into the back of his head. Turning a corner ahead of them he drove his bike behind a shed and crouched down. He could hear them running past and shouting out, but they passed him and ran off laughing into the distance.

Putting his hand to his head he could feel something sticky, and when he brought it round to his face there was bright red blood. It was running downwards and running into his shirt collar. His mother would be cross with him. With his heart skipping beats and scared of the blood that still seemed to be seeping out, he waited there, dabbing franticly at the wound with his handkerchief, hardly daring to move. Eventually he stood and looked out. The boys were nowhere to be seen. But worst of all, he realised that he'd shit himself.

He didn't think he would shit himself now, but the old fear, so disgusting, so embarrassing, was always there at times of stress. And this hot night in September, waiting for the battle that he knew was coming it was there in his body. With others around him grunting and snoring, he knew he needed to get back to sleep too, but his body resisted. Eventually he must have done, and dreaming again, he was briefly at home with the wife he'd married just before leaving England. He could see her face clearly, and she was calling out to him, saying something animated, excited, but he couldn't hear or understand what it was she wanted to tell him.

He was awakened by a kick; "Time to go mate." There was movement all around him, although it was still dark. He pulled himself to his senses, trying to shake off the dream. As he got himself together, the vividness of it faded until he could hardly remember what it was about. Around him the stale smell of men who hadn't washed properly in weeks mingled with the late summer dew. He checked his rifle, swallowed hard and fell in. In the pre-dawn darkness they were all moving downwards to the shoreline to board the waiting landing crafts.

In what seemed like no time at all he was on board, and the boat was weighing anchor and setting off across the straits. The sea was calm and he was grateful for that. Even in a short crossing he could feel seasick and he certainly didn't want that.
"This is the exciting bit now," someone was saying to him, "we're off to Europe. Have you been to Europe before lad?"
Wasn't Sicily Europe? Maybe it wasn't. In the gloom he could see the soldier, all of twenty five he guessed, certainly not much older than him, and talking like a veteran.
"No never before this."
"Aye. Real battle starts now."
"Yes." He tried to look excited, smiling, but it wasn't how he felt.
"We're gonna win the war from here alright."

Their conversation such as it was, stopped at a sudden booming and crashing of mortar and artillery fire. For a moment Tom thought they were being fired on directly, and ducked down onto the deck.
"Relax lad! It's our boys, scaring the Eyeties! Cover for us to land!"
Tom could hardly hear him over the crashing sounds, but got a rough idea of what he was saying. And then in what seemed like no time at all, they were preparing to land.

The shore was deserted. There was no enemy waiting for them. Five divisions of the eighth army stepped ashore on the Italian mainland unopposed. It felt eerie, stepping into an empty city. The civilians presumably were staying out of sight and the military were nowhere to be seen.
Suddenly, without warning, an animal was ahead of them; a large animal, like a big cat, staring fiercely.
“What the bloody hell is it?”
The big cat wasn’t waiting to let them find out. It seemed to make a sudden decision that it was no match for a squadron of soldiers carrying rifles, and with a snarl, turned and ran off out of sight at some speed.
“Jesus, is that what they have over here?”
“It must have come down from the mountains.”
“I hope there’s no more where we’re going. Must be the Eyeties secret weapon.”
Tom shared the nervous laughter.

For maybe hours they gradually moved unopposed out of the city, and into the countryside beyond. The land rose steeply at times and frequently the sea came into view below them with the sunlight shimmering across the water. He was hot once more, as he had been every day for weeks. As they moved, their own landing craft, way beneath them now, receded and then disappeared from sight as they moved further north. Gradually they seemed to be climbing upwards towards the mountains. He knew with some relief that the plan wasn’t to cross them, but they were moving into the unknown, and they were on their own now. There was no way back.

Suddenly there was a commotion behind them. Not an animal this time, but humans. A group of what he assumed to be Italians were shouting menacingly and pointing what they took to be rifles. And then they were all running together, the whole platoon, in disarray, away from the danger. Really scared this time, Tom kept running, not stopping for maybe a mile, until he felt safe. And all at once he became aware that his panic had caused him to become separated from his platoon. With a shock of realisation he saw that he was in the middle of nowhere, isolated in a foreign country.

Retracing his steps and finding the platoon before they were too far away from him was what he had to do. There was a ridge above a valley below, and he began to run back along this, thinking that was the way he had come. But suddenly, out of nowhere, in front of him was a soldier, not one of his own platoon, but an enemy soldier holding a rifle. Just as in his dream, the soldier came towards him with his rifle lifted to strike him over the head. In the fraction of a second before the butt hit him, Tom found himself wondering why the soldier wasn't shooting him, and whether he was actually still inside his dream. Then the force of the blow turned him round on himself, towards the valley below the steep edge he'd been running along. His body buckled and he had no power to stop himself falling before losing consciousness.

*

Slowly and painfully Tom woke to the buzzing of flies and midges in his ears. His head hurt. He was hot and sweaty and desperate for a drink. As his eyes gradually recovered their ability to focus, he could see that he was actually in a narrow valley, or maybe a dried out river bed. Above him on one side the ground rose steeply. It had to be the face down which he'd fallen. The other side looked as if it rose less steeply through what seemed like cultivated vines. Either way he couldn't see far, but gradually he realised that unless he stayed in the river valley, he would have to drag his exhausted body through the vineyards, wherever that led him. He remembered the soldier with the rifle. Did it actually happen? Had his dream come true? It was the only explanation; he'd scuffled with the Italian and been pushed over the ridge and steeply into the valley. Now, bruised and exhausted, he had to escape.

There was blood on his shirt. Somewhere he'd bled, and the actual sight of it triggered the feeling of pain inside, and he fell backwards into the damp earth of the valley. His consciousness drifted, and briefly he fainted. Coming to again, he pushed his right arm cautiously inside the wet shirt sticking uncomfortably to his shoulder, and his fingers felt a sticky mass of blood. For a moment the eight year old memory flared back, scaring him. He had no idea how bad the injury might be, and he didn't want to discover the worst. At least he was still alive.

There were birds in the sky twittering and squawking, and in his half conscious state he thought he could hear the high pitched squeal of a buzzard; definitely there were birds of prey. Perhaps there were vultures up there too. What did that say about him? Were they circling, waiting for him to die? Above him he could hear a 'klee klee' sound. He looked up, shading his eyes against the sun, and saw a large bird with an unusually white under-carriage and powerful wings. Was it stalking him?

He had to get out of the valley before it was dark. He'd have to take his chances climbing the more gradual upward slope, through the vineyards. Cautiously he stood and moved forwards. The vines seemed to be held up on wooden poles. He could use them to support his climb. Despite his painful shoulder he began a slow gradual movement, one step before the other, every so often leaning back on one of the vine poles for support, until he was in sight of the top of the ridge. Ahead of him was a kind of farmhouse. Even in his dazed state, he knew all the occupants had to do was to look in his direction and they would see him, but there was no choice, he needed help. And almost as soon as the thought had passed through his brain, he found himself once more facing a rifle barrel.

*

The donkey, tethered outside the old barn had suddenly become agitated. Needing to go out and relieve himself, Benito decided to check whether anything was amiss. The German soldiers had retreated north and something was definitely happening in the war effort. But not here, not in this corner of Italy, surely, where the daily movement of the seasons went on unchanged. The grape would need harvesting, and he knew it would soon be time to mobilise the villagers to strip the vines. He looked down across the shallow valley to the vineyard and the setting sun over the sea beyond, feeling pleased with life. He crossed himself. God had blessed him. Then for a moment, in the gathering darkness below, something moved. Alert suddenly, his eyes strained to scan the vines in the still warmth of the evening. There it was again; something was moving, and moving slowly up the slope towards him. And suddenly he remembered the reports of recent days about the animals that had escaped from Reggio Zoo. Could something have come up this far? He rushed inside.

Four sets of eyes from within the farmhouse looked up at him in surprise.
"Something moving outside! Could be an animal from the zoo," he said. "Stay in here – keep the door closed while I sort it. All of you stay in here."
From the lobby at the back of the house, he quickly found his rifle, loaded it and stepped out of the door, shutting it behind him.

With his senses alert to the slightest movement now, he waited on the courtyard, watching with rifle outstretched. Closer now, he caught another glimpse of whatever it was moving slowly up the slope directly towards him and to his astonishment the shape gradually settled in his vision to that of a human. Fifty metres away, not an animal, but someone was approaching.
"Halt!" he shouted, expecting a German soldier, and in the best German he could manage: *"Hände hoch!"* Slowly, the body emerged from beneath the vines, lifted its hands falteringly above its head, and fell forwards.

It wasn't what he'd expected. Cautiously he stepped forward a few paces, rifle outstretched, to reach the body. It wasn't wearing a German uniform. The khaki colour looked suspiciously English. There was a moment of shock before he shouted loudly for anyone to hear. The hens behind the house began squawking loudly and fluttering about in confusion while the donkey, disturbed again, stamped its hooves wildly and brayed noisily. A moment later, his two sons came running out of the farmhouse towards him. The English body stirred and tried to raise its head, but didn't seem to have the strength to stay conscious. There was blood on the shirt, and Benito suspected he'd been shot, but couldn't bring himself to touch it. Was this the start of an invasion?

"How many more of them are there out there?" he asked himself and anyone else who was listening.

"What is it papa. Who is it?"

"English! The English are here!"

The two young men joined their father peering into the valley through the vineyards in the darkness for any sign of further movement. Gradually the hens and the donkey quietened again, their noise replaced by the incessant crickets.

It was in Benito's head that he could shoot the Englishman and have done with it. They were at war after all. There would be no questions asked, and maybe anyway this one had got detached from his regiment. If there were English soldiers they must have landed in the harbour below, and would be trekking up the highway towards Naples, not coming into his farm. But it wasn't in his nature to shoot an injured man in cold blood and if there were more English soldiers out there, this one could be a prisoner, a hostage for their protection. He made up his mind.

"In the barn!" he ordered. His sons looked at him, at first not quite taking in what he meant.

"Get this man into the barn!"

Roughly and unceremoniously, one took hold of his arms, the other his feet and they half lifted and half dragged the limp body towards the old barn. The donkey stamped and fussed again, objecting to the disturbance. The soldier, half conscious again, groaned and muttered, seemed in pain and shouted out loudly when dumped on the floor of the barn.

The man needed to be cleaned up and his wounds sorted. That was a woman's job. Unable to stay in the farmhouse with all the activity going on, his wife had already come outside, followed by his eighteen year old daughter.
"English," he said, "There might be more. We'll need to keep him alive for now in case we need him. He needs cleaning up."
The women understood what he meant.

*

Drowsy, and struggling to rouse himself to consciousness, Tom was dimly aware of hands and of people around him. His shirt was being removed and his arm jerked out of the sleeve, making him wince. He couldn't keep his eyes open, but somewhere on the edge of consciousness he thought he heard a voice say *'mama.'* Then something cold and soft at his shoulder and a gentle rubbing of his skin. It hurt, and briefly he woke to see a blur of what looked like two women kneeling over him before he slipped once more out of consciousness.

The sound of movement woke him again. He couldn't make sense of it, and when he opened his eyes and looked around, he saw that he was in a place without windows, but that daylight was spilling in from what seemed to be large doors. There was a pain in his left shoulder, and when he lifted his right arm to it, he discovered some kind of bandage. Looking down in the dimness he saw there was some kind of bandaging on his upper arm and over his shoulder. But he had no memory of how it had got there. He tried to sit up, pushing himself with his right arm, but it was too painful and he flopped down. The barn broke up around him and he lost consciousness again.

The next Tom knew he was being wakened and there was sunlight streaming from an open door. Through it he could see two men. Someone else was right next to him, a young woman, half in the shadow. She was speaking to him in a foreign language and seemed to be offering him water from a large beaker. He sat up, supporting himself while she held the beaker to his mouth. Drinking the water rapidly made him realise he was actually very thirsty. There was still pain in his shoulder, and as soon as he'd taken the water he fell clumsily back again. He tried to say thankyou, but the words didn't come out. The woman said something else to him he didn't understand, and he thought he glimpsed half a smile before she stood and walked away from him to where the men were still standing. Silhouetted against the light from the doorway, he could see she had long hair. Then she was through the space and the men closed the door on him.

'Guards,' he thought, and it occurred to him for the first time that he was their prisoner; 'I'm a prisoner of war!' He began piecing together what had happened; the attack on the cliff top; the soldier with the rifle; the fall: they were all there again in his memory. But still he couldn't grasp how he'd got to where he was. 'Italians,' he tried to say out loud, 'of course – that's what they are – and I'm in Italy.'

Had they found him at the bottom of the cliff and brought him here? The effort of thinking made him drowsy and he drifted between sleeping and waking until he was once more interrupted by a sound from where the barn door was. This time there was a narrower beam of light coming towards him in half darkness, and eventually he could see it was a torch. When the light reached him he realised it was the girl again with more water, and he raised himself on his uninjured arm and drank noisily while she held the cup for him and watched while he drank. He couldn't see her face clearly, but he was aware again of the long hair which framed itself against something paler that she was wearing. Then almost as quickly as she came, she was gone, disappearing through the shaft of light which was swallowed up when she went.

Afterwards he must have dropped into a deeper sleep. When he woke again he was aware that it was dark outside, and he could hear something making a noise quite close, maybe something animal. He had an urgent need to relieve himself for the first time since he had been aware he was in the barn. The water must have gone some way to topping up his fluids after the loss of blood, and normal needs had resurfaced. He tried to look around him in the darkness, and dimly he could see the walls of the barn. If he could get across to the other side he could do what he had to without messing the area where he was laying. But when he tried he simply couldn't manage to stand. Instead he rolled carefully to the side, keeping his injured arm tucked in to protect the shoulder. The pain shot through him each time the weight of his body was on his injured side, and three rolls was all he could manage. Finishing on his right side, he unbuttoned his trousers cautiously and did what he could to avoid wetting himself, allowing the warm fluid to flow out of him. When he'd finished, he fixed his clothing and rolled back again, away from the wet area he had created, suffering the pain once more. He was pleased with himself; he could still achieve such a basic act despite his weakened state. Tired out by the exertion it wasn't long before he fell once more into a sleep.

At some point in the night he dreamed again. The same soldier was advancing towards him with the outstretched rifle. He could see his face, cadaverous, expressionless, and the rifle once more pointed upwards. In his dream he experienced the force of the impact, and it woke him with a start, sweating with fear in the darkness. Impulsively he tried to stand, but fell back. For a while, he could make no sense of where he was or what had happened to him.

4

'Have you noticed how infuriatingly sure of themselves men can be? Always convinced the other person or the other side is in the wrong. Always complaining about the referee when a decision goes against them, certain from the terraces that they know more than the trained official on the pitch.'

Anna stopped for a moment to look at what she'd read, and a vision of Ben shouting obscenities at the referee came into her head and made her shudder. She was glad she didn't have to put up with that anymore. But there was more she wanted to say.

The other day I had a prang in my car. The driver in front of me stopped suddenly; a man of course. It wasn't my fault and it shook me up. When we got out of our cars I could have coped with a civilised exchange of insurance details, but he was so sure it was my fault it really made me mad. So all you men out there reading this, think twice before being so cocky. It really turns women off.

Just writing it felt better. She gazed at the screen with satisfaction. It would fill the first half of her column nicely. Bound to get some responses too, which was why, although she knew he would object at first, being the sexist guy that he was, the editor was likely to pass it. She grinned to herself at the thought of the righteous indignation. And of course it would prove her point.

Outside it was a beautiful Saturday morning. The trees across the road were just beginning to show signs of autumn, and the sun was glinting from the windscreens of the passing cars. Getting some of the pent up anger out of her system into next week's article was definitely worthwhile, but the irritable feelings she'd known since Ben left was still there. Why had it had such an effect on her? It didn't really add up. It ought to feel like a release. Having the flat to herself again, not having to worry about his whims felt better. A lot better. It wasn't as if she actually missed him. Seeing a psychotherapist and getting angry had helped. So had the cry she had to admit. But it felt like something inside her still needed sorting and she didn't really know what it was. Underneath the anger it felt like something else wanted to take her over and she had to fight it off.

Her body felt sluggish, as if something was drawing her downwards. If she let go of the anger whatever it was might take her over. She definitely needed to get active. It had been the sort of busy week that prevented her getting to the gym at all. Now suddenly it felt like a need, so she went into the bedroom, changed into her track suit and put her running shoes on. She would do what she'd done before when she felt guilty about slacking on exercise; jog the mile and a half journey to the gym. Probably walk back after all the exercise, but that was no problem. If I'm really knackered I can catch a bus, she thought, locking the door of her flat behind her and stepping out into the street.

The journey took her past the local synagogue; a past life which no longer had meaning. All those Saturdays with her parents observing rituals were gone now. Too many fixed views, too much dwelling on the past. Life was for living now. The faithful were arriving, a sea of kippahs and a couple of those strange black Chassidic hats which even Ben, who had more of a Jewish consciousness than she did, and had several kippahs of his own, used to laugh at. *Meshuge* in the extreme; just crazy, especially on a beautiful day like this. But as she ran past there was still a tinge of guilt. It was something she did well. That message had come out with the psychotherapist. It was the Jewish thing too, and she would after all always be Jewish.

Her pace quickened, pumping up the adrenalin. Absurdly she imagined she was running from some ancient rabbi with his hat and long beard who was pursuing her, personifying all the disturbing thoughts the synagogue had stirred up. Gradually she calmed down, and by the time she reached the gym it almost felt like an anti-climax. The sweaty atmosphere inside was no match for the sunshine outside but she could be dutiful and respectful to her body and tone up all the muscles to make herself feel good again. The regulars talked about an adrenalin rush. Not something she'd ever experienced, but she could live in hope. For now it was enough to channel the energy and dispel the demons in her head.

*

Josh's first floor classroom looked out onto the large housing estate on the outskirts of the suburb which the school served. Students were arriving, mostly smartly dressed, but several with shirts hanging loosely over trousers. Getting the shirts tucked in was a daily battle against reluctant students. It was a battle he chose not to fight in his room. He had other battles he'd rather win first. Four weeks into term, he felt he'd made a reasonable start. Better than banking at least!
That had been anathema to him. Everything geared to making sales and achieve targets. Pressure from managers if he missed a target, even for one day, was something he hated. He couldn't understand why he'd gone into banking in the first place. Why on earth had he thought it would be something that would suit him? After four years he knew it wasn't the right job for him.

An idea had been formulating in his brain for some time that maybe, just possibly, he could retrain as a teacher. A bank customer he'd got talking had done it himself and encouraged him.
"You could get in easily, they're always advertising on the television. You've got a degree haven't you?"
"But I need to earn a living. Can't just train like that."
"Graduate teacher programme it's called. Train on the job. They'll pay you."
That sounded more attractive, more like a real possibility, so, when missing yet another target, it had been suggested to him, politely of course so there was no constructive dismissal, that maybe this wasn't

the job for him, he got the message quickly. And the school had taken him on. But it was far from an easy job. He was discovering that.

Children's voices made their way ever louder along the corridor until they spilled through the door and into his classroom. It still amazed him how many students seemed unable to judge the width of the doorframe, never quite avoiding crashing bags and bodies before falling noisily in some kind of heap into a chair, more or less oblivious of his presence. Mostly he said little as they arrived, content to acknowledge the few girls who grinned and flirted casually with him as they settled into the room.

His Year 10 English group were arriving. The start of the lesson still made him feel anxious. There was always the fear he wouldn't be able to get control it all when he was ready. So far he'd been able to settle things down when he'd wanted to and get some work done. But a large boy, named Jack Mackenzie but known by everyone as Mac was beginning to make himself difficult. This morning he took it on himself halfway through to stand and look out of the window.

"Sit down please Mac."

No response.

"Sit down please Mac!"

"Cool it man!"

"OK, but just sit down please."

Josh could see that there were girls playing netball on the pitch beyond the window which was attracting Mac. Clearly they were more interesting to him that the Steinbeck novel he was meant to be working on.

Without any sense of urgency, Mac turned himself round, shirt flap hanging loose, and grinned at him.

"Just watching the girls sir. There's some nice looking ones down there."

"OK Mac, but just sit down and carry on with your work please now."

"Do you like girls sir?"
It felt like a challenge, but he managed to keep calm, and resisted saying anything else, letting Mac sit down in his own time. He looked round the class, aware that he was being watched; judged to see how he would react. It was uncomfortable, and he didn't know if he'd got it right.
"I was just looking sir," Mac said as he sat down, backing away from the confrontation.
Josh continued watching him until he settled back to his work with obvious reluctance. Then there was another student wanting his attention, and the moment passed.

*

"I'd say you got that about right."
"Do you think so? I wasn't sure."
"I'd shout at the bastard if it was me. Send him out if necessary. Just trying it on. Don't let him win."
"What if he challenges me again?"
"Deck him! That's what I'd like to do."
"Don't listen to that nonsense Josh, unless you want to lose your job. Johnno wouldn't still be sitting there if he'd ever done that."
Johnno muttered incoherently and ignored the rest of the conversation. From the authority of being deputy head, Len Turner suggested he sent Mac out to him.
"You won't lose out in the long run that way."
"Thanks, I'll do that if he's a problem again. Meanwhile, I've got my Year 7 group. They're great fun; really lively."
"Enjoy it. But don't let them get too lively. The younger they are the firmer your control needs to be."
"OK. Thanks."

*

The dogs are different. Snarling more, face in your face. Not happy. Not sitting with Marco and lifting paws for strokes.
'Dogs sense things. You can see they know something.'
Marco senses things, but can't understand.

'A body. Buried in the valley. Shallow it must have been for the floods to unearth it like that.'
The dog won't come to him. He wants to get up and stroke it, black and brown, but it wanders off, following the two women. He sits there looking over the valley where the sun is shining.
"Marco! Marco!"
He looks round. Father Leo is coming towards him, calling his name. He smiles, pleased to see him. Leo pats him on his back. He likes it, giggles, feels better. The Father sits beside him on the seat looking out across the bay. He can see the sunlight shining on the water, a long way below them. It makes him feel happy, safe, what he's always known.
Things have changed for the better. He kicks his large heels, and watches grinning as Father Leo rocks backwards and then forwards again on the seat where they are both sitting.

*

There was a scuffling sound at the door a perfunctory knock. One of the younger members of staff came round the door followed immediately by a Year 10 boy.
"This boy Mrs Broad has been swearing!"
"I didn't, you misheard me." The voice tailed off in an indistinct complaint.
"I know you did, I'm not stupid."
There was more muttering. She stepped forward towards them, the teacher glaring and the boy observing his feet as if something important was happening down there. It was obvious she had to act, putting the boy outside to cool off, before calming the teacher down with a promise to act. Then she was outside the door to sort out the boy, by now reasonably contrite.
"Sorry miss."
"Mr Wilson says you were swearing."
"Not at him. He wound me up."
There was more muttering which sounded like 'gets on my tits.'
"What did you say?"

"Nothing miss."
"So you'll apologise?"
"Sorry miss."
"Not to me. To Mr Wilson."
Muttering again, but a clear nod told her he had capitulated, and the apology to the young teacher when it came was genuine enough to be accepted. Wilson's slight nod as he went seemed to serve as a grudging vote of thanks.

She walked across to the window and looked out over the school yard in the autumn sunlight, squinting through her glasses against the glare. From the front of the school she could see the trees, still green, but with a few leaves beginning to turn brown. Not a time of year she particularly liked. The excitement of the new term, the new students and the smart new uniforms were always tempered for her somehow with the thought of ending. Just around the corner from the season of mists and mellow fruitfulness was the season of dying off. Inside her there was a sense of unease, which she knew she was good at covering up. None of her staff would guess how she felt about autumn, unless it was Len Turner, known by all the staff as Twitter for his cryptic gossiping. No one else would have any idea how she might be feeling. In eight years of headship she'd got used to being seen not as Elizabeth Broad the person, but as 'the boss,' repository of everyone's fantasies about authority. Something about her reserved personality fitted her well for the role, although it meant she had to live with the loneliness that came with it.

With just thirteen year old Max at home, wise beyond his years though he often was, she found herself yearning for some adult interchange. Dramatic word 'yearning,' but it felt about right. Max had his friends, and when he wasn't on the computer, he was increasingly out in the evening. It left her peace to manage the mountain of paperwork, but with a feeling of being incompletely fulfilled at the same time, however much she enjoyed the job.

She turned the corner into the main corridor to find herself confronted by Len, shepherding some parents and a child around the school.
"Can I introduce you to our headteacher Mrs Broad, although only by name, I hasten to add!" It was one of his favourite jokes. The reference to the slim figure she'd maintained well into her fifties didn't displease her, and she knew he'd worked that out. She could still wear her dark hair shoulder length and was starting to enjoy the occasional flirtatious interchange once more. After nearly three years on her own, it was something she was just beginning to be able to do.
"Pleased to meet you. Looks a nice school."
"Very nice."
"And you're in year 6 are you?"
The little girl in front of her nodded and responded with a shy grin.
"Good. Hope you'll like what you see. Then you'll want to join us next year."
They moved off along the corridor, with Len continuing his familiar patter as he escorted them. He was much better at it than she was. The same stories never seemed to tire him.

There was noise coming from one of the English classrooms, which stopped almost immediately she entered.
"Is there a problem Mr Greenwell?"
Guilty faces in front of her told her there probably was, and the message was reinforced by the unnatural quiet, but Josh Greenwell wasn't going to admit it.
"Just a bit lively, but, I think we're all settling down now Mrs Broad."
"I'm always ready to deal with anyone who wants to disrupt things Mr Greenwell."
"Thankyou Mrs Broad."
She retired from the classroom and closed the door behind her. The absurdly formal pantomime of speech teachers used when students were present amused her, but didn't allay her anxiety about her enthusiastic new teacher.

Back in her office a few minutes later she glanced out of the window onto the PE class taking place below. A squabble had developed between two girls over the hockey game. A shrill blast of the whistle didn't resolve the problem, so the teacher marched across and separated the girls before some kind of fight developed. Apologies followed and the game resumed. Teachers as referees she thought. 'They saw that the wisdom of God was in her,' came fancifully into her brain from nowhere. In the end it was all about judgement. With a sigh she moved back to the desk to sign some paper work; the easy, boring bit of the job. Doing what she'd just done, and what she'd seen happen out of the window was much more important.

5

It wasn't difficult for Simon to work out that the new cellist in her low cut top was interested in him. She kept looking across, although she hadn't actually said anything. He chose to avoid her looks, and when she came to talk to him afterwards he was friendly, but a bit distant too.

"Hi, you're new aren't you?"

"Yes. Straight from college in Manchester. I'm Celia by the way."

"Oh, hi," he said again. "I'm Simon, violinist."

"Yes, I noticed you. Third desk isn't it?"

He nodded in agreement and looked at her a moment before continuing.

"So, new to London?"

"Oh no! My parents live in Barnet. Just studied up north. Well, not really that north, not like Royal Northern College, or Edinburgh or something."

"No."

The buzz of conversation round them filled the pause that followed. She smiled awkwardly. He smiled politely back.

"Well, must be off. Work to be done before the performance. Want to practice the allegro a bit more."

Her wave seemed slightly simpering. He could feel her watching him as he walked off with his violin case and scores, both carried in one hand.

'Why don't I like women?' he found himself musing to himself as he walked the short distance to the underground station and down the steps. The smell of stale urine was quite strong; he turned his nose up at it disapprovingly. The memory of school toilets was in the smell, adding to his displeasure.
'Why don't I?' he said again, almost out loud to himself, and then, quite quickly he realised that was wrong. He did like women. He loved their company, chatting and gossiping. Women certainly fascinated him, and sometimes he wondered what it might be like to be a woman, to dress up, to look good, to care about appearance in that very feminine way that as a male he knew he couldn't really match.

But he wasn't a cross dresser. He couldn't understand why some men wanted to actually pretend they were women. He knew at some deeper level that ultimately, he didn't want to be female. He was male, he felt it deeply within him; it was his core being. His excitement was male. He didn't want to be otherwise. But there was the problem. He knew what excited him, and had done since as long as he knew.

Opposite him now on the tube he was watching a guy in well cut pale blue jeans. A white guy, mid-twenties, clean shaven, no designer stubble, with dark hair swept back. He was with an attractive Latino girl, also in blue jeans with a blue tee shirt. Their arms were linked and they were chatting and smiling at each other. The noise of the tube meant he couldn't hear anything of what they were saying, but it was obvious they were partners. And that made the guy still more attractive, which didn't make any sense to him.

It was his stop. He squeezed his way through the gangway and stepped onto the platform. There was plenty of time to settle himself and play through the allegro movement he didn't think he'd quite got right yet and have something to eat before returning for the performance. It was just a short walk from the tube to his flat, some way out of the centre, but still hugely convenient for an orchestral musician's life style. The old Victorian terraced house where he lived had been turned into eight flats. His was the basement, small, but quite big enough for him. His orchestral salary wasn't enough to pay for it, so he had to do occasional session jobs, but there was plenty of need for a competent violinist. He also played in a trio that was increasingly gaining a reputation. Life was good. Except that he was alone, and he couldn't come to terms with how he could resolve that.

In his head, he wasn't quite a virgin. As a nineteen year old student he'd done a late gig one night, got carried away being Stefan Grappelli and also drank a bit more than usual. When he came out of the club, way after midnight, all the tubes had stopped. He couldn't afford a taxi fare, especially with the late night add on. Walking wasn't really an option. Panic began to rise in him as he realised how cold it was. An older guy he hadn't noticed had followed him out of the club. He wasn't old; not very old, just . . . well, lived in was how he would have described him, like the ancient mariner in his imagination. The polite enquiry as to whether he was stuck came as quite a surprise.
"Well, yes actually, I've missed the last tube."
"I did like your performance tonight. Like the great man himself."
"Grappelli, yes, thankyou."
"Look, I can see you're in a fix. I live not far from here, come back to my place for the night."
Quick decision time he thought, take the chance or get frozen.
"Well, yes, I am stuck, would that be alright?"
"Music man, it would be a pleasure. Alfie!"
Alfie held out his hand and he took it.
"Thanks, thanks a lot."
"It's just this way."
Clutching his violin case and smiling to himself with relief at not having to spend the night on the London streets, he followed.

Alfie was clearly, he realised, just a little drunk, like he was, but within five minutes they had reached quite an elegant street, and he found himself led up the front steps to a first floor flat beyond a large front door with what looked like an original Victorian stained glass window. It was clearly no back street dive, but something about the whole encounter was also slightly unnerving.

He settled himself on one of two leather sofas and waited while Alfie made him a coffee. In front of him was a large and very full bookcase, and there were a few books scattered around as if they'd all recently been consulted. Alfie was clearly a reader. His eye was drawn to a photograph on the wall of two men standing by a swimming pool, both wearing trunks. One had his arm round the other's shoulder, and both were smiling into the camera.
"That's me," Alfie said coming back into the room, "Some time ago now of course. On the right."
Alfie put the coffee down, handed one mug to him and sat himself heavily in the leather sofa at right angles to where Simon sat.
"Not quite as slim now, but still in good shape."
"Thankyou for putting me up for the night like this. I do appreciate it."
"No trouble. You're a fine fiddler – hope it's alright to call you that. And of course, you're very good looking. I'm sure you realise that."
It took a moment for it to register. The bargain. As he realised what he had let himself in for his heart jumped. Alfie wanted sex with him. He didn't know what to say or do. Making excuses now would make no sense. He'd have to sleep rough on the cold streets, taking his chance with other predators. Fear was beginning to rise inside him; he didn't know how to respond. His stomach felt tight. There was probably no way out but to resign himself to what was coming.

*

It was dawn when he woke. Outside the traffic was already moving and a pale light turned the darkness into shadows. Next to him on the bed he could make out Alfie's shape, laying on his side with his back towards him, breathing slowly and heavily. He eased his way out of the bed. His white underpants on the floor stood out against the darkness inside the flat and he slipped them on quickly. By the light from the window he could just make out the time on his wrist watch. Six o'clock. As silently as he could he moved over towards the door into the sitting room where he remembered he had taken off the rest of his clothes, by the side of the small table, next to his violin case. Hastily he pulled his sweater over his head and put on the jeans. With his shoes and the rest of his clothes in one hand, his violin in the other, he tiptoed to the door. It opened easily, but when the main door to the building shut behind him it clanged noisily and he thought it must wake everyone in the building.

Without waiting to put his shoes on, he ran barefooted down the steps, along to the end of the street and into the main road before stopping to catch his breath. There was a low wall on the corner, and he sat on it to finish dressing. It was getting light. The sight of early morning traffic and red London buses had never been more comforting. There was a bus stop very close to where he found himself. He walked along to it more calmly and managed to read the timetable, which told him a bus in his direction would arrive in five minutes. He joined the short queue with a tall woman in a hijab and two short white guys with elaborate tattoos. No one spoke as they waited for the bus.

"Since then, and that's six years ago, I've been. . . . . well I suppose you'd have to say celibate."
The insistent sound of sparrows outside became audible in the counselling room, above the background hum of the traffic. Patrick waited a few moments at the end of Simon's story, keeping the urge to say 'me too' well down before saying anything.
"Is that what you want?"
"I need to make some kind of sense of who I am."
"You seem to be owning being gay. Have I understood that right?"

"When I think of the Alfie experience it makes me hate it. That was gross, but I can't pretend that sex with a man isn't what, well, what turns me on. Not Alfie, but someone my age. I wish I wasn't gay but I don't think I can change it."
"Do you want to come to terms with it, maybe develop a relationship with another man? Is that how you want me to help you?"
"I'm really anxious, lots of the time, mostly about sex. But there are moments, with the music I play, when I can get to feel completely and totally at peace. If there is such a thing as heaven, for me, it's there. That's where I could die."
"Die?"
"Sometimes I think about it. Easy way out. How many gay men have killed themselves I wonder – more than straight men I guess, proportionally anyway. Like Tchaikovsky. Do you know he married? Wanted to try and cure himself that way! What must that have been like?"
For a moment he seemed seriously to be trying to imagine it.

"I've tried to think myself straight, if you see what I mean, but I know now that it doesn't work. It threw Tchaikovsky into a big depression and he nearly killed himself and about fifteen years later he finally did. I think about that sometimes. His despair must have seemed absolute. No way out. Trying to convince himself that somehow he could make it work as a married man. Disaster! His brother told him it wouldn't work, but he didn't listen, simply didn't want to believe it; thought his secret 'sin' as he called it could be cured by marrying a woman. It wasn't long before he left her. Being gay is so hard, and must have been even harder then."

He stopped for a moment. Drank some water from the glass beside his chair in the counselling room before carrying on.
"And this is my fantasy. Into Tchaikovsky's head, at the height of his despair as he seriously considered his own death, drifted the fragment of a melody, a beautiful melody that he didn't want to lose – played

sweetly, high on the violin. In his mind, he sees a beautiful young man playing it, the violin tucked under his chin and resting on his collar bone. Perhaps he is wearing a white open necked shirt, and Tchaikovsky can see his skin beneath. The young man's right arm guides the bow gently but firmly over the strings, and the fingers of his left hand form the notes he is playing. Tchaikovsky allows the melody to develop in his head, inspired by his vision of the young violinist. After a while he takes the violin from him and rests it on a table, although in his head the music carries on. Gradually they strip each other and fall naked onto a soft bed, while all the time the wonderful melody in his head carries on. And then with absolute certainty, he knows he has to go on living. Out of his homosexuality has come the most wonderful of all violin concertos. And it is amazingly beautiful. And for me, whether it's actually true or not, that's how he created the violin concerto everyone loves. He didn't die. Not then anyway."

"And you?"

"Oh don't worry, I'm not going to kill myself. I can play that concerto you know."

"With an orchestra?"

"Couple of times. Smallish venues."

"Any plans to play it again?"

"If I can. I love it." He stopped. There was silence in the room. "How did I get to tell you all that?"

"You seem to be saying you need me to help you come to terms with being gay. Maybe coming out. How many people know you're gay?"

"Would you believe I've not actually told anyone. Never, ever. I think some of the orchestra might guess. "

"But what you want is to come to terms with who you are in life. That's the task is it?"

Simon sat back again and breathed in deeply before replying.

"I think so, yes."

*

Marco's large shape is perched on one of the sideways seats at the front of the town bus. He is aware of the talking. He holds onto the rail as the driver changes gear to manage the steep slope upwards to the left. The sound of the engine obscures the words in the bus until the summit of the hill.

". . . . from the war"

"That far back?"

"So they say."

War. He hears 'war.' He knows they are saying war. A different sound, a different word. Scary. He wants it not to be war, to be 'alright Marco' with a smile and sometimes sweets. They are indicating towards him now. He smiles.

"He found it you know. Found its hand sticking out, so Signora Rossi said. The good father was with him."

They are engrossed. Not smiling at him. He wants their attention. He fidgets to attract them. Smiles again.

"*Va bene Marco! Giorno!*"

"*Marco*! *Giorno!*"

His smile widens. Everything is alright.

"Do you think he understands?"

"No. Simple. Born that way. Simple as a *bambino*!"

"'cept he's not little. Seems to get fatter every year."

"Well that's his syndrome isn't it."

He knows they are talking about him now. He likes it; fidgets again, rolls on the seat, claps his hands a couple of times and grins widely.

6

'Mrs Elizabeth Broad, Headteacher' said the door proudly. Josh knocked and waited till he heard her voice calling for him to come in before tentatively pushing the door open and stepping inside. She was sitting beside the computer screen on her desk wearing a dark jacket and white blouse, open at the neck. He caught a glimpse of a faint smile.

"You wanted to see me?"

"Thanks for coming along. You don't have a class at the moment?"

"Non-contact session."

She didn't offer him a seat, so he stood slightly awkwardly in front of her while she continued.
"OK. It's about the student in your tutor group who took an overdose. How much do you know about him?"
"Wesley Freedom?" He waited for her to nod before continuing. "He's been self harming too. Cutting his forearms. Always keeps his sleeves down so you can't see it, but Johnno, Mr Jones that is, saw it in the changing rooms. Family's got a social worker, and I think he has counselling through them."
"You're sure about that?"
"Oh yes. Wesley, doesn't say much. He keeps himself to himself quite a lot. But I've spoken to his social worker. I think it's under control."
A knock at the door was followed by the entry of the secretary with some papers for signing. Josh watched the process, wondering what was coming. Once the secretary left, there was no hiatus, and she surprised him by continuing from where she had left off as if there had been no interruption.
"We do need to be sure." There was a hint of accusation in her tone. "There's a team around the child meeting next week. I'll go to that myself, but I need a report from you about everything you know about the boy. Can you do that by this weekend please."
There was no doubting it was a command and not a question. He nodded, feeling slightly as if he's been told off without quite understanding why. She nodded back in response. The meeting had clearly ended. He had a ridiculous urge to bow and back out of the door in deference, but managed somehow to turn himself round and walk out, closing the door quietly behind him. The secretary in her office watched him go.

*

"Goes with the job. That's headteachers for you, they're all the same."
"But why should I feel as if I'd done something wrong?"
"Remember when you were at school. Going to see the head was always a punishment. Doesn't go when we get older!"

He watched Johnno sit back in his chair in the staff room with a knowing look. It didn't feel reassuring. He was already aware that Johnno was cynical in a way he had sometime experienced with banking colleagues. Obviously there were people like that everywhere, even in teaching.
"All she wanted was to ask me about Wesley."
"The lad that cuts himself?"
"Yes. Apparently he took an overdose as well. There's a meeting next week. She wanted some information from me."
"Is he back at school yet?"
"No. Still off. He's got a counsellor now."
Johnno's grunt suggested his opinion of counselling might be lower than his opinion of headteachers. It made him feel more uncomfortable than he'd felt in the head's office.

*

Wesley wasn't a small boy, but he looked tiny in the big black chair. Patrick watched him trying to sit still. Mostly he looked down, fidgeting with his hands. He waited for the boy's large eyes to look up at him.
"You're thirteen?"
Wesley muttered, agreeing quietly.
He began the halting conversation he knew he would need to conduct before approaching the difficult areas in Wesley's life. Direct questions would almost certainly close down communication and that was the last thing he wanted to do. Fifteen minutes of chat about Arsenal or Spurs, or X box technology or whatever. In time, before the end of this first session, he would ask some vital questions, but not till he was reasonably sure he might get some kind of answer.

With Wesley, it went quite well. He was happy to talk about his PS3, even a little bit about his mother from St Lucia, where he wanted to go one day, so after twenty minutes, a risk seemed worth taking.
"Those tablets; they were your mum's?"
There was a moment of pause in which Wesley looked at him directly, then dropped his head and muttered an almost inaudible yes.

"Did you look for them, or just find them?"
"I looked. In the drawer."
"Do you know why?"
Wesley didn't seem to want to answer this, or didn't know how to. He tried another route.
"Was mum out at the time?"
Wesley nodded.
"So you knew you wouldn't get caught too quickly."
Another nod. Or was it a shrug?
"Did you want to be caught?"
Tears began to form in his eyes.
"Wanted mum to find you?"
There was no question about tears now.
"Wanted to tell her something important about you?"
He nodded again. Patrick judged he had pressed hard enough for one session. Too much too soon and there was a real risk of engaging the boy's defences.
"OK, that's something we can talk about in the future."
He watched as Wesley took a tissue and blew his nose more noisily than he expected. He couldn't resist a slight grin. Patrick noticed it, grinned back, and made him laugh more. It was an important moment of connection, and he was in no hurry to press on. It felt like the beginning of an understanding. The last five minutes of chat about Arsenal and scoring goals seemed more meaningful as a result.

*

At the case conference Wesley still looked small to him. He was sitting there with his mother, an attractive West Indian woman, he guessed no more than 35. She looked lost and very anxious. He made a point of introducing himself and enjoyed the big smiles he got from both of them in return.
"I hope you'll be able to help him doctor," she offered, deferentially.
"Well, I'll certainly do what I can."
"He's a good boy sir, he doesn't mean any harm."
"Of course."

Opposite from Wesley and his mother, he could see another, older woman, maybe fiftyish, wearing a smart black suit; attractive in a wholly different way. Actualised was the word that came to his head – counsellor jargon again – knows who she is. He watched fascinated as she organised paperwork, organised people, with confidence. After a few moments, guessing her to be the headteacher, he went across to introduce himself. She smiled and stretched out her hand for him to shake.
"Liz Broad. Headteacher."

He had little to do at the meeting. He wasn't going to say too much in any case, as he didn't want to damage the confidence he hoped he was developing with Wesley. He spent most of the time surreptitiously watching Elizabeth Broad. She fascinated him in a way he couldn't quite understand. Was he attracted to her? A middle aged, power dressed woman in a black suit? Surely not. But she was good looking, no question of that. Stylish and interesting. Maybe it was the calm assurance she had, and gradually, running riot into counsellor mode, he thought he detected an underlying vulnerability. The combination of assurance and vulnerability, he was sure now, was what was attracting him.

She was looking at him. He shifted his gaze away, embarrassed, and focused instead on the intense, ageless social worker who was talking about the way forward. But he hadn't heard much of what was being said. Through his peripheral vision he managed to ascertain that the headmistress had moved her gaze away from him. She was watching the intense social worker in the multi-coloured linen dress affecting a pseudo Indian style. Once more he dared to look back again, trying to be less overt.

Liz was aware of the doctor, or counsellor, or whatever he was, who for some reason seemed to keep glancing in her direction. Other heads had told her that counsellors did a good job, but that wasn't quite her experience, at least not personally. The counsellor in the hospice hadn't done her any good. Quickly she stopped her mind going in that direction. Maybe this guy did know his business. How young Wesley developed would certainly be a test for him. At least he seemed more mature, likely approaching sixty, and in a suit and tie he was properly dressed for the occasion. Not like the social worker who was still talking.

What was that little grin about? Patrick's attention had inadvertently shifted back to the headteacher. It softened the austerity of her face, and he could see that there were tiny laugh lines radiating out from her eyes. She had to have a sense of humour. He managed to look away quickly enough as she turned back again in his direction, and then realised she wasn't the only one; every face in the room was now focused on him. He must have been asked something, and he didn't know what it was. He turned back to the social worker and asked for a repeat.

"Senior moment, I'm afraid."

The polite laughter was embarrassing.

"Perhaps you can give us an indication of what you can offer Wesley, Dr East."

"Yes of course. I'm a consultant psychologist from the Lady Mortimer Hospital. I've been funded to work with Wesley for six sessions. We've had one session together so far. I think it went OK?"

He waited for an affirmative nod from Wesley and also from his mother before continuing, "So that's what I'll be offering."

"Thankyou doctor. We're grateful for your help. Wesley said he liked talking to you. Says you like football."

Smiles around the room. Patrick felt embarrassment once more but rode it.

"Yes, he told me he supports Arsenal."

It felt like he was being politely indulged. Counsellors; not in the real world. He'd experienced it before. Something you just have to live with and get on with the job, or the patient, or the client, depending on the setting.

The meeting drew to a close. Wesley waved as he left with his mother. She was smiling, seeming happy.
"See you next week, Wesley."
He gathered up his papers, preparing to leave, before glancing around the room to look once more at the fascinating headmistress, only to find she had approached him.
"Thanks for working with Wesley. It does seem as if he appreciates it."
"I hope so. No guarantees of course, but I'll do what I can."
There was a pause before she continued.
"You're based at the hospital then?"
"Yes. I do some private work from home, but mostly it's at the hospital. That's where I see Wesley. There's a big black chair, and he looks tiny in it."

Awkward laughter. Was he rambling on, saying too much, when all she wanted was a polite closure? But she was smiling again. Maybe it was alright.
"And you, you're head of this whole school?"
"I am yes. There are more than a thousand youngsters here. Most of them delightful."
"A thousand children," he repeated, "God! How do you manage that? Rather you than me!"
"That's what everyone says. You've got to want to do it, but it's a great job."
"How long have you been here?"
"More than eight years. Enough time for it all to be my fault!"
"Indeed!"
"Well, see you again, I hope."
"Another case conference maybe?"
"Why not."

He watched her make her way through the double doors moving them elegantly with her outstretched elbow, before making his own way out down the central stairway, through reception and to the car park below.

There were a large number of children running about in the playground above the car park, enjoying a range of mostly well ordered activities involving footballs. It was a chill early autumn day, and he noticed they were almost all boys. 'Girls must be inside – quieter activities for them." Generally the boys were white, but a few had African Caribbean features, and some looked Asian. They all seemed to be well integrated, and he didn't sense any racial tension, but he made a mental note to check that out with Wesley. As he got in his car to drive out of the school, no one seemed to take any notice of him at all.

Liz settled her papers in her office. As it was lunchtime, she made her way down to the school canteen. Len was on duty, keeping his eye on the students making their way into and out of the queues for lunch. When he spotted her he made his usual wiping of harassed brow impersonation, although everything in fact seemed completely under control.

"Everything alright Mrs Broad?"

"Yes, just done the TAC meeting about Wesley Freedom. He's got a counsellor now it seems. Chap called East. Doctor at the hospital I think."

"Patrick East? Well he won't go west with him! Sorry. Poor joke."

She ignored his comment and continued.

"What do you know about him?"

"Not much. Don't think he's a medical doctor. Psychologist of some sort. Pastoral staff say he's a decent chap."

"Seems it. I've not come across him before. Thanks."

For some reason, she found herself still thinking about Patrick East. She was surprised to have found a counsellor who seemed to make some kind of sense for a change. Not that she would ever do it, especially after the hospice experience, but he was, perhaps, the kind of counsellor she wouldn't mind consulting herself.

Across the dinner hall two girls had started an argument. Their voices penetrated the other sounds in the hall, which quickly diminished in the expectation of something more interesting. It drew her sharply from her reverie, and in no time she was heading for the girls' table. Before she arrived, the voices were stilled, and the two protagonists made an immediate show of settling back to their lunches.
"No problems here I hope?"
"No miss. Sorry miss."
"There are better ways of sorting out problems than shouting at each other. Yes?"
"Yes miss."
She stood watching for a few moments, satisfying herself that they really had calmed down before moving away again. The usual background chatter in the hall resumed. No need for a counsellor here then, she thought to herself with some amusement.

When she got home that evening Max was sitting at the kitchen table playing a computer game on his laptop. When she walked in the door he acknowledged her with a grunt, barely raising his head from the screen, across which she could see some kind of cartoon figure in armour running and overcoming a series of obstacles.
"No homework?"
No response. No movement apart from his hand manipulating the figure on the screen.
"I'm just going upstairs to change and then I'll organise tea."
She didn't think he was consciously blocking her out, although at times it made her feel almost invisible in her own home. He was in his own world; typical thirteen year old. She longed to be able to communicate with him on some meaningful level, but knew really that wasn't going to happen, at least not in the immediate future. She knew he needed

to keep her at a distance, although it hurt. But did he really have the same kind of desperate need to make contact with her, as his mother, as she did with him, her son? Or was that an illusion in her head?

"What would you have done?" she said out loud to the picture of Guy she kept by the side of her bed, holding it in her hands, and looking at it. Guy smiled enigmatically out at her, but provided no answer.
"You're his bloody father, after all. Or at least you were."
The sound of her own voice and the unusual vehemence of her expression surprised her. From downstairs she could still faintly hear the sound effects of Max's computer game. She put the picture back down in its usual place beside her bed and walked across to the en suite. Her face looked back at her in the mirror. Are you angry, it seemed to ask. She took off her glasses, pushed her hair back behind her ears and looked again in short sighted close up. For some reason, the eye-liner under her eyes looked more smudged than usual. Had it been a stressful day? Nothing she could think of gave any reason why the day had been worse than any other. She took off her black work suit and hung it tidily in the wardrobe and put her glasses neatly on the dressing table before walking into the en suite to cream off the make-up. Then she washed and dried her face, found her glasses and put them on, bringing the bedroom back into focus, before slipping into a grey sweater and black jeans.

The landline telephone was ringing, so she hurried downstairs to answer. Max still playing on the laptop, ignored it. When she picked up the phone, a male Asian voice asked for Mr Guy Broad, and then assuming he was speaking to his wife, asked Mrs Broad how she was today. Mrs Broad put the telephone noisily back on its cradle.
"Crap?"
"So you are here after all."
But he hadn't actually left the computer, or even looked up from it.
"Thought it was."

She caught the faintest smile reflected from the screen of the laptop. But the words dried up again.
"Have you got some homework to do?"
"Mmm."
"Does that mean yes?"
"Mmm."
"Do you think you ought to get it done before tea?"
The usual pantomime of huffing and moaning followed as Max logged out of his computer game, put his lap top on standby and fussed about in the depth of his school bag, eventually producing some books and a biro.
"Need any help?"
"No."
"Well just ask if you do."
Max adjusted his position so he was sitting at the end of the table furthest from her, almost it seemed as if to keep her away from what he was doing.
"You could go to your room."
Sometimes he worked in what had been designed as his playroom and had since become his teenage room in which he had another computer and a television as well as other gadgets she hardly knew about.
"I'm alright here. Just let me get on with it."
The irritation in his voice and manner was obvious. It was so hard to get the balance right. What was going on inside his head? She looked at him for a moment without saying anything. At least for today he was prepared to sit in the kitchen with her. It hurt though that he wouldn't talk to her in any way seriously, that he'd moved into his own private world of school and friends which no longer had anything to do with her. Often now he wanted to be out with friends, increasing the loneliness she already felt. It wasn't as if she was ever short of work to do at home, and at least she knew she could cope with her own company. She'd had to for the past two and a half years or more, since Guy died.

*

Patrick couldn't face a visit to see his mother every evening. There were carers keeping an eye on her, and he knew she wouldn't remember even if he went. He needed time to sort out some of his case notes and for his own thoughts. His mind kept returning to the headteacher he'd come across at the case conference. Yes, he thought she was attractive, but why, after more or less giving up on relationships over the past few years did he feel himself interested again? He kept seeing her peering through those glasses of hers. Under the air of calm control, He was sure he was right in detecting something vulnerable. Divorced probably, he decided, and maybe quite recently.

The telephone rang and disturbed his thoughts. He picked up the phone.

"Who is it?" Unmistakably his mother. He could feel irritation rising.

"You rang me, you should know. It's Patrick of course."

"Patrick?"

"Yes, it's me, Patrick, your son."

"Did you want me?"

"You rang me. Are you OK?"

"Yes I'm fine thankyou. I've had my tea. Lucy made it for me. And a nice cup of tea. And there's some grapes here. I like grapes."

"Yes I know you do. Are you going to watch television now?"

"Pardon?"

"Eastenders. You know you like that." He was conscious of raising his voice in a way he didn't like.

"Is it on tonight?"

"Yes, make sure you don't miss it."

"Miss what?"

"Put the television on now and watch Eastenders."

"Alright, I will. So you're alright then?"

"Yes I'm fine. I'll see you tomorrow."

The conversation ended. Despite his frustration, he couldn't resist a brief smile. And shorter than usual he thought, that's some relief. His mind drifted back to the headmistress. He felt as if he wanted to get to know her, but no obvious way forward presented itself.

7

From his sickbed in the barn Tom's strength was gradually returning. The pain in his shoulder was becoming less intense. He could get up and walk shakily over to the corner where he had created a toilet for himself. His stream of piss no longer had a burning feeling, and he guessed his temperature must have come down. He was more readily able to eat the food the young girl brought out to him. There were pieces of tomato bigger than any he had ever seen before, even during his time in Sicily, some kind of pale cheese, and hard biscuit like pieces of bread. During the first days all he had felt able to do was pick at things, but now everything she brought went almost as soon as she left it.

At some point towards the end of the first week he'd felt the need to do more than piss. He remembered it must have been six or seven days since he'd managed it and he could feel the rumbling in his bowels to the point he knew he had to go. He hurried to his corner, crouched down and waited. At first nothing, even after tentative straining. Then he felt movement, and finally managed to pass a large hard turd. He looked at it in some triumph as he pulled his trousers up. It really felt like an achievement, and it was almost a shame to have to bury it under a clump of hay.

He became conscious of his personal hygiene. His mouth felt unpleasant and unclean and he was sure his breath smelt. He hadn't washed for ages and apart from where the girl cleaned his wound, he felt stale and sweaty. Probably he stank like some half feral creature. When the girl next came into the barn, he mimed cleaning his teeth and rubbed his hands together as if to wash them. She watched him quizzically for a few moments and then seemed all at once to grasp his meaning. Fleetingly she smiled before turning back towards the big door. A few minutes later she was back with a small bowl of clean water and what looked like a toothbrush, leaving them to the side of where he slept. He smiled with pleasure, and she responded with a gentle reciprocal grin before departing and locking the barn behind her.

He examined what she'd left. As well as the bowl of clean cool water and the toothbrush, there was a small tablet of what he took to be soap. The faintly carbolic smell confirmed his assumption. She had understood him well. First he wet the toothbrush in the bowl and set to scrubbing the scale off his teeth and tongue. His right arm was relatively unharmed, so he could be rigorous without feeling pain. He would have liked some toothpaste, but for now he had done what he wanted. When he'd finished spitting mouthfuls of water into the hay that was all around him, his mouth felt cleaner and fresher and maybe his breath would have stopped smelling too.

Then he took the bowl and the soap over to the far end of the barn, a little away from his toilet area. He reckoned the girl wouldn't be back for some time as she'd just been to see him, so it felt safe to strip his clothes off completely. For a moment he stood there naked, enjoying the feel of his body. With his right hand he touched his penis, suddenly conscious of it, and briefly stroked it. There was a stirring of life as it rose a little from its flaccid state which made him smile. But his purpose was to wash himself clean, so carefully he dropped to his knees and began to lather the soap in the bowl of water.

The speed at which even this hard soap gave him lather surprised him. With his right hand he was quickly able to soap his head and his lank hair, and round his neck and under his left arm. Then, gingerly moving his weak left arm across, he managed to soap his right arm. Rinsing took longer as the lather was so effective. It had to be soft water out of the hard mountain rock. Then he eased himself back to a standing position and soaped the lower part of his body, making sure he cleaned gently and proudly round his genital area. Once more there was the stirring feeling. His manhood was quietly alive and well.

Finally, he tipped what was left of the water over his head and let it run down his body. It felt good. He was clean again. For a few minutes he waited, enjoying his own clean nakedness and allowing himself to dry before pulling his clothes back on again. That was less pleasant as they were dirty against his clean body, but he knew he couldn't stay naked. After dressing, he walked back to where his bed area had been created, and sat down. He was surprised how tired he felt after the exertion of washing, but it did feel like an achievement. As he lay back on the bed, his breathing got heavier, and quite soon he was in a deep sleep.

He was in an open space, walking forward through what seemed like a swirling mist. A shadowy figure was moving about. He was aware of a feeling of anxiety, wanting to turn and run, but his legs were heavy and he couldn't lift them to move. Then out of the mist a soldier carrying a rifle appeared. In the dream, he knew he had met this soldier before, knew that something unpleasant and painful was coming, but felt powerless to stop it. Through some kind of slow motion the soldier reached him, and raised his rifle to strike him. In his strange dreamlike state he was conscious of trying to cower down, and of attempting to shout, but the words were stuck in his throat. He struggled to work out where he was. Had he woken up? All around him it was dark, but somewhere in front he could see a moving light approaching him.

Half conscious of someone moving about somewhere in the barn, and of a light somewhere, he tried to wake up, but unable to manage it completely, slipped instead gradually back into sleep again. Standing beside him, the girl looked at his sleeping form in the dim candlelight and listened for his breathing in the dark. Gradually it became deeper and more settled again. Once she thought he was fully asleep, she lifted the candle again to watch him for a moment. Then, very quietly, she made her way back to the big door and left the barn. Outside the donkey was moving about, seeming restless.

*

Marco can hear his name being called, but can't work out where from. He looks around trying to make sense.

"Marco! Marco!"

The old donkey, older than him, shuffles and stamps his back feet. Marco moves away, making sure he isn't standing behind it. He remembers the big kick and the big bruise on his leg, just above his knee. First it was red, then black, then yellow, till it gradually faded through dirty flesh colour to nothing. He remembers it hurt a very long time.

"That will teach you not to stand behind donkeys and horses."

He made sure he learnt that. Marco never stands behind the donkey. He won't be kicked again.

Still there are voices calling him. He looks round again. Still no one. Then he feels a tap on his right shoulder. He looks round smiling, wanting to be friendly, but there's no one. Then rustling behind him and a tap on his left shoulder. He looks round the other way. Still no one.

"Marco! Marco!"

The donkey stamps again, and he moves further away. Still no one.

"It's the hand. Coming to get you!"

Then the sound of running, then nothing. He looks around him, but there is no one to be seen. He can't understand what is happening. He turns back to the donkey, snorting and fidgeting. It turns its head towards Marco, and then away again. Cautiously he strokes the back of its neck.

*

Anna knew Sophie's wedding was going to be a difficult experience. The invitation, so welcome and exciting when it arrived, was gathering dust on her dressing table. Its meaning had shifted from celebration to something like a wake in her mind. She kept on reminding herself how glad she was that Ben had gone, but it felt skin deep. Underneath was a well of anger and indignation that he could actually walk out on her, and beneath that was a dark pit of hurt and loss that she couldn't allow herself to feel. She knew she wasn't ready for it. Not yet anyway.

Anyone else's wedding she could have sent a polite excuse and then stayed at home with Big Brother on TV. Easier and less embarrassing than going on her own and having to tell people she was no longer with Ben who had buggered off with another woman. But Sophie was a best friend. She'd already missed the hen night in Amsterdam the weekend after Ben walked out. No way could she have gone over there and had the sort of fun she'd always enjoyed in the past. But she couldn't miss the wedding.

On the bed she laid out her short black dress. Putting out the clothes, and getting herself bathed and ready for the wedding made her feel slightly better, but underneath the nagging hurt was still there. Ben was gone. Ben, the bastard lover who'd taken three years out of her life and then just walked out.

The invitation surprised Josh. 'The wedding of Jamie and Sophie' didn't mean anything to him until he remembered Jamie was an old friend from the banking days.

"That must have been quick," he thought to himself. But the opportunity of a day out was welcome, and he was happy to reply positively.

Should he be stuffy and wear his school suit and tie, or be a bit more cool? In the end he decided cool was how he preferred to be, make a fresh image for himself. Good opportunity. Might even be some single girls there. He'd been single too long.

"If Jamie can do it, and get married for God's sake . . wow! So can I"

*

Anna knew the bride looked lovely. Traditional white dress, but nothing flouncy, just something straight that emphasised her slim waist with a simple bouquet of white and yellow flowers. No headdress, so her beautiful long blonde hair could flow down her back. Unlike her own dark hair, which she'd tied back into a pony tail. Lightness against her own darkness. She couldn't help thinking it suited the way they both felt. How Jamie had to be proud of her. Good idea to choose a simple registry office ceremony and follow it up with a reception at a local hotel accompanied by family and friends. It was her idea of the best kind of wedding too. What she'd probably have herself – if anyone would have her that was, and if any bastard man could be trusted enough.

She stood in the sunshine, slightly apart, watching the bridal group outside the hotel as the photos came to their long winded end. Good idea to do that here as well she thought. The registry office was hardly attractive, even on a bright early autumn afternoon. Out in the grounds of the hotel they could pose against the pond and the artificial fountain. She'd tried to avoid the photos herself, but had been dragged into the 'best friends of the bride,' and then into the final 'everyone together.'

It was time for passing on the bouquet. A silly tradition - the bride throws it, and the girl who catches it is the next to get married and all that nonsense she thought.

"Come on Sophie, time to throw it to one of us."

"What do I have to do?" Laughter.

"You know! Throw out the bouquet so one of us can catch it. Got to do it properly. Shut your eyes. No peeping! Keep them shut." More laughter.

Sophie lifted the bouquet in the air with both hands.

"Shall I throw it now?"

"Nearly ready." The single girls gathered round in front of her.
"OK everyone? Right, now!"
Sophie lifted her arms and threw the bouquet in the direction of where she could hear the excited laughter. Anna watched the bouquet sail up into the air in an arc, and descend towards one of the bridesmaids. There was a little burst of applause. She looked from a slight distance at the happy recipient, bouquet in her arms, babbling excitedly about someone whose name sounded like Whippet who she would be marrying in the spring. Good luck to them she thought, rather them than me. What complete nonsense it all was.

Sophie was coming towards her.
"Congratulations! You look lovely. I'm so pleased for you."
"Anna! I'm so sorry to hear about you and Ben." They kissed.
"Don't be. Don't let it affect your day. I'm fine. Really!"
She smiled extravagantly, not at all believing what she was saying, but hoping Sophie would choose to believe her.
"Are you? It must be hard though."
She wanted to say, 'go away, Sophie, enjoy yourself, leave me alone,' but all she managed was "I'm OK, really. Isn't it a lovely day!"
And as soon as she'd said it she realised to her surprise that it actually was the most glorious late summer day. The September sun was shining brightly and it was warm without being too hot.
"Yes. Aren't we lucky!"
"You deserve it, Sophie."
"Thanks Anna, catch up with you later." Sophie was already moving away from her, waving and smiling pleasantly.

She walked off in the other direction, wanting to meet someone to talk to, and at the same time not wanting to have to say anything about her and Ben. The sun was reflecting her distorted image in the pond as she walked along the edge, and then another form materialised beside it. She turned to see a young man of about her own age.
"Haven't we met before?"

"I'm sorry?" Anna looked at him, not understanding.
"We definitely have met before. I'm sure of it."
Was he chatting her up? She looked at him cautiously.
"You drove your car into mine – three weeks ago. I recognise you. You were quite rude I remember. But I've forgiven you."
There was an accompanying smile, which looked far from genuine.
"Oh God! Not you again. I think we'd better avoid each other here."
"Well it was you who ran into me."
"You weren't very nice about it."
"Are you surprised? It was quite a shock."
"OK. Let's skip it. We're at a wedding party remember. If you don't mind, I'm going across to see some friends."
He watched her flounce away, twirling in her black dress and coming close to pushing past him. He caught a whiff of perfume as she went.
"Better than the scruffy jeans and sweater she was wearing when she hit me anyway. Quite nice legs really."
"Pardon?"
He'd almost walked into the bride's mother. She looked at him benevolently.
"Oops, sorry . . . I was talking to myself."
"Quite alright. As long as you're enjoying yourself. By the way you're not Margaret's son are you?"
"Margaret? No sorry, not me. I don't think I know a Margaret. "
"Well you do look like him."
And before he needed to say anything else she was off heading for someone else.

*

Simon found himself watching the young man talking to Anna. He thought his dark hair rather attractive, and enjoyed the saucy smile which seemed to make her a bit angry. Then aware he might be staring, managed to avert his eyes just before the guy turned in his direction and talked to his mother before wandering off again. She however turned back to him.
"Do you know I could have sworn that was Margaret's son."

"You haven't you got your glasses on mother!"
"Today? Of course not. I can manage perfectly well without them. It's your father who's got to make the speech, not me, I'm glad to say."
"He doesn't look anything like. Too young to start with. I thought Margaret's son was nearly forty?"
But his mother was already wandering off to talk to someone else, leaving him alone once more. He wandered off to the large double doors that led into the reception room and looked around. There had to be forty or fifty people mingling and chatting noisily to each other, celebrating his sister's wedding. Over the bar was the congratulations sign he'd put there, surrounded by groups of balloons. No one seemed to notice him. Then emerging through the doorway from the gardens next to where he was standing he spotted Anna.

"Hi Simon, you alright?"
"Sophie said things weren't going too well for you."
"Did she tell you Ben walked out on me?"
"Mmm. Sorry to hear that. You alright?"
"Not really, but I'm coping."
"Anything I can do?"
"No. Just got to come to terms with it haven't I. Just takes time."
"Who was that you were just talking to?"
"You won't believe this, but he ran his car into me a couple of weeks ago. Now the cheeky bastard's turned up here! God knows why. Have you seen him before?"
"No. Must be a friend of Jamie's. At least he's good looking."
"Is he? I didn't really notice. Got rid of him actually. Didn't want to have anything to do with him. Certainly not here. Not on Sophie's wedding day."
"So you don't want to chat him up."
Suddenly from nowhere she was angry.
"Fuck off Simon, that's not funny!"
"Sorry. Didn't mean to offend you."
"You go and chat him up if you want to."

Her words felt like a punch in the stomach. He was aware of an inane laugh coming out of his mouth, but he felt completely unable to say anything. An image of himself standing in front of her, open mouthed came into his head. It was as if he'd been caught out.
"I'm sorry Simon, I shouldn't have said that. It wasn't meant to be hurtful."
Still he just stood there looking at her.
"But you shouldn't have said that about me chatting him up. You know how quickly I get angry, especially at the moment."
"OK. Let's leave it. I just need . . ."
"Sure. I . . . I think Sophie's beckoning to me. I need to go. See you in a bit."
"OK."

It was all too obvious what she was implying. To him it felt like he was back in a dream he often had, where he was naked with every part of him exposed. Now suddenly it felt like his dream had come to life and he was horrifyingly exposed to everyone. He wanted to run, wanted to get out as fast as he could, but today of all days, at his sister's wedding, he was trapped. He went over to the bar to get himself a drink and steady himself down, only to find he was standing next to the guy he'd seen talking to Anna, the bastard who'd run into her car, and who had now led to his exposure. He felt himself trembling. Part of him wanted to punch him hard for everything he'd done. And yet rationally he also knew it wasn't the guy's fault. He'd done nothing at all to him.

Simon looked at the guy in profile, ordering his own drink. There was a hint of designer stubble covering his face; dark stubble, like his dark hair. He felt himself stirring and fleetingly imagined he was pressing his own lips onto the other guy. It was as if all his fantasies had suddenly materialised. He couldn't stay there, couldn't take the chance on what he might do, how he might react. He had to get away. But the other

guy had got his drink and was turning round towards him as he move away from the bar and brushed against him as he went.
"Excuse me mate."
"Sure." He heard his own voice break and go ridiculously high, making him feel like a schoolboy.

*

Later that evening Josh found himself asking Jamie who the girl in the black dress was.
"There's more than one, mate. What's she look like?"
"Well, short black dress, nice legs, long dark hair, tied back. Look, there she is, talking to Sophie."
"Anna. She's one of Sophie's best mates."
"What's she like?"
"Good looking, bit of a temper, but she's OK. Why, do you fancy her?"
"Not likely. Completely rude. Ran her car into the back of mine recently. Really stroppy – said it was my fault. I remember her name now. She wrote it down for me when we collided. Is she always like that?"
"Like I say, she's got a temper. Sparks just like that, out of nowhere. Jewish I think, might accounts for her being so dark. Sophie says she's a good mate. Her guy walked out on her not long back though. Bit cut up about it still. Might be why you copped it."
"OK. Maybe. Thanks."

Fuelled by a few drinks, he could feel the hint of a challenge. He stood a few minutes at the bar, watching Anna chatting to another less attractive girl. When she moved away he saw a chance. Nothing ventured and all that. He walked across.
"Anna . . . ."
"Mmm . . . .?"
"Anna, I'm, er, sorry if you thought I was rude."
She looked at him, uncertain, seemed to mutter something.
I . . . er . . .believe you're going through a bad patch . ."
"Christ almighty, what's it to do with you?"

Wrong move. Too familiar he thought. Try another tack.
"Er, I'm a friend of Jamie's. We used to work together . . ."
"Look, are you trying to stalk me or something?"
She was raising her voice now and staring straight at him.
"Can I make this any clearer? Will you fuck off."
Josh lifted his hands in surrender.
"OK, OK. Message received. No harm meant. See you around."
"In your dreams!"
Once more he watched her flounce off, noticing again the curve of her calves.

*

"When she said that I wanted to floor to open up under me. It felt like I'd been deluding myself; that everyone really knew all the time I was gay."
Simon was still distressed when two days later he saw Patrick.
"Would that really have been such a terrible thing?"
"Feels like I've been leading my life completely unaware of what others thought of me."
"Do you think they would have thought any less of you if they had known?"
"Not sure. But it's how I feel that matters surely?"
"Exactly. And that's where you can change. You've told me you think some of the orchestra might suspect it. No one else gay in the orchestra?"
"Oh yes! Flute and principal double bass."
The incongruity of the pairing broke some of the tension and he laughed.
"Partners?"
"Don't think so. Only musically. The bass player's got a shaved bald head. The flute's got lots of wild grey hair; older guy, eccentric."
"Anyone think less of them because they're gay?"
"No. Not at all."
"Wouldn't it be like that for you?"
"Maybe."

"Maybe?"
There was a pause. Patrick waited. It was some time before Simon responded.
"I hated secondary school. Because I played the violin, I got teased. At first that's all it was. I didn't like it, but I coped. Then it got worse. This lad called Mason used to get others on to me. One day a group of them took my violin – it was in its case – and threw it to each other over my head. It got dropped a couple of times and I tried to grab it, but one of them got there first. I was really worried it would break. I started crying, and that made it even worse. Other times I got tripped up. Kids would stick their feet out in front of me so I fell over. Once I hurt my arm. I thought I'd broken it and wouldn't be able to play the violin again. I told my mum I'd just fallen over. I was too embarrassed to say I was being bullied. Didn't want her coming up the school. In the end it was only sprained and healed up quickly, but it scared me."
Patrick waited, allowing Simon to continue his story.

"The school was an old one and there were outside toilets. One icy morning I tripped going up the steps into it. There was a big lad I didn't know coming out at the same time. I expected him to kick me or something, but instead he asked me if I was alright and helped me up; even picked up my violin for me. I cried a little bit, not because I was hurt, but because he was so kind. Brings tears to my eyes just telling you about it. In my mind now, he's the perfect, ideal man. Unattainable all my life so far."

He sat quietly. The tears welled in his eyes and flowed freely down his cheeks. Patrick let him stay in the moment before saying anything.
"So far."
"So far?"
"It's what you said. So far."
"You mean, maybe that ideal man might one day appear?"
"Seemed to be what you were saying. If you want it. If you let him in."
"If . . . .you mean . . .if I can be gay?"

"If you can accept yourself. Yes."
"It scares me. Really scares me."
Patrick waited again before responding.
"Coming out? Coming out scares you?"
"Yes. But not just coming out. It's bigger. I'm a private person now. No one bullies me. No one judges me."
"Is that how you want to stay? Are you happy?"
"No. . . no. Not really."
"Your choice. Your call for what you want out of life."

8

"In the end, it comes down to sex. Survival of the species. Darwin. Not complicated at all." Len Turner stopped to draw on his cigarette, standing, slightly compromised at the outside door of the staff room, holding it open slightly to let the smoke out. He looked round at his audience sitting inside on the shabby teachers' chairs that must have been there ten years or more and waited for the response. As usual Johnno couldn't keep quiet.
"Sex is all you think about Len."
"Precisely. It has almost nothing to do with us as individuals." Another long inhale on the cigarette, followed by the familiar dry cough. "We do what we have to do. OK, we've institutionalised it with marriage and all sorts of laws and rights – that's how we got our kids honey!" As he made the aside he pantomimed Groucho Marx with his cigarette. "All good clean stuff! But underneath the skin, we're just sexual beings geared towards propagating the species."

Josh sat back in his chair and listened with interest, taking his mind off the next struggle with his Year 10 group which would begin in five minutes time. Into his mind came the image of Anna in her short black dress. The unattainable Anna, who wouldn't have anything to do with him. He smiled to himself an involuntary smile, which Len spotted.
"I see you're smiling young man." He smiled back at Len without reply.

"Young man like you. Can't keep your mind off sex!" The voice was Groucho still, softening the impact before reverting to his own natural west country lilt. "No, you don't need to say anything, and I won't ask you. But it will be true."

As Josh's smile widened, Len gave him a knowing grin back, puffing once more on the cigarette and creating a smoke cloud, which he waved out of the door with his spare hand.

"Don't think it's only men. We know women enjoy sex. Magazines tell us now."

"Is that the only way you know?"

The stout French teacher sitting opposite Josh, who he'd discovered was called Jeannette, or incongruously Madame Hardcastle to his Year 7 group, laughed out loud.

"Oh yes, you can laugh, but you know it's a basic need. All of us, men and women, we don't just like sex. We need it. That's why we like it. Darwin again. Can't survive without it."

"Come on Len, you know that's not true for everyone."

"Isn't it? Think about it."

"Catholic priests?"

"Well we all know what they do." Groucho again, the provocation intended for Catholic Jeannette, but she didn't take the bait.

"OK, what about spinsters, single people. Plenty of those."

"Well there are ways and means." He indulged in more Groucho pantomime and a big overtly cheesy grin as if posing for a photographer before stubbing out the cigarette and throwing it unceremoniously out of the door.

"Must go. Bell rings soon. And anyway, there's always what Freud called sublimation."

Theatrically he brushed his hands together before flouncing across the staffroom and through the door into the school beyond.

"Bet he doesn't get much sex." Johnno offered his thought conspiratorially to Josh. "Rule of thumb. Less they get, the more they talk."

"Really?"

"Wait till you see his wife. Big and ugly. Nice woman, puts up with him, but you wouldn't fancy her. Talking about it helps him get through. All those brains – more than most – damned good teacher too. Kids love him. But doesn't know how to enjoy life. Right, better go and get organised for Year 11. Only came in for a cup of tea and had to listen to all that. See you."
As he went out, Josh heard him blow his whistle to control some noise in the corridor outside, which quickly stopped. He took the opportunity to go out to his own classroom and prepare for the Year 10 group.

*

The lesson started badly. Some of the boys seemed very excited and it unnerved Josh. There were catcalls at each other, and taunts at two well made up girls.
"Tell him to shut up sir!"
"He gets on my nerves, always the bloody same. Sorry sir, but he is. Mac – fuckin' shut it!"
"Ooh sir, did you hear that. Send her out!"
Josh wanted to control them, get them to settle down. He shouted.
"Now, will you all stop it and sit down. Now! I mean it."
It had some effect, but he had the uneasy feeling that some of the lads were smirking at him. He tried not to respond. Eventually there was a kind of sullen quiet in the room, enabling him to start the lesson. He wanted them to read two texts, comparing writing styles.
"Sir, this is boring."
"I'm sorry, but we have to do it."
"Why sir?"
"Because it's on the syllabus. Now read it please."
There was some sort of quiet for a few moments. Then suddenly, for no apparent reason, Mac stood noisily, crashing his chair back into the desk behind him, and walked over to the window.
"Mac, get back to your seat and get on with your work."

Mac ignored him completely and continued leaning with both arms on the window ledge. Provocatively he rested his head on his arms. It felt like a challenge he couldn't ignore.
"You can either get back to your seat and do some work, or you'll have to get out."
Slowly, Mac stood up, turned towards Josh, and pointedly announced:
"It's crap in here."
The quiet in the classroom edged perceptibly into a tense silence as everyone watched to see what would happen.
"Mac, get out of the classroom!"
"Right, I'm fuckin' goin'."
He moved clumsily back to his desk, grabbed his bag, swung it round his shoulder, making the girl behind move quickly to the side to avoid being hit. Then he moved to the front of the classroom, passed threateningly close to Josh and on towards the door, which he opened noisily and then slammed behind him. The door failed to fasten and swung back open again.

As it did so, the figure of Len Turner appeared.
"Everything alright Mr Greenwell?"
The entire class watched in awed silence.
"I've just had to send Mac out, Mr Turner."
"I think I've just seen his speedy exit, Mr Greenwell."
There was a touch of levity in the reply that relaxed the tension in the classroom and brought a few faint smiles. Len was onto it immediately.
"That's not a cue for the rest of you to stop working. I expect to hear that every one of you has worked really hard through the lesson. Let me know Mr Greenwell."
It wasn't entirely clear what Josh had to let him know, but he thanked him anyway. For some while after, nobody spoke, and the lesson settled to an uneasy calm.

*

"How did it go once Mac left?"

Len Turner's office, just off the main entrance to the school, gave him a view over comings and goings. There wasn't much he missed. But it was far from tidy. Josh looked around at piles of marking, a couple of footballs in the waste paper bin, odd items he presumed confiscated on the edge of the desk, and sun bleached pieces of paper round the edge of the notice board where the newer notices had clearly been place over them. On top of the filing cabinet were two water starved plants.

"Better. I felt in control again. Rest of the group seemed to respond."

"You need to be pack leader. If you don't do it someone else will. Be the boss."

"OK. Thanks Mr Turner."

"Len. Everyone calls me Len."

"Can I ask you something?"

"Of course."

"You said something about sublimation this afternoon. What did you mean?"

"Freud. You ever read any Freud?"

"No, can't say I have. Don't know much about him at all."

"Freud thought, I've no doubt rightly, that sex was central to human motivation, but not everyone has access to sex as that French woman was saying. Some people sublimate their sex drive into other things, like power, heaven forbid. I guess the likes of Hitler come into that category. He's not supposed to have had much sex, although I suppose he did have that Eva woman. Anyway, whatever, sex governs most of what we do. Take that guy you had to send out."

"Mac?"

"All that testosterone sloshing about inside him and nowhere for it to go. He can't make any sense of it, so he loses it. Makes a pest of himself in lessons, keeps getting thrown out."

"You think that's what goes wrong? He can't control his sexual instincts?"

"Well we all have trouble with that, but most of us as adults are better at managing it. The Macs of this world can't handle it at all."

He had to clear his throat before he could continue with his argument.
"We have this need to make life make sense. As if we're that important in the grand scheme of things. But it doesn't. Sure we can pretend that it does. Do things that seem meaningful, go into politics, become a doctor, or a nurse, or a teacher, heaven forbid! Even write a novel. Maybe we have to do something to stop us going mad, but in the end, it's all an illusion. Our only task is to keep the race going, though God knows what for, or rather, if he existed at all, I guess he wouldn't be able to explain what his creation was for! That's why sex is so central to all our thinking. And sublimation is the delusional drive that comes out of the sexual energy when we can't do it, or can't get enough of it," suddenly Groucho was back, only to disappear again as quickly as he appeared.
"Which leads us into doing things we think have meaning."

He stopped, looked at Josh and looked away again. Josh sat in the dowdy office listening to him, trying to make some kind of sense out of the bleak message he was hearing. He didn't know what to think.
"Not that I want to depress you. You're at the start of your career. Life's ahead of you." Len was bright again, as if coming out of a dark place in his head.
"But, never let the truth get in the way of a good story, I always say! If there's no meaning, we can make it up! You can make it all work for you. Do something exciting. Go bungee jumping or sky diving or something. You're young enough to do that sort of thing. Have a bit of fun in your life. Look!"
He pointed to a poster on the wall.
LIFE IS WHAT YOU MAKE IT
"You're at the start of your career. You'll do well. Make the most of it."
He bustled around the room for a moment, as if looking for something, while Josh watched him. Then, seeming to have found it in the form of a tattered looking book, he spoke again.
"You'll have to excuse me now."
"Well, thanks for your help, Mr Turner,"

"Len."
"I'm grateful for your help with Mac."
"Any time."
They left the office together and Josh headed for his classroom. He could see Len making his way to the staff room, taking a packet of cigarettes from his pocket as he went.

9

It made Leo feel very uncomfortable reading the Gazetta del Sud two days after following Marco down into the shallow valley. They'd certainly made the most of the story. "Priest finds body," or similar variations of the theme were all over the front pages, accompanied by a picture of himself. And that wasn't true of course; Marco had found it in the first place, but he knew if he told them that, Marco's life would become very difficult. They knew Marco had been with him, which was bad enough, but had assumed he'd just been taking Marco out for some exercise. Better at least to take the pressure himself, although he certainly wasn't enjoying it. And then it was all over the national press, his worst nightmare.

The photographers camped outside the vestry to get pictures; journalists wanted him to give them accounts of what had happened. He kept saying the bishop had told him to say nothing, and he couldn't go against the church's instructions, even if he'd wanted to, which he certainly didn't, but still they pestered him every time he appeared outside the door. He felt sorry for Marco, who couldn't understand what all the attention was about. It hadn't taken the press long to realise Marco couldn't tell them anything, but it didn't stop them wanting pictures. After initially enjoying the attention, he'd got frightened and wouldn't go out.

He discovered from the newspapers that Marco's hand had turned out to be part of a body buried some distance into the past. It would take forensic tests over a period of time to establish just when, and just what were the circumstances of the body's death. There were suggestions that it was probably a man, but no one was sure, and the police, even if they knew, weren't letting on. They sealed off the area down by where they'd found the body, where investigations of the area were ongoing. More than that, neither he nor anyone else in the town had any real idea. But it didn't stop the rumours, which spread much faster than any kind of real knowledge.

It seemed to him that the gossip which resulted was very Italian. He loved his country's ability to make a real fuss and develop improbable speculations out of nothing much. Sometimes people talked loudly on the street corners, in the town square and under the war memorial. Sometimes he noticed conspiratorial discussions in doorways and outside shops. For the men collecting the grapes from the vines, it replaced *calcio italiano* as the main topic of conversation, although not for long. Football would always reassert itself, the blues were just too much part of male Italian life. It amused him that there was no need to be shocked by any of the latest revelations about the prime minister in the face of such huge excitement in Sottomonte.

There was general agreement about why the hand had suddenly appeared now. The unusually heavy rains of the last year had filled the normally sedate stream at the bottom of the valley and the rush of water had washed away some of the embankment at the side. The hand must have become exposed once the heat of the sun had dried it out again. Nobody knew how long the hand might have been visible. It had taken Marco on his walks with the observational ability of a child to find it, and then when he'd followed him that day, anxious for his safety, they'd discovered the body between them. But everyone had their own theory about which long disappeared person the body might be.

Some of the older people talked to Leo about an old tramp who'd wandered through on his way to Reggio to find some kind of shelter

for the winter. He was told his predecessor Father Luigi had put him up for a couple of nights.
"Must have been twenty years ago at least."
"No, nearer thirty surely."
"You may be right, who knows. I bet it's him though. Got drunk and fell in the stream I guess. *Ubriacone*."
"Could be. But wasn't there that strange chap, all the way from Naples, who came here looking for work that autumn. That was more than thirty years surely."
"Could have been him too."
"Could have been anyone really I suppose. We'll know soon enough."
Darker speculations centred around a possible local murder, and various missing people were suggested, but all of these ideas seemed to result in someone claiming that the person was alive and well in the next town, or Reggio, or even Perugia, which didn't stop another suggestion surfacing with remarkable speed.

The very oldest remembered something about a soldier from the war, but that was soon dismissed. Just too long ago was the common consensus.
"Body wouldn't last that long in the ground surely."
More than ever, there was a general tendency for everyone to cross themselves; Hail Marys were on everyone's lips. He was happy to encourage that. Something in the very idea of finding a dead body stirred up disturbing thoughts in everyone.

It took at least a month before anything remotely like normal working returned to the town. The body had been exhumed and taken away for analysis. With it had gone the reporters and the photographers, leaving something like a return to peace behind them. Leo's sermons for several Sundays afterwards invited people to get back to normal and get on with their lives. And there was always prayer for the body, whoever he was.
"May his soul rest in peace, whatever the circumstances of his death."

"May his soul rest in peace."
They all said it. He knew that most of them meant it in a broadly Christian way.
He was pleased when something like normality returned, but it didn't stop people talking. Salvatore wanted the soul of the body to rest in peace too, but he knew Salvatore was also going round and saying to anyone who would listen that the old idiot, meaning Marco, shouldn't have been allowed to interfere with God's will.
"It's blasphemous," he kept saying, "interfering with the natural order of things."

Talking with Salvatore however disturbed Leo. He knew his memories went back a long way and sensed he had more knowledge about the body than he was prepared to say. Sun weathered and dark skinned with what was left of his hair covered by a dirty flat cap, he looked like a very old Sicilian, part Arab, part Spaniard. His mother had crossed the straits to Italy to marry his father after the first war. Approaching eighty five, his memories went back to the second war.
"Bad days," was as much as he wanted to say about it now, but the days of the German occupation still lived within him.
"Bad days. Don't want to live through anything like that again."
Was the body a German soldier? Leo knew it was possible.

He had another responsibility. Marco's mother was distraught. She didn't want to talk about what had happened to anyone. She stayed inside her house even after the reporters and photographers had gone. It took him some while to talk, to re-establish contact. He promised once again to keep an eye on Marco, who was in any case too scared to go far, and was also anxious about his mother. In effect, he realised, they contributed to each other's anxiety.

"I can take him up to the church, find him jobs to keep him busy. He'll be alright with me."

But first he had to get Marco into the church. He was alright on Sundays when everyone else was there, but the empty church was different, and initially he resisted. Leo guessed it felt cold and gloomy to him, going in from the sunlight outside, and he knew he didn't like the smell of incense. Sometimes, even on Sundays, it made him rub his nose violently, almost as if he had been stung. But in the end he managed to get him inside. Together they walked through to the vestry, where he had some church magazines that wanted stapling, and he got Marco laboriously and inefficiently fixing the sheets together in the order he laid them out for him. The end product wasn't as neat and tidy as he usually liked, but he decided that it was better to keep Marco busy and out of trouble. Later I can get him to sweep out the aisles; he'll do that OK he thought.

He worried about Marco's mother. She still seemed to be spending a lot of time sitting at home, not wanting to venture out into the sunlight. Not like her old self at all, and uncharacteristically, she locked the door and refused to answer whenever anyone came knocking, trying to stir her into talking about what was worrying her. Leo knew she only let him in because she didn't think she should keep a man of God out, but she was very unwilling to talk. It puzzled him. Did she too have some kind of knowledge, like he guessed Salvatore had, that neither of them wanted to share? She had said something about not stirring up old ghosts, but not much else. All he could do for now was to let her alone and keep trying to raise her spirits in whatever way he could.

In his quieter moments, the church was his sanctuary. Above the altar was a wooden crucifixion. It was at least a hundred years old. The sculptor clearly wanted to emphasise the pain and distress of Christ's suffering rather than any kind of beatification. Once he'd climbed up on a ladder to see it more closely. It was obvious from the care with which it had been carved that the sculptor was really in touch with Jesus' pain. Frequently he knelt before it, looking upwards and always he found it both awe inspiring and comforting. It was the supreme sacrifice that made the sense of the world. He died to save us all; and the imitation of Christ was his Christian mission. There was no shadow of doubt within him and he embraced it with all his heart.

10

The idea of clay pigeon shooting sounded like fun. It was certainly different from sky diving. On a whim, she rang up and booked herself a Saturday morning session. When she got there the place was in a kind of dip, and she had to walk down a steep embankment to get to the meeting point, where ahead of her she could see the small group of people who had clearly also signed up for the same activity.

As she reached the group, she looked around at the faces, and to her astonishment she could see once more that the guy who had caused her to crash her car and was then rude at the party was amongst them. At first, she wasn't sure whether to ignore him or acknowledge him, but quickly realised there was no way of avoiding him, so decided to take the initiative before he spotted her.
"Hi. We meet again."
"My God, it's you! Are we fated to keep meeting?"
"Seems like it."
"Can we just agree to be civil to each other for today?"
There was something in his tone she didn't like. Patronising, yes, that was it, bloody patronising, but she fought it down.
"OK. Why not."
She smiled. It was false, but she wasn't letting him spoil her day. Maybe he wouldn't be much good and miss everything. The thought brought a more genuine smile, which Josh responded to, unaware of the hidden thought.
"Looks like a nice clear day."
It was the first day of October. In the dip, and ahead of them, a bright early autumn sun shone through the trees.
"Have you done this before?" he said.

"Never. Something I thought I'd try."
"Me too. I was at a loose end this weekend, so I signed up. Something I've thought I might like to do, but guess I might be useless really. I'm quite clumsy, but I give anything a try once."

A kind of tractor drew up, with an open trailer behind it. They were all invited to climb onto the trailer to get to the shooting area. Anna got on first, and Josh followed her, standing next to her against the rail. Once everyone was on board the trailer was quite full, and he felt he was uncomfortably close to her. But the ride was short, although rather bumpy, and she noticed that he seemed to be doing his best to observe her personal space, rather than take the opportunity to be over familiar.

Once they reached the range, there was an overlong explanation of what to do and what not to do with the rifles and all the health and safety rules, before anyone could get started. Then it was Anna's turn first. She had to shout out 'pull', which felt quite silly, and a disk, more like a plate than a pigeon, shot out of a contraption by the side of where she stood and into the air. She followed the arc, trying to anticipate its trajectory, fired and missed. There was advice from the instructor beside her, again 'pull', and once more a miss. It took her five goes before she managed at last to make any kind of contact. When she did, breaking the clay plate into many pieces in the air, she felt a surge of satisfaction. But it was her only success in that first round.

Eventually it was his turn. She watched him taking in the advice from the instructor, noticed how well balanced his slim figure seemed to be as he raised the gun and shouted out 'pull'. But he too missed his first shot. Her satisfaction was short lived; it was his only miss. Every other shot blasted through the object in the sky. When he came back to where she and the other shooters stood, she couldn't look at him, sure he would be very smug. But he didn't say anything, and she was at least grateful for that.

She got better in future rounds, but he didn't get any worse. By the end his score was significantly higher than anyone else. 'Well done' she said without really meaning it.
"Thanks, but you did well too."
She couldn't answer. It sounded so horribly patronising again, and she couldn't speak to him in the return journey in the trailer. But when he asked her if she wanted to join him for a coffee afterwards, she agreed without quite knowing why.

"What do you do?" he asked, once they'd sat down with their drinks.
"Journalist. Work for the local paper."
"Herald?"
"Mm. Don't laugh, I write Rosie's Read. I use experiences like this morning to publicise local events and activities. A fortnight ago I went sky diving. And I do some interviews."
"Sounds like fun. Do you enjoy it?"
"Sometimes. Can be boring though. You? What do you do?"
"Teacher. Secondary School."
"Well that figures. Should have guessed."
She looked at him laughing.
"Why do you say that?"
"Well you can be patronising."
It took Josh a moment to register the directness of her response and the absence of any attempt to wrap the message up politely.
"Thanks a lot."
His smile looked forced.
"Well you did ask. That goes with the job as well I suppose."
"I'm only in my first term."
"Doesn't take long then."
She didn't look embarrassed at all.
"Do I shock you?"

"Actually, yes you do."
"Most people are surprised. Goes with being a pushy journalist I suppose. My last boyfriend couldn't cope with it. Walked out on me in the end."
"I'm sorry ..."
"Don't be! He wasn't worth it."

Josh thought her eyes said hurt as well as anger, but he didn't respond. He took a sip of his drink, and Anna did the same. For a while they sat in silence. He didn't know how to break it and felt anxious not to provoke her further. But at the same time he knew he found her fascinating. Eventually, unable to stand the silence any longer, he fell back on the old cliché.
"Would you like something else to drink?"
"Thanks. Same again."
She watched him walk over to the bar. For the first time she noticed that he seemed comfortable in his own body. No swagger. She liked that. Bit patronising, but perhaps that was just being a teacher. She could feel her resistance to him receding slightly, but at the same time it felt risky, and she resolved still to keep her guard. Another relationship was certainly not what she wanted right now. All men in the end are just the same, she reminded herself. She didn't smile when he came back with the drinks.

"So you're a teacher in your first term then. School to university then back to school was it?" He felt a force in her question, more like an accusation, but didn't want to be uncivil again.
"No actually. I didn't do that. I flunked out of university after two years and got a job. Worked as a waiter in an Italian restaurant for a while; wanted a break from studying. While I was doing that I learnt some Italian, and then the owner gave me a contact with his family in Perugia. I worked there for three months in the family restaurant. At first I was mostly in the kitchen, but eventually they trusted me to do a bit of waiting; when my language skills had improved enough."

“So you can speak Italian?”
“I can get by,” he said, “but I get lost if anyone speaks too fast.”
“Why did you come back?”
“Missed my family, missed England. . . and, well . .”
Josh hesitated, wondering whether to go on.
“Sounds mysterious.”
She seemed genuinely interested and he couldn’t help responding to a new sparkle in her eyes.
“I had an Italian girlfriend. Then I discovered she was two timing. She had an Italian boyfriend as well. That upset me, so I made up my mind to come back to England.”
“Do you miss Italy?”
“Yes and no. The climate, the beautiful hill top city I miss. But England is beautiful too.”
He looked at Anna, and she looked away.
“I got a job in a bank and finished my degree part time. Social life was good. But in the end it wasn’t for me. Then quite suddenly, one day, I thought I’d like to train as a teacher.”
“Teaching Italian?”
“No. Not much call for that. I teach English. But look, you must be getting bored with me telling you my life history. What about you?”
“Nothing to tell really,” she said evasively.
“There has to be,” he said, laughing.
“Maybe. But not now. Perhaps another time. Look, I’ve got to go now. Nice to talk to you in a civil way at last. See you around.”
“Can we meet again soon?”
“Maybe. I’ll call you sometime if you give me your number.”
“OK. Fine”
He hunted in his pockets for something to write on, but she produced her mobile phone with the intention of putting his number straight in. And with that, she was off, calling her goodbyes as she went and leaving him sitting at the table bemused at the suddenness of her departure.

*

She felt confused. He wasn't as rude and obnoxious as she'd first thought. She liked his openness and despite the patronising tone, she liked the way he spoke. She even felt guilty at rushing off when she knew really there was nothing to rush off for. The afternoon and evening stretched emptily ahead and she didn't yet know how she would occupy it. At the same time, she felt a deep resistance rising in her against men, who she knew in the end couldn't be trusted. Ben had been a mistake. It was a mistake to think she cared for him. She wouldn't use the word love. In the end she doubted if the word had much meaning between men and women, or any adult for that matter. Mothers might love their children till they grew into independence. It was part of the nurturing process. Beyond that, in the end, the responsibility everyone had was to take care of their own needs. Friends, at least amongst women, did matter. But men, she knew really, had to be kept at a distance, and that included Josh.

It was where she'd gone wrong with Ben. She couldn't understand how she'd allowed him to live with her, even for the short time it lasted. At least he'd kept his own flat, which obviously meant he wasn't that sure things would last any way. All the lies he told her, about only wanting her, about changing, and she'd fallen for it. At twenty five, a graduate with a professional job, how could she have got that so wrong? She wished she wasn't attracted to men in the first place. Was it easier to be gay? But she knew kissing another woman wouldn't work for her, even though for a time she'd thought about trying it. Her gay friend Jill said she was incurably heterosexual. It was a disease she had to accept.

There was also the Jewish problem. It had already occurred to her before Ben left her that perhaps one reason she'd allowed herself to get involved with him was his Jewishness. It had pleased her parents, and seemed like a kind of natural progression. Once a Jew always a Jew so to speak. So much heavy history hung over her. All the holocaust stuff her parents talked about, and that vague feeling of guilt she couldn't really explain. Her father called it survivor guilt, but it was her great grandparents who had died in the camps. She couldn't really understand how that applied to her, at least not intellectually. But there was a deeper feeling, somewhere below consciousness, where it did make sense. Her father talked about atonement. How could she possibly make up for something she had nothing to do with? But it felt important. Sometime in the future she knew she would have to work that out.

She took her mobile phone from her pocket and opened up the contact list. There was Josh's number that she'd recently entered. Putting it in had been a moment of weakness. She didn't need him. She didn't need anyone really. She had to learn to be properly self sufficient. By herself she was enough. Living alone was no big deal. There were more urgent things to deal with first. Her thumb stretched for the delete button.

*

"So you've deleted him?"
Patrick sat back in his black chair and looked at her across the counselling room in her black jeans and rust coloured sweater.
"I will do, yes."
He continued to look at her without speaking and waited.
"I said I will do, yes."
The anger flashed again. He'd felt it in both their previous two sessions. He didn't respond.
"Sorry. I'm not really angry at you."
"No?"
"It's just the way you looked at me. As if you didn't believe me."
"And you think I don't."
"I don't know. I really don't know what I think. I'm just confused."
"And angry?"
"I am. I feel really angry. I don't know why."
"Not sure what you feel for Josh?"

"It makes me angry that . . . that somehow I can't just treat him as a passing . . . whatever. And yet I hardly know him, and he's made me angry from the start when he made me crash my car. Wish I'd not got talking to him. He's confused me."
"Maybe you need to give yourself time. Let your feelings gradually emerge. Don't rush yourself."
"Maybe. But . . . I just feel so muddled. You know I was angry when Ben left. I was just getting over that and now I'm confused . . . and angry all over again."
She took a tissue from the box at the side of her to stem the flow of tears falling down her cheek. She hated it when the anger turned itself into tears in this way. It felt so out of control. It was almost like all the anger inside was bursting out, overwhelming her, but not being expressed in the right way. She could feel herself on the edge of shaking.

"I know I'm very emotional. Sometimes I wonder if it my background. I remember my grandmother, my father's mother, getting really emotional, especially when she talked about escaping from Nazi Germany as a girl, and about what happened to some of her family. Both her parents died in Auschwitz. I remember her crying about that a lot."
"And she was angry about that as well?"
"Oh yes. Very angry! Everyone was."
"So is that where you learnt to be angry?"
"The holocaust goes very deep in all Jewish people. Such a massive genocide. Horrible beyond belief. It's part of being Jewish. I can't see how it could ever be any different. It sort of defines us."
"And that anger is part of who you are?"
"Yes, but it's not helping me to make sense of what I need to do now."
"Maybe for now the answer really is nothing. Just see what happens."
For the first time she smiled faintly. Patrick read her thoughts.
"But you want to be in control of the process."
"You know I do. That's why this is so hard."

The session came to an end. As he watched her walking back to her car Patrick wasn't sure he'd been much help to her. She turned and gave him a fleeting smile before getting in and driving off.
He sat for a while and before he realised it his mind began to wander towards the headmistress he'd met at the case conference. An interesting woman, but married. He'd noticed the ring on her finger, which almost certainly proved the lie to his first thoughts about her being divorced. Self contained he thought, and for a moment allowed himself to fantasise about her in the counselling chair. The idea made him smile, but before he could get carried away any further a knock at the door startled him. When he opened it he was confronted by Hasan, dressed not in his usual casual taxi driver gear, but in what looked like a rather elegant middle eastern costume.
"Come from the mosque gov. Friday prayers. That alright?"
"Yes, yes, of course it is, come in."
Hasan's arrival, slightly early, banished all further thought of the headmistress in his counselling chair, and replaced it with Hasan's corpulent shape.
He closed the door and began his next session.

11

In his peripheral vision Josh became aware of movement. There was a figure making its way through the bushes at the edge of the school grounds. From the window of the staff room where he'd gone during his non contact period he focused his attention to see if he could pick out just what it was and after a minute or so he thought he spotted a school blazer. It looked like the figure within it was sitting, with its back towards the school, and seemed to be alone. There was no one else in the staff room to point it out to, so he decided to go across and look for himself.

As he moved across the yard towards the figure, some kind of sixth sense seemed to alert whoever it was to his approach. The person looked round and, not more than ten yards away, he could see a pair

of large frightened looking eyes staring at him from a face he recognised; it was Wesley Freedom. Before he could say anything Wesley turned away from him and moved deeper into the undergrowth towards the high brick wall beyond, but there was no way through, so there was no other option but to wait for Josh to reach him.
"What's this about. Truanting?" he said.
There was no answer. Instead Wesley sat down, seeming to gather inside himself, drawing his knees up to his chest with his arms across his body in an obvious gesture of unapproachability, and kept his eyes fixed on the ground.
"Are you going to talk to me?"
Still no response.
"We need to talk. You can't just stay here."
He waited, hoping he would talk, but still he was silent . He sat down leaving a gap of two to three feet between them. He knew he'd been present in school that morning; something must have happened.
"Has someone upset you?"
He turned and looked at Josh in a way that told him he was right.
"No."
"Look, how about we walk back to the school and talk about it."
No response again. Josh waited, and into the quiet came an unmistakeable sound: drops of rain falling.
"We're going to get wet if we stay here."
"So?"
Josh smiled. He resigned himself to getting wet as the rain became heavier. Then unexpectedly, more reaction.
"Why should I care?"
"Well, I don't want you to get wet. Shall we go in?"
Wesley looked as if he was thinking about it, and Josh thought he detected something of a softening. Was that a tear, or rain on his face? He began to be sure the boy was actually quite upset.
"Come on. I'll walk in with you. Let's talk about it inside."

Wesley hesitated for a moment, stood up uncertainly, and stood still on the spot before starting to climb forward and out of the bushes. He followed, walking behind at first, and then catching up with him to walk alongside. The rain had quickly become very heavy, and normally he would have run to the cover of the school, but Wesley continued to walk slowly, and by the time they were inside both of them were quite wet. To the right of the main entrance was a well used interview room, and he ushered Wesley into it.

"You might not want to talk to me, but I guess there's something worrying you."
Wesley didn't reply, but he nodded briefly, as if to acknowledge the truth of Josh's words.
"I need to see my mum," he said suddenly after a moment.
"Can you tell me why?"
"I just need to see her."
There was another silence. Josh wasn't sure what to do. And then to his relief, Len came into the interview room.
"I heard you were in here with Wesley, Mr Greenwell."
Josh related the events of the past few minutes. Len listened without speaking, while Wesley continued staring at the floor.
"So you want to see your mum, young man. Why is that?"
"I just need to see her. Now!"
There was a sudden exclamation on the last word which took Josh by surprise, but didn't seem to phase Len.
"And where is she now?"
"At home."
"So if I rang her and told her what had happened, that would be alright would it?"
For a moment Wesley looked surprised, but then nodded. It was Len's turn to be surprised.
"So you want me to ring her."
"I told you. Yes."

"OK, just keep calm please. We're trying to help you. Mr Greenwell, can you stay here with young Wesley, while I go and ring mother."
They sat together without speaking. Fifteen minutes later his mother arrived to take him home.

*

"You wanted to see me Mrs Broad."
"Yes, I did Josh. Come in and have a seat."
It was only the second time he had been in the head's office since his appointment in the summer, but this time it immediately felt different. She gestured to a comfortable seat by the far wall and he sat down. She took the seat directly opposite him and looked at him for a moment first over, and then through her glasses. There was a nervous feeling in his stomach and he felt, however nicely, that he was going to be told off. But the start of the conversation surprised him.
"First of all, I want to thankyou for bringing young Wesley back into school. As you now know, he's a student we're worried about. He might have done something if he'd left the school site. You did well there. Because of your actions we've been able to get his counsellor to talk to him as a matter of urgency. So well done."
He smiled, slightly embarrassed, and felt the need to deflect attention from himself.
"Is Wesley alright?"
"He's a troubled boy. We don't really know what's happening in his life at the moment. But you've definitely helped." She smiled, and looked directly at him. "Now, as it's nearly half term. I thought this might be a good time to talk to you about how you felt things had gone for you generally. I know you've been talking to Mr Turner and that he's mentoring you, but I also like to know about the progress of new staff as they see it themselves."
She stopped, sat back in the chair and seemed to be waiting for him to say something. Her dark eyes behind her spectacles continued to look at him unwaveringly. It made him feel nervous.
"Mmm, yes, Mr Turner's been very helpful. He's given me some good advice, and helped me with a difficult boy in Year 10."

"Mac."
She knew. Was that what she wanted to talk about?
"Yes. He's been difficult, and Mr Turner is helping me to deal with him better."
"I'm glad you're working at that with him. Don't be afraid to be clear with your boundaries. It's always hard when you start. I know the students like you, and you obviously care about them, as you showed with Wesley. You don't have to work at that. Just make sure they also know where they stand with you."
So this was it, he thought, she thinks I've not been strict enough. He was about to start apologising, but she carried on.
"Good class control needs to be like a cricketing net. Are you a cricketer at all Josh?"
"I bat a bit, yes."
"Well you'll know from net practice . ."
A sudden image of Mrs Broad in cricket whites came into his head and gave him a whole new image of her. He dismissed it immediately. She was carrying on.
"You hit the ball as hard as you like, but the net can cope with it. It gives a bit, stretches out against the impact, but the ball always stays inside. You've got to be like the net. Whatever the student hits at you, you can contain it. The boundary holds, but there's a bit of room for flexibility. After a strike, you can pick up the ball again and carry on. And the important thing is, that's what the students want too. Usually they call it firm but fair. You've got the flexibility, the fairness, which for some teachers is the hard bit."
Johnno, Josh thought, no flexibility with him. One reason the students didn't like him.
"You just need to make sure your net holds. That can take a bit of time to get right of course. But we're here to help out when necessary. Always ask if you're in trouble"
"Yes, I will do."
"We want you to succeed. It's in everyone's interest, and you've got the makings of a very good teacher."

"Thankyou."
"Is there anything you want to add to that?"
"No I don't think so. You've been helpful, thanks."
She smiled at him formally, and the smile carried the implicit message that the interview was over, so he got up from the seat and walked to the door. When he got there he turned to look back in case she wanted to say anything else, but she had already turned her attention to something on her desk, and didn't notice.

*

"Mum tells me you ran out of school one day last week. Where were you going?"
"Home."
The general chat over, Patrick had got to the point quickly. He was conscious that Wesley might be at risk of doing something to himself again. Under his loose sleeve, he thought he'd already detected a cut, but he'd come to that later.
"Why did you want to go home before school ended?"
"See my mum."
"Why the hurry?"
No answer. He was going too fast. Too direct. The straight line isn't always the quickest, he reminded himself.
"How is your mum?"
"She's alright."
There was something guarded in the answer, which Patrick noted, but again he held back.
"That's good. Remind me, does she go out to work?"
"Bakery. She works in the bakery."
There was a large local bakery not far from the school, which was obviously where Wesley was indicating she worked. Patrick guessed that would mean night shifts and early starts, probably on a rota. But he left that and followed an intuition.
"And your dad. He works there too?"
The change was immediate.
"He don't live with us no more."

Patrick waited, watched his face redden. There was something important here, but he had to be careful.
"But you still see him?"
"Sometimes. He comes round."
Another pause. Patrick stayed with it. Then Wesley did the work.
"I hate him."
Again Patrick waited, but stayed looking at Wesley directly.
"You won't tell?"
"Depends what you want to say. Remember I said if I thought you might be at risk I'd have to say something. But maybe I can help you sort something out."
Again there was a silence. Wesley was breathing heavily, struggling to decide what to do. Outside somewhere in the distance somebody trundled something noisy along a corridor, reminding Patrick he was in a hospital building. He was vaguely conscious of voices outside, but he waited for Wesley, until in the end he felt he had to break the silence himself.
"Would you like me to help you . . . if I can?"
Wesley nodded.
"You'll need to tell me."
Wesley moved his left arm along the chair, and it was impossible not to see the criss-cross markings on his lower arm. Wesley followed his gaze. It was almost like he wanted him to ask about it.
"Did you do that to yourself?"
Again Wesley nodded.
"How long ago?
"Yesterday."
"Can you say what triggered it?"
"Every so often he comes round and shouts at mum. Threatens her."
"Your father?"
"Mmm. He wants money. She has to give it to him. Case he hits her."
"Has he done that?"
"Not yet."
"You're scared he might?"

He nodded.
"Is that why you were leaving school the other day?"
Another nod.
"You knew she was home and you wanted to check she was alright. Is that it?"
"Yes."
There was a clatter outside as if someone had dropped a tray, followed by a silly laugh before it became quiet again. Inside the room, admitting what had happened seemed to have released something in Wesley and he was crying; quietly at first, and then less controllably for a while. Patrick let him cry, allowed him to ease the pressure. From the box beside him he took a paper tissue and handed it to him. He blew his nose loudly twice, the second time making a noise like a fart, which made him grin sheepishly, despite what he was feeling. Patrick laughed too before speaking again.
"I'll do what I can to help. Don't worry, I'll be careful. I won't let it be worse for you. Or your mum."
Wesley smiled, thinly.

12

Wearing a tee shirt and underpants, Simon sat on his bed with his feet over the side, flicking without enthusiasm through the collection of pictures he kept in the drawer beside his bed. Cut out from magazines, they were photographs of men, mostly in their twenties, that he'd found over the last couple of years, and which at the time had excited him. They'd been used to satisfy his otherwise barren sexual life. Mostly they were men in various stages of undress, advertising deodorants, hair gels, soaps and items of male clothing.

Someone had left a gay magazine on the train. He took it home with him and cut out a couple of photos but he couldn't bring himself to buy a copy. The embarrassment of standing in front of a shop assistant buying a gay magazine was more than he could bear. He couldn't even bring himself to take out a subscription online. Until recently he hadn't quite allowed himself to know, really know, in every part of his being. It might be an extended adolescent phase. He'd read about boys' boarding schools where homosexuality was said to be rife. Most of those involved, in the end grew out of it, found themselves a woman and got happily married. Maybe he was bisexual? Occasionally he noticed a girl with nice features. Maybe he could develop an attraction for women if he tried hard enough. It was what lots of people had done. Maybe for some people it had worked, and of course they weren't going to let on if it was the case.

But at twenty five, it had gradually dawned on him that wasn't going to happen. It was why he'd gone to see Patrick, and Patrick was giving him the difficult message he knew he would have to hear. He was gay. That was that; as much a fact as if he was blind, deaf, or paralysed. His sexual attraction was for men. Homosexual was what he was, not even bisexual. He liked women, but he wasn't attracted to women. The full awareness of it was sinking in. And with it came another recognition. Actually, he didn't want not to find men attractive. That was him, that was how he was. Coming out was the problem. Yet in the circles in which he moved, he knew there wouldn't be a problem. He'd be accepted for who he was. The problem was in his head.

And in having the courage to find a partner. Where did he start? Sometimes he noticed dating columns in the newspapers. There were 'men seeking men' columns as well as the usual straight adverts. Sometimes quite a few in fact, and he'd been tempted to respond. But always in the end he'd held back, scared of finally admitting he was gay. It didn't feel safe. There were so many terms of abuse for gay men it had to be a bad place to be.

He put his pictures back in the drawer at the side of his bed and stood up. In the mirror he could see himself. He was slim, he kept fit, he knew he was far from unattractive. He could fancy himself. The thought amused him, made him laugh out loud. Did that mean he was narcissistic? He didn't really think so. He wanted another man to fancy him, make love to him, and he would reciprocate. The thought excited him and stirred him deeply; it felt like he was at a turning point in his life. He didn't want to continue the old insular ways but he wasn't yet sure how to move forward.

*

Josh knew that Anna fascinated him. He found her attractive in a different way to any other woman he had known, and he couldn't quite understand why. Certainly he was intrigued by her unjustified anger at him. She basically blamed him for something that was her fault, and with an insurance claim working its way through the system, there could be more fireworks from her yet. He couldn't win her over in the ways that had worked in the past. Always before his charm, his good looks, had meant women found him irresistible. Since he was an eighteen year old sixth former, a succession of good looking girls had allowed themselves to become involved with him. Flattered by their adoration he began to develop the illusion of himself as a kind of Casanova figure who could win over any girl he chose, have a brief sexual relationship and then move on.

But he was also uncomfortably aware that despite his charm, he kept himself at an emotional distance. He boasted to his colleagues at the bank that he could 'love them and leave them.' It was what his father used to say. Male colleagues seemed to be jealous, but he suspected that they also secretly admired him and it flattered him still further. But a feeling of dissatisfaction had begun to creep in. It was behind his decision to give up his career in the bank for what he hoped would be a more satisfying role as a teacher working with teenage children.

Just before leaving the bank he'd started noticing an Irish colleague called Kathleen. She was large breasted with longish blond hair, blue eyes, and very pale skin; different from girls with darker complexions he usually preferred. At first he wasn't sure if she was his sort, but her short skirts revealed shapely legs, and he found himself attracted.

"You'll get nowhere there," Jamie said one lunchtime.
"Wanna bet?"
"Confirmed virgin that one. She'll end up a nun."
"A nun?"
"Catholic. That's why she's Irish."
He laughed. "Watch me," he said, determined now to see how far he could get.

She was at first resistant, as predicted. It only made him try harder, and after a time she allowed him to take her out for a meal.
"I like you Josh," she told him over a pizza, her blue eyes staring at him, "but you have to understand I'm a practising catholic."
He knew already what she was telling him, but he smiled innocently.
"I'm not prejudiced."
"You know what I mean."
He did, but he wasn't giving up. A week later he got to kiss her, and she allowed him to fondle her breasts through her blouse. Sometimes she sat cross legged in front of him and he could see a fair bit of her thigh. Once he thought he spotted a stocking top, and because he couldn't be certain, it aroused him even more. He didn't think she would be much good as a nun.

But the messages she gave out were very mixed. No amount of charm got him any further. Eventually things drifted, and the relationship came to an end. He thought she didn't seem particularly upset, possibly even less than he was, and that disturbed him. It wasn't that he'd got emotionally involved he told himself, he just hadn't been able to succeed. Jamie's laughter didn't help.
"Didn't believe me, did you?" he said smugly over a pint. "Steer clear of the blondes."
But since then, he hadn't been in a relationship. It was the longest time without since he was in the sixth form. And now there was Anna, a new and differently unsettling challenge. He wanted to get to know her, but risking his feelings again felt scary.

*

Simon noticed a new face in the first violins, a young man of about his own age. His penetrating blue eyes held for slightly longer than he might have expected when they first met at rehearsal. Was that him, with his new determination to be open, or the other guy, or both of them?

Afterwards, packing away the instruments, he noticed the newcomer looking towards him again.

"Do we go for drink now?"

The accent was very pronounced. Eastern European he thought. He liked it, enjoyed the increasingly cosmopolitan makeup of the orchestra.

"Watch the brass players. Follow them!"

"So, nothing is new there."

"Afraid not. I'll come with you."

"Thankyou. Takes a while to get to know routines."

Simon felt excitement. A connection perhaps.

"Simon Smith."

He stretched out his right hand.

"Stefan Paminski. From Poland. Pleased to meet you."

He took Simon's hand and held it, again a fraction longer than he might have expected.

"Your English is good."

"It's OK." Stefan shrugged his shoulders, "but not perfect. Originally from Krakow, but I am in England for more than year now."

In the pub, Stefan stayed with him, seemed to want to get to know him. He felt himself liking it. Once the trombones had cleared the area round the bar, ahead of the queue as usual, he managed to get to the front and order drinks. 'Just juice,' was all Stefan had asked for, but he got himself a pint, expecting to enjoy the rest of the evening. When he got back to the table, Stefan had been joined by two other members of the orchestra. Jealously, he was hoping to be able to chat to Stefan himself. He sat down and passed the juice to him, taking a long draft of his own beer. One of the cellists, rotund, with short blond hair and piercing blue eyes was holding forth about her holiday to Cyprus; 'Oh my God it was hot! At least forty two degrees and weak air conditioning. Good pool though.'

The words washed over him meaninglessly, but Stefan seemed to be politely taking it all in and nodding in the right places. Surely he couldn't possibly be interested in all that nonsense? A sly grin when the cellist, with her eyes closed, was saying she really thought she might die at one point, confirmed it. The grin pleased him, felt conspiratorial, and made it easier to cope with the interminable monologue. Eventually the other woman, slimmer, with an anonymous face, old fashioned floral jeans and plimsolls, announced she was getting another drink, and did anyone want one too. There were no takers, and he hoped that might mean they would go soon, but the cellist, not satisfied with Cyprus, started on about how wonderful Florence was for another ten minutes before flouncing off, followed by the friend.

"Whew! I thought she'd never stop."
Stefan grinned at him again.
"Now we talk, yes?"
"Yes, I hope so."
"Tell me Simon, where you are from?"
"London. Through and through. And you?"
"Small town. As I already tell you, not far from Krakow. It is called Oswienczim."
"That sounds hard to say."
"Germans thought so too. That's why they called it Auschwitz."
"Auschwitz! You come from Auschwitz?"
"I grew up about two miles from camp. Not then of course. Years after I am born."
Simon looked at him in horror. He didn't know what to say.
"I usually say I am from Krakow. It's easier."

"Auschwitz. Is it still there?"
"Camp is now memorial. Museum to the killed, with big motto over gate. 'Work make you free.' German joke I think. Actually, do you know, there are two camps. Birkenau, real killing camp, is two kilometres away. Main gas chambers were there. But now it's just, do you say, derrict?"
"Derelict?"
"Yes, derelict. Nothing left but few huts. It is also museum. You can visit. Railway lines from Oswienczim still go there, through big columns. Like film 'Schindler's List.' But no trains now, of course."
"You grew up with all that?"
"We know it is there, yes. Evil things done by Germans in my country, but past. Not modern Germans."
"The past still affects us."
"Of course. But we have to come to terms. Absorb past into present. Learn and move forward."
"It's not always easy."
"Of course, but we have to try. Can't live always in past."
He thought of his work with Patrick. Coming to terms with the past, coming to terms with yourself. Weren't they related in some way? Unless you could do that, you couldn't move forward with life. It seemed to be taking on a deeper meaning for him.
"We are understanding each other well, yes?"
He smiled. It felt right. He really wanted to get to know Stefan. He offered to get them another drink and this time Stefan wanted a pint.

He brought the beer back to the table and put one glass down in front of Stefan, unintentionally putting a hand on his shoulder as he did so. Then he sat down with his own glass.
"So now we can be boyfriends?"
The phrase shocked Simon. Did Stefan mean what he'd said, or was it just his imperfect English?
"You mean . . ."
"Of course."

He stretched out both his hands and put them over Simon's bowing hand, which rested on the table beside his glass. It excited and shocked him at the same time, but he made no attempt to withdraw his hand.

"Is easier to be gay, here in England, than my country. Church." He raised his eyes upwards. "Everyone is church, and church says homosexual is wrong. I am bad man because I like man not woman. Here you have equality. Gay rights. Civil Partnerships. You can be 'out', is that how you say it?"

He took a sip from his beer, trying to stay calm.

"You like to come home with me? Shag?"

He found himself spewing out his mouthful onto the table between them.

"I say something wrong?"

"No. No."

Suddenly he was laughing, and Stefan began laughing with him. He couldn't speak for a while. The laughter had released the growing tension and excitement within him, and surprisingly he felt better. Eventually he managed to regain control of himself.

"No, it's just the way you said it. We don't quite use that word – shag . . ." he laughed again, "in that way. Quite like that."

"Sorry, I didn't . . ."

"Please Stefan, don't apologise. At least you made it clear what you meant."

He paused, took another sip from his beer, trying to get a grip on his feelings.

"You want . . . " Stefan paused before mischievously repeating, "shag?"

"Yes, I do. But you'll need to excuse me. I'm not experienced."

He paused, and their eyes met in a mutual smile.

"Not experienced at all."

He felt an almost irresistible urge to lean forward and kiss Stefan. He knew that he wanted him. *Really* wanted him. It was new, and he was ready now to let it take him wherever it led.

Stefan's hands were on both of his again, reinforcing the intimacy.
"We go?"
"Yes, we go."
As they walked out, he could feel the eyes of one or two members of the orchestra unobtrusively watching them. He looked for the place inside where embarrassment had always been, and it wasn't there.

13

Rosie's Read for Halloween wasn't progressing particularly well. She had twenty four hours to get three hundred words to the sub editor, and for once couldn't dash it off with her usual speed. She sat at her desk in the office and stared at the blank screen. Silly, overblown occasion anyway she thought, devils riding on the night before All Souls, for God's sake. What a stupid tradition! She'd already deleted a couple of half hearted efforts which sounded more like a girls' own story. Her mind kept drifting. She thought of Ben and got angry. She thought of Josh and got angry. Nothing was helping until the phone rang. It was from the office. There was a young lad perched on a ledge above what used to be Woolworths, overlooking the high street. Police were closing the street. It would be a good story.
"Too right. Thanks for that. I'll be there in no time."
Anna took no time in getting her coat, running out and into her car and driving off even faster than usual.

Within five minutes she was at the end of the high street, but the road was closed. Two well built police officers, one with an over large stomach, barred her way, and weren't prepared to accept her reporter's card as justification for entry. She swore at them under her breath, backed up and found a spot on a verge to park the car. She could find a way in on foot. Once inside the cordon she could use her usual journalistic approaches to get as much information as possible, and sure enough she was able to get through. She knew that if the lad, whoever he was, jumped off the ledge, the story was likely to make the national news. She wanted her local part of the story.

As she approached the empty Woolworths building, an over ornate late nineteenth century edifice, she could see the boy above, standing on quite a narrow ledge which jutted out from a sash window on the second floor. He was crouched down precariously clutching the edge of the window. It was easy to see that a fall from that height would be fatal. Around her, there was a fire crew, preparing what seemed to be a landing pad, no doubt hoping to catch the boy if he did fall, or jump. She approached a nearby woman police officer and presented her press card. The officer was young, and didn't seem prepared to tell her much, but she gathered the boy seemed to have got in via a small hole in a window round the back, broken open by vandals and not properly repaired. Once inside he must have made his way through the empty building and up to the top floor, where for whatever reason he decided to climb out onto the window ledge. No one yet knew who he was, or why he was there.

"He looks black, maybe West Indian?" she offered, hopefully.

"We don't know yet."

"But you can see he's black by looking at him, surely."

"You can draw your own conclusions if you want to."

She resisted one of her tantrums against officialdom, knowing it would be unhelpful. Instead she tried a different approach.

"He must be very scared up there."

The officer couldn't deny that, and looked genuinely concerned. Sensing a way through to more information, she waited.

"We're trying to contact his mother."

"So you know who he is."

"I can't tell you that."

"But you do know."

"I can't tell you that."

She knew a brick wall when she felt it, but it was a breakthrough. They knew who the boy was. She would find out too.

Since it was half term week, Josh was in town. He wanted to get some more clothes for the forthcoming winter, something he'd been putting off, and this morning he'd finally got round to it. Parking before the police closed the high street meant he couldn't get back home the usual way, and he would have to make a considerable detour, so having deposited his purchases in the car, he decided to walk back in to see what the problem was. He couldn't get beyond the police cordon, but he could get close enough to see a small group of police and fire officers gathered outside the old Woolworths building, looking upwards. Following their eyes, he spotted the figure on the second floor ledge. At first he could only make out the shape of what looked like quite a young person holding onto the window frame and facing away from him. He watched trying to grasp what was actually happening, until there was a shout just in front of him and the figure on the ledge turned its head to look. Confronted for a few seconds with a face, Josh could see not only that whoever it was had African Caribbean features. He could also recognise a face he knew. The boy on the ledge was Wesley.

He made his way quickly to the nearest police officer and explained what he knew, and was ushered forward to the officer in charge, who wanted to know what information he could give them. It was little more than a name, but enough for them to deal with identification. He wanted to do more.

"Officer, I've talked this boy round before. I'm a teacher and he's in my tutor group. I think I might be able to help."

"I'm sorry sir, we have to send for a specialist negotiator for this."

"How long will that take?"

"Probably an hour or so."

"But he might jump or fall in that time! You can't just leave him there."

Anger was rising in him. He wanted to help, and felt himself being denied. But the officer had recognised the potential for solving the problem too. He wanted to know Josh's details before radioing

through to headquarters for advice. He waited impatiently while the formalities were negotiated.
“Right sir. I’m told you can talk to him from the window inside, but no more than that until our specialist team arrive.”
“Thankyou. That’s fine.”
He was led round the back, where the police had opened a side door into the shop, and up the flights of stairs leading to the old storage room containing the large window where Wesley was. The officer with him told him he would have to wait inside as well, but that he could talk to the boy from the window vantage point. Suddenly there was fear. Could he really do something? He knew he had to try.

Looking out from the window, he could see below the fire crew with their makeshift landing pad. It seemed incredibly small, and certainly no guarantee of safety if the boy fell. Cautiously, he stretched his head out a small distance. He could see Wesley now, in front of him, further from the opening than it had seemed from below, some five or six feet he guessed. The ledge itself was perhaps eighteen inches wide, and too shallow to turn safely. Kneeling on one knee and facing away from the opening, to get back to safety, Wesley would have to edge himself backward. His position was precarious. It would only be a matter of time before his muscles became tired, and he could no longer support himself.

Instinct told Josh that his first contact was vital. He couldn’t risk scaring the boy. That in itself might make him fall. He had to ease himself as gently as possible into the boy’s awareness, and calling out his name might not be the best thing. From this height, also, although there was noise below, it wasn’t so loud at his height and he wouldn’t have to raise his voice much. Simply projecting it a bit would probably be enough. “I’m here to help you,” he said tentatively.
There was no discernible movement, no change to Wesley’s position. He could see that the boy had one free hand that was not holding on to the window frame. He had an idea.

“Lift your free hand a little if you can hear me.”

He waited, anxiously. Then to his relief, the hand obviously lifted a couple of inches.

“I know you’re Wesley. It’s Mr Greenwell, I’d like to help you.”

There was no obvious response at first. Then movement. It seemed as if Wesley moved slightly towards him.

“Wesley. I can help you sort this out. Like I did last week.”

At first nothing. Then for the first time, Wesley spoke.

“It didn’t help, did it.”

“I don’t know Wesley. I’d like to try again though. If you come back in.”

“He still keeps coming round.”

He couldn’t make sense of this. He waited for a moment, to see if there was more that would help him understand, but there was nothing.

“I’ll help in any way I can Wesley. You just need to come in.”

“If I fall. If I kill myself. Then they’ll have to stop him.”

“Come back in Wesley. That will sort it.”

There was another slight movement, and this time, unmistakeably, Wesley inched back a small way towards the opening.

“That’s it, Wesley. That’s what you have to do. Just keep moving back gradually.”

“How do I know you’ll sort it?”

“I give you my word Wesley. I’ll do everything I can, honestly.”

“How can you?”

“We’ll find a way.”

There was no response for a moment, but Josh hoped he was considering what he was saying.

“You promise?”

He was getting somewhere. The boy didn’t want to jump. The danger now was stopping him from falling before he was safely back inside.

“I promise Wesley. Whatever you want me to do.”

Slowly, small movements at a time, Wesley began to inch his was back to safety.

Anna had managed to join the fire crew beneath the window. She had managed to find out the boy was Wesley Freedom from the local comprehensive. Strangely ironic name she thought to herself as she wrote it down on her notepad. Rumour also had it that there was a teacher from the school trying to help him, and looking up, she could see someone was talking to the boy, trying to encourage him back in. She'd worked out from information she'd got that it had to be nearly an hour the boy had been up on the ledge, and she guessed he couldn't stay there for too much longer without tiring to the point that he fell. The thought made her shudder.

There was movement on the ledge. It looked as if whoever was talking to the boy was getting somewhere. Slowly but surely, he seemed to be easing his way back towards the opening. It didn't look easy. Presumably, he'd got out there without any thought of getting back. Now he seemed to have changed his mind. She kept watching, transfixed, and like everyone else, willing him to succeed. Suddenly there was a loud noise. A police or ambulance siren approaching fast from a distance startled her and everyone else watching from below. The boy seemed to sway outwards. There was an involuntary intake of breath from everyone on the ground.

Wesley had almost reached safety and Josh's hopes were rising when the siren startled both of them. It made him jump, and then he watched in horror as it seemed as if Wesley was about to slip away from the window. Somehow, he managed to regain his grip, but was now suspended even more dangerously outwards over the road.

"Hold on!" he blurted out, "I'll get you!"

Ignoring his instructions from the police and moving too quickly to be restrained by the officer, he jumped up onto the window sill and out onto the ledge alongside Wesley. Holding onto the frame with one hand, he stretched his free hand out towards him.

"Ease your way back. You're nearly there. I'll support you."

He could feel Wesley's body continuing to ease its way back to safety, inch by inch, until he was in the opening of the window. The police officer who had accompanied him was ready. Quickly he pulled him towards him, and Wesley was safe.

Then it was Josh's turn to get back inside, but it wasn't initially very easy. Although he was holding on, his weight was suspended at the wrong angle. He couldn't let go of the window frame or he would have fallen himself. Gradually he had to ease himself back towards the window, using all the strength he had in his supporting arm to manoeuvre his weight back into balance. Once he'd done this, he could ease himself downwards until his head was below the level of the top of the frame, and then use his body weight to literally fall back through the window, at the same time as releasing his grip on the outside. He knew all too well that if his feet slipped in the process it would be him not Wesley falling into the firemen's landing stage below. He paused for a few seconds, managed to co-ordinate his actions, and fell with a crash into the storage room within.

Anna below was astonished to see the figure of a man suddenly jump onto the ledge and appear to push the boy back in through the window. Adrenalin surged within her as for a moment she feared that first the boy then the rescuer might fall to their deaths. The drama of the man having to ease himself back into the room was if anything greater than seeing the boy disappearing into safety. The applause around her which followed was entirely spontaneous.

The fire crew packed away their equipment and drove away from the scene. The police were preparing to reopen the road now it was obviously safe to do so. She watched it happening, keeping her eyes open for the opportunity to get more information. The black woman arriving in a police vehicle she assumed would be the boy's mother, but didn't get any chance to intercept as she was ushered away by a police officer. Gradually the road was becoming normal and the first cars were making their way back through the high street. Shoppers began to move about their business again as if nothing unusual had happened minutes before.

She was about to approach the building again to get what she needed when she spotted the familiar face of Josh coming round from behind Woolworths and talking to a police officer. Before she could talk to either of them, they were inside a patrol car and driving away. 'Has he been arrested for some reason' she thought to herself, and made a mental note to check that out too. Then, as she stood in the same spot, another officer appeared and she asked who the boy's rescuer had been. He wasn't prepared to stop, but as he breezed past her he gave her the information she needed:
"If you were standing here a moment ago, you saw him. He's just driven off with my colleague in the patrol car."
Josh the rescuer? Perhaps there really was more to him than she'd given him credit for. In her mind again she had a vision of his form stretched out from the window looking for a brief moment as if he would fall crashing to the ground, seriously injuring or even killing himself. Not everyone would have done that. He'd risked his own life for someone else. Suddenly the sensible reporter side of her clicked back into action. She needed to check her facts. Did the officer really mean Josh? She needed to be sure.

Close to where she was standing, the boy and his mother were now emerging from the building, and being escorted into another police patrol car. She would have liked to talk to them, but there was no chance. Then realising that two officers would still be remaining once the car had driven away, she approached them.
"Can you confirm something for me? I've been told that the person who got the boy back in from the window up there was a Mr Josh Greenwell, a teacher at the boy's school. That's correct?"
"If you say so, yes."
"So, why was he up there in the first place?"

"Told us he knew the boy. Probably one of his teachers. He did a good job anyway."
She had what she needed. Her contact with him could help her with the story. She was also seeing him in a new light.

*

The noise of a donkey making a braying sound somewhere just outside the barn woke Tom. Blearily he roused himself, struggling for a few seconds to make any sense of where he was or what had happened to him. Although it was dark and gloomy inside the barn, some light filtered in through various cracks and gaps, and he could tell it was daylight. As he came to, he knew also that he was feeling better. His arm no longer hurt, and he could lift it without pain. He had no idea how long it had taken him to get even this much better, but it had to be weeks rather than days. That he was a prisoner of war in all but name, trapped in the barn, was gradually becoming clear to him. He had no idea how long it might be before he would be free and how he would get home. His only comfort was that at least he was being treated as well as could be expected, and he was given something to eat on a regular basis.

It was always the girl who came to see him. She had dressed his wound until it was virtually healed; she brought him food, made sure there was water to drink, and water to wash himself. He had sorted out his own toilet arrangements now at the far side of the barn, and the girl didn't try to interfere with that. He didn't blame her. From where he had his bedding place he didn't think there was any kind of lavatorial smell, but whenever he uncovered the thin coating of hay covering it, there was the foul stench of his own shit. It embarrassed him having to use such a makeshift toilet. Once, the girl had come in while he was hunkered down over it. She'd gone back out straightaway and he was grateful, but it didn't stop him finding it difficult.

Now he was well enough, he could think about what he'd left behind. Just before his posting, his wife told him she was pregnant. That had to be at least three months ago. His child would be born in the spring, and he wasn't likely to be able to see it until well after it was born. The thought depressed him, but at the same time, there was something to look forward to. He was going to be a father.

Some while ago, he didn't quite know how long, he'd managed to mime to the girl that his clothes, his khaki uniform and his underwear, were very dirty, very smelly. It was the first time he'd seen her smile, quizzically, as he tried to get her to understand what he wanted. Then a light seemed to have dawned, she said something that sounded like *sporco*, and did her own mime in turn, which made him laugh. He thought he'd understood that she wanted him to take his clothes off, and he guessed she meant she would wash them, but as he started to unbutton his stinking tunic, she stopped him. A little more mime and he got the message. She would go, sparing his blushes, and hers he guessed, then come back once he'd taken them off. At least he would be able to cover himself up with the coarse bedding she'd brought him some while back.

And sure enough, a few minutes after he'd done his strip tease and was waiting shyly and expectantly under the blanket, she was back. In her arms she carried some replacement clothes, which he thought must have been from one of her brothers. She put them in a neat pile beside him.
"Thankyou," he said almost hidden under the blanket.
"*Prego, prego,*" she replied, as if to say that's alright. He smiled.
She gathered up the clothes he'd taken off without any apparent recoil at what to him was an awful smell, and smiled sweetly back at him. He smiled again, feeling that at last he'd managed to communicate with her. It felt good.

The clothes made him laugh. There was an ancient grey shirt, smelling of sweat, but nowhere near as bad as the smell of the shirt he'd just taken off, and there were a very baggy pair of greying trousers with a cord tied round them as a makeshift belt. With the size of the trousers he knew he'd need it to stop them falling down. There was also a baggy, dirty cream coloured piece of clothing that looked like a cross between shorts and underpants. He slipped them on first. They were big enough for two of him, and they reached almost to his knees, but didn't feel too uncomfortable. Then he put on the shirt and trousers. There were no socks or shoes, but he thought he could manage well enough. He wasn't at all cold.

There was a thin crack at the far end of the barn, close to where his toilet area was, and with one eye pressed against it he could see out. Tom assumed the crack looked out in a different direction from where he knew he must have come. He couldn't see the vines he thought he remembered when he arrived, and there was no view of the dip down to the valley into which he knew he must have fallen before climbing up the slope to where he was now. But he could see leaves on the ground, and although it was still bright and most days the sun seemed to be shining, there was a different hue to the sky. It looked like it was becoming autumn and he calculated that it had to be well into October. He knew he was at the southern tip of Italy, and maybe through the winter the weather would be mild.

The great barn door opened again and the girl was back. When she saw him, she laughed once more at the sight of him in his new clothes. He knew he must look strange, and she was enjoying it. He couldn't resist an exaggerated pose, as if he was a model and it brought on the laughter again. Managing to communicate with her, even in a small way, made him feel less alone.

14

Anna was glad she hadn't deleted Josh's number. As soon as she thought he might be able to answer, she rang it. He was surprised and pleased to hear from her.

"I didn't think you'd ring me back."

"Why not?"
"I wasn't sure what you thought of me. Pompous teacher and all that."
Wanting to get straight to the point, she ignored his remarks.
"I've heard you've been a hero."
"What do you mean?"
"I'm a reporter remember. I get to find out these things. And I was there. I saw you climb out of that window and get the boy back in just as he might have fallen. Can you tell me anything about why he climbed out there in the first place?"
"Well no, I don't really know. He was there when I spotted him. I was doing my shopping. I know him from school of course."
"Do you teach him?"
"I'm his form tutor," he said cautiously.
"Has he seemed upset lately? Can you tell me anything more about him?"
"Nothing I guess you don't already know, like his name and so on."
"OK. But I'd love to do an interview with you about what the experience was like. Guess it beats sky diving for the adrenalin rush."
"You could be right there!"
"Look, how about tomorrow afternoon, Saturday. Can we meet for a coffee, say four o'clock?"
"OK, sure, I've got nothing planned."
She sorted out the venue and then finished the conversation. She had to get herself organised. This was a good local story and she didn't want to lose out. Maybe after all he might just be worth getting to know a bit better.

Josh for his part was surprised. He was certainly keen to get to know her, but thought she was dismissive of him. How strange that climbing out of a window to rescue a boy should have changed things. How weird too that circumstances kept throwing them into each other. First the crash, then the wedding party, then the clay pigeon shoot. Now this. Like living in a Thomas Hardy novel, he thought wryly. Would

Hardy have created a plot like that? Surely not; it was too circumstantial even for him.

Anna was already waiting for him at the cafe when he got there, and even bought him a coffee. It didn't take her long to take a notepad from the large handbag she was carrying and start asking him questions about his experience. She wanted to know every detail of what had happened.
"It's just for 'Rosie's Read', my column in the Herald."
Len's words came into his head; 'Never trust a journalist.'
"I won't use everything you tell me. I'll select the most readable bits out of the profile I get from you," she reassured him.
He was careful, saying nothing about Wesley and sticking to his own experience. He watched fascinated as the pencil in her hand scribbled down his words in the strange looking marks of her shorthand.

She was closing her notebook, sliding the pencil along the spine and putting everything away in the large handbag on the floor. As she leaned forward he caught a glimpse of the black bra holding up her breasts. The stolen glance excited him. As she sat up again, her dark hair fell forward, partly covering her face. She flicked it back with a swift hand movement, but a small strand she missed remained. Delicately, she picked it off and eased it into place, smiling at him.
"Thanks. I appreciate your help. I've got my article for next week now."
He smiled back. Outside the autumn evening was already getting dark. Despite all his experience, he wasn't sure how to continue. She seemed to be ending the meeting, and that wasn't what he wanted. He resorted to the usual stalling tactic.
"Another coffee?"
"No thanks."
He nodded, but his disappointment must have been obvious.
"But, what say we make a date?" she said.
"OK. If that's what you want."
She bristled slightly.

"It's what you want isn't it?"
"Yes, sure, of course. Isn't that obvious?"
"Just wanted you to be straight about it."
"OK. When?"
"I'm busy next week, and you're back at school. How about next Friday evening?"
"OK. I'll take you for a meal."
"Fine. You sort it out and text me the details."
He smiled, and watched as she stood up and eased her coat round her shoulder. She smiled back, and stretched out her hand, which he shook, feeling slightly uncomfortable with the gesture. It felt false and unnatural, but it was better than no contact, and anything more didn't yet feel appropriate.

*

As he drove into school on Monday morning for the new half term Josh wasn't anticipating being a celebrity. Word seemed somehow to have got round that he had gone up onto the ledge to save Wesley. Several students surrounded him as he walked from his car to the school.
"You're a hero, sir!"
"You saved that little black kid."
"That's really cool, sir."
It surprised him and embarrassed him.
Some staff seemed to know too, and Len offered one of his dreadful puns.
"I hear you stopped young Wesley's flight to freedom."
Josh didn't know what to say, and no one else round them laughed. Len apologised for the bad taste joke.

At the staff briefing that morning, Mrs Broad referred to what she understood to have been his courage in 'saving one of our very troubled students' There were murmurs of appreciation, which embarrassed him still further. She said she didn't yet know what the problem had been, but had been in contact with Wesley's mother, that he was physically unharmed, thanks to Josh, but social services were involved now and Wesley was continuing to see Dr East. At the end of the briefing she smiled at him without making any direct comment, except to say she had to hurry, but she would speak to him later. It felt like some kind of appreciation that she'd mentioned him in the briefing.

He noticed the difference in his classes too. It felt like a new kind of respect. There were the inevitable questions at the start which took up five minutes or so of each lesson. He allowed that, deflecting most of it by saying he knew little more than they did. But he noticed once he wanted to get the lesson started, there was less problem getting classes settled, almost as if he'd gained a new status overnight. He really did feel like a school celebrity. Even in his Year 10 group, Mac's usual sullen defiance was different. He didn't say much, but he responded as politely as Josh judged he could, and got on with what he was asked to do without complaint.

There weren't many black students in the school, or in the area as a whole, and he hadn't noticed any kind of racial tension, but he did notice that those that were in the school seemed to want to talk to him. It was almost like he'd crossed an unspoken divide in saving one of their own, and his approval rating as a white teacher had risen accordingly.

"Wesley's mum is really grateful," one girl said to him.

"You're a hero, man," said a large boy, with what seemed like heroic pretensions himself.

"You're a good teacher, sir, we like you."

He liked it. It surprised him too, but strangely, it also disconcerted him.

*

Having followed up Wesley's disclosure with social services, Patrick felt he ought to let the school know himself. He was sure the headteacher would want to know and preferred to go in himself rather than telephone. 'Face to face is always preferable,' he told himself. It seemed the natural and courteous thing to do.

Reporting in at the entrance hall, he found himself directed to a small room accessed from a corridor to the side of main entrance with 'Interview Room 2' written on the door. He sat down, and a minute or so later a tall man with greying hair and well cut moustache and announced himself as Mr Turner the deputy head.
"Can I help you Dr East?"
"Well actually I just wanted to let the headteacher know how things had developed with young Wesley Freedom."
"I think she's quite busy now. Can I help?"
"Well, I met her at the case conference, and she phoned me afterwards on the day Wesley ran out of school. I believe he was found by a member of your staff."
"Mr Greenwell?"
"I think so, yes. After that I saw Wesley, and he told me some things about his family life which I think your headteacher needs to know."
"OK. I'll go and see if she is free."
"Thankyou."
Waiting in the interview room, he wondered whether he should after all have just told the deputy rather than worrying the headteacher. Was this something to do with status he asked himself, but that didn't feel quite right.

Len Turner knocked and put his head round the already half open door of the head's office.
"Dr East from the hospital wants to talk to you about Wesley Freedom. Says it needs to be you, but I can get the information from him if you would prefer me to do that."
Liz looked up from her laptop where she had been revising the school self evaluation form. She knew it had to be done and had hoped to get on with it without interruption that morning. But she found herself looking up and smiling.
"It's OK Len. I don't think he'll want long."
Len looked mildly surprised as he nodded.
"I'll get him brought up."

"Thankyou."
She stood up, waited until Len had gone and then took the mirror from her handbag to check her makeup and hair. Absentmindedly she cleaned her glasses, put them back on, and looked across the hard play area where boys in PE kit were running round in a wide circle. In the middle of the circle Johnno stood with his whistle ready.

Patrick didn't have long to wait before the deputy was back.
"She will see you. I'll point you in the direction of her office."
He stood and followed Len out of the door and up the central staircase to her office.
"Just knock and go in."
He knocked and walked through the half open door to see her walking towards him with her hand outstretched.
"Dr East. How nice to see you again."
"Likewise."

She pointed to the small group of chairs to the side of her office, clearly intended for interviews. He sat down, and she sat opposite him, smiling through her glasses.
"I'm sorry, but I feel a bit guilty interrupting you like this."
"Not at all. Len, my deputy that is, said you wanted to talk to me about Wesley."
She was still smiling at him. He smiled back, politely he hoped, before explaining how he was working with Wesley, and that he had already arranged to see the boy again. She listened without interrupting, her eyes fixed on him.
"Thankyou for that, I'm glad he's being well monitored. We've been worried about him."
There was a brief silence, and he wondered if it was his cue to leave. He moved as if to stand, when almost it seemed on impulse, she offered him some tea. He accepted.
"OK. I'll ask my secretary."

She stood and walked over to the telephone on her desk to arrange it. He watched while she had her back turned to him, but carefully looked away as she returned to sit opposite him again.

"I, er, just wanted to ask you about the work you did at the hospital."

"Of course. I'd be pleased to explain. We don't see many of your students though. There's Wesley of course, and there is another we've seen recently, whose name escapes me for a moment. I only saw him once myself."

"Don't worry about the name. It's just useful to know that you see our students when there is a problem."

"I just wondered if you had any more children."

"Me?" she said with a surprise smile, "Oh, just the one, he's nearly fourteen, but I don't think he'll need your help, I'm glad to say."

"Oh, I'm sorry, I didn't mean that. I meant any children from the school you were thinking needed my help. I'm sorry if you thought that was personal."

His discomfort looked like it amused her and she grinned.

"Oh, that's alright. It was me who misunderstood you. But yes, I do have a son. He's here at the school. Copes very well with his mother being the head. Better than me I think. He just ignores me if he sees me. Stays with his friends mostly. Loves IT; typical lad I suppose."

Relieved he hadn't offended her, he relaxed back in his chair, and relaxed his caution as the tea arrived in large mugs, not at all the polite cups and saucers he had expected.

"Refreshing!"

"The tea? Hope so."

"No, mugs. Not what I expected."

"Ah, I might be a woman head, but this isn't a girls' grammar school of the nineteen fifties. Shame on you Dr East."

"You're right. Showing my prejudices. And it's Patrick. Please call me Patrick."

"And maybe that's one of mine. Doctors are always to be addressed formally."

"Not that sort of doctor. I have got a doctorate of course, but I'm a psychologist. And a psychotherapist."
"And I'm Liz."
There was a pause. It felt as if neither of them quite knew what to say next.
"So how long have you been head of this large school?"
"Too long. More than eight years now. Since my son was five. I waited till he was at school before I thought I could take on this kind of challenge. I do really enjoy the job, but it's hard work. Sometimes I worry about Max, but he always tells me he's fine. He's always on the computer."
"Does your husband work long hours too?"
She paused and looked down, which he noticed immediately.
"I'm a single parent. That's why I worry about him."
"Oh, I see."
But it felt wrong as soon as he said it. He didn't really know what to say next.

"I'm telling you more than I ever tell anyone this soon into a conversation." She smiled ruefully. "I guess it's your psychotherapeutic way."
"Sorry, I don't mean to be intrusive."
"It's OK. It's nice talking to you." She paused, as if wondering what to say next. "My husband died actually. Nearly three years ago."
"I'm sorry."
"I suppose I've got over it now. Mostly that is."
"Always takes time."
"He was ill for some time. I knew it was coming."
"Doesn't make it much easier when it happens."
"You're right. But I've told you more than I should have done already. Thanks anyway for listening."
She stood up and stretched out a hand, a little precipitously he felt. It was obvious she wanted the meeting to end, as if she'd exposed too much of herself.

"It's not a problem."
He smiled and stood too, shaking her hand warmly.
"Perhaps we'll meet again."
She smiled. "Next TAC meeting for Wesley I guess."
"No doubt. I'll look forward to it."
He passed Len at the doorway to her office, and made his way back to his car.

"He's a decent guy," she said to Len once Patrick had gone.
"For a psychiatrist, yes, you could say that."
"Psychologist is how he describes himself. How much do you know about him?"
"Works at the hospital. He's done work with our students in the past. Lives in the town. Seems something of a loner actually. I believe he's been married in the past, but not for a long time. I don't think he's got any children, despite the job he does. I think there's an old mother though, going a bit senile so they say, but she doesn't live with him."
She looked at him in amazement.
"How do you know all this?"
"Aha. Keep my ear to the ground and my nose to the grindstone. Just pick things up."
"But you remember them."
Len tapped the side of his head knowingly and grinned.
"Anything else I can tell you?"
"How's the young lad, Josh Greenwell doing."
"Something of a celebrity at the moment of course. Can't do anything wrong. I think it's helped him with his classes. Done wonders for his street cred, and, sensible lad that he is, he's making the most of it. He'll be a good teacher."
"Thanks. That's good news."
"Aye, aye cap'n. Will that be all now?"
She aimed a playful blow at him as he went, grinning.

She could feel a buzz of excitement in her. Was it about Josh's good progress? She didn't think so, but quite why she felt excited wouldn't surface. She gathered her thoughts ready to see Josh again.

When he arrived he was conscious of being offered the same seat as before half term, where she'd had her previous little chat with him. He waited as she smiled through her glasses.

"It isn't often we have heroes on the staff."

Josh wondered how many more times in the day he was going to be embarrassed, but smiled back.

"It really does seem like you saved Wesley's life, and that you were very brave in doing what you did."

"It wasn't really as much as everyone is making out. You just do what you have to when the time comes."

"Well you certainly did. I'm not sure everyone would have done. I've spoken to Wesley's mother again, and she wants to meet you and thankyou. I take it that's alright with you?"

"Yes, of course, but she doesn't need to . . ."

"Actually, I think she does," she said, cutting him off, "it's part of her coming to terms with what has happened. You almost certainly saved his life," She said again.

"Of course I'll see her. I'd be pleased to."

She sat back for a moment and smoothed her skirt before continuing.

"Has it been a strange day for you?"

"Yes, very strange actually."

"Wesley is still being seen by Dr East. As I'm sure you will have guessed, there are a lot of problems at home that led him to think about killing himself. I expect by the end of the week everything will settle down, but use this opportunity to reinforce all the things we were talking about before half term."

He thanked her and stood up. She followed him out of the office and he could see her eyes were smiling. Had he changed even in her eyes?

*

As he waited for his appointment with Wesley, Patrick couldn't help feeling relief that it was still possible for him to be talking to him. Along with the relief there was guilt. He didn't quite blame himself, but he felt he must have under reacted to how distressed Wesley really was last time he'd seen him. And he also knew he hadn't spoken to him about suicidal thoughts, especially after his earlier attempt. He had broken a rule of counselling. Always check suicidal ideation, that was the jargon phrase, and he hadn't done it. If Wesley had fallen to his death, he would have carried that thought around with him for the rest of his life. It wasn't only Wesley who owed a great deal to the schoolteacher who saved him.

The knock at the door broke his thoughts; Wesley with his mother. As soon as she was through the door, she was speaking to him.
"Have you heard doctor?"
"I have. I think Wesley and I need to talk."
"I need to explain to you doctor."
He ushered them both to a seat and closed the door.
"I don't know what he tell you before, but it about his father. He's been coming round making life difficult, wanting money and that. Nothing I said stop him."
"And you were giving him money?"
Wesley stayed silent, head down, looking at the floor, not seeming to want to get involved.
"In the end I did, yes. Then I find out it about drugs. He's spending money, my money, doctor, on drugs for hisself. Was that right? I tell him no. He won't take no, so we have a argument. He start hitting me, and that when Wesley run off. I couldn't stop him doctor. Then his father take the money out of my purse and go out of the house. I have no money left. Next I know policeman is at my door telling me Wesley up in the Woolworth building. He take me there, but when I get there, the schoolteacher has save him. He a fine man that teacher. Wesley's headteacher arranging for me to say thankyou."

She stopped. Patrick noticed there were tears in her eyes, and watched as Wesley slipped his own hand into his mother's, comforting her.
"The police have take him away. After what Wesley done. Then the social worker come, and she helping now. Life going to improve for us now, thank the lord. It going to be different. Wesley be alright now."
"It'll be alright mum. It will. I won't do that again. Not now."
Patrick waited for a moment before responding. He smiled at Wesley.
"Thankyou Mrs Freedom. I would still like a chat with Wesley. Can you go and get a cup of tea in the cafe along the corridor. Come back in half an hour?"
"Yes doctor, I will do that. You be a good boy now Wesley."
And with that she got up slowly, picked up the bag and coat she'd been carrying and left.

He knew that social services had taken over the case but he still wanted to reassure himself that Wesley really wasn't going to try to harm himself again, however much things might be under control at present. He smiled before beginning, and Wesley smiled back, a more relaxed smile than any he'd seen from him.
"Despite what's happened, you look calmer now. Is that true?"
Wesley smiled again, nodded, swung his feet forwards. Somehow, he also looked younger.
"Now he's gone, yes."
"You're less worried now."
He nodded.
"What about these attempts to kill yourself? You got pretty close last week."
"I know. Mr Greenwell saved me."
"Do you think you'll try that again? Seriously?"
"No. Too scared." There was a sheepish grin on his face.
"It was really scary?"
"Mmm."
"How has that affected you?"

"I'm alright now."
It looked promising, but he knew he couldn't afford to relax just yet.

15

With recovery came a gradual recognition of how isolated he really was. There was literally no one Tom could talk to. Just a girl, perhaps his own age or even younger, who looked after him and came to see him for a few minutes three times a day, but who couldn't speak a word of his own language. He knew there were others. Vaguely he remembered there were others on the day he had staggered into their place, wounded and ill, unable to understand anything that was happening. Occasionally he saw them with one eye pressed against the crack between the timbers of the barn he had come to think of as his prison. He'd seen a well built older man he guessed was her father, and two younger men. In his imagination they were the girl's brothers, but he had no way of knowing if he was right, and he couldn't ask her. He'd never seen another woman. If there was a mother, she must spend virtually all her time inside the house. Maybe that was how it was with Italians.

That wasn't how he wanted to be with his own wife. He imagined them out together in England, after the war, with her pushing the pram and him walking alongside her. In the pram, his son would be giggling and laughing. Strangely he could imagine the child he'd never known, always a boy in his imagination, but he was losing touch with the image of his wife. The picture of her wasn't clear any more. It was distressing at first. He wanted to have a clear idea of her ready for the time when he got back, and she was there to meet him at Dover, or wherever he eventually returned. But he knew that she was bound to look different anyway, and that was difficult.

The young Italian girl was becoming more interesting to him. With no way of knowing anything about her, he could put all his fantasies on her without any fear of contradiction. Even though she was his captor he became increasingly attached to her in his head. Now she was used to him, she smiled and used sign language so that up to a point they could communicate. She never seemed to look any different; always there was the same shapeless dark dress, falling to calf length and through which he could never see any indication of her body shape. It didn't stop him imagining what was beneath. She began to feature in his daydreams as he lay back on his makeshift bed. It encouraged him to try and develop a relationship with her.

One afternoon when she came in with his lunchtime meal, he tried to use words for the first time.

"Thankyou. This is my lunch."

"Mi scusi?"

"I" pointing at himself, "thankyou," he said, pointing at her.

She smiled without understanding. He tried again, pointing extravagantly at her and repeating 'you.'

"*Io*," she said pointing at herself.

He repeated it after her, and pointed at himself.

"*Io*," he said.

"*Si*!" she said, pleased.

From somewhere he remembered that '*si*' meant yes.

"*Si*," he repeated, and then ventured, "*Io* Tom."

She beamed, and indicating him repeated "Tom!"

It was pronounced with a kind of shortened second syllable after his name, but there was no doubt she'd said Tom, and knew that it was his name. They smiled at each other. Inside, the tight pressure of loneliness eased just a little.

*

It was irrational. He knew it was irrational, but he kept thinking about his meeting with the headteacher; Liz, as she'd told him he could call her, and on her own, like him; completely absurd to think that something might develop between them. Five years alone was a long time. He remembered she'd said three years for herself, and there was a son. He stopped himself. This was stupid thinking; it was nothing to do with him. He was getting carried away.

His mother of course had been on her own well over fifty years. She'd had her brief flirtations as she called them, but never lived with anyone else, probably never had any significant physical contact with another man since his father died, sometime around his birth. How had she coped with that? He knew he couldn't. Even in these five years he'd had his own little 'flirtations' to use his mother's word. Which to him meant a bit of social contact with a woman, or women, and in one case a bit of kissing. But no sex; not for five years. He wondered if that would ever happen again. Would anyone want to make love to him at his advanced age? His clothes were relatively fashionable, and he had plenty of energy, but when he looked in the mirror he saw the older man he just didn't feel on the inside. Mirror, mirror on the wall, mirror that told all. He was no longer the fairest of them all. He was mostly grey, there were plenty of laughter lines beside his eyes, and worst of all, there were signs of neck scragging as his mother called it. Thank goodness he'd never smoked, and that he wasn't too thin.

Into all his musings came the sound of his mobile, and his first thoughts were of Liz, although as he immediately realised, she hadn't even got his telephone number. His second, more gloomy thought was confirmed when he looked at the screen. 'Aged P' it said. His irreverent tribute to his favourite Dickens novel told him it was his mother.

"Are you alright mum?"

"Of course. Why shouldn't I be?"

"Because you've just rung me. You don't usually do that."

"Why not?"

"I don't know. You just don't"

"I thought you wanted to talk to me."

"Well it was you who just rung me."

"Oh. Shouldn't I have done?"

"No, it's perfectly OK," he lied, "I just wanted to know what you wanted."
"Shall I put the phone down then?"
"Have you had a drink yet this evening?"
"I don't drink, you know that, it's not good for me, and you shouldn't either."
"Drink a cup of tea, I mean."
"Cup of tea?"
"Yes, are you in need of a cup of tea?"
"Yes, I could do with a cup of tea."
"Well put the kettle on, and I'll be round to see that you're alright later."
"Yes, I will do that. See you later."
'Aged P disconnected' his phone said, and he couldn't help agreeing. His excited mood during the minutes before her call quickly dissipated.

*

Max was as usual on his laptop playing some game or other when Liz got home. She could hear the synthesised voices and the sound effects that formed the usual aural backdrop of home life.
"I hope you've done your homework."
If he heard her at all he ignored her.
"I've got plenty to do tonight. Don't let me down by not doing your work."
She made her way to the kitchen. A few seconds later, to her surprise he was in the kitchen with her.
"Mum. Did that black kid really try to jump out of a sixth storey window?"
"You know I can't discuss that with you."
"I'll take that as a yes then. And . . .Mr Greenwell saved him?"
"Max, you know I can't take the risk of you going in tomorrow with an authoritative version from me."
"People expect it anyway," he muttered as he wandered out before doing an about turn and coming back into the kitchen.
"Mum."

"What now?"
"Can I go out with Neil after tea?"
"Where?"
"Just up to his house. He's got a new game."
"Yes, if you get your homework done first, and back by nine thirty."
"OK. Thanks mum."
And he was off to the playroom again to get his homework done, she hoped.
I'll check it in few minutes, once the tea's made!"
It seemed strange still to call it Max's playroom. It was his work room now, but the name had stuck since she and Guy first set it up when he was still quite small. Computer games are what he plays in there now, when he should be doing his homework.

Her mind drifted back to the conversation with the psychologist. How had she told him so much about herself in such a short space of time? And about Guy; something she rarely talked about. Maybe it was his training. Not that she really minded. He seemed a decent guy, but not married, no commitment; what did that tell her about him? He certainly interested her and she wanted to get to know him, but caution was necessary.

She became aware of Max calling her.
"Mum, have you gone deaf? That's the third time."
"Sorry Max. I was miles away."
"I know! Is tea nearly ready? I've done all my homework and I told Neil seven. It's nearly that now," he said, appearing round the door.
"You only need a couple of minutes to get to his house don't you? And anyway, here's your tea. I've not just been daydreaming out here."
She watched him sit down and speed eat his way through two sausages, a fried egg and some tomatoes without surfacing till he'd finished. Too many fry ups, but sometimes it was just easier. At least she made sure she cooked a healthier diet for them both at weekends.

But it was still it was a bad habit she ought to break. Guy wouldn't approve.

The meal over, it was coat on and charge for the door to play the new computer game, leaving her to her own company. She didn't mind the quiet. There had been plenty of that since Guy died, and she was used to it. The loneliness was harder. Tonight there was plenty of work to get through, which was good. It helped to fill the giant space that had been Guy. On the wall behind her work desk was a photo of him before he got ill. He was smiling at her holding the camera as she took the photograph and now there he was in front of her smiling for ever more. Except there was no Guy anymore. The real man was gone. She knew in every part of herself that she would never see him or hold him again. The finality of it appalled her. For many months she simply hadn't accepted it; not really. Early in the morning after he died she remembered distinctly looking out of their bedroom window at the still starry sky and wondering on which one he'd landed. That kind of fantasy thinking seemed incredible to her now, but at the time that was what she believed. How could she, as a rational woman without any religious belief have thought that? And yet she did.

At least now she could look at his photograph without crying. It had taken perhaps two years. None of her staff could ever have believed that, not even Len. Still she talked to him, or at least to his pictures. And in that first difficult year of loss she'd written a series of poems to him. They were kept in her desk as a private communication between the two of them.

She sat down at the desk and switched on the computer. Her mind wandered as she waited for it, staring at the picture.

'I know it would really upset you if you had any idea how much I've suffered for you. I'm glad really that you don't. I wouldn't have wished that on you. Max is quite the young man now. He misses you. Doesn't tell me, probably because he doesn't want to upset me, but I know. I can see it in his face sometimes when he doesn't think I'm looking. He misses you alright.'

With a start she pulled herself out of the reverie. The computer was waiting, and there were staffing calculations to be done. She needed to be ready before discussing it with Len. But first her emails needed to be checked. There was something from Suzy her older sister. Usual happy family stuff and something about how she and David were planning for retirement. It seemed astonishing to Liz that her sister was nearly sixty. How soon the age of flower power had turned into settled middle age. Late middle age really. She didn't feel anywhere near wanting to retire herself. She was after all the younger sister, and after eight years, there was still plenty she wanted to do in the job. How in any case would she manage retirement on her own? School was a lifeline.

Suzy's email, the first in ages, was also about Simon's recent success. Prestigious appointment to the first violins of a London symphony orchestra apparently. Well she knew he was good. She and Guy had been very impressed a few years back at a concert he gave as part of a trio. Seemed however that Suzy was anxious now about him getting a partner and settling down. She looked at Guy and raised her eyes upwards. 'Nice lad if I remember,' she said out loud though I think I've only seen him once since you went. I will go to one of his concerts soon." She closed the email, pulled a tissue from the box she always kept on the desk and wiped her eyes.

16

"Sorry, I am third floor," Stefan said as they reached his apartment building somewhere before midnight; "and no lift."
Struggling for breath because of the climb, because of the anticipation, and from carrying their violin cases, Simon thought incongruously that they must look like gangsters from an old black and white movie.

The inside of the flat hardly registered. His brain was too excited to take anything in. Stefan was already ushering him into the bedroom.
"Not worry. You will like. Shag is fun."
There was a large double bed the in the centre of the room dominating everything around it. He was warm from his exertions and felt overwhelmed. It made it easier that Stefan took the lead.
"We take clothes off, yes?"
It was an expectation rather than a request, which Stefan standing now on the opposite side of the bed was already fulfilling. He followed suit, and in no time both were naked. Stefan got onto the bed and gestured for him to follow, which he did, almost coyly.

The shock of a man's body holding his was intense. For years he'd imagined this moment, longed for it without any real expectation that it would happen. Now at last it was real. Stefan's mouth was seeking out his to kiss him, and he could feel the warm smoothness of his downy hairiness on his own body. Drawn into the magical excitement, his experiences gradually blurred and his body became indistinguishable from Stefan's. There was no sense of time. All he was aware of was energy building and building to a moment of wild ecstasy when they both came within seconds of each other.

At some point he knew he must have fallen asleep. When he awoke, it was already daylight, and he was alone in the bed. For a moment he couldn't quite work out where he was, until the memory of the night flooded back into his brain. He smiled to himself, a satisfied smile. On the far side of the bed he could see the two violin cases, as if they too had enjoyed their night together. He imagined smug grins emanating from the happy violins within, maybe sharing a duet or two.

The figure of Stefan appeared in the bedroom doorway. He was still naked from the waist upward but was now wearing a pair of bright red boxer shorts.

"So you wake, sleepyhead. I am making coffee, toast, breakfast fit for sexy beast, yes?"
"Yes, sure, sounds great. What time is it?"
"Now you want to know. Would you be believing half past eleven?"
"Jesus! That's late!"
"You come through for breakfast?"
He got himself out of the bed and put on his underpants. He wasn't sure whether to dress further, but a touch of returning modesty made him put on his trousers and shirt before walking through to the kitchen, where Stefan had not only made coffee and toast. There were boiled eggs and what looked like sausages and some jam too. Stefan was already sitting at a small table with a view over the high street below, and he sat down on the chair opposite.
"You enjoy, yes."
"I will enjoy. I am quite hungry. Long time since I've eaten anything."
Stefan smiled at him indulgently. He looked at the sausages, which somehow weren't quite sausages as he had always known them.
"What are these?"
"Kielbasa! Polish speciality. You like them?"
He bit into one, and wasn't quite sure, but said he liked it anyway. Anything would taste good for him now.

For a while they ate breakfast quietly together without speaking. It was a bright morning in early November and the sound of Sunday traffic drifted up from the road. Opposite there were trees turning brown and glinting in the sunlight. Simon breathed it all in, glorying in a special morning in his life.
"So, shag was good."
He smiled again, and nodded enthusiastically.
"I am glad I could, how do you say, initiate you?"
"Yes I count myself initiated now."
Impulsively he raised his coffee cup, and Stefan raised his in a mock toast, laughing together like schoolboys.

An hour later, looking very much as if he hadn't gone home since the night before, he was on the bus back to his own flat. The bus driver inquired sarcastically whether it had been a good party as he got on, but he just smiled and sat down, losing himself in his own thoughts. He remembered he'd agreed with Patrick that coming out was a task. Well he'd done more than that in one way and discovered for himself how much it was right for him. He was sure he'd changed the course of his life. He guessed the way some of the orchestra had looked at him as he'd left the pub with Stefan would also make it easier to be more open with them now. It felt somehow as if he had just opened up some giant double gates onto a world of bright sunlight, and at that very moment, the bus turned a corner and the afternoon sunlight streamed into the window where he was sitting, illustrating his thoughts. It felt like a confirmation.

Stefan had been full of energy and encouragement for him. Maybe they would make love again. But as soon as the clichéd phrase entered his head he knew it was wrong. They hadn't 'made love.' The sex they had enjoyed didn't arise from a loving relationship. He grinned to himself; Stefan called it 'shag,' and crude as the word was, it was about right really. He didn't mind that, he didn't do puritanical thoughts. In the long run though, he knew he wanted a loving relationship and it wasn't going to be with a woman. He believed now that in order to achieve what he wanted, he would have to come out fully. Yes, he decided, he and Stefan might shag again. Why not? Just the thought of it aroused him once more, giving him an inner sense of satisfaction, and he was glad he didn't have to get off the bus for a couple more stops.

*

Tom's existence in the barn was little more than long stretches of time in which he had nothing to occupy him apart from his one eyed observations through the hairline crack in the barn construction. It was getting colder and increasingly windy and unpleasant draughts blew into the barn. He kept on hoping that winter this far south, if he had to face it, would be mild. He calculated that it must already be November, but he couldn't be sure. In the early days he was rarely conscious and more or less time than he estimated may have passed. He wondered whether his regiment had made it through Italy to Rome, and whether the Italians had surrendered. When they did, surely his captors had radios and would get to know about it. That would be when they released him. It couldn't be otherwise.

He wanted to see his wife again, and be there in time for the birth of the baby. By now she would be quite big with the child. He wondered how much she thought of him. Did she know he was missing, or did she think he might have been killed? That was a sobering thought which he didn't like at all, but there was no way of getting a message to her. No one in the world, apart from this Italian family, knew where he was. It was the girl who kept him from losing hope. He was getting increasingly fond of her, and now he'd managed to tell her his name, he wanted to find out what hers was. He didn't expect her to be a Dolly or a Daisy, but he had no idea of any Italian names and couldn't begin to guess what it might be from her appearance.

When she came in somewhere around midday, with something for him to eat, he spoke to her straightaway.
"*Io* Tom!" he said proudly.
"*Si, lo so.*"
He knew that she was saying yes, and her body language told him she still recognised his name.
"Your name?" he said, tentatively and pointed at her, "*Io* Tom, and you?"
She didn't understand at first, continuing to put the food she had brought him on the straw beside him, while the donkey outside stamped and snorted, probably sensing food and wondering if it was his turn as well. He tried again;
"*Io* Tom, and you?"
She seemed suddenly to grasp what he was saying.

"*Ah, si, io sono Lucia*."
He loved the way she said it, emphasising the '*io*' and smiling broadly at the same time. He felt a surge of pleasure at knowing her name, which he repeated straightaway.
"Lucia! *Io* Tom, you Lucia."
"*Si, si, ha ragione*!" She paused looking at him, seeming to scan him all over before repeating, "*hai ragione*," in what felt like a more sorrowful, gentle tone. Then, almost as if she'd said too much, she set about clearing the morning utensils. As always there was no food left. What she brought him never felt like enough for him, and even on the rare occasions when he didn't like what she brought, he still ate everything voraciously.

He wanted her to stay with him a little longer, but had no way of asking. Even if he had been able to ask, he had no way of knowing whether she would. In fact he suspected she wouldn't, and guessed that her family outside would come and search for her if she stayed too long.
"It's better when you are here," he said, pointlessly.
She looked round and smiled at him, without looking as if she was trying to understand what he'd said, before moving quickly to the door and slipping back into the world outside.

His spirits fell. It would be hours now before he saw her again. There was nothing to do, nothing to read, and no point in asking for anything, even if he had the words to ask. Knowing her name was a small achievement, and from now onwards he determined to greet her with it. But it went nowhere to easing his loneliness and his fears for his future. He stood up and began pacing the barn, something he'd read that prisoners did in their cells. Now he was doing it. Pacing it out, he worked out that the barn was probably ten yards long and about eight yards wide. At least he had more space than what he imagined were the usual tiny prisoners' cells. He had to be grateful for that, but it didn't help his mood.

It couldn't have been more than fifteen minutes after the girl left when, more noisily and decisively than usual, the barn door opened again. Tom was pacing at the far end of the barn, but the noise startled him, and he was already looking towards the door when once more a figure appeared silhouetted in the door frame. He could see straightaway that this time it wasn't the figure of the girl, but a man carrying a rifle. He watched, frozen to the spot, as the man, still in the doorway, lifted the rifle to his shoulder and pointed it at him. For an awful moment he feared the man was going to shoot him. He stood completely still, and for some reason raised his hands above his head. The man also stood still, keeping the gun trained on him for what must have been at least thirty seconds before lowering it slowly and retreating back through the door, bolting it again behind him.

Tom sunk down onto his bedding area with his head in his hands, shaking, trying to compose himself so that he could even think, so shocking to his whole system was the experience. Eventually his logical thinking abilities began to reassert themselves, but he was at a loss to understand what had just happened. No shot was fired and no orders were given. He didn't think he'd done anything wrong, and the man didn't react as if he thought he had. It was all confusing. All he could think of was that he was being intentionally scared, made to realise that the man was in charge, and watching his every move. A difficult message, but one he had to accept. He was the prisoner.

That evening when the girl returned with his meal and another change of clothing he was still too shocked to remember his intended greeting. She didn't use his name either, and there was no further attempt at contact with him. She left the clothes in a pile beside his bedding and scurried quickly out of the barn. He could only assume that the family had somehow suspected that some kind of relationship had begun to develop. Maybe she had talked about him to them, even told them his name, and that had alarmed them. The appearance of the man with the gun, who he assumed to be one of her brothers, must have been intended to frighten him, while the girl had been warned off. All he could do now was wait and hope that Lucia would in time be prepared to talk to him again.

*

Patrick's telephone had been ringing for a few seconds before he registered it. Aged P the screen told him. He didn't really want to answer, but his sense of duty told him he ought to.

"Hello mother."

"Patrick?"

"That's me. What can I do for you?"

"I've been thinking."

He found that hard to believe, but waited to see what followed. Nothing did. He tried a prompt.

"What have you been thinking?"

But the train of thought had gone and the conversation that followed rambled through what she'd been doing at the day centre, to what she'd been eating and drinking. He listened dutifully for several minutes, adding minor interjections to keep the flow of conversation going before deciding to bring the conversation to an end, when suddenly the initial thought returned.

"I've been thinking about Christmas."

It was the last thing Patrick wanted to think about. Unhappy ghosts of Christmases past lived inside him. Christmases when his mother seemed unable to rise out of a melancholy state of mind and the lights inside the house seemed insufficient to dispel the winter darkness.

"It's still early November. I'll work something out and let you know. Don't worry about it."

"Worry about what?"

"Christmas. What you were just saying."

"You know I never like Christmas."

He resisted the urge to say why raise it in the first place. Instead he chose a diversionary tactic.

"Make yourself a cup of tea. Put the television on, that will cheer you up."

The conversation came to an awkward end, leaving him feeling guilty. How many times had he told his patients that they weren't responsible for their parents? But they weren't the only audience for the message; he was also talking to himself. For all his training that feeling remained unresolved. He knew it wasn't his fault she hadn't remarried when his father failed to return from the war. He'd fought hard all his adult life to keep her emotionally separate as if somehow she would stifle him otherwise. Guilt was the result. He knew too it had affected his ability to develop close relationships with other people. He could recognise now how it contributed to the breakdown of his marriage with Laura and to his difficulty in building lasting relationships since then. It felt bleak, and the thought of Christmas encapsulated the emotional gloom.

*

Quite often, walking through the front entrance into the school felt like leaving the real Liz behind and becoming Elizabeth Broad the headteacher. Sometimes it felt like trying to cut out the individual particularity of herself, but she knew there had to be something of a delusion involved there. The real secret wasn't to lose yourself in some alien persona but to channel your essential self into the confines of the role.

"People respect you because you know who you are and what you stand for," Len told her once, and she'd been grateful, but wished she had his confidence. There were times when a nagging sense of inadequacy gnawed at her from the inside. Nobody else spotted it she guessed, which in a way almost made it harder. The months after Guy died were especially hard. She knew she had to be a good capable mummy for Max, though often she didn't feel like it. Yet his smile, even in the worst times felt like a flickering light at the end of a dark tunnel keeping her going. A woman down the road happily took him to school with her own son and then looked after him until she got home. After she'd left him, the tears flowed in the car on the way to work.

Sometimes great shouted bucketloads of them, and once or twice she had to pull into a layby, unable to continue driving for a few minutes.

As well as her briefcase and laptop in those dark months she always travelled with a ready prepared bag. There was a convenient cul-de-sac a few hundred yards from the school. She had her routine; no make-up on when she left home. Then, with no one around to see her it was face cleanser, foundation cream followed by make-up. It felt like a mask of office. She drove the last few hundred yards to the school looking, she hoped, calmly authoritative. Len guessed she had some kind of system, but being Len, he never asked directly. At least he was always there, a sympathetic presence when she needed him. He was much more than Twitter.

Two weeks after Guy died she got the call from OFSTED.
"HMI Mr Blunt wants to speak to you," her PA said. It was Monday morning. They were coming Wednesday and Thursday for a full inspection. How nice, how very caring. Somehow she managed to get through the grilling about targets and the attainment of boys, but it left her exhausted afterwards. She couldn't understand why she felt so tired. It was an altogether bigger tiredness than she'd expected from an inspection. Only later did she learn that extreme tiredness was part of the grief process.

'Good with some outstanding features' was the verdict. Better than she'd expected, but even Dickens couldn't have made up HMI Mr Blunt. Reading glasses on the end of his nose, erratic hair that wouldn't quite stay in place and a faintly musty smell. His sharp intellect was certainly not matched by the ability to communicate on a human level. He lived up to his name. There was no smile even when giving positive feedback to the governors.

*

Through Tom's narrow viewing place there were no trees visible, but leaves were settling from somewhere. On the ground they were yellow and brown and the wind gathered them in clumps by the building parallel to the barn where he was. The donkey that seemed to spend most of its life tethered to the far end of the barn and outside his line of visibility had been noisier lately, sometimes braying discontentedly as it sounded as if he was led off, presumably to do some kind of heavy lifting work.

The autumn fall seemed to mirror his mood. In the three days since the incident with the rifle he hadn't managed to re-establish contact with Lucia. A feeling of intense loneliness gripped his stomach, made all the worse for the brief promise of some respite in being able to communicate with her. He felt homesick and desperate for some kind of human contact to go some way to easing the long hours he spent on his own with nothing to do. If only there was some way of getting even a pen and some writing paper, he might feel better, and the idea took root in his brain almost to the point of obsession. He had to try and get some means of writing down what was in his head. But the first barrier was regaining contact with Lucia, and the next was communicating his need through the language barrier that separated them.

He was preoccupied with these thoughts and moving round in the barn when Lucia came in with his breakfast. He smiled, as he had done for the last three days, fearful that once more there would be no response. But his spirits rose suddenly when the smile he had begun to despair of ever seeing again was once more on her face. He smiled back and instinctively, before he was able to restrain himself, he stretched out his hand and touched her arm. The warmth of the connection with another human flowed through him like a current, and he was unable to resist the tears that came into his eyes. She looked at him uncertainly, but didn't pull her arm away.
"Lucia," he said out loud, wishing he could say more. Then, feeling embarrassed, he removed his hand, but she didn't recoil from him.

Back in thinking mode, he decided to try his luck further.

"Lucia," he said again, "*io*," pointing to himself, "need writing paper." As he did so he mimed writing with his right hand.

She looked at him at first uncomprehendingly. He repeated the mime.

"Write, with pen?"

Suddenly she seemed to understand.

"Penna? Vorresti una penna?"

"Si, penna," he said copying what he heard as her pronunciation of pen and accompanying the Italian words with a still more vigorous mime. He was speaking Italian and being understood! He felt elated.

"And writing paper." His mime became more elaborate, as with his right hand he mimed the action while simultaneously miming a sheet of paper with his left hand. She seemed to grasp his meaning. Nodding and smiling, she copied his mime of writing.

After she left the barn, he felt more hopeful. The thought of getting a pen and paper had a positive effect. The idea of writing a letter to his wife might become a reality. He had no idea how the letter might actually get to her, unless somehow he could find a way of asking Lucia to post it. Did they even have a postal service in Italy? He just didn't know, but the thought of actually writing a letter felt like a step forward, a kind of reconnection with his past life. In a strange way it made him feel more human again. Even more significant was the fact that Lucia seemed to want to communicate with him again. Against logic, for some while he kept his eye on the barn door for her reappearance although he knew he would have to wait until the next time she brought him something to eat.

When the barn door opened he was absurdly full of anticipation. Had she brought him pen and paper? It felt more important than anything she might have brought him to eat or drink. At first there was no evidence of anything, making him anxious, but once she had put down what she was carrying, her hand disappeared deep into the pocket within her dress and produced a small pencil, no more than three inches in length, and a few sheets of what looked like letter writing paper. She bent over and put them at the side of his hay bed, while he stood in front of her. So strong now was his excitement and so pent up were his feelings that as soon as she stood, he leaned forward to kiss her on the cheek, but his movements didn't co-ordinate with hers, and instead he found himself kissing her full on the lips.

The kiss was over in a moment. He pulled himself back as soon as he realised what he'd done and looked at her, scared of what her reaction might be, scared that she would go and avoid any further contact with him; even send her brother to kill him. She didn't recoil from him but in her eyes he could see fear, and also something else he couldn't understand. It was as if she was puzzled, maybe struggling to understand what had happened as much as he was. She stared at him for some moments without saying anything, as if she was trying to absorb what he might have meant by his action. Then she gesticulated gently towards where she had placed the pen and paper as if to say 'here is what I've brought you' before turning and walking back to the barn door at some speed.

He didn't know what to make of what had happened. It didn't feel as if she thought he'd gone too far, although it had at first been his fear. It was almost as if she accepted, even expected his action and didn't have any strong feelings about it. He remembered that he'd seen what looked like fear, but that might have had more to do with her family than what had happened between them. She didn't actually seem to dislike him, but she didn't seem to particularly like him either. He wondered if in her eyes, he was after all just the English prisoner in the barn.

He sat down and picked up the paper and the pen. It was the first time in weeks he'd had anything with which he could put down his thoughts and try to record what was happening to him. And now he was so confused by what had happened he didn't know what to write. What could he write to his wife and the child, his child, which she was carrying? By the spring he would be a father and he would have a son, or maybe a daughter. In the end it didn't really matter which; more than anything he wanted the war to come to an end so he could be released and return to them. That was how he would start. He would say how much he wanted the war to be over. With the pen in his hand he began to write down his thoughts.

At some point during his writing, possibly as a result of the excitement built up in him dissipating, he realised he must have dozed off into an uneasy sleep. Once more he found himself walking along the ridge with what he took to be the soldier coming towards him. He was aware though in his dream at some level that this was different, and as they were close enough to interact he realised that the soldier was not male but female. The whole atmosphere had changed. He wasn't about to be hit with a rifle. Instead the female soldier, whose face he was unable to see, lifted her arms and put them around his neck. He felt no resistance to this, but waited until her lips met his. He was conscious of a touch, no more, and then at that point the dream came to an end, and he awoke to the sound of the donkey braying outside.

It took him several minutes to bring himself fully from the dream. In front of him was the paper on which he had written two lines. Outside was the continuing sound of the donkey, clearly disturbed by something. Inside it was light enough to see dimly, but darkness was rapidly taking over, and he knew at this time of year it would soon become completely dark. As he came to, he wanted to believe that the female soldier in his dream represented his pregnant wife waiting for him at home, but he was uncomfortably aware that the girl Lucia was also involved somewhere, and that he was developing an attraction for her. He revisited in his mind the kiss he had given her earlier. Had that really been accidental, as he had believed at the time, or had he without realising it arranged for that to happen? He thought back to her responses; the quizzical look. What had that really meant? Was she more aware than he was? He didn't know any longer, and his doubt made him feel even more vulnerable.

Outside the donkey had calmed down, although he could hear it moving and snorting and shifting its feet about. In the darkness of the barn, it was too late now to be able to make use of the paper and pen. It would be morning before he could continue the letter. After his exhilaration earlier, he felt lonely and isolated again, and scared not only that Lucia would once more turn against him, but also that his own feelings weren't completely under his control. All he could do for now was lay back and think and hope that as night wore on, he would be able to sleep.

*

It took several weeks for the authorities to confirm anything, but for some time the rumour had been gaining credibility in the town. The body was a soldier from the war, and an English one. There were very few locals who had been alive during the war, but those who were didn't seem to have any memory of any kind of English troop movement in the area, although German soldiers had been seen. The war seemed to have passed them by. There was hardship, but those who had land and could grow their own food survived reasonably well through a combination of eating what they grew and bartering for what they didn't have. Leo knew that had been the case with Marco's family, sustained by the vineyards and their extensive land. But no one had any idea how the body of an English soldier came to be at the bottom of such a remote valley nestled under the Aspromonte.

An officer from the *carabinieri* let it slip there had been a letter in his pocket, and that they were trying to trace his identity with the English government. In time, it might be possible to trace his family in England. Leo hoped that would mean a Christian burial after all these years. Was there a wife, did he have any children in England, and how old would they be now? He sat outside the church looking down over the valley towards the sea. All around him the leaves on the trees were turning golden as he offered up a silent prayer to God for providing such a lovely afternoon.

Without warning the figure of Marco was in front of him, gesturing and seeking his attention. It was obvious almost immediately he had something to show him. He stood up and followed him round the other side of the church from where the mountains were clearly visible. Knowing Marco's powers of observation were frequently amazing, he waited while he pointed excitedly up into the air. At first he could see nothing unusual. Then, way above them he spotted a large bird gliding downwards and into view. At first he assumed it was a larger than usual buzzard but as it came closer the white underparts with their dark streaks and the short rounded wings told him it was almost certainly an a*quila fasciata,* a Bonelli Eagle. His father claimed to have seen one on a trip up into the mountains, but they rarely ventured out of the Aspromonte itself. Seeing one this far down gave him a real sense of privilege. It was truly one of God's special days.

Together they watched it circling and then swooping down in a soaring motion to take its prey from the ground no more than a couple of hundred metres in front of them. As it climbed back up into the air and then into the distance of the mountain beyond, they could see in its beak what looked like a rabbit; certainly more than a small rodent. Once there was no longer a danger of scaring the bird off, Marco clapped his hands together wildly and grinned. But his control earlier confirmed once more Leo's belief that there was greater intelligence inside Marco than most people were prepared to believe. He patted him on the shoulder, sharing his excitement.

17

The anger that had felt like it was overwhelming her after Ben left seemed at last to be abating. Maybe the psychotherapy has helped after all Anna thought. Suspicious as first, she found that talking about her feelings, even to a male therapist, had helped her get back into control. And discovering that the young schoolteacher wasn't after all as bad as she'd first thought had also helped. Even when she'd had to concede to the insurance company that the accident was actually her fault, she could still recognise that he had kept calm against her verbal assaults and that in saving the young boy from jumping off the window sill he had actually been very brave. Whether she pursued any further relationship with him was another matter, but at least she felt now she had an open mind. And knowing him had after all gained her a good story for her column, despite the sub editor's naff contribution. 'Teacher to the Rescue' was hardly an inspiring headline.

She was sitting in the first floor cafe above the local M&S store with a view almost opposite where Josh performed his rescue act. Except that it had been one floor higher than she now was. That seemed quite amazing. She could never have done it; not climb onto a ledge at that height. The thought of it made her shudder; it was a different league again from jumping out of an aeroplane. Today it was windy. Leaves swirled about in the autumn air and it felt colder outside than the relatively mild twelve degrees.

She was on the point of leaving when someone, walking past her table, slipped and fell beside her, dropping a cup and making quite a crash in the process. A young man in a flamboyant yellow waistcoat looked up bemused as if he didn't quite know how he had come to be semi prostrate beside her. Before she could actually gather her senses to do anything he had manoeuvred himself from the floor and onto the seat opposite hers. Almost as quickly an assistant from the coffee bar was on the scene checking his state of health and offering a replacement coffee, which he accepted. As another assistant made her way across with a mop and bucket, she watched as the young man drew himself together and smiled across the table at her, still with a bemused expression as if to ask 'how did I get here?'

"Are you alright," she asked, belatedly, not yet sure whether to smile, and instead affecting a concerned voice. He was the first to smile.
"Everything still working I think. Bruises maybe, but arm is good." He flexed his right elbow cautiously.
"I'm glad you're alright. That was quite a fall."
"I think you call it spectacular," he said, grinning now and beginning to enjoy the benefits. Anna noticed his blue eyes looking at her, not quite penetrating, but observant. Delicately he fingered his blond hair, checking the gelled upward spikes had survived the fall unharmed.

His replacement coffee arrived, brought by the manager and accompanied by enquiries as to his state of health and appropriate fussing. Once more he reassured her all was well and thanked her for the coffee. It was 'on the house' she told him and there was more if he wanted it.
"What is 'on the house'?" he said to Anna once she'd gone.
"Free. No charge. It's to compensate you for the fall."
Something about his appearance and his obvious unfamiliarity with the English expression made Anna ask if he was German.
"So, sorry! No, no. Allow me to introduce myself. Stefan Paminski, from Poland."
And with the introduction, he stood up and held out his hand. She lifted hers as if to shake his, but instead he took her hand, lifted it to his lips and kissed it. Taken aback and impressed at the same time, she managed to introduce herself.
"Anna. I'm Anna Rosenthal."
"Ah, I see, you are German."
"No, I'm English, but my grandparents were German. Hence the name."
His combination of easy manners and old fashioned formality was disarming.
"I am from Krakow area. Not so far from Germany, especially before the war."
"My family is from old Silesia. Not far indeed."

"So we are both now in England. But maybe distant cousins, meeting here by chance because I fall over by your table."
"My grandfather escaped to England before the war. His parents weren't so lucky. We are a Jewish family."
"Death camps. I am sorry. I know about that. My town is Oswienczim."
"Auschwitz! You are from Auschwitz?"
She felt herself recoiling inside, wanting to end the conversation and go. But the inquisitive journalist over-ruled the great scar from the death camp experience she shared with all Jews. What had he seen? Worse, what had his family seen?
"Many unhappy memories in my home town."
Had his grandparents watched the train carrying her relatives on its terrible journey?
"Eating, opening a window, or just walking dully along," she said suddenly, out loud.
"Please?"
"It's from a poem. English author, Auden I think. About how ordinary people go about their business while awful things are happening around them. What you've been saying about your family's experiences in the same place where so many of mine were exterminated. It just came into my mind."
He wasn't smiling. It occurred to her he didn't know quite how to react to what she was saying.
"One of the greatest evils of history, and your family were kind of spectators. That's really strange."
"Strange for me too. Survivor guilt is what you call it?"
She nodded. He was touching the raw nerve directly now.
"You don't have to be Jewish, or German. Polish for me, English for you. We are here talking. All those six million, they died. We respect and remember, not let it happen again. Move on with our lives."
"I feel we ought to have something stronger than coffee to drink to that."
He smiled, but his mouth hardly moved. It felt as if something very significant had happened between them, although she couldn't exactly

put it into words. But now she needed to move away from the dark areas they had just visited.
“So what brings you to England?”
He smiled again, more widely this time as if he shared her need to move away from the heavy legacy they’d inadvertently shared.
“Music. I come to study. I am violinist.”
As he said this he made an extravagant mime of playing.
“Classical music?”
“Yes, I play in Symphony Orchestra. I am proud to be first violins.”
”Look. I’m a journalist. You know I’d really like to do an article about your experiences for my column in the local paper. Could we meet again for that?”
“Of course!” His eyes lit up with obvious pride. “I am always ready for fame!” He laughed out loud.
“Well that’s one way of describing it. A week of local interest perhaps.”
He laughed again, standing up in the process and took her hand once more for a formal farewell kiss. Slightly embarrassed and amused at the same time, she let him do it. Then he was off, out of the coffee bar and downstairs. She stood and looked out of the window into the street and waited till she could see striding away into the wind with a long black overcoat held tightly round him.

Anna wondered whether she liked him. He was certainly different from most men she met, with his antiquated Eastern European customs. Vaguely she remembered seeing her grandfather kissing hands like that, but it seemed odd in a young man. Strangely it felt almost intentionally not sexual. Was he gay? It made a kind of sense. In any event, he felt entirely unthreatening. The interview would be interesting, and now she had her next weekly column sorted.

Talking about Auschwitz had stirred up again all those thoughts she wanted to keep at a distance. Supposing her grandparents had not escaped from Germany in 1938, but been taken to Auschwitz, or Belsen or Birkenau or any of the other camps for that matter, like six million others? Death would have almost certainly been their fate, and she wouldn't exist. The living breathing conscious self sitting calmly in a local cafe drinking coffee and talking to a guy who grew up in the place where it all happened would not exist. Involuntarily she shuddered. It was more than just men that made her angry. The disregard for human life made her profoundly angry.

And now because of a series of freak coincidences, she'd allowed herself to arrange a date with Josh. She wasn't sure how she felt about that either. From hating him she knew she had moved to finding him more interesting. She wondered if even when she was angry with him she had at the same time, without realising it, found his looks appealing. That was the strange sort of thinking she was learning from Patrick but it seemed plausible to her now. Perhaps he no longer made her angry; maybe there was more to her anger than just men. But he was egotistical and probably self centred. How involved did she really want to get? Part of her was ready to give him a chance. Another part was very anxious that this could leave her vulnerable to being drawn into a relationship which would then be hard to get out of. She needed her defences ready.

The waitress was clearing the cups from the table.
"Seemed to take a shine to you love, didn't he."
It took a moment to grasp what she meant.
"That guy with the flashy waistcoat. Seemed keen on you!"
Inane gossip wasn't what she wanted at that moment in time. She stared hard and walked out without making any response.
"Please yourself then. I should be so lucky!"

*

Out on yard duty, Josh hadn't expected the wind to have such an effect on children. He watched the eleven and twelve year olds throw themselves about almost as if they were mirroring the leaves falling all around them in the gale. They were running and chasing about wildly. He found it amusing but also slightly disconcerting. Up on the top yard where the older boys were kicking footballs about, the same frenetic movement seemed to have affected them, while more senior girls, huddled together in small groups looking as if they were unaffected by the wildness around them, revealed through high pitched squeals and laughter that they too couldn't resist the effect of a force so primal as an autumn wind.

It was Friday, the day of his date with Anna. The excitement and the wind seemed to be in tune with the excitement inside. He wanted to score after his recent bad experiences, and he did after all quite fancy her. Quite a lot actually, he had to admit. What he should wear? Casual, but not too casual; that would match the restaurant he'd chosen, and which she'd agreed to. Don't overdo it for the first date. It had taken a while to get this far. All too easy to mess it up at the moment, and he really didn't want to do that. Keep calm, act cool, don't get too excited too soon he told himself. That had to be the way.

A young face was looking up at him, waving. Someone wanting to say hello drew him back into the present.
His reputation since the rescue had remained high. All manner of students greeted him warmly in their own slightly uncouth way as he moved around the school, shouting out, waving or just grinning as they passed. It must feel like this to be a celebrity he thought. A couple of times Wesley had walked past him and just waved without seeming to need any further communication. He was happy with that.

He tried to remember what she looked like, and was surprised to discover that beyond generalisations like dark eyes and hair he couldn't exactly picture her in his mind. He would recognise her again, he was sure of that, but the detail of her face escaped him. He would have to make a conscious effort to put that right when they met. She had a quick temper, no doubt about that. Was it one of the things that made her attractive to him? More of a challenge than the other women he'd known in the past, certainly; the hunter instinct perhaps? The thought made him smile.

There was movement back into the school. He hadn't heard the bell himself, but obviously the students had. Len Turner was making his way from the top yard, shepherding students down in the process.
"All seems to be going well with you now young man," he called out into the wind as he got close.
"Yes thanks, it does."
Two large girls passed, both talking together and laughing at the same time. When they saw him, both of them grinned and waved extravagantly.
"You're a star now with the students of course."
"Seems so."
"Use it well. It won't last forever. But they do seem to like you anyway. Once you've got into their hearts you can do almost anything."
Their paths diverged as they entered the doors into the school, and Josh made his way to his next class.

*

The wind was still strong when he arrived at the bistro in a side street just off the town centre where he was meeting Anna. He was cold waiting outside, and relieved when she arrived quite soon after him, her dark hair blowing in the wind. He had no difficulty recognising her, and noticed once again that she had chosen to wear black, not this time a dress, but trousers and a smart silk blouse which she revealed once an obsequious waiter had taken her coat and showed them to the table he'd booked. Once they were sitting she smiled at him over the table, and it crossed his mind how little of her smile he had seen so far. Suddenly he didn't quite know what to say.
"Thanks for coming." It felt like a fatuous comment as soon as he had said it. But she smiled again and assured him she was pleased to be with him.

Which was true. Despite her uncertainty, and fears that the whole idea was a mistake, looking across at him she could see that he'd obviously made an effort, something Ben rarely did. It felt reassuring. It wasn't an effort to smile and for the moment any anger seemed to be in abeyance. But still she wasn't entirely comfortable; something she couldn't define still didn't seem right about the meeting. Once the waiter had brought the menus and asked about wine she tentatively moved the conversation forward.

"Who would have guessed, when our cars collided that day that we would be sitting here having a meal together in this nice bistro?"

His grin had just a hint of satisfaction she thought, as she waited to see if he would respond.

"I feel as if I need a glass to drink to that," he replied, and conveniently on cue, the fussy waiter returned, rearranged the glasses and poured. Once he'd gone, they followed Josh's suggestion. Was it all pretence? She really didn't know.

"So you're a schoolteacher, and a local hero. And you've invited me here to thank me for getting you in the local press." The accompanying grin was consciously mischievous. "But I'm off duty now, so you can tell me about yourself, safe in the knowledge it won't appear in next week's herald."

She watched him smile, but he didn't rise to the bait directly.

"What do you want me to tell you?"

"Anything interesting really. Give me a better idea of who you are."

"And you'll tell me more about yourself afterwards?"

"Of course," she lied, determined to keep the journalistic approach, off duty or not.

"OK." He sat back and took a sip of wine without any kind of ostentation. "Twenty seven. Single of course. Had girl friends before, but no really long term relationships . . ."

"Meaning?" The response was sharper than she really intended, so she softened it with a smile.

"University girl friends, three or four since, including the Italian girl I've already told you about. No more than a few months with anyone."
Was he lying? Or just being factual?
"And I did an English degree."
Had he forgotten that he'd told her he didn't finish his degree, and then completed it later? It seemed like a bit of dissembling. But he was carrying on.
That's what I teach now, to students at the school. But I guess your degree is English too, being a journalist."
"It isn't actually. Languages for me, French and German; not that I use them much now. I'm a very English based journalist."
"No desire to travel then?"
"Oh yes, definitely!" How could he have thought she wouldn't want to do that?

He watched her nod her head vigorously. Did he detect some regret, a sense of something unfulfilled perhaps? She intrigued him. She was interesting, but cool and detached. It felt like he was opening up to her, but the opposite wasn't really happening. Not yet anyway. The waiter arrived with their food. For a while the conversation stopped as they tried what was in front of them, agreed mutually it was good, raised their glasses to their friendship, a word which he noticed she emphasised, and began eating. He watched her without saying anything for a short while, finding her increasingly fascinating. Her choice had been steak, and he noticed how she seemed to attack it with her knife and then thrust it into her mouth almost with a degree of urgency. She was certainly a fast eater, which he knew he wasn't, and he was anxious that he would still be eating long before she had finished. He didn't think he could speed himself up, so instead he decided to try to get her talking to slow her down.
"So how about you?"
She looked up almost as if surprised that someone was in the bistro with her. For a moment he wondered if she was going to reply at all.
"Oh, me, quite boring really. Not much to say about me."

"Well I know you're a journalist, and you've just told me you speak French and German . . ."
"Badly. Rusty since uni I'm afraid."
"Better than me. Schoolboy French is my limit."
"But you speak Italian. You told me before."
"Yes, I do, but my French is very primitive."
He really wanted to ask about boyfriends, but he could sense evasiveness, and couldn't quite bring himself to ask the question directly, half wondering if she would attack him with the steak knife if he offended her. She had almost finished, and he was no more than half way through. He decided the best course might be to work his way through his plate as fast as he could and wait for her to speak when she was ready, but more quickly that he expected, she picked up the conversation.

"Yesterday I interviewed a guy who grew up in Auschwitz."
"The death camp?"
"Well, not in it, but in the town where the camp was. Not at the time, he's young, our age group. But can you imagine that?"
He nodded in amazement, not quite understanding why she had suddenly started talking about that.
"It's called a Polish name now, which I can't pronounce, but don't you think that's awful?"
It was more a statement than a question. He didn't feel the need to respond. She hesitated and then continued.
"Some of my family died in there. Jews exterminated by Hitler. Part of my inheritance, like all Jewish people."
He didn't quite know what to say. Sorry seemed inadequate. He looked in what he hoped was a sympathetic way, while she carried on.
"I'm from a Jewish family. Not that I'm religious. My parents go to the synagogue and that was part of my experience as a child. I dutifully had my Bat Mitzvah ceremony when I was twelve, and I can do a bit of cursing in Yiddish."
So the Auschwitz bit was about telling him she was Jewish. . . .

"Being Jewish is completely in my blood, literally, but I'm not religious. I don't practice it."
"Not at all?"
"Not practising, no. Doesn't seem relevant anymore. The idea of some kind of external God you pray to doesn't make any sense. We're born, we live our lives as best as we can. We die. That's the end of us as far as I'm concerned."

She sat back, taking another sip from her wine and watched him finish the last of his food, surprised at herself for saying so much so quickly. At least he'd listened, but she wondered now what he would be thinking. Not that it mattered too much, she was who she was. He was sitting back, having finished his meal at last, presumably trying to take in what she'd been saying.
"So no life after death?"
"Absolutely not; makes no sense to me. Do you believe anything different?"
"I don't know really. I do believe there's something spiritual in all of us. This hard factual here and now world we inhabit isn't all there is. That's where creativity comes in. And that's what lives on."
She was suddenly conscious of sitting across the table looking at a man she hardly knew and talking about issues of life and death. It seemed very strange.
"We've got really serious haven't we?" he was saying now, and she had to agree with him.
"Life's a serious business, and we're being honest with each other. No point in just small talk."
"None at all."
In spite of her intentions, she knew she had actually revealed a lot about herself already, and it felt OK to do so. He was after all a decent guy, even easy to talk too, and maybe once you got to know him, not too patronising, given he was a school teacher. But definitely not her kind of man she decided, even though more polite, more thoughtful than Ben ever was. She would miss the spark with someone like him.

They were coming to the end of the meal, and she knew she didn't want another course. No desserts, she'd had enough and was adamant about that, despite his protestations. Then he told her he wanted to pay for the meal, but she wouldn't accept that either, so they split the cost in half and settled it that way before leaving the restaurant through the door which the waiter held open for them.

Outside the wind was still blowing hard. He would walk her to her car, he told her, and she didn't object. Something traditional quite appealed to her, as it had with the Polish guy, although this time she knew there could be ulterior motives. This guy certainly wasn't gay. It was two or three minutes walk to the car park, and they didn't speak against the noise of the wind. At one point she noticed he put his arm briefly round her back to guide her round the corner. She didn't like it, but let him do it without complaint.

As they approached her car, she pressed the automatic control and watched the lights acknowledge the doors were open, then turned to face him.
"Thanks for the company. You chose a nice place. I enjoyed it." The accompanying smile was as non-committal as she could make it.
"Thankyou too," he said, uncertainly, as if he didn't quite know what to do next.
"Bye then. I'll text you." She waved briefly, ducked down into the car and closed the door. Through the rear view mirror, she could see him still standing, as she drove away.

As he watched her car disappearing into the distance, Josh couldn't quite work out how he felt. Yes, it had been a pleasant meal, and they hadn't argued this time. But she puzzled him. She'd shared the Jewish inheritance with him, and talked about Auschwitz. That had been surprising. Otherwise very little about herself. He couldn't really work her out. Yes it was true he found her attractive. Those dark features, Jewish features he now knew, made her very good looking. And fate did seem to keep throwing them up against each other. But whether she thought all that much of him, he really wasn't sure. Perhaps accepting the date was more out of politeness. Maybe he should let her fade out of his mind, wait until someone else came along where he could be successful. And yet . . . it was male wasn't it, to enjoy the chase, to find the woman who is hard to get the most attractive? Maybe he didn't have to give up just yet. She had said she would text him. Why was that? She didn't have to. Would she want to meet him again? He didn't know.

Well at least he was company for the meal, she thought as she drove back home. Probably not really my type though. Suddenly, out of nowhere, her mother's voice came into her head.
'Oy, oy, Anna you know what? You *kvetch* too much!' Was that what she was doing? Never being satisfied? What would her mother have said about him? A pleasant young man perhaps, nicer than Ben? Yes she would complain that he wasn't a nice *Jewish* boy, but she'd like him. Perhaps that was the problem. Ticked too many of the wrong boxes. Not Jewish, but otherwise too much like the clone her mother might have created for her. Well that wasn't what she wanted. She'd text him as she'd promised, but probably to tell him that was it.

Her mind drifted, and out of nowhere a strange new idea began forming in her head. Why not go to the death camp where her great grandparents had died? Would it help her to come to terms with the inheritance she hadn't asked for, but which she couldn't avoid? Was that sensible? Atonement; making up for something, making up for not being there, and dealing with being Jewish. Maybe this was something she needed to talk to Patrick about. But just thinking about the possibility was having an effect on her. It suddenly felt very important.

She knew Jews went to Israel. Stood at the wailing wall and, well wailed. She couldn't resist a slight smile at all those deadly serious frummers in sober religious clothes making all that racket over what was left of a wall destroyed two thousand years ago. But maybe it made more sense than she'd allowed before. Once upon a time Christians had gone to holy sites too. And Muslims had their pilgrimage. Didn't they call it the Hajj? For serious Muslims it was very much alive. Why not for her? By the time she got home she had more or less decided that she would go to Auschwitz, and quite soon. It would be her pilgrimage to honour the dead in her family, and to respect all Jewish suffering. *Tschuve;* unbidden, the word came out from within her. *Tschuve*; it would be her day of atonement. She felt calmer thinking about it. It was definitely the right thing to do.

18

Simon hadn't believed it was possible to enjoy so much sex. After the years of self imposed abstinence he was enjoying a riot of indulgence. Stefan encouraged him all the way, treating him as a kind of protégé, although there was very little difference in their ages.

"You are fast learner," he said, "and I am good teacher. We play and afterwards we play again!"

Which is what they did. Sometimes there were interludes in which they practiced their violins, and sometimes they played duets together. Life was fun. He sent a text to Patrick: 'Have found partner. Enjoying time together. Thanks', and got a brief reply: 'delighted.' Just the one word felt like a validation, absolving him from any vestiges of guilt, which he admitted had in any case very quickly dissipated. There were no regrets.

He was aware their relationship was for now. He could live with that. They were master and student, friends with a lot of integral sex, but not long term partners. Stefan was clear about that from the start, and despite having some feelings of jealousy at the thought some other guy might in the future get what he was getting now, he knew realistically he was one partner in a succession of 'lovers' who had made their way through Stefan's life.

"Why I like sex with you? Because you are innocent, fresh face starter. And I like you."
"But you'll move on, have other lovers."
"I am not faithful lover. I like many. Variety is spice of life you say in English."
So there was no doubt in his mind. He knew from the start that one day he might climb the stairs to the flat in an ecstasy of anticipation, only to find someone else enjoying Stefan's bed. For now, he felt as if he could live with that, but a dream was developing in his mind. There would be a wonderful lover, a man who loved him and wanted the same kind of committed relationship that he did. He knew some gay men were like Stefan. There were some straight men who wanted to fuck as many women as possible, and never seemed able to settle with one partnership. Lived for 'shag' as Stefan might have put it. But there had to be other gay men like him. Now thanks to Stefan, he would be ready when the right guy came along.

He enjoyed having their secret within the orchestra, although he suspected most of the violin section, firsts and seconds, had grasped the situation. Gossip being what it was, if a few guessed, most did. And so what? He was enjoying the excitement of it, a kind of playful coming out, which at the same time, at least in his imagination, put him surreptitiously centre stage. It seemed only a small step from here to coming out fully. The gay bass player did seem to be looking at him differently, and he wasn't quite sure how he felt about that, but he was feeling so chilled about life now it didn't really worry him.

At the back of his mind, he was aware that he would need to make a decision about whether to tell his parents. He knew he didn't have to, and they probably wouldn't find out otherwise, but now it felt more complete, almost more clean, to be honest with them. It would avoid the pretence of having to make up half stories when they wanted to talk about girl friends. It had always been uncomfortable subject at home. A life where he could be fully himself stretched out ahead, and he was thankful to be in a profession where colleagues would think nothing less of him as a result.

*

Before going into her own bedroom, Liz liked to check on Max. He might be thirteen, but he's still my child she told herself. The side lamp was on, but he'd fallen asleep in bed, and the computer was off, or at least on standby. A huge poster with some kind of mythical creature looked down on him from above the bed, but she noticed there was also a photo of a grinning girl of about his age in shorts and tee shirt pinned to the bottom of it. A holiday snap, which the girl must have given to him. So he's starting to be interested in more than computer characters she thought, before turning out the light and closing the door.

Inside her own room, the only pictures involved Guy. Beside her dressing table there was a photo of them together and next to her bed, her favourite picture of him.
"Max has a picture of a girl on his wall," she said, "you'd be proud of him."
Guy smiled back at her unchanging, and without warning, she could feel tears welling in her eyes. Why now she wondered? Brushing them away, she undressed, walked into the en suite and switched on the shower.

Afterwards, she dried herself, put on her nightdress and got into the large double bed. It felt as lonely as it had for the last three years. She looked at him again, smiling, wanting to take comfort from him, but tonight the spell wasn't working. The tears were welling again. It hadn't been a particularly difficult day. She'd kept herself occupied, nothing especially sad on the TV, and no mournful music. She couldn't really understand what had changed.
"Why am I crying again tonight Guy?" she said to his picture. And from nowhere, into the silence around her came the word 'Max.'
"Why Max?"

The knowing smile looked out at her.
"It's the girl isn't it?"
She was beginning to sob quietly now, not wanting to wake Max, but crying more deeply than for maybe a year, maybe since the last anniversary. She allowed herself to cry, until the body convulsions eased. Taking two tissues from the box beside the bed, she dried her face and cleared her nose. It was midnight. Her body felt heavy, filled with the dull ache she knew so well now. Stretching her arm across the width of the bed. It felt like there was no end to it. Loneliness inhabited her.

*

Tom woke to the sound of rain outside. It always had an effect on him. In his dream he'd been with his wife in England, and she was close to him. It was as much a feeling as a visual dream and he knew on waking that the dream involved a sexual experience. The first time he'd made love to his wife it had been raining outside. The sound of the rain had filtered into the end of the dream, no doubt as he'd gradually become conscious of the rain on the barn roof. He looked around him. The barn was still dry, but there was a dripping sound over by his toilet area. I'll get wet pissing, he thought. At least it might help to improve the smell.

He put on his top clothes so he was presentable in case Lucia called in, and went to look outside through the spy crack. He could see that it was wet on the pathway outside. The rain was heavy and persistent, but it was, he calculated, somewhere in the middle of November, and rain was normal, certainly in England. Why should it be different here in Italy. He knew it had to mean his barn would become damp; it would hardly be surprising if it didn't.

There was a sound at the barn door. Lucia was entering, so he made his way back to the bedding area in readiness for what she might have brought him to eat. He watched her close the door and walk across to him in the gloom. As usual there was bread, and a large red tomato.

She put it in front of him and smiled. Then from within the folds of her dress, where he knew she carried things, she withdrew something. It was a picture of a bird, hand drawn he guessed. *'Io'*, she was saying, pointing to herself and miming drawing or writing. She wanted to tell him she had drawn it. *'Aquila,'* she said. Did that mean bird he wondered? He repeated the word, and she corrected his pronunciation until he got it right, putting the accent on the first syllable: *'aquila.'* She smiled at him approvingly.

The bird in the drawing was large. Some kind of mountain bird he assumed, probably from the area where he was incarcerated. It had wide wings, and she had drawn it with a white undercarriage, as it might be seen from below while the bird was in flight. He had to admit it was a good drawing, even thought he couldn't really identify what kind of bird it was. Then he remembered the large bird flying around just before he collapsed in the valley. It was like that he thought. As far as he could remember from his hazy state at that time, it was a good likeness.
"Good," he said, "very good."
"*Ti piace*?" She smiled, pleased. "*Buon*?"
The word stirred a memory from the little French he had done at school. "*Bonne,*" he said, "good!"
"*Buon*!" she repeated.
"*Bonne*!" he said again, and she replied "good." So pleased were they to have understood each other they continued saying the words, his being French rather than Italian, but neither of them knowing or bothering about that.

After she went, he felt better for a short while, buoyed by the brief communication, but it left him feeling even more dissatisfied. He was growing very fond of Lucia, his only contact with the world beyond the barn door and he wanted to spend more time with her. In the long hours of loneliness it was what he clung to, against any kind of realistic hope. He sat back and listened to the sounds outside the barn. The incessant rain continued. The donkey was restless again, moving about, stamping and snorting, and he could faintly hear voices outside. They were always men's voices. Very vaguely he remembered the men who had first captured him when he arrived back in September. He'd also seen the man with the rifle who came to scare him, and he'd seen more men with the one eye that could look out from his viewing place, but still no other women.

Feeling the effect of the dampness in the atmosphere, and colder than he'd been before, he sat down to write more of his letter to his wife. He was disturbed to discover that that he could remember even less about her. Precisely what colour were her eyes? Were they blue, or more grey? And when she let it down, how long was her hair? Had she grown it longer since he last saw her? He knew what her smile was like, and it made him smile thinking about it. She was shy, and she'd never allowed him to see her completely naked. In his whole life he'd never actually seen a woman naked. He regretted that and knew that was something he wanted to put right when he got back. For now he tried to imagine her without her clothes on, imagining moving downwards from her face, to her rounded breasts with the nipples he loved, and then down to the slim waist. Beyond that he imagined the bush of hair covering her most intimate part, and wondered if it would be the same colour as the hair on her head. Probably it would be. Then he worked his way down to her legs, with the sturdy thighs and the shapely calves, down to her small feet.

Thinking about it, with the rain falling steadily outside, excited him, and took him in his mind away from where he was. And in his excitement, he found himself also conducting the same imaginative act with Lucia as his subject. What would she look like without her dowdy clothing? The thought, with its forbidden element, stirred him even more, and he allowed himself to imagine her taking off her clothes in front of him and standing in the barn to let him see her whole body.

His thoughts were suddenly interrupted by the sound of voices outside, much louder. Quickly the excitement drained from him, and for a moment he was scared, until he realised it had no connection with him. Some kind of farm activity was being organised, and the donkey, stamping and snorting even more now, seemed to be part of it. It was astonishing how much noise one animal could make, and now, even though the sound was diminishing, it was still braying loudly. He guessed it was complaining about being led away to work in the rain.

19

It was the next TAC meeting when Patrick saw Liz again. He'd been looking forward to it, and to seeing her again. He knew he wanted the chance to talk to her. When he entered, she was talking to someone else, but he managed to catch her eye so that she briefly acknowledged him. Wesley and his mother were there already, and the warm smiles they both gave him suggested things had moved very much in the right direction. The course of the meeting seemed to establish that too. Mr Freedom was no longer on the scene, and Wesley and his mother were both beginning to settle into a better life. The effusive thanks from her for all the support she'd got from him and the school pleased and embarrassed him and, he guessed, Liz too.

After the meeting, it seemed natural to enquire how Wesley was settling back into school.
"Well he seems to really like you," she said, "thinks you've helped him to make sense of things again. So thankyou for all you've done, he's a different boy. He should do well."
"I've liked working with him. How's Max?"
"Like a thirteen year old, what do you expect? All computer games and iPods and never without the mobile!" She smiled, but formally, in role he thought, and the meeting seemed to be coming to a professional ending.

"Liz, I was just wondering," he paused, trying to gauge the likely reception for what he wanted to say.
"I was wondering," he said again, "if, well, could I take you out for lunch one day?"
Suddenly she looked slightly flustered, out of her professional mode. But she answered quickly.
"Well, yes, that would be nice, why not? But you do know headteachers don't get lunch breaks. Ten minutes for a sandwich if I'm lucky. It would have to be a weekend meeting, is that OK?"
"Of course." It certainly was, better than he'd hoped.
It wasn't difficult to agree on the forthcoming Saturday. It was almost too easy.

'What am I doing' she asked herself as she made her way back to the office, but at the same time there was an excitement, an adrenalin buzz she hadn't felt for quite some time. Had she really just made a date? Len met her on the corridor.
"TAC meeting go alright?"
"Fine thanks Len."
"How was the doctor?"
Did he have some sixth sense?
"Yes he was there. He's done a good job with young Wesley."
"Knows what he's doing I think. That's what the grapevine says anyway."
"I think that's right." She hesitated. Should she tell him? Everyone told her he couldn't keep secrets, but for her, he'd always been discreet. It would help perhaps to share it with someone, and really there was no one else she could tell. Certainly not her sister.
"Len, would you believe, he's asked me to lunch?"
"Yes, actually. He's seemed to want to talk to you since he's been coming here. Good. I'm pleased."
"You'll keep that to yourself won't you?"
The joker was back. Big wide grin, mime of zipping across the teeth.
"Soul of discretion!"

It made her laugh, somehow normalised it.
"Thanks."
"You'll tell me how you get on?"
"That's your price for keeping it to yourself is it?"
"Of course. You know me."
She did, that was the secret. Keep him on the inside, knowing what was happening, and he'd keep things to himself. Knowledge is power and all that.
"It's a deal."
They laughed, and absurdly shook hands on it before she disappeared into her office.

*

She was asleep in her chair when he went in. The television was on, far louder than comfortable, a clear reminder of how deaf she was. The remote control was on the table beside her, so he picked it up and turned the sound down low rather than off, not wanting to wake her. There was no response. No stir of her head stretched back against the chair with mouth half open, snoring quietly. He sat down in the chair opposite her and picked up the Daily Mirror from the table. The front page was filled with a grinning picture of some glamorous celebrity he'd never heard of and an article about her sex life. Stories like that aroused his puritanical side and he put it down again in disgust. Immediately she stirred and snorted. Her arm twitched, making him realise there must have been more forcefulness in his action than he realised, but she didn't wake, and soon the regular breathing returned.

He watched her for a while, experiencing a strange mixture of what felt like tenderness, together with a feeling of recoil from how aged she was now. The mother who had brought him into the world was now the old woman sleeping in the chair. Her facial skin looked as if it needed the creases ironing out, and her hands were blotched and rough. On both her feet, the bunions she always complained about had stretched out the old slippers she was wearing into ugly bulbous protrusions. He couldn't imagine a greater contrast with the airbrushed celebrity on the front page of the newspaper.

And now he knew her memory, even her identity, was diminishing. When she woke she would probably know who he was, even if she got his name wrong, but what was happening around her wouldn't make a lot of sense. Moderate dementia he knew it was called, a medical euphemism which really meant a kind of midpoint in personality disintegration. That sense of ego, the 'I am' of existence which so often got in the way of experience with some of his clients but without which at some level it wasn't possible to function, was fading in her. He knew there was still a sense of here and now, but where she had come from, and where she was going to, the context of existence which made meaning; that had more or less gone.

It struck him then how much of a paradox existence involved. Really being alive meant being able to put aside the ego and opening out to a greater sense of self. It stood at the heart of what people thought of as religious or spiritual experience, and to him meant living fully. And yet to stay human, anchored to the world, to the here and now, needed a sense of 'who I am' in the context of time and place. His ancient mother, snoring in the chair, could still exist in the here and now, but most of what made sense in the world was disappearing.

Although, he remembered, she could still sing. Old songs, established in her memory for decades and remembered by heart, she could still access. And from the outside it looked to him as if she did, for a while, regain a connection, especially when she was singing in a group at the day centre. The communal connection, through singing at least, was not yet gone. He thought of churches, and how important music was to religious experience. It was the connection again, and he knew that his own experience of music was about connection, often at a level beyond words.

She was stirring, coming round from the sleep. Her arms moved on the chair and her eyes opened.
"Patrick, is it Patrick?"
"Who else do you think it is?"
"It's you, of course it's you."
"Just called in to see if you were OK. You were asleep."
"Must have just dozed off."
He resisted telling her she was sound asleep. In the past she would always have denied it, giving him amusement. Now he guessed she would just accept it with a grunt or a nod, and somehow the thought made him sad. Another loss. He couldn't tease her anymore. It would go straight over her head. Instead, realising it had become gloomy, and the room was lit mostly by the flickering television, he stood and put the light on.
"Get's dark early now," he said, for want of something to say.
"What day is it?"
"Tuesday. Last Tuesday in November."
"Is it November?"
"It is. Cup of tea?"
He was raising his voice to what seemed a very high level, but at least she was hearing him tonight. Not always the case. He turned the TV up to a level he thought would be comfortable for her and watched as she turned towards it, as if almost forgetting that he was there in the room with her. He went into the kitchen to make the tea, and while he was at it, decided he would make her something to eat. She would have had a meal at the day centre, but that was some while back.

Almost as if he was sixteen again, he wished he could tell her about his date. Every part of him knew it was completely absurd, but the feeling was there inside, like an old script, wanting approval for what he was doing. The realisation astonished him, and as he waited for the kettle to boil and the toast to brown, he could feel a kind of unravelling of other occasions when he felt that same sense of unrequited desire for approval. The recognition seemed both new and not new, like seeing something you've always known, but knowing it now at a different level, illuminating the knowledge in a new way. He felt stupid, pathetic, like he'd discovered something really quite unlikeable about himself; an inner neediness lurking under the surface of his daytime consciousness. Had others noticed it? He felt suddenly quite exposed.

He took the tea and the toast and put them on the table beside her chair.
"Thankyou dear," she said.
"That's alright."
He sat down again in the chair opposite her and watched as she picked up one of the pieces of toast and bit into it. A few crumbs fell onto her lap. She brushed them away with her other hand before turning her attention back to the TV, watching it intently, no longer really noticing his presence in the room.

He sat drinking his tea, his eye drawn again to the celebrity on the front page of the newspaper. It looked like she wanted to be noticed. How different was that from his need for approval, his need to be noticed? More extreme certainly. He didn't need his sex life to be a tabloid front page. Not that there was any sex life to report. He laughed sardonically and his mother, noticing him laughing, laughed as well. That's being noticed I suppose, he thought.

"Thankyou dear," she said again when the toast was gone, "You are a good boy."
Notice and approval together! He laughed at himself again, and once more she laughed, before turning her gaze back to the TV. He drank his tea and then got up to leave. It was always difficult. Common sense told him his presence didn't make much difference. The TV would keep her happy for the rest of the evening, but it didn't stop him feeling guilty every time he left her. He knew he would tell a client something like 'feel the guilt and do it anyway,' and that's what he did. But he also knew from the inside how difficult it was.

"Bye, see you tomorrow."
"Are you off now?"
He nodded, waved again, and made his way out of the door. Outside the strong wind felt like it was trying to blast all the guilt away.

*

Lucia's picture of the large bird, or *aquila* as he was trying to call it, began to represent freedom to him. He thought there had to be lots of *aquila*s outside, probably robins and sparrows like he was used to in England, although through his spy hole he couldn't remember ever having seen one, or heard them twittering outside. He had to admit though that until she'd given him the picture, the thought of birds hadn't really entered his head.

He wanted to be able to ask her about the bird life but he didn't know how to. And the more he thought of her, the more he developed his mental fantasy of her naked. So much so that it began to scare him how much interest he had now in his sexual urge. He began to imagine making love to her and how soft and gentle love making might be with her. The persistent rain outside seemed to be merging his memory of his own limited sexual experiences with his wife, and what he was imagining with Lucia.

He waited anxiously for her reappearance through the barn door, wanting urgently to see her. What he would say and how he would communicate he didn't know, but he was sure now he had to make some kind of contact with her. He paced up and down for what felt like hours, just pacing without pause even to look out of his spy hole. At one point he went across to relieve himself, but quickly got back to pacing, tiring himself out with it, but not stopping. Still she didn't come and he had no way of knowing how much time had passed. He could hear outside that the rain still fell, and it added to his anxiety. Then suddenly there was the familiar noise at the barn door, and she was on her way in. He stopped mid pace and stared across to where she would appear, desperate to catch sight of her once more.

As she entered, he could see she looked surprised to see him away from his sleeping area. She closed the door and then stopped beside it, as if unsure how to proceed. In her hands he could see the tray with something for him to eat, and he realised the need to make some kind of acknowledgement. He waved in her direction, and then moved across to his usual place, so that she could walk over to him as she always had. He waited till she put the tray down beside him and then stretched out his hand to take hold of her other arm. The suddenness of it shocked her, but she didn't recoil from him. He smiled, and with his other hand stroked her reassuringly, trying to allay the fears he knew she was bound to have.

"Sit down with me," he said, hoping she would understand his meaning from his action, and after a moment of hesitation, she seemed to grasp what he wanted and cautiously sat down beside him.

With her next to him now, he continued stroking her arm, until he thought the fearful look had gone from her eyes. She didn't struggle, didn't seem to want to get away from him, and gaining confidence, he turned more fully towards her so that he could stroke both of her arms with his arms. Without fully realising what he was doing, his stroking became more emboldened until he was approaching the area of her breast, and becoming more aroused. Briefly she allowed him to do it, before lifting both her hands to stop him.

"*Non troppo rapido*."

Her movement stopped him and broke the contact, bringing him back to himself. At the same time he thought he grasped what she had said.

"Not rapid?"

"*Non troppo rapido,*" she said again, her tone confirming in his mind what she seemed to be saying. Once more she lifted her hand in a gesture which clearly said stop. He sat back, calming himself, controlling his breathing, not really wanting to force himself on her, but at the same time with a feeling of disappointment. Still holding her hand out, obviously keeping him at bay, she stood up. Then she stretched out her hand towards him briefly, touching his arm in a repeat of his first gesture. It felt hopeful, although her face looked scared as she hurried away from him and went out of the barn. The door closed behind her more noisily than usual. In a dazed state he stayed seated in his bedding area for some while after she had gone. Gradually he became aware that the rain outside was less heavy. He tried to focus on what had happened, but his mind was too excited to manage it.

He didn't know how many hours he paced about again after she left. As the autumn had worn on and the hours of darkness increased, he spent more and more of his time with only his imagination for company. He was used to it now, but the fading of the light earlier and earlier was always depressing. In his agitated state, he dreaded the perpetual gloom of the day becoming darkness once more. It was cold and damp in the barn and he wanted to warm himself, and pacing was the only solution available to him. He was impatient for her evening visit, desperate to see her once more, wanting the physical contact he'd lacked for so long. What had happened on her last visit made him want it even more, so that when he heard the sound of the barn door opening and saw the light she carried moving towards him he became almost uncontrollably excited. She was close to him. He could feel her presence and could see her shape vaguely in the weak light. He waited till she set down what she'd brought, and then as before stretched out his hand towards her, this time more eagerly, almost desperately.

She didn't seem to resist his touch. Again he motioned for her to sit down beside him on the hay pile. She took care to put the light down and then did as he was asking, without any apparent second thought. In what light there was, he could see her face closer than he had seen her before. She looked different. The expectant, puzzled look was still there, but she looked somehow younger, only just into adulthood. Before it hadn't occurred to him that she might actually be good looking in her dowdy peasant clothing, but now she seemed even beautiful. He lifted his arm to stroke her face, and she let him do it, but still she didn't smile. He could feel his excitement rising again within him, but resisted it. Although part of him now really wanted to force himself on her, something else within him couldn't do that. He knew there were soldiers who raped enemy women. He didn't want to be one of them. And his survival instinct told him that was likely to lead to certain death. The memory of the man with the rifle was still vivid in his brain.

Instead, he wrapped both arms round her. At first she didn't respond, just let him hold her. He held on tightly, his desperation seeming to shift into a kind of child need to hold and be held, and after a few seconds, as if she'd understood his need, he felt her arms gently rising to hold him. The quiet tenderness of her action released something in him. He found himself unable to resist tears, and he felt his body shaking. Now it was like she was holding him, not the other way round, holding him until the crying passed.

Eventually she seemed to need to break free and he felt her removing herself from his embrace. As she did so, he was able, dimly, to see her face again. It looked as if she was smiling at him. She stretched out her hand now and stroked his brow for a brief moment. Then she stood up rapidly and took one of his hands into hers, squeezing it in what felt like a gesture of comfort. For a moment he resisted her obvious wish to free her hand again, but when she moved her other hand to ease his grip, he let her go, aware of the danger of being too needy. Then, all too quickly, she was gone, taking the light with her, and he was alone in the dark with his feelings mixed and confused, but at the same time comforted by her touch.

20

"I'm going out for a while tomorrow lunchtime," Liz said to Max on Friday evening, "I'll leave you some lunch."
"Meeting?" he said on the way to his computer.
"Kind of, yes."
She finished clearing the kitchen and then went through to the living room to turn on the television. A loud commentator was introducing contestants for some kind of game show. She changed the channel, only to find a football match, and had to change several times more before deciding on something about portraits in art which she'd saved earlier. Normally it would have engaged her attention, but she couldn't settle to it, and after a few minutes turned it off again.

It reminded her of what it was like after Guy died. For weeks she was constantly agitated and couldn't settle to anything. At work she could cope, but discovered much later how Len had managed communications for her, saving her from a significant number of problems. She in turn thought she'd managed to protect Max from most of her grief, although she knew he couldn't be unaffected by her mood. But when she was alone, her concentration was non-existent. For a few weeks she couldn't even tolerate music, preferring silence, which seemed to reflect the emptiness she was feeling inside. Tonight, some of the same agitation was affecting her again. But it was different. She knew she wanted to have lunch with the doctor, Patrick, as she knew she would have to start calling him, whether anything came of it or not. It would be her first date since Guy and she didn't want to miss it. He seemed interesting and she felt she'd like to get to know him.

There was also guilt. Everywhere she looked around the house, Guy was looking back at her, husband of more than twenty years, father of her son. Was this date two timing? Should she be going at all? At least in theory Guy would approve.

“You’ll find another man,” he said, not long before he died.
“I don’t want anyone else.”
“After I’ve gone, give yourself time. Then, if someone comes along, take the opportunity.”
“I don’t want anyone else. Only you.”
“I wouldn’t like to think of you alone for the rest of your life.”
“You’re my husband.”
“Now. But not I’m afraid for much longer.”
She remembered the rueful smile on his face and the pain he was in. It still upset her thinking about it. She hadn’t wanted anyone else in the three years since he died. But ‘take the opportunity’ he’d said. She looked up at his picture. ‘Is this the opportunity then?’ she said out loud. ‘am I doing the right thing?’
She didn’t know. Maybe it was all too soon.

Max was in the room. She hadn’t noticed him coming in.
“You alright mum?”
“Yes, yes, I’m fine. Why?”
“You just look, well, you know.”
She did know, and so did he.
“Just one of those moments, Max. I’ll be fine.”
He nodded, carried on through to the kitchen to get the drink he’d obviously come for. Then back to his computer. Was he aware of her talking to Guy’s photographs? She liked to think she’d kept it from him, but he didn’t miss much. She needed to calm herself down somehow, and on an impulse decided to go for a walk. It was something she seldom did in the dark, but just for tonight perhaps it was a good idea. A short walk round the immediate area; it felt like a way of settling herself.

Outside it was still windy. In the light of the streetlamps she could see leaves still falling and swirling about. Only the occasional car passed her. She paced it out, wanting to channel her energy into activity and dispel the agitation. Clouds were scudding across the sky in the wind

and every so often, just for a brief moment, she could see the moon. It was almost full, and surprisingly bright. It seemed to radiate hopefulness beyond the ceaseless activity and helped to calm her mood. Her walking pace slowed, and she became conscious of breathing more deeply, allowing her to think more clearly. What was it about the moon that had such an effect on her? Not the female cycle now, surely, she was more or less past that. The very intermittence of the moon's appearance seemed to reinforce its power. The great unblinking eye was watching down on her like it was playing peek-a-boo between the clouds. 'I'm here, I'm always here,' it seemed to be saying. The night after Guy died it was there. No wind and no cloud that night. Stars and coldness, an endless and unchanging universe, and the moon seemed to have a message for her:
'Those you love die, and you die, but I'm always here, beyond all human life.' She knew she'd found the message weirdly comforting that night, giving her strength for the sadness and loneliness that followed.

Afterwards work took over, giving her purpose and helping to make life make sense again. She couldn't go along with Len's belief in the meaningless of existence. She actually found it hard to believe that was what he really thought, despite all his protestations delivered in a range of assumed voices. Life was full of meaning. The trick was not to think your own life was too important. We were all part of a whole and her role, after Guy, after he'd left her on her own, was to carry on for Max and for the generations of children in the school.

And now? What was happening for her now? Something to unsettle her maybe, change things again. It was exciting and scary all at once. The moon which had not appeared for a while from behind the clouds, was suddenly directly in front of her, above her own house as she came back from the walk.
"Look after me, moon," she found herself saying, "Take care of me."

Was that a prayer? Maybe it was. She turned the key in the lock and went in. Was she mad? Praying to the moon and talking to Guy's photographs? Four hundred years ago they'd have burned her as a witch! Even today there was no way she could tell anyone that.

The television was on. Max had come down and found a football channel. He would hardly notice her entry she thought, but to her surprise, he did.
"Hi Mum."
"Hi Max. You OK?"
"Fine, how about you?"
"Me? Yes, I'm fine. Just needed a walk. Fresh air after work."
Had he picked up something in her mood? Not something he usually did, or at least not that she'd noticed before. He nodded and turned back to the football, apparently satisfied with her answer. She went through to the kitchen as shouts from the TV and a joyful shout from Max seemed to suggest the right team had scored. Guy smiled down at her.

*

By morning Tom knew the rain had definitely stopped, but it still felt damp and also colder. There was less activity outside, a pattern he'd noticed after every few days, and gradually it dawned on him these days were probably Sundays. But there were no sounds of bells or other signs to suggest it was Sunday. This morning he also noticed that Lucia seemed to come later, and guessed that was also consistent with Sunday, although it wasn't a pattern he had noticed before. He waited anxiously for her arrival; he was hungry, and he wanted to see her, still hoping she wasn't going to change towards him as a result of him getting closer to her, being too friendly.

His letter to his wife was now well underway. At the top of it, squeezed into the space between the top of the page and where he'd first started writing he'd written her name and address, and then underneath he'd written 'from a barn somewhere in Italy.' It felt like the opposite of one of those schoolboy addresses in which he followed his address by 'England, the world, the universe. But it was the same kind of affectation as if to say, 'I could be anywhere.' After that, the letter went on for two pages, and it occurred to him he could go on indefinitely, but if he was going to try to get Lucia to send it back to England for him, he would have to stop somewhere.

He was thinking about how he might finish the letter when the sound of the barn door distracted him and he looked up to see Lucia. She seemed to be at the door some time, and he presumed she was bringing several things into the barn for him. Then, when he saw her, she was wearing a smarter looking dress than usual, and he realised he had in fact seen the dress before. The obvious deduction was that this was her Sunday dress. He thought once more that she looked more beautiful than he had realised, and she smiled at him as she approached, encouraging him. It didn't seem like his recent behaviour had changed her attitude towards him. If anything in fact she seemed more friendly, casually comfortable with touching his arm and stroking his hair as she bent over to replace his food plates. He let her do it without any other response than a mutual light touch, not wanting to overdo the familiarity too soon and too early in the day. But she seemed in no hurry to go and he took that as a good sign.

Then she was gone, leaving him to eat his Sunday breakfast alone. She had also left him a change of clothes, so after eating, he did his daily wash in the lukewarm water she'd also left, and put on the clean clothes, leaving the dirty ones ready for her collection. He felt better. He didn't like changing as infrequently as he did now. His animalistic existence in the barn made him feel only slightly better than the donkey outside. But he also knew that building his friendship with Lucia, getting some kind of physical rapport, even though he couldn't really talk to her, was helping him to feel better about himself and giving him more energy. The difficulty was actually using the energy. All he could do to exercise was pace the length and breadth of the barn, up and down, side to side, until he grew tired of it, or until he needed a rest.

Lunchtime came. She appeared briefly in order to give him something more to eat, remove his breakfast things and take his dirty clothing. At one point he stretched out a hand to touch her. She caught hold of it with hers, gave it something of a squeeze and then politely but firmly pushed it back towards him. The message was clear. Not now, it's daylight, maybe later. He couldn't say anything to check that out, but the message nevertheless became fixed in his brain. 'We can get closer after dark.' He was sure that was the message. He only had to wait till she came in the evening and they could sit and hold each other for a few minutes, perhaps more. The evenings, the dark nights he hated, now took on more promise.

In the afternoon, tired from all his pacing, he lay down on the bedding area. His mind drifted into sleep and then to dreaming. Once more he was walking alone along the ridge and he could see ahead of him another person. But as they got closer, he could see once again it wasn't the soldier with the rifle approaching him, but a young woman in a grey calf length dress. In his dream he knew he was becoming excited by her. They were close enough to touch. She lifted her arms into the air provocatively, inviting him. Now in the dream she became naked, and her breasts stretched out firmly towards him. He thrust himself forward, conscious of an erection, before waking in a sweat.

For a moment he wondered if he'd had a wet dream, but although he was still hard, he hadn't ejaculated. He considered finishing himself off to ease the tension, but already he was subsiding, so he allowed it to happen, waiting for his body to calm down. He felt uneasy, not in control of himself. Uncomfortable feelings were stirring all the time. Living in the barn, spending so much time on his own, unable to talk to another human, it felt like a part of his mind was diminishing, that he couldn't quite hold onto it. More and more an animal instinct for survival was taking over his brain.

The light was already fading outside, and it was quite dim in the barn. He knew it had to be approaching the darkest time of the year. He didn't think Christmas had passed. There had been no sign of Christmas celebrations so he guessed it was early December, maybe three weeks before Christmas. The thought saddened him. He was sure there was no way he would be released before it. All he had to look forward to for the moment was the reappearance of Lucia at the barn door.

*

"I've decided I need to do my own pilgrimage."

Anna sat in the black chair opposite Patrick, aware she was easing her way to telling him the whole picture gradually. It didn't quite feel safe for some reason to tell him everything at once. Maybe she was still coming to terms with the decision herself. She was aware of him looking at her, waiting for her to continue.

"I've done a lot of thinking. Things I need to come to terms with. Anger particularly; and where it might come from."

"Coming to terms with anger."

He was probing into what she might be trying to say, reflecting her words back to her. It felt uncomfortable, and she could feel the anger was on the edge of rising into the room, but she held it back.

"The anger I've been feeling since Ben left; that's probably been there since long before that; back in my past. I've realised I need to try and come to terms with it. Maybe that's partly what caused Ben to leave me."

A memory opened up in her mind: she was shouting at Ben, beside herself, while he stood opposite her, across the living room, staring wildly. 'You're always fucking angry, always shouting at me. I can't take this much longer,' he was saying.

"He didn't like me getting angry."

She stopped, stretched for a tissue from the box on the table beside her and blew into it loudly, not wanting to cry. She looked at Patrick, waiting, almost daring him to respond.
"What are you feeling right now?"
"Fuck you! Fucking angry."
She was still holding the tissue and buried her face in it, resisting the tears she knew weren't far away, not wanting to admit them.
"I'm sorry, I didn't mean to swear at you."
She watched as a faint smile appeared on his face as if to say it was alright, before carrying on, more composed.
"I know I have to sort this out. I can't go on like this. I've made a decision."
"The pilgrimage?"
Still she held back, feeling embarrassed to say it out loud.
"I need to go where my great grandparents died. Where my grandparents and parents could have died; before I was born. I want to go to the Auschwitz museum."
The word museum softened its impact in her head.
"And that feels really important?"
"Yes. It does. Maybe it doesn't make sense to you, but it's like I said, a pilgrimage. Honouring the dead. The people whose genes I've inherited. And nearly didn't."
Imagining her own non-existence felt impossible. She could manage the idea of time before and after her, but without existence, there was nothing to hold onto. Without her own being, there was no sense, nothing, a void scarier than death itself.
"Do you know when you want to go?"
"Straightaway really. December, dark time of the year; feel like it really was for them."
Saying it felt like a validation. The opposite of the scary void. Now she knew that she would do it.

*

"Tonight I have work to do. Maybe later in week."

They were packing their violins away. The long slow last movement of the Tchaikovsky sixth that had finished the concert was still in Simon's head, but Stefan had been humming the march movement with all its rhythmic energy, which surprised him. It didn't sound like he was in a reflective mood for whatever work he might have to do. However, a night on his own would at least give him some time to catch up. There were Christmas arrangements to sort out and presents to organise since he'd accepted the Christmas dinner invitation from his parents.
"Simon, my friend, I will see you very soon. For now it is *do widzenia*."
He accompanied the farewell with an exaggerated Slavic kiss on both cheeks. It wasn't something he'd done to him before. Then he was off out of the stage door before he could say or do anything else. Work didn't seem a likely explanation. He was too excited. Simon couldn't help being suspicious. Another date seemed far more likely. He sighed. It was bound to happen sooner or later. He just hadn't expected it so soon.

He was making his way slowly to the exit, when someone called out to him.
"Coming for a drink tonight, Simon?"
"Well I wasn't going to."
"You're very welcome."
He hesitated, unsure whether to join the group. It was some while since he had. Since the evening he met Stefan in fact. On impulse, he decided after all it might be a good idea.
"Well maybe for a short while."
"Good. It's the usual."

The pub filled with the buzz of excitable post-concert musicians. He got himself a drink and sat down with the three who had invited him, two young women and a young man, all string players. They were enthusing about the concert, so he listened politely nodding appropriately, without actually joining in, until one of the young women, an attractive violinist, brought him in directly.

"On your own tonight, Simon?"

He smiled, nodding his agreement.

"You seem to have become friendly with Stefan lately."

It felt like an invitation. He hesitated. There was loud laughter from the other side of the room as if someone had told a crude joke. He swallowed, making an instant decision.

"Yes. We've been good friends. Lovers actually."

He could feel himself colouring up. He looked down into his beer waiting for disapproval.

"We did wonder. Night off tonight?"

It was someone else's turn to colour up. The young violinist, realising what she'd said, apologised to him immediately, while the others laughed. Despite his embarrassment, he couldn't help laughing too and saying it was alright, no offence. They were all laughing and suddenly it seemed normal. He'd just told three people he was gay and they were all laughing round the table as if he'd told them he'd been practicing his violin. Relief surged through him.

"I'm glad I've told you."

"Did you think we'd mind?"

"Didn't you think we might have guessed?"

The laughter this time was polite, but it eased his lingering embarrassment further, and the conversation moved on. It felt huge. He'd shared it and a trapdoor hadn't opened up beneath him. At the same time it felt like no big deal. He was gay, living his own life. They were . . . well, whatever they were, he didn't know, and they were all drinking together talking about the symphony they'd just played, written by a gay man, as if nothing of great significance had just happened. There was some sort of irony in that he thought.

"Don't you think it's about love and death?" the young violinist was saying.

"Isn't everything? Love, or sex if we're honest, to perpetuate the species, before our own death. That's what life is."

He sat back with his beer unable to subscribe to that biological view of existence. He wouldn't be perpetuating the species. Did that invalidate him? Surely we were about more than that. Wasn't the very existence of the symphony evidence for that? So was the violin concerto. But he nodded in the right places and let them talk. Even though he guessed Stefan was by now having 'shag' with some other guy, it didn't feel bad. More a quiet sense of satisfaction that he'd managed to come out for the first time. He knew there would be more difficult moments in the future, but for now, it was an important achievement, a first step.

21

Everyone told Anna that going in December was mad. She would be perished in the central European winter. The icy Siberian winds would cut through her. But she knew that was what the holocaust victims, six million Jews, had experienced, and there was a need in her to experience for herself what it must have been like, even though she would be wrapped up in warm twenty first century clothing, while they had been at times half naked and at best wearing clothes offering almost no protection against the weather. So it was a strange disappointment to arrive in what the hotel staff told her was a 'mild spell.'
"Better this week. Two degrees. Not even freezing in daytime. Last week minus twelve."

It was slushy and unpleasant underfoot. Half melted snow froze again at night, leaving ice patches for the morning which made walking difficult. Sometimes it must have been like that in the camp, when her great grandparents and all the other distant relatives were there. Walking alone would have been treacherous, quite apart from all the other indignities.

There was a line of taxis waiting in the rank directly outside the hotel. She had been told that for a fixed fee, agreed in advance, any one of them would take her there, wait for her as long as she wanted and bring her back. The trip would include both sites, Auschwitz and Birkenau, and the cost would be reasonable. She was surprised to discover that the two were not actually the same camp. Both names were part of her family history, spoken of as a place of great evil throughout her childhood, but it hadn't penetrated her consciousness that they were actually separated by about two kilometres.

The driver of the first taxi in the rank was a stocky Eastern European man in early middle age. A woollen hat came down to his eyebrows and a scarf was wrapped around his neck.

"Hello!" He greeted her cheerfully as she approached.

"Auschwitz?" she asked, tentatively.

"Please. I take you. Bring back when ready. Hundred and fifty zloty." He gestured towards the interior of the cab. She was prepared for any expense. It was what she had to do.

"Please."

The driver got out, opened the door to the rear compartment of the cab, and she got in, relieved to discover that he had at least some English. She didn't think trying German would be a popular choice.

"How long to get there?"

"One hour. Maybe less."

Suddenly she felt apprehensive. The determination that had got her this far felt for a moment as if it was draining away. Yet she was in a warm taxi, not being herded from the *Umschlagplatz* into a crowded train, in many degrees of frost, travelling to almost certain death. The thought produced an involuntary shiver.

"You are cold?"

He turned up the heating without waiting for her reply.

"Thankyou. Yes a little."

"Not too cold today. Last week very bad."

She nodded, and wrapped herself up tighter in the scarf and coat.

She didn't want him to talk, and he seemed to understand, turning his attention away from the rear view mirror to the road ahead of him.

The city of Krakow was retreating behind her and they were moving out along the highway into the open countryside beyond, towards the camps that had become her pilgrimage. The scenery was more undulating than she expected. The Poland of her imagination was a vast flat land, more like East Anglia or Northern France. There were no hills of any significance, but it certainly wasn't completely flat. She could see industrial works in the distance. Chimneys and smoke rising into the air, which made her think about the gas chambers, but these were clearly working plants and not sinister.

Her mind wandered. What would her parents think if they knew where she was going? It had been a clear decision not to let them know. They would never go themselves. Once, some time ago, she'd suggested it, only to be told she was being morbid. The holocaust hung round the necks of all surviving Jews like the ancient mariner's albatross, but for her parents, no way were they going to explore the past. It was there, hung there by the Nazi goys, but it wasn't their fault, they didn't need the *tschuve*. And they would, she was sure, hold it against her if they knew she'd been. Her mother would think she was trying to show them up. No, she couldn't tell them, although it would be hard to keep it to herself when she saw them again.

The taxi was pulling into a car park. There were a couple of coaches and a few cars and just beyond was a building, like a museum site. Not what she expected.
"I wait here. You come back when ready. Then other site."
She got out of the car, thanked him, and as she stood, not quite knowing where to go, he pointed to the entrance. She followed the direction he indicated and went through the doorway. Once inside, she could see the ticket office ahead of her, and incongruously she thought, what looked like a tea bar. Definitely not what she had expected, but she bought her ticket, ignoring the tea bar and the offers of a guided tour. There was even a film of some sort being played and

a few takers within. It felt like a commercial enterprise. She wanted to experience what it must have been like for the Jews who died here.

Picking her way through everything she found herself walking through doors at the other end and into an open area. Ahead now was the gate she had expected to pass through straightaway, with its inscription in black ironwork. *'Arbeit macht frei'*; work makes you free; except when it was a concentration camp. Crossing under that inscription as a Jewish prisoner meant death. Once she walked through barbed wire, way above her head height, surrounded her. It began to feel more like what she was searching for. The camp stretched out ahead, like some kind of army barracks. There were huts where she assumed the prisoners must have been housed, and she made her way to the nearest. It didn't matter that she had to work it out for herself. It was what she wanted to do.

Because the temperature was just above freezing, the snow and ice of the previous week was slowly melting and it was slushy and unpleasant underfoot. Everywhere looked dirty and dreary. There was a wind which made it feel colder than it probably was, and she pulled her coat round her, feeling slightly guilty doing so because she knew the Jewish prisoners couldn't. The experience was unpleasant, so to get out of the wind she went into the nearest hut, which was filled with photographs of prisoners, and soon she worked out that the huts were memorials classified by their nationalities. Maybe she could find photos of her own relatives. She began searching out the German huts to find any Rosenthals, and in the second hut she found some. A sombre man and woman stared out at her across the decades, and there was also a young looking woman: Elsa who couldn't have been any older than she was now. She stood there looking at the faces but there was no way of knowing whether they were her relatives. In Germany she knew her name wasn't an uncommon one, but it was beginning to feel as if she was getting closer to the past she was seeking.

Just beyond was another hut, not identified as any specific nationality. She went in. There were many hundreds of suitcases piled in huge glass cases; suitcases Jews had carried with them into the camp, with clothes and belongings she assumed, still expecting to survive. And in another glass case were what looked like crutches; and wooden legs! It shocked her. Even though she knew how inhuman the Nazi regime had been, seeing the evidence of such cruelty to invalids, maybe some who had fought for Germany in the first war, was overwhelming; she had to go outside.

The door opened out straight into the direction of the wind and the coldness struck her immediately, bringing tears to her eyes. She held onto the side of the hut for a moment to steady herself. She wanted to get out, get away from the awful place, but within her was a determination to continue however hard it was. She needed to visit as much of the camp as she could, had to make the experience a part of her. It was her pilgrimage, her *tschuve*. She waited, gathering her strength, before walking across to the next hut. Again there were rows and rows of stern faces looking out at her. Did they understand what their fate would be? How was it possible to come to terms with it? She was struggling with it herself now. It was unimaginably horrible.

Ahead now was the block which the inscription told her housed the Auschwitz gas chamber. At first she wasn't sure that she could go in but after a pause found the courage to enter. Inside the door she was taken aback by noise; laughter, even merriment. She couldn't at first work out where it was coming from, until she saw a small group of a few adults and what looked like teenage children apparently laughing and joking. Anger was rising in her. How could they be so insensitive? They seemed to be Spanish or Italian, she wasn't sure which. She must make them stop.
"Shut up! Have some respect!" she shouted in English, guessing they wouldn't understand, but knowing they would pick up something from the tone of what she said. Immediately the noise stopped, and all of

them looked at her in surprise. One of the adults seemed to have understood. 'So sorry, not offence' he said, looking shamefaced. At least it felt like some kind of vindication.

But the anger had changed her mood. She could still feel it boiling inside her as she made her way round the other huts, round the awful cell blocks and outside to the place where the plaque told her executions had taken place. She had wanted to get rid of the anger, and now here it was still, working away inside her, and the more she thought about it, the more she could feel it. Feeling more disturbed now than before, she began to make her way back to the entrance block and to where her taxi was waiting, not even sure if she wanted to go to the other camp at all.

Suddenly in front of her was a hut she didn't think she'd visited and it seemed to draw her in to take at least a cursory look. She stepped inside. Beyond the doorway was a central corridor between two vast glass display cases, one on each side, stretching the entire length of the hut and loaded way above her head height. She looked around in astonishment. Each case was piled high with shoes, and suddenly it felt as if the weight of all those shoes was pressing down on her. This was the weight of her inheritance, the life and death of all the Jewish wearers of all those shoes was what she was carrying. A great wave welled up inside, overwhelming her with bitter tears for all the lost souls whose shoes surrounded her. She fell to her knees and cried out, unable to stop herself, and sobbed uncontrollably. No one came in, and gradually the crying subsided, replaced seamlessly from somewhere in the long distant past by the words of the kaddish: *'Yehei shmëh rabba mevarakh lealam ulalmey almaya.'* She found herself saying it aloud over and over, 'may His great name be blessed for ever, and to all eternity,' As she repeated it, the ghostly presence of all the wearers of all the shoes in the vast mountain around her seemed to enter her soul bringing a peace beyond the words. She had no idea how long she was on her knees, but eventually she stood, shakily at first, and made her way to the exit. The chill wind outside struck her again, but didn't affect the calmness inside her.

Slowly, in a world of her own, she made her way back towards the entrance gate. Its cruel message, sculpted with such an absurdly artistic curve, was highlighted now against a sky filled with heavy clouds. Then she was back, through the incongruous visitors' centre, out of Auschwitz and back to the taxi.
"We go Birkenau, yes?"
"Please, yes."
She sat back in her own world as he drove.

The route passed a working railway station, disturbing her again with its echoes of what she had imagined, and then in just a few minutes he was stopping again, this time in a vast parking space outside the chilling gates with high towers either side, familiar from all the photographs, with a railway line passing through. She went in. It felt even more bleak than Auschwitz and again she felt cold in the chill wind which blew across a vast expanse of derelict land stretching out in front of her.

There were a few huts near the entrance and beyond that nothing but empty space. How many Jews had died here? It was incalculable. As she walked out into the camp, it felt like walking on the bones of those who had died, and bending down, she realised it was literally true. Everywhere there were tiny shards of bone which could only be one thing. These were her ancestors, Jews across the century who had died where she now stood. But unlike the tears she had experienced with the shoes, she could feel anger at the awfulness of it rising again.

There were hardly any other visitors, but a short way ahead she became aware of an old man, walking with the help of a stick and supported by a younger woman. She watched for a moment as he stopped, took a handkerchief from his pocket and wiped his eyes before carefully putting it back into the same pocket. The woman noticed her watching and called out to her in a language she didn't understand. Unsure whether the greeting was friendly or not she made a gesture indicating her lack of understanding, and the woman tried again.

"*Sie sind Deutsch*?"

It felt like a need to communicate. She responded in German.

"Nein. Ich bin Englisch. Ich kann aber Deutsch verstehen."

Encouraged the woman began talking. The man was her father she said, and his parents, her grandparents, had died in the camp. She told the woman about her own relatives and the woman translated for the old man. To her surprise, when he heard her story, he visibly made the sign of the cross on himself.

"Where are you from?" she asked.

"We are Roma Gypsies by birth, from Bohemia. Now Czech Republic."

"Not Jewish?"

"Many Roma Gypsies died here. Many of our family. Not only Jews."

The old man bowed to her gently, almost graciously, as if he understood. Gypsies too? It was another revelation. She watched a faint smile appear on his face as his daughter translated the conversation for him. He half nodded, half bowed again.

"Your German is very good," the woman was saying.

"My grandparents were German; German Jews. They escaped all this by resettling in England."

She stretched her arm out indicating the camp around them as she spoke.

"We are pleased to meet you. But now I have to take father back to car. It's very cold. Don't want another death here."

A harsh sounding laugh accompanied the grim joke, and she held out a hand as if it was a peace offering. It felt strange shaking hands with the Roma woman, inappropriate somehow, almost like a distancing when she wanted to share the experience as a fellow sufferer. Then, once more the old man bowed before they began walking across the railway sleepers towards the exit.

So much dignity in sorrow, she thought to herself as she watched him moving along the railway line where so many Jews had got off the train that brought them straight into captivity and death. So many Jews, and so many others she now knew; a mass of suffering humanity. How could this have happened? The wind blew hard into her, but she stood her ground, knowing there was much she had to think through. Instinctively she knew something important had happened inside her and she needed to come to terms with it.

22

Josh's attention was disturbed from marking his Year 10 books by a knock at his classroom door. He looked up to see a familiar face through the glass, motioned Wesley to come in, and watched as he opened the door and slipped through it, closely followed by another young boy.

"Can we speak to you?"

"Of course, what is it?"

It was a dull afternoon in early December. He'd heard the bell for the end of school ring several minutes earlier, so it was strange that the two boys were still around the classroom blocks. He waited for Wesley to continue.

"You saved my life, right."

He nodded, slightly taken aback by the directness of the statement.

"And you helped me get it sorted out afterwards, so my problem's sorted with my dad, right. We need you to help sort out Elijah's problem now."

As he said this, Wesley indicated the slightly dishevelled black lad standing next to him.

"Elijah's gettin' bullied. There's a kid called Mac in Year 10. Keeps stealin' things off him and pushin' him.

Elijah's scared to go home in case he's still out there."

"You want me to come out and see?"

The boys nodded. He put his pen down beside the pile of books and stood up.
"Show me where you think he is."

They led him out of the classroom and beyond the main gate. He looked up and down the street. There were groups of students still making their way home, and a small group of lads some distance from the gate. Elijah pointed to the group.
"He's with them."
Deciding to act more confident than he actually felt, Josh walked purposefully towards the group, while the boys stayed back by the gate. Mac was directly facing him as he approached.
"There's a Year 8 lad claiming you're bullying him, Mac. I hope it's not true."
"What if it is?"
"Then, I'd like you to stop. You're a lot bigger than he is."
He watched as Mac's friends pantomimed shock horror at his words and one of them waved a finger at Mac as if he was a naughty boy. Mac grinned, disdainfully.
"We'll have to see then won't we. Saving little boys again then, hero."
The words were cutting and intentionally hurtful. Impulsively, he stepped towards Mac menacingly, wanting to intimidate him.
"Just make sure it stops. That's all."
He knew it was a deliberate threat, and for a moment it made him feel better. Mac's friends made mock scared sounds as he turned to walk back to Wesley and Elijah standing at the gate. He knew the shock of his action would have startled Mac, but he wasn't totally sure if it was the right way of handling things.
"I've spoken to them. I'll watch as you walk past."

As the boys walked together uncertainly past, the group remained in a close knit cabal, looking as if they were studiously avoiding any kind of contact. Once they'd gone, he was aware of Mac looking scornfully at him. It made him feel uncomfortable as he walked back into the school to continue his marking.

It was Thursday evening. For once there was no staff meeting and no parents meeting. One thing he hadn't anticipated when he decided to go into schoolteaching was the sheer amount of work outside the classroom it would involve. Marking, preparing work, and what seemed to him endless meetings more than doubled the amount of work, and the sheer pressure of it was making him increasingly tired as the term wore on. 'You'll get used to it. It's not as easy as banking you know' was what Len told him. Actually, he thought to himself, banking involved pretty long hours too, but there was something unrelenting about the teaching role that was different altogether. Then there was the emotional pressure, like what he'd just been dealing with for Wesley and his young friend with the biblical name. Going out on a weekday evening was more or less a thing of the past.

Except tonight. An old banking friend had invited him out for a drink and a chat, and he'd accepted. Nothing seemed to be happening with Anna. She'd texted him, but seemed very non committal, so why not? He told himself he'd make sure he got home by midnight, then all he had to do was get through Friday and he could relax for the weekend, or at least until Sunday, when he knew there would be more books to mark. He hurried home from school, leaving everything locked away in his classroom, in order to be ready for Dave who was picking him up at eight and driving him off to a club. He knew from the past that Dave was good fun, and it seemed like a welcome change and a bit of a lead in to the Christmas period at the same time.

He should have remembered. Being on time had never been one of Dave's strengths, and it was nine o'clock before he arrived, without any reason or excuse for his lateness. But in no time they were on their way to the nearest local as a prelude to 'a great night out clubbing,' as Dave put it. There was a moment of anxiety for Josh and he had a vision of Friday morning school following seamlessly and exhaustingly on the end of the night out, but despite his fears, the overwhelming anticipation of what might be forthcoming was too great. It felt like a return to the old days of freedom. Three pints went down in no time, and in more relaxed mood and high spirits they were ready for a night at 'Flirts'.

The club was a local one, only open Thursdays to Saturdays. They left the pub, both talking excitedly together. Like a pair of school girls, he thought as they hurried the ten minutes down the road to the club, where a giant of a man stood on duty, and scrutinised them as they went in. He'd forgotten how much noise a disco in an enclosed space could make, but it didn't take long before the whole atmosphere enveloped him. The place seemed full of girls dancing in skimpy dresses. Many of them looked like teenagers, probably seven or eight years younger than he was. It made him feel old, but maybe he didn't look old, so he pushed down his reservations and joined the throng of dancers on the main floor. The music was continuous; one number ran into another without pause. Soon he found himself warming to it in every way, so that it made sense for the girls to be wearing as little clothing as they actually were. The boys he hardly noticed as the adrenalin pumped through his body giving him boldness and energy.

It wasn't too long before he began to make eye contact with a girl he thought might be nineteen or twenty. She was wearing a very short dress whose colour kept changing with the movement of the lights. She didn't seem to be with a particular partner, so he engineered his own dancing to coincide with hers. She was clearly prepared to acquiesce with his manoeuvring and when he began to put his hands on her waist to enhance their pairing, far from objecting, she responded by putting her arms out towards him and moving her hands along his sides. He had no idea how long they danced together, but eventually they both seemed to tire together and eased themselves away from the floor towards the door to the yard outside. He could see Dave still dancing across the floor and judged there was no particular hurry. There was time for a bit of fun with the girl.

The chill outside came at first as a relief. He watched her pull her short coat round the shoulders of what he could now see under the street lights was probably a yellow dress, and flick her long dark hair over the back of the coat. Even though they were now outside, the sound of the disco was still very loud and any kind of conversation was difficult. He had to be content with the occasional shouted word and with sign language. She aroused him, as much because she was a young female as anything else about her. He would have liked to take her to bed somewhere, but there was no car, and nowhere else they could go. He wasn't going to be fully satisfied tonight, but still wanted as much as he could get.

He moved his head towards hers and she responded. It was the first time he'd kissed a girl for several months. It felt good. Gradually his hands moved round her back then down her body and over her backside. He tried to lift her dress so he could put his hands underneath but she pushed him firmly away from her, breaking the contact. It cooled him, and he let it happen, aware that he'd reached the limit of possibility. He breathed out sighing, while she smiled at him knowingly.
'Let's go in for another dance, she mimed, and with her arm indicated that they should go back inside. It made sense. Use up the frustrated energy. He nodded. She took his hand, grinning, and led him back in.

The wall of sound inside hit him and kick started the adrenalin again. He began dancing wildly, first with the girl and then with another group of other girls, dancing between them as they looked on with surprise as he cavorted ludicrously between them. He could see Dave again, and made his way across to him, still moving wildly, and to his delight, Dave joined him in an equally erratic way so that they were gyrating together near the centre of the dance floor. A group of girls and boys began clapping rhythmically at them. It felt good, like it always used to, and for a while he had the feeling that everything around him, everything in the world was good.

Gradually the energy ran down. The pace slowed along with the music, and it became quieter. It was obvious to him the club was about to close, and he looked at his watch. It was gone half past two. With a start he remembered he had to be at work the following morning. He grabbed Dave and pointed at his watch. Dave nodded, and they made their exit.
"I'm working in the morning," he said
"Me too. Good night though. Looked like you scored."
"Yeh, great."
"What would your kids think, eh?"
He grinned to himself. It had been fun.

Once Dave had gone, it was well past three o'clock. He felt very tired as he set the alarm, realising he had just four hours sleep before he had to get up again for work. It was too late to worry about that now. He drifted into sleep thinking of the girl and stirring once again at the thought of kissing and fondling her.

When the alarm woke him, it seemed like he'd only just fallen asleep. His head felt heavy and he struggled to get out of bed. There was an unpleasant stale smell on his body which he didn't recognise at first, but which had to be from 'Flirts.' He guessed the inside of the club hadn't been exposed to daylight for years. The shower removed the smell and helped to bring him to his senses, but it still felt as if he had a hangover, although he knew, surely, that he hadn't drunk all that much. His body was sluggish, and didn't seem willing to hurry to get ready for the day's school. The morning began with his Year 10 group, and he wasn't looking forward to it, especially not with the dull ache which seemed to be taking root somewhere inside his head. From a drawer in the kitchen he found two paracetemols and washed them down with a full glass of water, which he realised after he'd drunk it that he really needed. It helped, but he couldn't as yet face eating anything before getting into his car and driving off.

"Good night last night then?"
"How do you know?" The question coming almost as soon as he walked into the staff room shocked Josh.
"Have you looked at yourself in the mirror this morning?"
Johnno was grinning at him. He made himself some tea from the urn and took it with him to his classroom to get ready. His head felt heavy, like a hangover from a past life, although he was still sure he hadn't drunk too much. Maybe it would fade as the day progressed, but in the meantime he had to be ready for Year 10.

His mind went back to the altercation with Mac the previous evening. It had been a kind of stand-off, and he feared it may resurface in the lesson this morning. He tried to dismiss the thought as he prepared for the day, needing longer for each job as his brain simply wouldn't move at its usual pace. His own tutor group was already arriving for registration, noisy and excitable, jarring his brain with their sound. Two girls walking past him stopped to ask if he was alright, making him even more anxious about what he looked like, so between the end of registration and the start of the lesson he made his way along to the gent's toilet at the end of the corridor and splashed his face with cold water. The shock of it helped to clear his head, but he still didn't feel ready as the group began drifting in, most of them looking as usual as if they'd not been out of bed long themselves. Was that what he looked like too? Did he look as unready for work as they did? But no one commented, and in their somnambulant way, they made their way to the usual places and waited. There was no Mac. He began to think he was in luck. At least he wouldn't have to deal with him in his present state, so he drew the class to attention and began the lesson.

Two minutes into his introduction the door banged open noisily revealing Mac. He came into the classroom, slammed the door shut again behind him with no attempt to apologise for the interruption or for his lateness. Instead, he made his way ostentatiously to his usual seat, greeting other students on the way, but ignoring Josh completely.
"Have you got anything to say Mac?"
Despite the sudden anger he was feeling, he tried to make the question as reasonable as possible under the circumstances. Mac rotated his head to right and left as if looking for the answer somewhere in the room around him. Eventually, after an intentionally dramatic pause, he replied as if in complete innocence,
"No. Should I have?"
"How about, 'sorry I'm late sir'?"
"Oh, really? I hadn't thought of that."
He could feel his anger rising as Mac stared defiantly at him without attempting any kind of civil response, but still he managed to hold it in check.
"You need to say something by way of an apology if you want to stay in here this morning."
Tension filled the classroom, but nobody dared say anything or get involved. Mac continued to sit nonchalantly in his seat without making any response. He knew he had to do something, so he walked up the classroom aisle to where Mac was sitting till he was in front of him.
"Last chance Mac. An apology, or you have to go."
Still there was no response. He waited for a moment, then made a sudden decision, stretching out his hand and putting it firmly on Mac's shoulder, making as if to manhandle him out of the classroom. The reaction was instant. He scrambled to his feet and turned towards Josh, pushing his hand away at the same time.
"Don't fuckin' touch me!"
One fist was raised now and aimed directly as his head, and for a moment he thought he was going to be on the receiving end of a punch. Then Mac seemed to think better of it, swearing directly at him again several times before shouting at him again.

"Think you're a fuckin' hero!"
Then he pushed his way past him to the front of the classroom, pulled open the door and disappeared out into the corridor. There was shocked silence which he broke by sending a reliable student to fetch Len. He felt too stressed to continue the lesson straightaway, so told the class to take out their reading books. A brief period of clattering and rustling was quickly replaced once more by silence.

He was grateful when Len with his usual efficiency arranged for another teacher to cover the group and took him off to find out what had happened. Explaining made him feel better for a while, but within a few minutes all the energy seemed to drain out of him leaving him feeling even worse than he had at the start of the morning. Len wanted to know how much physical contact there had been between him and Mac, and he couldn't exactly remember.
"I think I tried to move him out of his seat, but I didn't hit him at all. He swore at me, several times."
Mac had disappeared. Probably run home, was Len's guess, gone to tell his parents his version.
"Don't blame yourself. The boy's an unpleasant individual at the best of times."
"But we were getting on alright," he replied. "Mostly he was settling down in my classes; till I blew it."
He explained about the night before, but Len didn't think he'd got that too wrong. Or at least that was what he said. But he knew, really, how much better Len would have dealt with it all.
"Don't be hard on yourself. Lads like him are unpredictable. Why not go to the staff room. Take a break. Looks like you need it."

He knew he did. It felt as if he staggered along the corridor, and flopped into one of the ancient staff room chairs. Thankfully, no one else was there. He felt terrible. Not just physically, although his headache was worse, and his body was feeling increasingly heavy. More than anything he believed now that it was his fault the whole incident happened. Getting carried away and staying out too late had affected his judgement so that he'd failed to keep his cool with Mac, and the more he thought about it, the more he felt responsible for setting himself up in the first place. If he'd reported Elijah's problem rather than trying to deal with it himself, he wouldn't have wrecked his improved relationship with Mac. He'd got over confident, the whole idea of being a hero had gone to his head, inflated his ego. What was it Wesley had said yesterday to get him to interfere in the first place? Something about saving his life? It wasn't Wesley's fault, but he'd risen to the bait. Now he felt well and truly deflated.

At lunchtime Mrs Broad wanted to see him. He knocked on her door timidly, but when she called him she was pleasant enough.

"I've had Mac's father in to see me. Claiming you abused his son. Don't worry. I know you didn't. Others in the group have confirmed what happened. He's gone away more angry with his son than you. I've excluded him for now. You'll get an apology on Monday before he returns." She paused, looking directly at him, and he waited in fear of what might be coming. "But we do need to talk about it."

"I know, I should have sent for help. That's where I got it wrong."

His heart was pounding and his head painful, but he was glad he said it, and relieved that was also what she thought. She was reassuring him, even telling him he had the makings of a good teacher. But he was struggling with the praise. He wanted to turn it into a confessional.

"I was stupid last night. I stayed out too late."

To his surprise, she looked at him and smiled broadly. There was a pun somewhere there and briefly it made him smile.

"Do you want me to tell you off for that?"

Then he felt stupid, immature again.

"No not really."

"But you do look unwell. Can you get through the afternoon?"

"I think so. Yes."

"Then go home after school and sleep it off."

He had an impulse to tell her it wasn't a hangover, he wasn't drunk, but he couldn't tell her about Flirts. She wouldn't understand, and it didn't really seem worth it. He thanked her and left the office.

She watched him go, feeling somehow like his mother. How old was he? Late twenties. Was that how Max would behave one day? Getting ratarsed? On a Thursday! She walked over to the window. Outside children ran around in all directions in the pale December sun. She smiled to herself. However old we are, something of the child, like those running around out there, always stays with us; it was part of our essential being. Getting us into difficulties sometimes, like Josh Greenwell, but it was also where all that life enjoyment came from. Was that what she could feel gently simmering inside her? A date for heaven's sake! How long since she'd been on one of those? She didn't really want to work it out. Just enjoy the nervous excitement it was giving her. At least her date was a Saturday.

23

Anna lay on her bed in the hotel in Krakow that evening and tried to get warm. It was as if she could still feel the chill wind blowing through her, but she knew really it was what she had experienced that had chilled her so much. There she'd cried, but now she was just exhausted, beyond tears. The *idea* of the holocaust had been a part of her understanding of the world for as long as she could remember. It was part of her whole existence. Now it was more. She'd seen the killing fields for herself. All those faces of the dead, their suitcases and their false legs, their spectacles and their false teeth, but more than anything the cabinets full of their shoes. The shoes haunted her. In her mind she kept seeing them. Shoes meant walking, movement, even escape, and that was what all the owners of the shoes had not been able to do. Millions of them, millions of Jews. Her race, her family had died there, and so had thousands upon thousands of gypsies from all over Europe. It was still her story, and she knew the Jewish loss had been greatest, but it was bigger, much bigger now than an abstract concept signalling the persecution of Jews. In her lifetime there had been other attempts to destroy whole peoples. She thought of Kurds and Bosnians, and it horrified her.

This was everyone's horror across the centuries, and everyone was to blame. Maybe we all needed to atone, just for being human, because our very humanity contained within it the potential to do unspeakable things. Hitler was just the worst example; there was also Saddam and Milosevic and Stalin and Genghis Khan, centuries and centuries of them, able to do unspeakable things because ordinary people followed them and allowed it to happen. Maybe all those dictators were manifestations of the evil in all of us, the serpent within. It was a terrible thought, and into her mind came the message from the Talmud: 'whoever destroys a single soul, he is guilty as though he had destroyed a complete world.' Each small act of destruction is significant. We all carry the guilt.

But there was another text, almost the antidote: 'whoever saves a single soul, it is as if he saves the whole world.' That was where there was hope. And out of nowhere came the act of saving she had seen; the young schoolteacher who had taken her for that meal. He saved a young boy, and risked his own life in the process. Had she been too hard on him? Was she trying to keep him at a distance for her own reasons? And why after all had she saved his telephone number? On the bedside table was her mobile phone. She picked it up to check whether his number was still in it, and on an impulse decided to send him a message. He was perhaps worth another try, at least as a friend.

*

When Josh woke on Saturday morning after what felt like a heavy sleep, the headache was more or less gone, but he still felt bad. 'A sadder and a wiser man' his grandmother used to say without any idea where the phrase came from, but he didn't really feel all that much wiser; just foolish for letting himself down. And still he was sleeping on his own. He sat up in bed, and as a matter of habit looked at the mobile phone he always had next to him. There was a message. He opened it.

Been to Auschwitz.

Will phone when back. A.

He looked at it, surprised, taking a moment to register who A was. Of course, Anna, she'd talked about Auschwitz at the meal. She said she'd text, but he didn't think she would. For a moment it made him feel even worse about his night club experience, but he persuaded himself that he didn't know she would still want to contact him. And anyway he'd learnt from the experience.

Auschwitz! Eastern Europe in December! The reality of it suddenly struck him. What was it like there now? Cold surely. He hoped it hadn't been too unpleasant for her. Quite why she'd wanted to go he couldn't really understand, but accepted that for Jews it had to be important. He guessed that if any of his relatives had died in the camp he would probably be the same; except maybe not in December. It made him feel cold even thinking about it, but the thought that she was still interested in him, even if only as a friend, cheered him considerably as he lay back and enjoyed a few more moments in bed before getting up.

*

"Well this is nice."

She looked across the table at him, smiling, looking as if she meant what she had said. He made a mental note to himself, 'not a psychotherapist today'.

"It is isn't it."

"Have you been here before?"

He'd chosen a pleasant bar where he knew they could get a drink and get to know each other.

"I think I once brought my mother here, a few years ago, when she could appreciate it."

He could see her looking, wondering what he meant.

"She has dementia. Not Alzheimer's, but similar. She struggles to make sense of things now."
"That must be difficult for you."
"Sometimes, yes."
How had he got to talk about his mother so early in the conversation? He knew he wanted to move away from the subject.
"She's quite old now, late eighties, lives close to me, but I don't want to bore you with all that today."
"It's alright. I don't mind. I thought we were just talking. Getting to know each other a bit."
"Yes, that's true."

He felt the conversation drop for a moment. She smiled across at him again, and he smiled back. She was certainly attractive. He wondered how old she was. There was at least one child. Did she have any others? He plucked up courage to explore it discretely.
"And you have a son, Max."
"Yes. He's thirteen, nearly fourteen actually, will be in January. We thought we couldn't have children, and then, after we'd given up, along came Max, a wonderful gift."
"Is that what it means?"
"Oh, I don't know, but that's what he was. And still is. Don't know what I'd do without him. But you need to tell me about yourself too. Do you have children?"
Was that an avoidance? But he kept to his resolve about not asking too many questions and answered hers.
"No, unfortunately. Just never happened for me. But I work with quite a lot of children. I sort of kid myself that makes up for it."
"Me too."

There was something about her smile that seemed to draw him in and the surroundings faded somewhere into the background. It was different from anything he could remember experiencing before. He found himself telling her about his own background with Laura, and the fact that he'd been on his own for 'some while now,' without specifying exactly how long. It felt like she was drawing him out like he drew information from his patients. Quite quickly she knew more about him than he knew about her, and he didn't mind. But he did want to know whether there was anyone else in her life apart from Max. He needed to find an opening.

"So, it's you, and Max, at home?"

She nodded, but didn't answer immediately. The pause felt suddenly uncomfortable.

"For three years. Almost."

He waited for her to continue.

"As I think I mentioned before, Guy, my husband, died nearly three years ago. But I'd rather not talk about that. Not now. Not here."

She smiled again, but he thought for a moment he could see her eyes filling.

"I'm sorry. I don't want to be intrusive."

The vulnerability he found curiously attractive was for a moment fully exposed.

"Can I get you another drink?" he said.

She nodded, grateful that he'd recognised the need to give her a moment of space. While he stood facing the bar, she found a small pack of tissues in her handbag and wiped her eyes carefully, not wanting to smear the make-up. His sensitivity appealed to her. He was easy to talk to, prepared to be open with her. But talking about Guy was still difficult. Next month it would be three years. Sometimes it felt like an eternity, and sometimes almost like yesterday. She was cross with herself, convinced she should have come to terms with it all by now, but all too aware that she hadn't.

He was coming back with something to drink. Another orange juice, although if it wasn't for driving she could really have done with something alcoholic.

"So, tell me about Max."

She was grateful he'd found a way of changing the subject. It was never difficult to talk about Max, and she chattered on, regaining her equilibrium while he listened and seemed to enjoy hearing about her son as they sipped their drinks.

She was warming to him, feeling very much like she wanted to see him again. A good friend perhaps. Someone to ease the loneliness she'd felt since Guy. Maybe one day she would be able to tell him about Guy, but not today. He was looking at her, smiling, Seeming to enjoy her company too. Strangely, she wanted to touch him, a little human contact she knew she'd missed over the past three years. Not sexual of course, just, well touch. His hand was on the table, next to his drink. Not a young hand, and not a hand that looked like it had known much physical work. A clean attractive hand though, gentle. There were veins standing out on the back of the hand, and hair, manly hair.

He was saying something to her while she was distracted by his hand.
"Sorry, I was miles away."
"I noticed." He smiled. "It's alright. I was just checking that you were still OK for time."
"Yes. I'm not in a hurry. Nothing else planned for today. But what about you?"
"Same. I don't need to rush off."
She hoped he wouldn't. But surely they couldn't sit in a bar all afternoon.
"Do you like jazz?"
She didn't really know, hadn't heard much at all.
"Yes, I do," she said, wondering what was coming, but not wanting to miss it, whatever it was.
"There's a club, not too far from here. I think there's a Saturday afternoon concert today. Won't last long; just an hour or so. Would you like to go?"
"Why not?"

She could feel adrenalin surging through her as he suggested taking her and bringing her back to her car afterwards. It was feeling more and more like a date, and it was just a bit scary.

The journey was in fact nearly half an hour she noticed, but didn't mind. He didn't say much in the car, just looked at her occasionally and smiled, almost as if she was a trophy he'd collected. It disconcerted her slightly, but she didn't say anything, not wanting to spoil the moment. Eventually he turned into an almost full car park behind what looked like some kind of social club. Once he'd parked the car, he came round to her side and helped her out almost as if she was an old lady and indicated the way across to the entrance.

Inside, there was a large hall with seats set out in tables, and at the far end a stage with a grand piano, a set of drums and a double bass lying on its side. She could feel a buzz of anticipatory excitement around the body of the hall as they made their way to a table. He checked the two seats he had chosen were free before they sat down.
"You've been here before," she said.
"Couple of times, yes," he said, and almost as an afterthought, "It's good," as if to justify bringing her.
"You're not a regular?"
"Not exactly."
She wasn't sure whether to believe him, but although one or two others around the room nodded to him in apparent recognition, taking a sly look at her in the process she noticed, there was no overt acknowledgement. Maybe he had told the truth.

There was applause. A large black man in a trilby hat came on stage and sat at the piano, followed by an equally large white man with braces curving over a white open necked shirt which held his stomach in place. He picked up the bass and began strumming it rhythmically. This seemed to be the cue for another, smaller black man who came in to further applause, made his way to the drums and joined the bass player with quiet rhythmic drumming. Finally, a slim younger white man with curly blond hair and carrying what she thought was a saxophone came on stage to yet more applause. By this time the pianist had joined the bass player and the drummer with block chords, and then the saxophone began playing a lively piece which she couldn't recognise as any particular tune. Eventually he seemed to come to the end of the piece and bowed to the audience who clapped enthusiastically while the tune passed to the pianist. His tune was followed by more applause and led into a bass solo which, predictably by now, received yet more applause. Finally the drummer launched into a very noisy and quite frenzied solo which ended with loud applause and led back to all four players rounding off the piece. She noticed Patrick clapping enthusiastically and smiling at her again. She smiled back and clapped along with him.

That seemed to be the pattern for what followed, with solos usually occurring in the same order, and always ending with audience applause. She did notice though that people didn't seem to mind talking during the playing, and that the musicians didn't seem to have a problem with it. Between numbers, the pianist, who seemed to be the leader of the group, told incomprehensible jokes in a deep throaty voice. The audience seemed to find the jokes funny, as did Patrick. He turned to look at her after each joke and she smiled dutifully, although what most amazed her was the repetitive nature of the whole event. The ageing audience in strangely unfashionable clothing seemed to think it was wonderful.

"They're good aren't they," he offered at one point and she nodded, although what was really good was being there with him and enjoying his enthusiasm. That was what she didn't want to end.

It was dark by the time the concert ended. 'That was really good today' seemed to be the general opinion, and Patrick smiled almost like a schoolboy in evident pleasure at taking her to such a successful event.

On the way back he could hardly contain his pleasure, sure that she had really enjoyed the concert and happy to be in her company.
"Wasn't the saxophonist good," he said.
She nodded her head and smiled, which he took as confirmation. The music was still playing in his head as he drove. He was very aware that some of his good mood was the result of being with Liz.

As they approached the place where he knew she had parked her car, he began to wonder how he might ask to meet her again. It was some years since he'd last been out with a woman, and the wrong side of sixty, as he knew he was, it seemed somehow not quite right to be presumptuous. Years ago, he told himself, he would have been direct. By now he would probably have moved his hand across to her side of the car and engineered some form of contact. But it was the head of a school he was sitting next to. The thought of it was slightly shocking: a date with a headmistress for heaven's sake! Could he ever have imagined that?
"My car is just round this turning on the left," she said suddenly. They were back. Should he get out, or let her get out of the car? He turned left into the car park, which was now largely empty.
"That's my car over there."
He drove across, parked beside it and switched his engine off before realising she might think that presumptuous. She turned to face him.
"Thankyou. It's been a lovely afternoon."
She was looking directly at him now and he returned the gaze. The eye contact lasted, and infinitesimally, not entirely consciously, he moved his head towards hers, sensing at the same time that the same thing was happening to her. He stretched his arm towards her, ready to embrace, still keeping the eye contact, until holding back was no longer an option. For a moment his eyes closed and his lips met hers in the gentlest of brief kisses that couldn't be interpreted as mere friendship. She hadn't resisted, and when he looked again, he could see his own excitement mirrored in her face. His hand found hers, and he took it.

"Does this feel good?" he said.
"I think so, yes,"
"Can we meet again?"
"Please."
"Shall I phone you?"
She nodded in agreement, looking almost bemused.
"I need your number."
He watched as she seemed to register what he was saying, then, opening her handbag, she took out a card.
"Those are my work numbers."
From her bag again she found a pen and wrote something on the back of the card.
"That's my home number."
She smiled, looking at him again as he took the card, and for a moment he thought she might be going to initiate another kiss. Then, seeming to think better of it, she said quickly,
"I must go now," and before he could say anything else she was out of his car and into her own beside his. He waited while she started the engine, put the lights on and drove off.

He sat back in his seat quietly and breathed out deeply. Then breathing in again he could smell her perfume still in his car. Strange that he hadn't really been conscious of it before, and now she was gone the smell lingered like a memory. He breathed it in again. It made him feel good as he sat there looking out onto a hedge in a town car park. In his hand he was still holding the card she'd given him, and he switched on the courtesy light to look at it. One side had her name and qualifications together with the school contacts. Very formal and proper. He turned it over. On the other side she'd written her number, and underneath it, a single kiss. It made him smile as he turned the courtesy light off and started the car engine.

*

Anna wasn't sure now quite why she had suggested they met again. She knew it was an impulse, prompted by thoughts about his rescue act, but was there anything more to it? Did she really want to develop a relationship with him? She didn't know, but the idea of another meeting in a local pub seemed a safe enough way of exploring it further. At least he wasn't boring, and when she got there he was already waiting for her. Ben would certainly have been late. She got herself a drink and sat down opposite him.

"I guess you're wondering why I contacted you again."

"Well in a way, yes."

"Those series of coincidences when our paths crossed. I've been thinking about that, amongst a lot else. I'm not a believer in fate or anything like that, but I didn't want to lose touch with you. I thought we might be able to be friends; just friends."

She knew she had emphasised the word friends. It felt safer, and anyway, that was what she wanted, but not wanting to be too remote, on another impulse, she took a risk.

"Even though you made me crash my car."

He accepted the joke without over-reacting, and they both laughed together.

"But seriously, you know where I've just been. It's had a big impact on me. I knew it would, but I didn't anticipate quite how much. Is it all right if I share it with you?"

It all felt different. It seemed possible to talk to him, like a friend, without anything else getting in the way.

She began to tell him what it had been like, leading up to her experience with the shoes.

"When I saw the shoes, the words of the Kaddish came into my head."

For some reason it shocked her for a moment that he didn't know the Kaddish was the prayer for the dead. Her mother's words came into her head unwanted; 'What do you expect, he's a goy!' But she dismissed them without letting them affect her. He seemed to really want to know.

"It's not as if I'm religious. I'm not a believer at all. And yet those words about God. At that moment they meant something important.

'May his great name be blessed for all eternity.' When I say them again now, I can feel it. Not with the intensity of then, nothing comparable. It doesn't make sense to me that I responded like that, but I know it was very powerful . . . in that place."
"Do you think it might have something to do with that word eternity? The difficulty we have with really believing in our non-existence."
"I hadn't thought of that."
"And believing that our existence just ends when we die. Death challenges our desire to believe that life has meaning. What's it all for, if at the end we just die?"
"Everything all the wearers of those shoes tried to do in their lives, ended in that death camp. That's just too awful to think about."

She felt herself physically recoiling. Her whole body moved backwards as if the thought had literally hit her, and it struck her at the same time that she didn't believe in a meaningless universe. Somewhere, there had to be a way of making sense of it all. And he seemed to be struggling with the same need.
"If we believe in God, even a vengeful god, there's a way forward to making some sense of it," he said.
"Especially a vengeful god," she said. "He can make the Nazis atone for their sins. They might burn in hell. And just in case there isn't, the Nazi hunters have done some of the work for him. Hunting them all down to make them pay."

She knew as she said it that the vision of a vengeful God was something she carried within her. However much she said she didn't have a religious belief, that idea was firmly there. She wanted justice in the world. Maybe that was the source the anger she was learning to control but didn't want to lose. Was that why the prayer felt so important? All those victims' deaths would be atoned?
"So do you really believe in God, when it really comes down to it?" he said. "Is that, in the end, how life makes sense for you?"

"I really don't know. The whole experience has shaken me. It seemed easier before I went."
She took a sip from her drink and looked at Josh. His face was serious. It looked like he was struggling to make sense of things too.
"There's a deputy head at my school who says he thinks life is basically meaningless. All we're here for is to perpetuate the species. I can see where he's coming from, but I can't really accept it. Too bleak for me. We're human, we've got this consciousness. We need to look for patterns in what happens to us. We actually need to try and make sense of our existence. Why did all those people die in Auschwitz? How can we atone for it, and so on."
That word again. How important it seemed to be now. Bigger than just the Jewish experience.
"Do you know, that was why I went to Auschwitz. It felt like I needed to atone personally. *Tschuve* is the Hebrew word and that seemed full of meaning for me. It still does."
"Do you think you achieved it?"
"I don't know. It was a powerful, disturbing experience. I'm glad I've done it."
"The holocaust is your personal history because you come from a Jewish background, and you have to make sense of it through that background. Whatever you actually believe, you can't change that. None of us can. But maybe the experience is the real point."

His words seemed to make a sense she hadn't considered before. Maybe it was the experience that made the meaning, which she could only interpret through who she was. An image of the vast bone covered wilderness of Birkenau came into her head. There seemed no end to it. Then she saw again the old Romany and his daughter holding onto him against the wind and the desolation, and in that moment she knew it was human contact which made everything make sense. That was what she had to hold onto. He who saves a single soul . . . . She looked across the table at Josh, calmly drinking his beer. How had she got him so wrong? He was altogether different from how she judged him before.

"You know, I guess you're a good teacher."
He looked at her and laughed. It seemed a strange development from the conversation they'd just been having.
"Why do you say that?"
"You think things through. You're very calm."
He laughed again.
"Not all the time."
He was tempted to tell her about Mac and staying out late because of the night club, but it seemed almost trivial in comparison with what she had experienced, despite the fact that it had had a significant effect on him, and he was still coming to terms with what it meant for him. He certainly wasn't going to tell her about flirting with the girl, even groping, which he assumed would lower her opinion of him, so he kept it to himself.
"I guess you're just being modest. What you did to save that boy in the Woolworths building must have had an effect. I've been thinking about that, and how brave you were."
It felt good to hear her say that, but he also knew it was just that kind of thinking which had helped him to come unstuck with Mac. He wanted to play down her comments.
"It's nice of you to say that, and yes, I did get feted for a while, but it soon passed. Children have short memories."
"Well I've remembered it, and I know a lot of people couldn't have done what you did."
He could feel his cheeks reddening, and he was blushing. He put his hand to his face to try to prevent her noticing, but it only drew her attention to it. She grinned at him, mischievously.
"Are you blushing? I don't believe it!"
She was laughing, which despite his embarrassment, he liked. There was a softer side to her, and he could access it. He laughed with her, saying something about not wanting to get too big headed, which she

seemed to like. It felt for the first time that at least they could be friends.

The conversation moved on in a more light hearted way. They talked about Christmas, and she told him how she would be with her parents during the break, which she wasn't looking forward to. He was tempted to suggest a meeting over Christmas, but didn't want to risk it. He would leave it to her to say whether she wanted to meet him again.

"I've enjoyed talking to you, we must do this again sometime," she said.

"Me too."

He waited slightly anxiously for what might be coming as she hesitated before speaking again.

"You know, I got you wrong. You're nicer than I thought you were. Much nicer actually."

She leaned forward towards him and kissed him on the cheek. He put his arm round her for a moment to draw her towards him to respond in a brotherly way. It felt good, and the smile she gave him afterwards offered just a hint of something a little more than a sisterly reply. But he kept his caution, making sure his smile was no more than affectionate.

"I'll ring you," she said. It felt like she meant it.

*

Max was in, watching the television in the living room when she got back.

"Thought you'd gone out with your friend."

"I did. Got back about half an hour ago. 'Spose there's nothing to eat is there?"

"Have you looked in the fridge?"

He looked at her as if she was speaking a foreign language. But she couldn't help feeling a touch of guilt at getting back after him, so she went into the kitchen to make him a sandwich.

"Don't expect it every time," she said as she brought it to him.

"Thanks, mum."
She watched him tuck into it, turning back to the television, before making her way upstairs to change.
"Well, that was different," she said to Guy as soon as she entered the bedroom. It felt important to share what she had been doing. She felt guilty. For the first time in her life she felt as if she had been two-timing. She'd never done that before, not even as a student. One relationship was always finished before a new one started. But when did her relationship with Guy end? It didn't feel like it had. Yet the kiss in the car, brief as it was, had changed her.

She looked at herself In front of the mirror. The figure was still reasonable although she wouldn't mind being a bit slimmer, but she was OK as she was. Taking hold of her breasts in the palm of her hands, she looked at herself face on and then from each side. They were still good, not too large or small. She was proud of them, and she knew Guy had liked them. They had liked him touching and fondling them. But no one had touched them for three years, and no one apart from Guy for thirty years. Was that going to change in the near future? She knew now it was possible.

She couldn't deny the feelings stirring within her. Sex had always mattered and Guy had been such a good partner. How much she missed sex was something she couldn't tell anyone. There was just no one close enough to share it with. The idea of a sex starved headteacher was embarrassing. Was she close to ending the drought, on the edge of the monsoon maybe? Exciting, but scary too, with the hint of excess the thought carried. And she was anxious it might not be what she really wanted.

From downstairs Max was calling out. She went to the door to hear more clearly what he was saying. Someone on the telephone. She hurried downstairs.
"Who is it," she asked as she took the phone from him.

"Man. Didn't say," he said disinterestedly and turned back to the television.
"Hello Liz, Patrick here. Hope it's alright to ring you so soon after our meeting."
"Yes, yes of course."
"I was just wondering if we could fix up something else."
She didn't hesitate.
"Yes, that would be nice. Did you have anything in mind?"
"If it's a nice day tomorrow, I was wondering if you fancied a walk. There's a countryside walk near where I live. Wrap up warm. Takes about an hour and a half. Have a meal out maybe, then come back to my place for a drink or something."
The 'or something' made her feel nervous and excited at the same time, but she held her feelings back. She could worry about that tomorrow.
"Yes. OK. Yes, I'd like that."
"If I give you my address, could you come over about twelve?"
"I'll have to sort out Max, but yes, I think I can do that. Can I text you to confirm it?"
"OK. Look forward to it."
And he was gone. She stood with the phone in her hand with a mixture of emotions running through her head. Max was still watching the television, oblivious, but she would need to make sure he was OK if she was going to spend the afternoon out on a date.

Suddenly Max turned away from the television as if something had occurred to him.
"Mum. Forgot to say. Do you mind if I go over to Neil's tomorrow afternoon? His dad's going to take us bowling. Said I could go over for lunch first."
Was this a sign? Such a coincidence was hardly believable.
"Yes of course. What time will you be going?"
"About twelve if that's OK."
"Of course. That sounds good."

"Thanks mum!"
"Do you need any money?"
"Well, I wouldn't mind . . ."
"I'll give you ten pounds spending money."
"That's wicked mum. Thanks."
"I might be going out myself as well. Take your key just in case you get in first."
"OK." He'd got what he wanted and was back to the television.
She went into the kitchen and sent Patrick the text, saying she would probably arrive nearer twelve thirty. It would be easier if Max was out first.

24

Stefan was at least honest with him. After the last concert before Christmas, there was the usual orchestra get together. He came over with his beer greeting him cheerily and sitting down.
"It is two weeks, yes, since we were together."
"About that, yes, but it's OK, I think I understand."
"Sure, you know me."
The sparkle in Stefan's eye told him some kind of disclosure was imminent.
"Truth is, there is other in my life now."
The directness was amusing.
"We could have, how do you say, threetimes?"
Simon laughed, but he was shocked.
"You mean a threesome?"
"Threesome, yes, not perfect, my English. I need practice."
Even though the whole idea shocked him, he couldn't resist exploring the idea further.
"Have you really done that before?"
"Of course. Sex is much fun. In English you say more is merry, yes?"
He had to admit that was true. In his head, before coming out, before his experiences with Stefan, he'd always believed intellectually that whatever was agreed between consenting adults was OK. He just

hadn't been able to apply it to himself. Now he was being offered the opportunity to experiment further. A small part of him wanted to say 'why not?', but there was a larger part of him was telling him there were limits he didn't personally feel able to exceed. He needed someone to develop a relationship. But that wasn't Stefan's world.
"So threesome is not you then, Simon?"
"No, I don't think it is, sorry."
"Not sorry! But maybe I find one more, we go two by two, yes?"
"You mean, you'd find another partner for me?"
"Maybe, yes."
"That I could meet in my own flat?"
"You want that? I arrange it for you."
He nodded, uncertainly. Was he setting himself up as a dating agency for him? But let it go for now, he could always say no later.

Stefan was getting his violin out of its case.
"Enough sex." He grinned broadly. "For now, is music."
He was tuning up, and rosining his bow with the almost manic speed Simon had grown to expect from him. Then he was up on his chair ready and calling out to everyone in the bar that he would play *zigeunerweise*, which he knew meant gypsy style, and in no time a melancholic tune was filling the bar and causing most of those present to become quiet, listening. Simon thought it sounded more Jewish than gypsy, but was impressed with how big he could make his tone. Then the tune changed, and although still minor key, became gradually faster and more rhythmic, so that everyone began clapping their hand in time. On and on the music went, with Stefan moving up and down on the chair seeming to become increasingly animated until with a flourish he drew the music to a close. The applause was instantaneous, and there were cries of *encore, encore*.

"We need cimbalom," he shouted over the sound, "but here is piano." He was pointing to an old upright to the side of the bar. One of the percussion players dutifully stood, and to raucous applause went across to the piano.

"Is E minor start, OK?"

With great exaggeration, the pianist began some basic chords which on the out-of-tune piano sounded not dissimilar to the cimbalom he'd remembered hearing in a cafe in Budapest. Stefan rose to the challenge and the pianist found a way of accompanying him through another wild number.

Simon looked around the room. The bass player was unzipping his instrument and was soon strumming along in time with the other two, and the clapping continued with each number they played. To his ears, there was little difference between any of the pieces, but it didn't matter. The atmosphere had been transformed from a quiet Christmas drink to some kind of Eastern European extravaganza. He didn't mind. What was happening around him seemed to mirror the excited but confused feelings inside. He had found his true sexuality, thanks to the man leading the celebrations. Now he needed to find boundaries that felt right for him.

*

It became dark once more and with it Tom could feel his agitation rising. He wanted to see her again. He wanted to be able to touch her, to end his isolation. He sat on his bedding area with his arms wrapped around his knees, waiting. He knew that he was hugging himself and at the same time rocking backwards and forwards. As he sat there in the darkness, it felt as if his mind was disengaging from his body and wandering freely. It wasn't like a dream now, more as if he could control what was happening and he could conjure Lucia into his imagination. She was naked once more. He could see her face looking at him, and her breasts, firm and warm standing out in his direction. His eyes shifted to the curve of her legs, moving from her feet upwards to her thighs and beyond into the soft darkness of her pubic hair, bushed and inviting in front of him. Although he was aware at some level that this was his imagination, that he was conjuring it up, it felt real, as if he could almost stretch out and touch her. The familiar stirring was in him, the old excitement was there. The rocking back and forward became more intense, and he could see her face smiling at him, inviting him to be with her, wanting him, and he knew it was true. He wanted her and she wanted him, and everything would be well.

A noise at the barn door startled him. Then the flickering light. She was coming out of his imagination to meet him. Or was she coming into his imagination. He didn't know. He drew himself out of his enclosed position to be ready to greet her. She was smiling as he knew she would be, and in her hands as well as the candle, she was carrying something on a tray. He watched in anticipation, barely containing his excitement, as she put everything down and turned towards him. He stretched out his arm towards her and she smiled again, returning his greeting so that he knew she really wanted him as much as he wanted her. He put both his arms round her, pulling her towards him, feeling the closeness he'd missed for so long.

She was still in his arms. He pressed her closer and then down towards the bedding. He was aware that she was saying something which he knew had to be encouragement and it felt like she was struggling with the enjoyment of it. He was on top of her, laying over her excited, almost to bursting point. Vaguely he was aware that with one hand he was fumbling with her clothing, while at the same time holding her in place with his other, helping to ease her struggling. There was strength in his body which hadn't been there for as long as he could remember, and he could feel the power coursing through him as he was thrusting uncontrollably. He was in another world, all his loneliness, all of his fears became as nothing in the ecstatic movements of his body over the woman who was saving him and ending his isolation. Then a great sense of release overcame him, making him thrust once or twice more before falling sideways from her and laying on his back catching his breath, and at precisely that moment, the donkey outside began braying. The sounds got louder and louder as if the animal was working itself up into an orgasmic spasm of manic laughter, before calming back down to its more usual snorting and stamping.

As the noise from the donkey died back he became aware from somewhere in the darkness of the barn a sound like sobbing. In the flickering light of the candle the figure of Lucia was standing away from his bedding area and adjusting her clothing. At first he couldn't understand what was happening. Was she crying? After she had done so much for him? He eased himself up on his elbow and stretched out towards her with his other hand, but she recoiled away from him. As she did so, he noticed with surprise that his trousers and his undershorts were around his ankles, leaving him exposed. He pulled his arm back and as quickly as he could and dressed himself properly again. A kind of awareness of what might actually have happened began to surface in his brain. Lucia was still standing a short distance from him, not seeming to want to leave the barn, but keeping a space between them. He tried to speak, wanting to say something but no words came out. He checked the button fastening on his trousers again, making sure he wasn't indecent in front of her.

The sound of sobbing seemed to have stopped, but the light wasn't good enough to see her face. Then he was aware that she was moving, circling him he thought, which didn't make sense until he realised that she was moving towards the candle light, but avoiding him in the process. Suddenly she snatched at it, and as the flame reared he could clearly see for a moment her frightened face looking towards him in terror. It shocked him. She moved quickly towards the barn door, opened it and then slammed it shut behind her. He sat back on the bedding. At that moment he knew with an absolute certainty what had happened. He'd done everything he told himself he wouldn't do. His brain couldn't, wouldn't make sense of it. He sat there in the darkness, unable to do anything.

There was a commotion outside the barn door. Shouting, a male voice, strident, insistent; a female voice, seeming to be arguing with him. The door flew open and again there was light. He could make out at least two bodies moving, and there was more shouting. Instinctively he got to his feet, and as he did so there was a flash of light and instantaneously an immense crashing noise engulfed him. His whole body felt like it had been smashed by something impossibly heavy. In less than another second the same sequence of events repeated themselves, and with the second smashing into his body he was knocked to the ground. There was a sharp pain in his side. He tried to stand, but his legs wouldn't work. In his ears now was a loud screaming from the female voice. He wanted to stretch out towards her in case it was Lucia, but he couldn't do that either. Now the screaming was right beside him and there were hands somewhere on his body, and then the screaming began to seem more distant.

His mind was drifting, and he was aware of a feeling of floating, like dreaming again. The soldier was on the ridge with his rifle held in the air, but this time it didn't seem like he was going to hit him. Somewhere in the dream was Lucia, but he couldn't make out where. Then suddenly, from nowhere, there was the large bird again, *aquila,* like a great eagle, which seemed to sweep him up and carry him off into the sky. He felt held, although he didn't quite know how, and soon it was possible to look down on everything below. He could see the ridge with the soldier, the barn, and even the donkey. Gradually, they faded into the distance, everything became remote, and at last it felt like he was free.

25

It was far less warm at the weekend. They were both wrapped up with coats and scarves and gloves and boots, but the wind chill made it feel even colder than the two degrees above zero that it actually was. Dutifully she walked along beside him, and it was beautiful scrunching through the carpet of leaves and enjoying the moments when the sun made all too brief appearances between the clouds and illuminated the almost bare trees. Neither of them said very much, and they didn't touch, but walking beside him felt surprisingly easy. After half an hour she felt very cold, and didn't quite know how to tell him, so it was a relief when he raised it himself.

"Are you cold Liz?"

"A bit, yes."

Speaking was difficult. Her face was too cold.

"Do you want to shorten the walk and have something to eat."

"Could do," she said. Out of nowhere a pleasant looking pub came into view.

Afterwards she realised Patrick had actually planned things so they were within five minutes of his house. A swift walk through the cold and they were there. They stamped their feet vigorously in his doorway and she stood behind him while he turned the key in the lock. Once the door was open, he stepped aside so she could walk in ahead of him. Something about walking in felt illicit, like an extra-marital affair. She was already married. Guy was her husband, and the message inside her head told her dying didn't make that any less so. She felt conflicted. What she was doing felt wrong and right at the same time, but she didn't feel able to tell him all that.

He sat her down in the living room and went into the kitchen to make them a drink. While he was gone she looked around. There was a large TV screen and a CD player in one corner, two large comfortable matching sofas in a kind of rust colour, and an untidy bookcase. The walls were unremarkable in magnolia, but to her surprise there were no pictures or photographs; so unlike her own house. She was about to walk over and inspect the bookcase when he was back with the tea, placing it on the small table between the two sofas before sitting himself down on the other sofa, adjacent and at right angles to where she was sitting. He smiled and picked up his tea.

She felt herself smiling back, but she could also feel a tension and anxiety rising in her. What would they talk about? How were they going to spend the time ahead of them?
"This is nice," she said, feeling the need to say something and indicating the room.
"Do you think so? Sometimes it feels a bit bare, but I can't think how to improve it."
"Maybe you need a woman's touch."
What was she saying? That sounded far too forward. And sexist too. But he just laughed and didn't comment.
"Most evenings after work I just come in here and watch the television; or play music. Maybe read."
"On your own?"
"Mostly, yes. I am single you know."
He smiled; more or less grinned.

The thought of him being alone most nights affected her. At least she had Max. Mixed blessing though he sometimes was, she couldn't imagine where she would be without him. Almost instinctively, she lifted her arm across as if to comfort him, resting it for a moment on his, before a sense of propriety seemed to take over and she lifted it again, once more feeling she might have been too forward.
"You can touch me you know."

The smile she gave him felt childish, embarrassed. He stood, walked across in front of her and sat down again on the same sofa, leaving a minimal space between them.
"You don't mind me sitting here?"
She was surprised that she didn't. She wanted, needed his male presence, and it was she who moved her hand across to find his. But there was guilt.

"I still feel married you know."

He nodded, looked at her sympathetically as if understanding what she was saying. He pressed the hand she had already offered him.
"How long is it now?"
"Nearly three years. Will be in January."
He didn't say anything, seeming to be absorbing what she said.
"It makes this difficult," she said.
He was nodding, almost sage like.
"I can't go too fast."
And then strangely, belying what she had just said, she turned towards him, embraced him, and soon they were kissing passionately. It felt as if something had burst open, freeing her.

Afterwards they moved apart, looked at each other.
"That wasn't too fast?" he said.
She wanted to say 'I don't know what came over me,' but it felt too clichéd, too trite, so instead she apologised.
"What for? I'm happy."
They laughed together before kissing again.
"Passion originally meant pain," she said, when they separated once more.
"I know. I often think that. Sometimes I even think, without pain there would be no passion."
"That makes sense."
He was holding her again, looking at her intensely.
"Do you want to come upstairs?"
"No. Not yet. It feels too soon. Sorry."
He nodded looking as if he entirely accepted what she said, but she knew there was disappointment too.
"Not that I don't like you. Maybe next time."
"Maybe?"
"Yes, maybe, I'm a staid headteacher, remember." she said flirtatiously.
"And a very attractive one."

"And you're a good looking doctor. We could be from a Mills and Boon novel."
He didn't know what she was talking about and she had to explain, losing the joke in the process, but they laughed together anyway, and in her mind 'maybe' turned more towards 'probably,' however scary it felt.
"But now I ought to get going."
"So soon?"
"I'd like to be home before Max if possible."
But it was harder to leave than she anticipated, and she couldn't hold back from a further embrace before going.

*

"Everything OK boss?"
It felt like one of Len's little fantasies when he called her boss. She also knew he was fishing for information.
"I'm very well thankyou Mr Turner, and you?"
Play him at his own game. Make him work for his information. But he was smart. He had his way of finding things out.
"I'm very well Mrs Broad, and it's nice to see you looking so well lately. Like the cat got the cream if you don't mind me saying so."
The irritating Groucho impression was back, complete with mock cigar. But she could stall for a little longer.
"Well, our contextual value added score is over a thousand in this year's figures. That has to be good news for us."
She knew it wasn't what he wanted to hear. He knew that anyway; part of his role to know. She wanted to make him be direct. Which he was.
"And Dr East? He's well?"
If she let him know anything, she knew there would be rumours. Secrecy wasn't his strong point. Loyalty and integrity when it really mattered she knew she could rely on, but the staff didn't call him Twitter for nothing.
"Well I hope he is. Are you asking me for a reason Len?"

She grinned at him artlessly, but she could see he took it as an unspoken communication.
"You know I'm interested in your well being."
Layers of meaning. Yes he was, she knew he wanted her to be happy again. He was also very interested in knowing the detail. For someone who claimed to believe life was essentially meaningless, he was surprisingly interested in looking for meaning. But he obviously realised she wasn't going to tell him anything yet, and made his exit with a smile and another fake cigar mime.

And, she thought to herself after he'd gone, there's really nothing to tell. He'd taken her to a jazz club and then invited her round to his house. They'd kissed. Yes she liked him, but that was all. And yet the feeling of anticipation was running like a back projection in her life now. It excited her and confused her in more or less equal measure. It felt like she was emerging from a lengthy period of semi-darkness and out into dazzling sunlight.

It was one of those bright cold December days she loved. She went from the play areas to the field where excited Year 7 boys ran around after a football, back into the bright gym and then into the classrooms. Everywhere the sun seemed to be shining on her. Her office felt bright and the Christmas decorations she'd allowed her secretary to put up this year really did seem to suggest a season of goodwill. Len was right, she did feel well, and it must be apparent on the outside, but ought she to feel so well? Three Christmases ago Guy was dying. She couldn't imagine that she would ever want to celebrate Christmas again. Could love really be so fickle? 'You will get over me. There will be happy Christmases in the future,' he told her. But her guilt felt very real. Three years was not long, and now she was two timing, on the edge of adultery even, and tonight it might happen. Already it was prepared. Max was staying overnight at his friend's house, and very excited about it. He'd got his clothes and everything else he wanted in his overnight bag in school with him so he could go straight home with

Neil after school. Unless their paths crossed during the day she wouldn't see him till tomorrow evening. His first night away from home and he was really looking forward to it. But he did think about her too.
"You will be alright Mum, won't you?"
"Yes Max, I'll be fine."
It was the answer he needed to carry on with his own life, while she knew secretly she was planning to bring another man into the house. The guilt felt bad. And yet she was still going to do it. How weak willed and deceitful was that? She knew when she opened the door to Patrick, let him in and kissed him even before they were out of the hallway that she was bypassing the guilt in favour of her own desire.

She made him a coffee and sat with him at the kitchen table to drink it.
"You look good," he said.
"Thankyou."
"Where's your son?"
"Staying with a friend tonight."
He looked directly at her registering what she was saying. She looked down, away from his gaze for a moment, before re-engaging.
"We have the place to ourselves."
He nodded appreciatively, seeming to understand what she was implying. She didn't know what to say now, so occupied herself with drinking the coffee in front of her. He helped her out by making some small talk about 'nice house' and the mild weather while she regained her composure.
"Would you like to come through to the lounge?" she said after a while, standing at the same time.
"The assertive headmistress," he said, laughing and standing himself, and at that moment, she knew that they wouldn't be going into the lounge but upstairs into her bedroom.

He followed her through the hall, past the door into the lounge and up the stairs without saying anything. Only once they were inside her

room with the door closed did they engage in any further physical contact. It felt almost as if, whether Max was there or not, she had to respect his presence. But soon they were kissing again, and then undressing. She was faster than him, jumping speedily into her side of the bed and pulling the clothes up to her nose so she could watch him struggling to get his shoes undone, laughing inwardly to herself as he did so. Finally he got into the vacant side of the bed.
"You've still got your glasses on."
"Of course, I wanted to watch you. But I'll take them off now you're here."
She lifted them from her face and put them on the table beside the bed before turning back to him. He was ready.

*

Afterwards, lying beside him, she could feel the deep inner sense of fulfilment she'd missed for so long. Sex really is good for you, she mused. It was warm in the bedroom and his arm against hers was perspiring. At some level too she was aware of an indefinable male smell she'd not experienced for three years. Someone else was breathing beside her in the bed in which she'd slept alone for so long. Without her glasses on, only her immediate surroundings were in focus, providing a cocoon in which for that moment it felt like all her needs had been met. She sighed with satisfaction and at the same moment the body next to hers made a sound suspiciously like a fart.
"God, are all men the same?" she said out loud.
"I don't aspire that high," he said with a hint of sleepiness in his voice.
"What?"
"God. I'm not God."
She gave him a playful thump on the chest and he cried out in mock pain before pulling her close to him and kissing her once more, softly on the lips and eyelids, disarming her, before lying back again. 'I like this man,' she thought to herself. 'I could do this again.'
"And again," she said out loud without quite intending to, so that he half sat up again and kissed her as before on the forehead, the eyes

the nose and then the mouth, more firmly this time, and she could feel the stirring again within her.

He stopped and raised his head a few inches above hers and looked down at her so that she could see his face still in focus. She smiled, and he smiled back.
"Do we have to get up yet?" he said.
She looked at the clock. Quarter past eight.
"Not unless you want to."
"I'd better go home soon though."
As soon as he said it she could feel a sense of disappointment, but it did feel too soon to spend the night together. He was right. She nodded, and he lifted the duvet back and stepped out into the blur beyond her.
"Alright to go in here?"
"En suite do you mean?"
"Mmm. Is that OK?"
"Of course, why not?"
"Just checking. Didn't want to intrude."
She smiled at his delicacy and lay back again. Shortly she heard the sound of running water. Then he was back, moving about, she assumed dressing.
"Aren't you getting up yet?"
She felt for her glasses at the side of the bed and put them on. He was there at the side of the bed, dressed in his shirt and trousers, looking down at her, so she slipped out of the bed and made her own way into the bathroom, grinning at him as he watched her naked body crossing the bedroom.

When she came back he was sitting on the side of the bed tying his shoe laces. Dressing, she was aware of him watching her, and for the first time felt slightly embarrassed. How strange she thought, to be more conscious of getting dressed than getting undressed. Then briefly

she sat at the mirror to adjust her hair. In the reflection she could see that he was still watching her.
"You're watching me," she said.
"Of course. You're worth watching."
She laughed. "I'm an older woman."
"You're my headmistress."
She turned to him and pulled a face before turning back to the mirror. Then with her hair done, she walked down the stairs, and he followed her into the kitchen, where she put the kettle on to make them a drink.
"Was that your husband?" he said suddenly, indicating the photograph of Guy on the wall. She nodded, waiting by the kettle and watching him stand and turn to look at it more closely.
"Nice looking guy."
Calling Guy a guy was something that had amused them both when he was alive. Now it felt uncomfortable, although she knew he hadn't intended any insensitivity. She let it pass with a quiet affirmative and sat down with him at the table. Something of the guilt feeling had resurfaced though and he picked it up.
"You OK?"
She decided to be honest with him.
"Just feeling a bit guilty."
"Guilty? Why?"
"Part of me still feels married to Guy."
"Was that his name?"
She nodded, and put a hand on his arm resting on the table.
"I know it must seem strange to you. We were married a long time."
"Do you need to talk about him?"
"Not now. I'm not ready yet."
His manner told her he accepted what she said. She did want to talk to him about Guy, but guessed she wouldn't be able to do it without breaking down in front of him, and that was definitely something she didn't want to do. Not now.

Then, all too soon, with one further kiss, he was off into the December night. She waited at the door until he was out of sight before going inside. Suddenly the house felt desolate, just as it had after the funeral wake, when everyone had gone home and left the house to her and Max. Tears welled in her eyes and for a while, still in the hallway, she cried. Was it grief for Guy, or relief that her life was moving forward again? She dried her eyes and walked into the lounge, taking a photograph of Guy with her.

"I've just fucked another man," she blurted out. Astonished, she immediately put a hand over her mouth in disbelief at what she'd said. What am I saying? She looked down at his picture, smiling at her as always, and the gentle, kind Guy was back in her memory. Am I trying to shock you? Why would I want to do that? It didn't make sense.

She lay back in the chair and closed her eyes. In her body she could feel again the movement of being with Patrick. It felt good, she knew it had been what she wanted, and that she would do it again. But where was Guy in all this? She had to find a place for him.

26

"Things seem to be settling down nicely for you Josh Greenwell. No problems with Mac in your classes now."

He was sitting in the corner of the staff room marking a set of books. Len's arrival provided him with an opportunity to stop for a moment, which he didn't mind at all.

"He's noisy occasionally, but nothing I can't handle. Even does a bit of work!"

"First term nearly over. Eventful I'd say, but successful too."

The praise felt good.

"Thanks. You've been very supportive."

"And how's the love life?" he said, sitting down alongside him, obviously wanting to get into conversation.

"Nothing much really. Too busy doing all this."

He indicated the set of books in front of him to illustrate his point.

"Nothing with that young reporter. Rosie is it?"

"You mean Anna. 'Rosie's Read' is the name of her column. No, she's a friend, but I think that's all it is."
"Thought you really liked her."
"Mmm. I do. But I'm not sure what she thinks of me. We're still in contact though."
"Still hope then?"
"Maybe. I'll have to see how it turns out."
Len looked at him quizzically and stood up again, seeming to want to say something else.
"Well, other love lives seem to be flourishing," he said cryptically, "but say no more for now."
He tapped his nose ostentatiously as he walked across to the door, then turned back to him with a knowing look before leaving. The strange throwaway remark was puzzling, but he dismissed it as Len being his usual provocative self and turned back to his books.

It hardly seemed more than a few minutes before Mrs Broad came into the staff room.
"Josh, how are you. I've been wanting to speak to you."
He watched her as she moved across the room at some speed and sat next to him on the same seat Len had occupied. He couldn't help noticing that for an older woman she was good looking. It hadn't occurred to him before and he wondered whether she was wearing something different, but nothing obvious stood out.
"Dr East tells me young Wesley is really improving. He owes his life to you, and he knows it."
She beamed at him, her eyes shining beneath the glasses. He felt embarrassed.
"I only did what I had to. Anyone would have done the same."
"I'm not sure they would. But the point is you did save him, and you can be proud of that."
"Thankyou."
"And you're developing into a good teacher. It's been quite a term."

He thanked her again, and she beamed once more before getting up and moving swiftly to the door as if on a mission.

He put his books down, reflecting that both the head and the senior deputy had between them prevented him from getting his marking finished. He walked over to the window to look across the quiet playground to the bushes where he'd first spotted Wesley. Quite an important observation as it turned out. And rescuing Wesley he was sure had helped him to be accepted as a teacher. Strange how it had all happened. Some people would call it fate.

*

"What does death mean to you Patrick?"

She was lying in his arms, in his bed. Despite the weather having got colder again, it was warm in the bedroom and the duvet only half covered them.

"Were you asleep?" she said.

"No, just allowing my mind to float a bit."

"Did you hear my question?"

"Of course. Honestly, I wasn't really asleep."

He lifted his free arm and put it round her shoulders, but she nudged him.

"Not that one. I asked you what death meant to you."

"Did you?"

"I thought you were asleep."

She was grinning.

"Do you really want to know?"

"Of course. I wouldn't have asked you otherwise"

"It's the end. There's nothing beyond. Life is here. Afterwards – nothing."

"Sounds bleak."

"Does it?"

"Mm. Yes. What's the point?"

"Everything. Being alive. Understanding; especially ourselves. Living fully. Really living."

"And relating to others?"
"Of course. That's one way we define ourselves. Like this. " He grinned, moving over onto his back and smiling up at the ceiling. "This is an unusually serious post coital chat!"
"How many have you had then?"
He grinned again and waited before replying.
"One or two."
He looked at her, feeling smug, and she laughed out loud without saying anything. Instead she got up to go into the bathroom, and as he watched her disappearing into the en-suite, she turned and poked her tongue out at him provocatively. It was his turn to laugh before turning his gaze contentedly upwards to the ceiling, feeling no incentive to move anywhere, wanting to stay in the moment.

He was still lying on the bed when she came back with one towel wrapped around her body and another round her hair. He watched her dry herself with the large towel before bending down to take some clean clothes from her travelling bag beside the bed and get dressed before putting her glasses on as if it was a final act.
"How do I look?" she said.
"Wonderful. My favourite headmistress. Do you know how attractive you are?"
She came towards him, putting one knee on the bed and bending over to kiss him on the lips.
"Patrick."
The tone suggested something else was coming.
"How many lovers have you had?"
"Why do you want to know?"
"Is it really one or two?"
He realised she was referring back to his flippant comment earlier.
"You think I'm well practiced do you?"
She walloped him playfully on the arm and grinned.
"Let's just call it maturity," he said, wanting to laugh it off, but she didn't seem to want to give up.

"I'm serious."
"Why do you want to know?"
"That sounds suspiciously like counsellor speak."
He was beginning to feel slightly uncomfortable.
"Does it?"
"You know it does."
"What if I said 65?"
"I'd say you were boasting!"
"What if it's three?"
"You're just lying. Playing games with me. "
Her tone of voice was different now, petulant in a way that felt unpleasant.
"I don't want us to have a row. It's not helpful. Talk about it tomorrow."
The mood had changed, and he didn't quite know how it had happened. He sat up, suddenly conscious of his nakedness, suddenly feeling less than decent. He hurried into the shower as if it was a refuge and let the water drench him while lathering himself vigorously with the soap.

Later, while they sat in the kitchen having breakfast he wanted to let everything settle and carry on as normal. That he was sure would be the best way. But to his surprise, she didn't let it rest.
"Is this our first row?"
She was looking directly at him. It felt almost like an accusation.
"Are we rowing?"
"What else is it?"
"Slight difference of opinion maybe."
"Patrick. Why won't you be honest with me?"
He thought for a moment, surprised to discover it was a question he hadn't considered.
"The truth is, I don't really know; and I'm embarrassed to have to tell you that."

"What would you say if one of your patients said something like that to you?"
It was a good question. He grinned at her, still feeling embarrassed.
"Ever thought of counselling?"
"Is that an avoidance tactic, Dr East?
"Certainly not." But as he said it he knew really that it was.
"Well then, do you have an answer?"
He felt cornered, and knew he had to make a response.
"I think I'd say something like, 'what might happen if you did know?'"
"So what might happen? To you that is."
"Like a patient anaesthetised and laid out on the table."
"That sounds familiar, but I'm not sure I understand you."
"It's Eliot. Prufrock; a line from the poem."
"Was it a serious answer, or another avoidance?"
He felt pinned down. Laid out on the table, out of control. Exposed. It felt like she was softening towards him, but the intense spotlight was uncomfortable.
"If it's going to be safe for me, risking a relationship with you, I have to know I won't just be another girl friend to be discarded after a few months. You need to understand that."
"I do, I really do. But I have to feel safe too."
"It's not me who's had all those relationships."
"Is that what's wrong? I shouldn't have told you."
"But you have to. It's not the past. It's now. Living in the present, like you said upstairs. I've got to know you're really here, and honest with me."
The words hurt. Instinctively, he could feel she was right, piercing through his defences to a part of himself he thought he'd resolved, but knowing at that moment that however much he said it, even believed it, being completely open still eluded him sometimes. In the counselling room he could do it. There he was always in the present, building the relationship with the patient on the interaction in the room. But what had Laura said? 'I never know what you're really

thinking. I'm not sure I've ever really known you.' Maybe it wasn't just Laura.

"What are you thinking?"
Was she reading his mind? She'd moved her position so she was crouching in front of him and looking up at him through her glasses, which made her eyes look bigger and more open than they actually were. For a moment he returned her gaze before looking down at the grey sweater rippling over the grey skirt and her knees peeping out from beneath.
"Nothing really."
He looked again at the unnaturally large eyes and held the gaze for a moment longer. It felt uncomfortable and important at the same time.
"I was just thinking about what you said."
"I want this to work. I really do. But you're going to have to learn to understand yourself as much as you do all those patients of yours."

*

It occurred to Simon that he hadn't seen his sister Sophie since her wedding, so the reunion at their parents' house for the Christmas period felt quite special. He'd always been able to talk to her, more than anyone else in his family.
"So how's life for you and Jamie now you're a married couple?" he asked her as they sat together round the breakfast table. It wasn't that early, but they were the only two up. She enthused about the honeymoon in The Maldives where they'd both gone snorkelling and ate and drank too much in the evenings.
"Then back to normal life, and a bit of a diet."
Between them on the table was a tin of biscuits. He took one and put it beside his cup.
"And you," she said eventually, "still single?"
It was his opportunity. If he could tell anyone, it would be her.
"Well, not exactly."
"Ooh, that sounds exciting. Anyone I know?"

"Don't think so. I've had a bit of a fling with another violinist in the orchestra. From Poland actually."
"Simon, that's really exciting! What's she like?"
"Actually Sophie, it's he. Stefan. He's a guy."
He watched her face register a moment of surprise. Then she smiled, at first almost apologetically, and then more brightly. It didn't feel forced. His hands were on the table in front of him, and she put both of hers on top of his, still smiling.
"Really?"
"Just a brief affair, yes. It's helped me come to terms with things. Helped me accept that I'm gay."
"Well you know I'm always your sister. Anytime you need me."
She stood up from her seat and embraced him. It felt good, warm. It was what he wanted.
"I've got to tell mum and dad, sometime over the next couple of days. Do you think they'll be OK?"
"It will take them time. Don't leave it too late."
He nodded, and at that moment his mother appeared in the kitchen, wearing a strikingly pink dressing gown and with her usually well groomed hair conspicuously uncombed.
"Goodness, is that the time! I'm never up this late."
He grinned at Sophie. It was a remark they'd heard on and off through their childhood. Hearing it again lightened the atmosphere for them both.
"You two are up early. Catching up on your lives then?"
That too was familiar. They recognised it as her attempt to be let in on the conversation. Sophie came to the rescue.
"Something like that mum, yes. Simon's been telling me about his orchestra and how well they're playing now."
"Oh, I'm so pleased. All that money we spent on your musical education's been worth it then."
He knew she wanted him to be grateful, which he was, but it was hard when he had to keep on saying it. He was tempted to make an offhand comment, but didn't want to cause a problem which might make the

conversation he knew he had to have even more difficult. Instead he let it wash over him, and changed the subject.
"Can I make you a drink mother?"
"Oh, Simon, that would be nice. A strong coffee please dear."

She sat at the table and began chatting to Sophie while he busied himself with the kettle and looked out of the window at the other end of the room. Outside, Napoleon the cat was on a wall, stalking some birds feeding just ahead of him. He watched as the tail lifted, the haunches moved energetically from side to side and the cat pounced forward. Almost all the birds flew off at great speed, but one small sparrow was less fortunate. The hunt successfully completed, Napoleon ran off with it firmly in his jaws.
"Nappy's just caught a bird," he called out.
"Oh, dear, that's always happening. But it's his nature. Nothing we can do about it."
"As long as he doesn't bring it in," said Sophie.
"He won't dear. He'll take it up the garden and eat it probably."
He watched Sophie pull a face and grinned before turning back to the kettle. His mind drifted to Stefan, and he wondered what he might be doing. He knew he'd gone to Warsaw for Christmas. 'Celebrations in *stary miasto*,' he'd told him, 'old town centre, rebuilt completely after Nazis.' Simon didn't think he would be much concerned about the architecture. No doubt he would be finding himself a lover or two for the Christmas break, then come back to England in the new year in search of another. Sex and music seemed to comprise just about everything that interested him. He was just one in no doubt hundreds of men who would flit through Stefan's voracious sex life, but he didn't mind. In a strange way he knew that he'd gained more out of their relationship. Stefan perhaps wouldn't even remember him in the years ahead, whereas he could never forget his first lover. He'd changed his life and that would always be special. His own life stretched ahead of him. He felt nervous, but it was exciting too.

"Hasn't that kettle boiled yet?"
It had, and lost in his thoughts he'd ignored it. He set about making the coffee. His father came into the room carrying his copy of The Independent and stretching as he sat at the table.
"Coffee for me too Simon, there's a good chap."
Suddenly it occurred to him. Was this the moment? Both of them there together with Sophie to support him? It seemed too good an opportunity to miss. He put the coffees on a tray and carried them to the table where they were sitting, gave the drinks out and took his place at the table.

Stirring his own drink for longer than usual, he weighed up how to manage it. His father was opening out the paper, getting ready to read it. If he didn't act now, the moment could be lost.
"I'd like to talk to you all," he said.
His father looked up, surprised. His mother put her coffee down and looked at him.
"Do you want me to stay here?" Sophie said, unsure.
"I'd much rather you stayed."
She gave him an encouraging look and stretched out her hand to his reassuringly for a moment, which his mother noticed.
"Has something happened?" she said.
"Not exactly, but I need you both to know something." He stopped, not quite sure how to continue. They were both looking at him and waiting. There was no way back now.

"Over the past month or so, I've had an affair."
"Well what's wrong with that? Not as if you're married or anything is it?"
"Dad, just listen, please." Sophie was helping him out.
"The affair's finished now. It was with another man."
There was silence. He looked at his father, reading an internal struggle between his liberal conscience and the old fashioned stance he knew he actually took on so many things.

"Another man?" His mother looked as if she really hadn't quite understood.
"Simon's telling us he's gay mum. And as far as I'm concerned, it makes no difference. He's still the brother I love."
He wanted to hug her again, but stayed in his chair, allowing his parents to come to terms with what he'd said. There was another silence before his mother spoke again.
"Yes Sophie, that's right. He's still our Simon." She stood from her seat in the bright pink dressing gown and came round to his side of the table to give him a hug. As he responded, he could feel tears of relief in his eyes. His father was standing too, stretching out a hand to shake his almost as if he'd just won a prize or something. He let go of his mother and took his father's hand willingly.
"Same goes for me son. No difference."

Then it was Sophie's turn to hug him again. He felt overwhelmed with relief as much as anything, but the silence that followed felt uncomfortable again until Jamie, with impeccable timing chose that moment to come into the room. Oblivious of any atmosphere, he wanted to know if he was too late for breakfast. Then, noticing his mother-in-law's dressing gown, he couldn't help commenting.
"That pink dressing gown is . . . . well, quite something."
Simon couldn't miss the opportunity.
"Isn't it. I'm thinking of getting one myself actually."
He waited for the joke to penetrate. Sophie got there first, then his parents. Jamie laughed too without knowing quite why.

27

She was asleep in her usual chair when he went in on Christmas morning, so he walked straight through to put the kettle on before coming back into the living room to see her.
"Happy Christmas mother."
There was no answer. Around her chair were a few Christmas presents she hadn't yet opened. He wondered if she'd sat down in the chair

with a view to opening them and had then fallen asleep. In any event the sleep seemed to be a sound one. Maybe she didn't sleep very well the night before. Maybe she kept thinking she heard Santa's sleigh bells he thought, laughing to himself at his own unspoken joke. She was fully dressed, so she must have got up and sorted herself out. Yet strangely there was no evidence of her having made herself a drink, or any kind of breakfast. He knew she seldom ate much first thing, but this seemed unusual.

He went closer, but still she didn't stir.
"It's me, Patrick," he said, and then a few moments later, "can you hear me?"
For the first time he felt anxious. It didn't seem possible to rouse her. Yet she was obviously breathing; deep breaths, in and out, in a slow rhythm. He felt her pulse. Possibly less strong he wondered. With his interference she would surely have woken. Was there something more seriously wrong? He spoke to her again, more in a kind of desperation than with any expectation of a response. For certain now he knew she needed help.

Trying not to panic, he walked across to the telephone and began to look for her telephone book to call the doctor, until it occurred to him it was Christmas Day and no one would be there. A simple 999 call would be more appropriate. He could feel his hands trembling as he picked up the receiver of her old phone and pressed the nine button three times. It was something he'd never done before. Always in the past he'd contacted specific services. This was different and urgent. So worried was he now that he struggled to give the information the woman at the other end of the phone asked for, forgetting for a moment the house number and then muddling up the post code. Eventually he managed to do what he had to do and put the receiver back on the base.

A feeling of helplessness overwhelmed him. All he could do now was wait for the paramedics to arrive. He thought about making the tea, but knew he wouldn't be able to drink it in his anxious state. He sat down in the chair opposite where she was sitting and looking, he thought, surprisingly peaceful. Was this the end? Was she going to die? Was this finally going to be the end of the aged P? He knew one day this moment would arrive, but it was always a few years away. It was a shock he hadn't expected. His mother was in trouble and it was Christmas Day. He could feel his body struggling to contain the fear, and he couldn't keep still, so the sharp rap on the front door was a relief as well as a further shock.

He let in two paramedics, a man and a woman, and watched in a kind of stupor as they began to examine her, and had to be asked twice what her name was. Everything felt unreal as they gently searched for any responsiveness in her, before the male paramedic hurried outside and returned with a stretcher. He answered a few basic questions and discovered where they were taking her before the ambulance drew away. Neighbours at their doorways were watching as he set off on the familiar journey he'd never expected on Christmas morning.

It surprised him that his impulse wasn't to drive as fast as possible. It was as if inside him an inner calmness had risen to the surface, over-riding the feelings of anxiety and panic, and he could once more think clearly. The change simply welled up from within him. His breathing steadied. It was almost as if he'd sat in on one of his own counselling sessions and was now putting it into practice.

The roads were almost completely clear. Only through the town were there any pedestrians about. Two young men in party hats like leftovers from the night before staggered across the road in front of him, supporting each other and waving to him meaninglessly as he stopped at a traffic light. An older woman hurried along the pavement beside him on some unknown quest. Otherwise there was no sign of life. The clock on his dashboard told him it was 09.33 as he pulled off the road into his usual place in the hospital car park. A nurse greeted him as he entered the building, showing no apparent surprise at his presence on Christmas morning. It was a disorientating experience to be on the receiving end of the hospital's complicated bureaucracy, but his calm didn't desert him.

He sat down waiting for news, unable to really concentrate on anything. Christmas had never been a time of year he enjoyed, and this year seemed unlikely to be any different. Liz wanted to spend it with Max and later with her sister. He declined the invitation to 'call in.' It was too soon to intrude on her Christmas plans. He hadn't even met Max and doubted whether he even knew of his existence. The visit to see his mother was going to be his only contact with anyone. Now he was spending it on a hard chair in one of the waiting rooms of his own hospital. Fleetingly it occurred to him he might go to his office and catch up on some paper work, but he soon dismissed the idea as unrealistic. It seemed heartless, even to him. He needed to be available when someone came out to report on whatever tests they might be doing on her. And in any case, he'd never be able to concentrate on work.

Even the volunteer shop was closed for Christmas day, so he made himself a barely drinkable coffee from the automatic machine and sat with it warming his hands. Only the occasional porter and nurse passed through. It felt quite surreal to be there. He checked his messages. There were two. One was an advertisement. The other was a happy Christmas from Liz, a return message from his, with a smiley face and two discreet kisses. For a moment he smiled. Should her text her back with his news? He thought about it. Did he want her sympathy via text? Would it spoil her Christmas? In the end he decided on a scaled down version: 'Mother not too well this a.m. Taken her to hospital for check up. P.' That would do for now. The reply came back quickly: 'Hope she's OK. Speak soon. Liz x.' Even that helped. It was some kind of contact as the wait went on.

The hospital chaplain walked through, looking more resplendent than usual and acknowledging him with an ostentatious hand wave; a fatuous man, spreading Christmas cheer. He wanted nothing to do with any kind of organised religion. He was with Marx on that one: opium of the people. Except it wasn't even that anymore. Why have religion when you can have the real stuff; at a cost of course. Coming to terms with death was the ultimate challenge of life. It was the end of the personal journey. What mattered was to make that journey as meaningful as possible.

He was so deep in thought he didn't notice a nurse standing in front of him.

"Mr East?"

"It's doctor actually."

Why did he say that? He hated it when others did it. Was he really as bad as them?

"I'm sorry sir, I didn't realise."

"No, no, it's quite alright. I'm sorry I said that."

She looked at him perplexed for a moment by the mixed message before continuing.

"The doctor would like to see you now, sir. Please follow me."

She led him along a corridor and into a side office where a young Asian looking man he had never seen before sat behind a desk.

"This is Dr East, Mrs East's mother, doctor."

She ushered him in and then left, leaving him with the doctor.

"You are doctor?"

"Of psychology, yes. I work here, but not exactly medical."

"I see. Please take a seat. I have to talk to you about your mother."

"Yes of course."

He sat down, feeling disorientated and waited for the doctor to speak.

"Your mother has almost certainly had a stroke. She has not regained consciousness. Until then,"
He paused. Patrick waited. It looked as if he was unsure how to say the next part of his message.
"I should say if she regains consciousness. She is eighty eight, yes?"
He nodded in agreement and waited.
"We have to accept that she may not. Another stroke is also possible at her age."
"I see. What would that mean?"
"You want me to tell you directly."
"Please."
"She may need life support. She might not survive."
"I see."
"We will just have to wait and see how things develop. I'm sorry to have to tell you this."
He smiled apologetically and stood, standing and stretching out his hand to shake Patrick's. The interview was clearly at an end, and Patrick stood to shake his hand.
"What happens for now?"
"We will keep her monitored. Keep you informed."
"Can I see her for a moment?"
"Of course."
The nurse who had brought him into the office was now waiting outside again.
"Please take Dr East to see his mother."
"Thankyou doctor."
"Not at all."
A nurse collected him and led him to a ward, and within that to a side ward. Inside, propped on a bed, was his mother, looking peaceful, but with drips and tubes everywhere. The nurse smiled almost as if apologising before leaving him with her.

He sat down on the chair beside the bed. It was quiet, and he could hear her breathing, shallow but regular. Should he talk to her? Would she hear him? He didn't think so. Briefly, he took the hand nearest to him. It was wrinkled and bony, a very old hand. It felt alien, so he placed it by her side again feeling uncomfortable. He looked at her face, lined with age, and the thinning grey hair. This was the mother who had born him and brought him up alone when the father he'd never known disappeared in the war. He couldn't have survived without her, but there had been no real closeness. Keeping her at a distance had allowed him to be a dutiful son. Calling her the aged P was distancing too. It was safer like that. Otherwise it felt like she would suck him into quicksand, where as hard as he tried to pull his boots out the more stuck they became, and he could imagine himself slipping further and further down until his head went under and he drowned. The thought made him physically shudder.

But what had that cost him? How much had it interfered with his relationships? More than he cared to admit maybe. Had it affected his life with Laura, and with other women since? Was that what Liz was trying to tell him? He looked back at his mother, lying quietly on the bed. How could such a frail woman have had so much power over him?

He had no idea how long he'd been sitting with her before the nurse was back. He stood up.
"You'll call me if anything changes?"
"We will, yes."
"Thankyou."
He nodded before leaving the room and making his way back to where he'd parked the car.

Liz rang shortly after he got home. When he told her what had happened she wanted him to go round. At first he still wasn't sure whether he should go.
"I thought you wanted to spend Christmas day with just you and Max."
"But you can't spend Christmas Day on your own now."

"I've done it before."
"But not like this. Please. I want you to come."
He looked around him at the bareness of his own house. He really did need to get out.
"You sure it's alright?"
"Yes. Come when you're ready."
"But what about Max?"
"He'll be OK. Don't expect him to say much though."
It was a relief to give in. He needed company; especially her company.

There was a bright Christmas tree in the centre of her lounge.
"Max decorated that."
"All of it?"
"Oh yes. He isn't always on the computer. Just most of the time."
"He's done a good job."
"He can be very creative."
"Where is he now?"
"On the computer of course! He'll be having Christmas dinner with us. Then his friend is coming round and they'll probably go on the computer together. I've bought him a new game," She put her hand on his arm. "You'll meet him later."

It worked out how she'd said. Max was friendly but a bit distracted at the Christmas dinner.
"I guess you really want to get on and play your game," he said, wanting to communicate.
Max nodded and smiled, taking another large mouthful of food.
"What time is Neil coming round?" she said.
Max grinned, unable to speak for a moment, his mouth too full. Eventually he managed to say 'three o'clock' before taking in yet more of his dinner.
"Well you don't have to rush. It's only quarter past one now."

Neil arrived just after three, and they disappeared into Max's room. They sat together on the same sofa and he told her what had happened. Sharing it felt important. At some point his eye was drawn to the tinsel around each of Guy's photographs. She saw him looking.
"Max did that. He likes to decorate his dad's photo. It's the second Christmas he's done that."
"Nice touch," he said, not quite sure if it was what he really thought.
"You still haven't told me what happened," he said.
"Another time maybe."
"Well, I've offloaded to you. Maybe it's a good time for you to tell me about Guy. You've told me, kind of, that he was quite ill at the end."
He was aware it was one of his counselling type invitations, but she didn't pick it up. Just stood and walked to where the wine bottle was.
"More?"
He nodded his agreement, and she brought them across a glass each. For a short while they sat in silence. He was conscious of waiting, leaving the initiative to her whether she said anything or not. Eventually, she began speaking.

"I don't know how he kept going for so long. So much spirit. He just wouldn't give up even though he knew he was dying. He talked to me about what might happen after he was gone. Wanted me to find someone else once I'd got over him. That was hard. Then one day he came home and told me he'd nearly knocked a girl off her bike. Probably fell asleep and lost control of his car for a moment, maybe because of the drugs he was on. It scared him. That's when he knew he couldn't keep going. Next day he was admitted to hospital. I think he gave in then. Each time I went to see him he seemed more distant, less able to communicate with me. Almost as if I was a stranger he'd met briefly somewhere. Now I think it was his way of detaching. At the time it upset me a lot; like he was disappearing before our eyes. It was hard for Max.

A week later I got a call at four in the morning. They thought I ought to go in. It was strange – unreal. I didn't just get dressed and go, I got into the shower first. Sort of denial of the moment probably. When I was drying the phone rang again. I needed to come straightaway they said. I got Max out of bed and into the car. When we got there he was no longer conscious, just breathing heavily and infrequently, almost stopping and then picking up again. It went on for what seemed like ages. I just sat on one side of the bed and Max on the other. We kept talking to him. It didn't look like he could hear us, but the nurse said the last sense to go was hearing, and I wanted him to know we were there with him at the end. I told Max that daddy was about to go to Heaven. I wanted him to have something positive to hold onto. He wanted to know what it was like there and if we could visit him, but I just said we didn't know. I was trying to hold back my feelings because of Max, but every so often I had a terrible urge to scream out. Max kept looking at me and checking me out. I'm sure he knew how distressed I was inside.

It got light outside. The window beside his bed must have faced east because I could see the sunlight streaming in. It seemed completely incongruous to me that it should be so bright outside when inside something awful was about to happen. I just couldn't make sense of that in my head. Eventually, about nine o'clock, he took one breath in and then let it out really noisily. I waited for the next breath, but it didn't come. It must have been a minute or more, and still nothing. I panicked, calling out for the nurse. Max looked at me wondering what was wrong, but I was so upset I couldn't comfort him. One of the nurses came up to me and I just pointed at Guy. She checked him over, looked at me and just nodded. I won't forget that nod. It confirmed everything I'd feared for so long. She straightened him in the bed, checked that his eyes were closed and put his hands together in front of him. Then she did a lovely thing. She took Max with her on some excuse I can't remember, pulled the curtains round the bed and left me with Guy for a few minutes.

I sat beside him and took one of his hands in mine. Then something bigger than tears seemed to well up inside me. Something quite primal just came out of me and I howled out loud. I've no idea how long that lasted, but I was completely out of control. I couldn't stop myself. My lovely, wonderful Guy, after thirty years together, was gone. Eventually I gained some control. Max came back inside the curtains with me. We just sat there with our arm around each other crying together."

Throughout her story, he sat quietly next to her, holding her hand, not wanting to interrupt. Now she seemed to have come to a stop. He let the silence hold for a while in case she wanted to say anymore, but she didn't. After a while she looked round at him and muttered something like sorry.
"I've not told anyone that before," she said, "not like that anyway."
"It's OK. I'm glad you have."
"We were very close, a great partnership. I didn't believe there would ever be anyone as good again. You see why I have to be sure."
He nodded, wanting to reassure her, trying to follow his own advice of being present in the moment without falling into the counsellor role. But somehow what she was saying made him feel uneasy.

"That night was cold and starry, and there was a full moon. I looked out of my bedroom window at the moon and stars and found myself wondering where Guy was. 'Where has he gone now?' I remember asking myself. It was a real question; not rhetorical. I couldn't believe he was no more. I still wonder about that sometimes. I know you find it hard."
"For me, there is no God and no existence after death. We're animals; all living things die. It's inescapable."
It felt hard to say that after what she had just been telling him and afterwards he wished he hadn't been so brutal, but she seemed to be able to accept it.

"It's not difficult to understand though how humans all through recorded history have needed some kind of belief system. I know I did after Guy died. It feels less important now, but then I had to hold onto something."
He nodded. He could accept conscious awareness of delusion as opposed to blind faith. But it wasn't that simple.

"I can't accept people just die and disappear," she said.
It felt like a challenge. He wasn't quite sure how to react. He waited for her to continue, falling back on what he would do in the counselling room.
"I wrote a poem this weekend."
"I didn't know you wrote poems."
"Not often. Times of change in my life. Ways of making sense, understanding me."
"Do you want to show me?"
"If you like."
He watched her walk across to a drawer and take out a sheet of paper. As she came back towards him there was a tentative smile in her eyes which made her look very vulnerable. She handed him the paper. On it was a finished handwritten version of a short poem. He read it while she sat on the edge of the sofa, next to him.

FULL MOON

A clear night sky
and a full moon
are always you.

Sometimes, on such a night
I feel your ghost
gliding softly through me.

There's no anguish now.
Only gentle warmth
and a reassuring presence

As if death was never more
than your sweet breath
on a moonlit night.

He read it through twice before saying anything. Finally he turned to her.

"It's very beautiful."

"I thought you would struggle with the idea of a ghost."

"I thought of it more as the spirit of a person that lives on after them," he said, "through those that live on."

She smiled. He could see that she looked relieved.

"I'm glad you understand."

"It's about Guy of course."

"Yes, but more. About moving on. About finding where Guy fits in my life now."

It felt uncomfortable. Her relationship with her dead husband was still hard for him. It felt like however hard he tried, the shadow, or ghost as she put it, would still be there. He would never have believed that he could be jealous of a dead man.

"I don't understand," he said uncertainly.

"I can't just forget about him, pretend he didn't exist. I need to make sense of it. Moving on takes time. Surely, doing what you do you should know that."

He could see she was hurt, but he was struggling to grasp why.

"It's so much easier with my patients," he said, almost as much to himself as to her.

"But don't you understand. It's because of you, because of us, that I can move forward. You have to see that. When we first met, when we kissed for the first time, it felt like I was two timing. At least it's not like that now."

"Two timing?"

"Yes. Like I was still married to Guy, but having an affair with you. You've just got to be patient with me if you want this relationship to work."

He let the idea sink in, trying not to struggle against the strangeness of it. They sat together in silence for a while, and he was aware of her looking at him. He looked again at the poem, which he had laid down beside him.
"Is Guy still a reassuring presence?"
"Yes, absolutely, in here he is."
She held her right hand across her breast.
"In the days before he died, he told me he hoped I would find someone else one day. I didn't believe that would happen. Not till I met you. Now he's like a long gone friend, still helping me to move forward with my life. Surely that makes sense to you."

He held out his hand towards her and she took it and as she did so something inside him seemed to shift and he knew all at once that Guy wasn't any kind of threat to him. The only real threat came from inside himself. It was in his power to destroy the relationship or to allow it to develop, not in Guy's. He looked at her and nodded. She released her hand from his and wrapped her arms around him. He responded in the same way and for some reason his eyes filled. He tightened his grip round her, not wanting to let go.

"I'm a slow learner," he said eventually, "you'll have to allow for that."
"As long as you do learn," she said, breaking the contact and looking at him again.
He knew his tears would be apparent and he felt embarrassed, tried to hide by looking away, but she noticed.
"The Japanese say that only a true warrior cries," she said.
Her words released more tears, so that she took him back into an embrace that was almost maternal, and he allowed himself to be comforted in a way that felt entirely new. Inside he knew that he was changing in ways he didn't yet understand. It felt welcome and scary at the same time.

28

"I'd like to introduce Leticia Niveau who joins the languages department as a student this term."
A nervous looking young woman wearing a grey sweater and a black skirt sitting uncomfortably on one of the upright chairs responded to the head's introduction with an attempt at a smile and a murmured hello. The accent was distinctly French. Josh found himself wondering how she would cope with some of the louder boys in the school; and how they would cope with her.

"How are things going with you and that journalist," Len asked him after the briefing.
"We're still friends. Nothing more at the moment."
"Still interested? In something more I mean."
"She's a fascinating woman."
"Is that a yes?"
Josh didn't answer, merely flapping his arms inconsequentially.
"Helps to know what you want." He performed one of his exaggerated Groucho smiles before walking off.

The French girl was standing by the notice board scrutinising it. He walked across to her, wanting to make contact.
"I'm Josh, English department. Everything OK?"
"Yes, I think so. I am told to wait here and I will be taken to the French department."
"This is your first practice?"
"In England yes. In France I 'ave taught 'istory and English."
The accent was very noticeable.
"Well, I hope you enjoy your time here. If you need any help just ask."

He made his way to his classroom to call the first register of the term, aware he had allowed himself to be slightly late. When he got there the sleepy faces told him they'd found it as hard to get out of bed as he had. A couple of girls were gossiping animatedly, but the usual hubbub was absent, and most barely answered their names when he called them. Trying to get the group engaged in telling him about their Christmas holidays had fallen flat and no one laughed at him when he asked what Father Christmas had brought. They would wake up later, he knew. By the afternoon the challenge would be to stop them talking too much but they sauntered off to their first class like zombies.

He felt like he was trying to wind himself up like in one of those dreams where his feet felt like they were stuck in concrete, but the feeling gradually diminished and as the morning progressed he warmed again into his role. By lunchtime when he found himself dealing with a Year 8 girl in tears because her dog had died over the weekend he was back into his stride and felt as if the holiday had never been. By the end of the last lesson he felt really tired, more like he'd been working for a whole week rather than just one day, but he told himself he would mark the holiday homework he'd collected before going home. He made himself some tea and sat down with the pile of books in front of him.

As he was opening the first one, Leticia came in and sat down in a chair near where he was sitting.
"Are you tired?" he asked her.
"A little, yes."
"First day is always tiring."
She nodded. In her hand she had what looked like a text book. As he watched she crossed her legs and began reading it. In the process her skirt rode up a little, attracting his attention. He tried not to be obvious, but despite his best efforts, his mind was no longer fully on the exercise books in front of him. At one point she looked up to see him glancing across at her, and feeling slightly compromised, he felt he had to say something.
"Not my favourite job. Marking I mean."
She smiled. "I know what you mean."

"Your English is very good."
"Thankyou. I am trying 'ard to perfect it."
He smiled back, reflecting that her English was a lot better than his French, or even his Italian.

His mobile phone told him he had a message, and he opened it. Anna. His heart skipped a beat. Nothing for a few days and now just as he was ogling a French girl, she'd contacted him.
Happy New Year to you. Anna x
It was 5th January; a bit late, but better late than never. His text had gone to her on New Year's day. He looked up to see Leticia gathering her things together, preparing to leave the staff room. She gave him a friendly wave and he waved back and watched her walk out of the door. With the distraction gone he could get on with his marking.

Except he was now thinking of Anna. At least she was thinking of him. But why did she still matter? He conjured her up in his mind wearing the little black dress she had worn at the wedding party back in the autumn. She'd attracted him, but she was also rude and offhanded, as she was when they'd bumped into each other again at the clay pigeon shot. That side still existed in her. But after their last meeting when she told him about Auschwitz, he also knew there was much more. She was interesting, and hard to get; quite a combination. Was it worth bothering? Why not pursue the French girl, see if he could have fun with her. Good looking and probably sexy. Why not? But perhaps that would be too easy. Like in the night club; he'd held himself back there. Sex mattered, but not like that, not with a pick up. It wasn't what he really wanted anymore.

He looked at the clock; half past four. He got out his phone, opened up Anna's number and pressed the dial button. He let it ring once, and then suddenly he wasn't sure and cut the call. He stood looking at the phone. Should he or shouldn't he? Did he have the courage? Maybe yes after all. He was about to try again when the phone came to life

and with the ring tone the inscription *'Anna R'* came onto the screen. He answered.
"Is that you Josh? Did you just call me?"
"Er no, well yes, I wasn't sure if . . ."
"Is that no or yes?"
Courage. That was what he needed. Be straight.
"Er, yes, I did try. I wanted . . ."
"Yes."
"I wanted to know maybe if you'd like to go, well, sky diving."
It was the first thing that came into his head, something he knew she'd done.
"Why not? You know I've done it before of course."
"Yes, I remember. That's what was in my mind."
"I could book it at the airfield again. Maybe Saturday, if they can fit us in that is."
"Saturday would be great."
"OK. I'll call you back when I've done it."
"Sure. Great. OK."
And with a cheeky 'bye' she was gone.

He cut the call and stood looking at his phone in disbelief for a moment before jumping in the air and flapping his arms like some great bird at precisely the moment Johnno came in, dressed in his football kit and looking flushed and sweaty from running around.
"Practicing for the PE department then?"
Once more he was embarrassed. It seemed to be his lot for the day.
"Just getting a bit of exercise," he said sheepishly.
"I see," said Johnno, obviously not believing him as he walked across to the kitchen area. "You can help me with football practice if you like. Get you fit."
"Not quite me thanks."
"You're all soft, you English teachers."
"At least we haven't got footballs for brains."
"Cheeky young bastard!"

He knew from Johnno's tone he hadn't really upset him.
"Twitter tells me you've taken a fancy to the new French student."
"Not really. She's good looking though."
Johnno was back into the main staff room with his tea. Josh noticed he hadn't offered to make him one.
"Nice legs," he said as he sat down, stretching his own muddy pair out in front of him.

While Johnno sat drinking his tea Josh settled back into his books and it was six o'clock by the time he finished, leaving school in time to catch the bus which stopped outside the school at ten past. At least he could leave his work behind him for the evening as he'd prepared all his lessons for the following day. It was a straightforward journey from the school to where he lived, and it saved him always having to take his car.

He stepped onto the bus to a surprise greeting. Wesley and his mother were sitting together on the seat behind him.
"Mr Greenwell. It good to see you!"
Mrs Freedom, all smiles took her opportunity to tell him how well Wesley was doing now.
"He's a new boy, Mr Greenwell and it all down to you."
"Well I'm sure he's worked hard himself to make progress."
It was their stop. Time to get off. As they passed him Wesley's smile, so like his mother's, seemed to fill his vision. It felt good. They turned to wave him at him through the window as the bus drove off. He waved back, feeling proud to seeing them together looking so happy.

29

The guest conductor for the concert on the second Saturday of January was ostentatious and officious. Simon looked at the raised eyebrows around the orchestra with some amusement. But once the rehearsal got going it was obvious he knew what he was doing and everyone settled down to the task. Nielsen's third symphony, which closed the programme was one of his favourite pieces. He loved the energy of the opening movement and the triumphant almost hymnlike finale. The symphony also required a soprano and a baritone for the beautiful slow movement, so they rehearsed all the other movements first before the soloists arrived and took a break before working on that movement.

Stefan acknowledged him in a friendly way, but the greeting was one that confirmed to him that he needn't expect anything more. It didn't bother him. Stefan was welcome to his threesome, or however many it turned out to be; probably boasting anyway. He gave him a cheery wave without making any attempt to engage in a conversation. His attention was drawn to a large young woman, dressed casually in black. She was big all over, with pink hands, a pink face and a large voice. It didn't surprise him to discover she was the soprano who was also performing the song cycle in the first half.

The baritone didn't seem to have arrived yet. He was feeling a bit sorry for him without having met him yet. His part in the symphony lasted about four minutes, and he guessed only a young singer still developing a career would have accepted the role without any other engagement in the evening. They were just about ready to go in and rehearse when a slim young man wearing a tight pair of blue jeans hurried across to the conductor with all the signs of apologising. He watched, immediately fascinated unable to avoid staring.

"Eyes off, he's mine first!"
He turned to see one of the female violinists grinning at him, obviously as interested as he was. The banter made him feel accepted. It was a benefit of coming out he hadn't expected.
"Suppose he's gay?"
Something completely irrational made him suspect it. But maybe it was wishful thinking,
"You're going to find out then?"

"Do you think I should?"
"Depends how subtle you are. But if he's not, send him my way."
"Perhaps he's bi. Then we're both in there."
"Simon! I can't believe you said that!"
He blushed, shocked himself. The influence of Stefan had rubbed off a bit.
"Sorry. It just slipped out."
"Made you blush, hasn't it."
They made their way back into the hall to continue the rehearsal. She was right. He could feel himself getting warm and loosened his already open collar.

They were going to work on the song cycle first. The big soprano stood centre stage and the conductor raised his baton as if about to start a race, and in no time at all they were into the opening music. She was good, and the conductor stopped them only occasionally. When it was over the orchestra erupted into spontaneous applause. She turned shyly to acknowledge their appreciation. Then it was time for the slow movement of the Nielsen, which gave him the chance to hear the good looking young baritone sing.

Afterwards he could feel energy and excitement racing through him. He made his way directly up to the young singer and congratulated him.
"Thankyou, that's nice of you. I'm Daniel," he said.
"Simon. First violins."
"Yes. I noticed you."
"Really? Third desk, I'm fairly anonymous."
"Oh, I don't think so."
Something about his smile seemed to indicate another layer of communication.
"I was delayed this morning. Everything's been a rush."
Have you got somewhere to stay yet?" he said impulsively.
"Well no, I haven't actually. . . ."

"My flat isn't far. I could put you up . . . ."
"That's very kind. Thankyou."
Although he tried to suppress it, he could feel excitement within him. It was just a friendly offer to a fellow musician he told himself, nothing special.
"We could go back and chill for a few hours before the concert."

They got back to his flat. He took some salad from the fridge and some bread and cheese which they ate at the kitchen table. He couldn't help feeling even more strongly that there were unspoken messages. Eventually it became necessary to organise the sleeping arrangements.
"I could make you up a bed in here, or . . . . you could share mine tonight?"
It felt an astonishingly bold thing to say. He wouldn't have dared before Stefan. There was a second of agonising tension as he waited, and was rewarded with a smile of acceptance. It couldn't have been more different from Stefan.
"I thought you'd guessed." At that moment Daniel looked no more than about eighteen, but he knew he had to be at least in his twenties.
"I haven't slept around much. It's not what I really want."
"Nor me. I'm not very experienced either."
Daniel looked at him surprised.
"Seriously. I've only been out since just before Christmas."
"How did we get to be here?"
"I've changed. I want to be open now. I have to find my true self."
Without warning, he could feel tears leaking from his eyes. His vision of Daniel fractured with them, and he was aware he must be looking at him wondering what kind of man he'd just agreed to share the night with. He pulled a tissue from the box on the small table between the chairs where they were sitting, wiped his eyes and blew his nose as politely as he could, which was still sufficiently loud to be embarrassing.
"Please don't think I do this often. For some reason I feel quite overcome."

He smiled, looking cheekily over the tissue still being held at his nose, and Daniel laughed out loud. It seemed to relieve the tension.
"I'm sorry. I'm not really sure what came over me then. A few things together perhaps. And sitting here with you Daniel is part of it."
"But we hardly know each other."
"I know. It's just realising I suppose, that it can happen. This I mean."
"Picking up someone?"
The words hurt. It didn't feel right, but he didn't know how to say it wasn't what it felt like.
"You might find this strange, but I've never picked anyone up as you put it before."
"I'm sorry, I didn't . . ."
"No, please, let me explain. I've been picked up, but only twice, the only sex I've had. Once a long time ago, one night stand, an accident really. I was naive. Then a short affair with another member of the orchestra before Christmas. That's all. . . in twenty five years."
He could see Daniel looking at him across the space between them, not sure how to respond. In the silence that followed he wondered if he'd said too much, exposed himself too quickly, but enough to push Daniel away before anything happened. The confidence he was feeling only a few minutes earlier was all gone.

"My story's very similar you know. I've had two lovers, neither for long, and I'm twenty four. It's hard when you're shy as well as gay. Oscar Wilde called it 'the love that dare not speak its name.' Seems like both our stories."
He paused for a moment and looked directly at him. Then without any apparent signal, they were both standing, embracing and kissing each other, stepping out of their mutual aloneness and closing the divide between them. Erect and excited, he led Daniel into the bedroom.

*

"This doesn't have to be a one night stand," he said as they lay in his bed afterwards with their arms round each other. His body felt satisfied and calm in a new way, with his energy spent for now. Daniel

turned towards him and kissed him gently on the cheek. Stefan wouldn't have done that, he thought. Either he would have wanted more 'shag', or he would have been jumping out of the bed wanting to do something else. He was energetic and daring and fun and great to be with, but this felt different.
"Maybe not. See how it goes."
But the smile which accompanied the words encouraged him. He stretched his hand out across Daniel's chest and sighed gently. He was in no hurry to get out of bed, even though the concert was just three hours away, and Daniel seemed to feel the same. They lay there together without talking for several minutes. He couldn't stop himself smiling at how strange and how wonderful it was.

Eventually, and reluctantly, he extricated himself from Daniel's arm, lifted both feet over the side of the bed and eased himself upright. On the floor in a pile beside the bed were his clothes. The sight of them made him smile. In another pile not far from his were Daniel's clothes. On top of the pile were his boxer shorts. He picked them up in amusement; the face of a cartoon character grinned out at him. He threw them at Daniel.
"Mickey Mouse pants!"
"My mother bought them for me! Rude not to wear them."
"She doesn't inspect them does she?"
In no time at all, Daniel was out of the bed and wrestling with him. They grappled with each other for a few seconds before falling back on the bed, where the laughter subsided into a sustained kiss. Energy and excitement pulsed through his body. He was unable to hold himself back and Daniel responded. The sex this time was even more overwhelming than before, his whole body and brain absorbed in the expression of his sexuality.

Afterwards they lay quietly together for a few more minutes almost perpendicular across the bed. When he opened his eyes, Daniel was

looking at him. For a few moments and they lay there gazing at each other.
"Did we just make love?" he said.
"I think so."
He stretched out his hand, full of hope, and Daniel responded.
"But now, I think we'd better get up. Concert starts in two hours."
"Bloody hell!"
"Get your Micky pants on."
"Fuck off!"
"No more! Not yet!"
They were laughing like two schoolboys as they moved around quickly, washing and getting into their concert clothes. Then they stood in front of the mirror and inspected themselves and each other.
"A handsome pair if you don't mind me saying so," he said, "and I won't tell anyone what's underneath . . . as long as you fuck me again."
They giggled together, and Daniel threw a mock punch at him. Then Simon grabbed his violin, Daniel made an exaggerated singer's cough and they dashed down to the tube station.

*

He'd never heard of Nielsen, but when Liz suggested it he didn't object, though classical music wasn't something he understood that much. Some of the tunes were fine; the European anthem and that similar sounding tune Neil Kinnock used as a labour party theme in the eighties, but not much else affected him.
"Don't fret Patrick," she said, "You might like it more than you think, and I'd like to go to one of Simon's concerts. He's been inviting me for a while."
"Is he a violinist?" he said
"Yes, how did you know?"
He shrugged his shoulders non committally. "Just a guess. More of those aren't there?"
"Yes. He plays in the first violins."

The orchestral players were making their way onto the stage. They were sitting some way back but he thought he could recognise Simon amongst the violinists.
"That's him," she said, spotting him too, "the one with the blonde hair."
"There are a lot of them," he said.
Then with no apparent warning a violinist in the front row stood and a wind instrument played a long sustained note, quickly joined by the others. A dreadful noise he thought.
"Tuning up," Liz said.
He nodded again. Then it was quiet for a moment before one more violinist entered and suddenly, without him doing anything, the audience applauded. The violinist responded by bowing and then sat in the unoccupied seat at the front of the violins. Again there was quiet for a moment before a youngish looking man with a large crop of frizzed hair entered. Once more there was applause and a deep bow before a silence settled as he stepped up onto a rostrum and lifted his stick into the air. The music began.

"Well, what did you think?" she asked him afterwards.
He knew that something had affected him, especially the symphony, even if he did think that some of the orchestral antics were a bit weird, but he was saved from saying too much by the appearance of a young man coming towards them in the orchestral uniform of black suit and black tie. Liz smiled at the young man before turning towards him.
"This is my nephew Simon, who played in the first violins tonight."
He looked at Simon and smiled in recognition, stretching out his hand, but leaving it to Simon to decide whether he acknowledged him or not. Simon took his hand.
"We've met before. Several times. Patrick has been my counsellor."
"Really, you never told me."
"I didn't want to break confidences. It had to be Simon's choice to acknowledge me."

As he spoke another blonde haired man approached them, carrying a violin in one hand and a bag of some sort in the other.
"Simon! How are things? Good concert, yes?"
Liz looked at the newcomer, already changed from his concert clothes, and wearing low cut blue jeans and a grey sweater revealing his slim figure. He put down what he was carrying on one of the seats, obviously intending to join the conversation.
"Stefan, hello! Yes. This is my Aunt Elizabeth and Patrick my counsellor. Stefan and I have been good friends."
"He is good violinist, and yes, good friend."
"Actually, we were lovers for a while. This is Stefan I told you about, Patrick."
"Only good things I hope! He is good lover," he said, rolling his eyes upwards in appreciation and blowing a kiss in Simon's direction, "and now we move on, but still friends I hope."

Liz watched the interchange with some surprise. The shy Simon she had always known being open about his sexuality and with this flamboyant man was a revelation. She noticed Patrick was smiling with obvious satisfaction. Out of the corner of her eye she spotted another young man approaching them, and when he was nearer she recognised him as the baritone from the symphony. Stefan noticed him too.
"Tonight you are singing well. I like it very much."
As he said this, she watched with amusement as the irrepressible Stefan took the singer in a bear hug and kissed him on each cheek. The singer, obviously less extrovert, smiled, but was clearly uncomfortable.
"Thankyou. Just a small part, but I enjoyed it."
"Small part is good. Without small part is no symphony."
"It was a good opportunity for me."
"Daniel, this is my Aunt Elizabeth and Patrick my counsellor. They were in the audience."
"Stefan was right, you did sing well," she said, reassuringly.

"Daniel and I just met today. I'm putting him up tonight. Saves him travelling back."
Stefan's reaction was immediate and enthusiastic. He stepped back a pace, raised both hands to head height in a dramatic gesture before speaking.
"Bravo! I teach you well my friend. I congratulate you both. *Kochajmy Się*, as our poet says," and aware they were all looking at him without understanding, "It's meaning, yes, 'let's love one another!' Mieckiewicz, our very great poet." He kissed his own hand and lifted it into the air as if to the poet.
The words were a cue for two more bear hugs, one for Simon and one for Daniel, with the obligatory Slavonic kiss.

She watched all this with increasing amusement as the two recipients of the hugs tried hard not to seem uncomfortable, but clearly failed. She could see Patrick, who had been quiet for some time, watching with what she guessed was equal amusement, and probably pleasure.
"You are Russian, Stefan?" she ventured.
Another cue for histrionics. He made a show of looking scandalised and for the first time overtly camp as opposed to dramatic before responding.
"Not Russian, please no! I am Polish, from near Krakow. But now I have to go. It has been pleasure meeting you."
He stepped back, clicked his heels together and saluted to Patrick and Liz before lifting his violin case in one hand, his travelling bag in the other and making his way with some speed to the exit.

"Well, he's certainly quite a character," she said, following him out with her eyes as he went.
"He was fun to be with. Taught me a lot," Simon said, and then realising the potential interpretations in what he said, coloured up. She noticed that he looked as if he wanted to hide somewhere. Polite laughter helped to cover his embarrassment as they made their way to the door.

"Well thanks for coming to our concert. Glad you enjoyed it, and good to meet you."
"Good to meet you too Daniel, and nice to see you again Simon."
They all shook hands. Simon and Daniel made their way to the entrance and went off towards the car park, where Daniel was giving him a lift back to the flat in his car.

Only after they'd gone did she feel able to look at Patrick, and as soon as they did their laughter for a while was uncontainable.
"We shouldn't be laughing really. I'm sure he's been good for Simon. You wouldn't believe how shy he used to be when he was growing up."
"I suspect that other young man, the singer, will be good for him too. I guess he'll be ready for someone like that now."
"That's quite an assumption."
"Well he did imply they were having a relationship."
"Starting one perhaps. But it's early yet."
"OK. Guess you're right. But it's nice to speculate."
She looked at him and smiled again.
"They were certainly an interesting few minutes. But you never know what will happen."

30

The phone call at tea time was disturbing. Somebody from the foreign office telephoning him and wanting to talk to his mother, and then discovering she was very ill in hospital, asking if he was next of kin. How was he to know if it was genuine or not? The distant voice reassured him that a proper identification would be made available to him, but wanted an appointment to see him. After a few irritating security questions, Patrick could get no further information. He put the phone down puzzled and anxious. The reassurance that he wasn't in any kind of trouble was only partly reassuring and didn't resolve any of the mystery. Why should someone from the ministry want to see him, or more accurately, his mother?

The appointment was for the following day. He thought about contacting Liz, but quickly decided that was hardly fair. At least he had no clients booked who would have to be cancelled. His concentration would hardly be at its best, and he knew that in any case he'd struggled recently to keep up the intense concentration needed for counselling. He switched on the television and tried to watch a programme about string theory but failed completely to understand it. Even playing a Miles Davies CD didn't calm him much, and his sleep that night was disturbed. He was glad the appointment in the morning was early and he didn't have to wait long.

By the time the knock at the door came he was very tense. There were two of them; a middle aged man in an official looking dark suit with thinning hair and a long face. Like an undertaker, was the immediate thought that came to mind. With him was a younger looking woman in a grey suit whose face hinted at a smile without quite achieving it. Their passes announced Desmond Price Williams and Sarah Jamieson, ministry officials. He invited them into the living room.

Refusing his offer of a drink, Price Williams began by getting straight to the point.
"We should really be talking to your mother, but as we understand she is very ill and you are next of kin, we will talk to you. Your father Thomas East served in Italy with the eighth army and was reported missing in 1943 we understand."
He looked at Patrick for confirmation.
"That's what I've always understood. I was a baby. I never knew him."
Price Williams looked directly at him, making him feel quite uncomfortable.
"We have recently had communication from the Italian authorities which suggests that the body of your father may have been found."
"May have?"
"We think so, but it hasn't been confirmed yet. It is a very long time ago, and you'll understand . ."

What he was to understand remained unspoken, but the word decomposition entered his head.
"The body was found in a small town just north of Reggio Calabria, deep in southern Italy. We understand your father was in the first wave of landings across the straits from Sicily to Reggio and went missing shortly after that. He was assumed killed in action."
He nodded his acceptance of the detail. Price Williams turned towards his companion.
"This may be upsetting for you . . ." she began.
"It's a surprise, but it's a long time ago."
"Of course. But we do understand this can still be upsetting."
"Yes." His mind was struggling to absorb what he was being told.
"The body . . . your father's body, was of course . . . but a letter was found on his person. It was in a plastic wrapping inside the pocket of what remained of his tunic. It helped us to identify him."
"A letter?"
"Addressed to your mother, Mrs East. The Italian authorities passed it on to us via the British Embassy, and from there our records tracked it to you; or to your mother to be precise."
"How was he found?"
She looked towards Price Williams. It occurred to him she was checking permission for how much she could say. After a moment Price Williams continued himself.
"We don't know the details, but it seems a local priest was out walking in a valley and noticed something unusual. Apparently it was a very wet autumn, and rain had washed earth away. From there an exhumation took place."
He didn't know what to say. It all seemed too much to take in. He sat looking at them, completely lost for words. Eventually Jamieson spoke again.
"Will you be able to tell your mother?"
"I'm not sure if she will recover consciousness. They think she's had a stroke."

Why did he say that? He knew she'd had a stroke. The CT scan had made it very clear.
"I'm sorry."
For a moment he wondered if she was going to pat him on the knee, but in the end all she did was smile at him sympathetically.
"Are you all right?"
"Yes. I'm fine. It's just, well, a shock. Not what I expected."
How many times had he heard a patient tell him they were fine? Now he'd done it himself, and he knew he wasn't.
"You may need to see a counsellor. Talk it over with someone professional," she said gently, but slightly mechanically, as if it was a stock response.
"It's what I do!" he said laughing. He would have called a gallows laugh himself.
"I'm sorry?"
"I'm a counsellor, a psychotherapist. It's my job."
"Then you know how important it is . . . and how to access it we hope."
They both nodded approvingly, but his mind was elsewhere as he began to absorb what he'd been told, wanting to know more.
"Yes, but the letter, can I see the letter?"
Once more Price Williams took over.
"We can't let you keep the original, but the Italian authorities took a copy of it. The original is quite damaged."
He looked in astonishment as Jamieson produced from his file both the original letter, looking very fragile in a plastic wallet, and a version on ordinary paper like any photocopy. He reached out to take them both, looking at them eagerly, but knowing he would need to be in private before reading the letter. He handed the original in the wallet back, but his mind was also moving on.
"The priest who found him. Do you know his name? Can I contact him?"
The woman produced a piece of paper from her folder and studied it for a moment.
"He is called Father Leonardo Morelli."

"The local priest?"
"Of the town, quite a small town I believe, just north of Reggio, where the . . where he was found."
"He speaks English?"
"I'm afraid we don't know that. It's not very usual in southern Italy, but priests are educated, and it's possible he can. We just don't know."
"Can I contact him?"
"We can put you in touch with the Italian embassy. That's the best route."
"Thankyou."
"Well, this is my card. We'll get back in touch with details of how to contact the right person at the embassy. Both of them nodded before getting up to take their leave. He showed them out, feeling dazed, as if something quite large had hit him on the head.

He sat down, taking the photocopied version of the letter, his father's letter and looked at it. There were two sheets of paper. One was filled with a large scrawling handwriting. The other was half filled and signed. It didn't really look like the handwriting he had seen from the few examples of his father's writing his mother had kept. It was scruffy and the lines of writing veered downwards to the right hand side of the paper. But circumstances were clearly very different. He was anxious to read what the letter contained. At the top of the letter he had written his mother's full name and the address. It was the one he remembered from his childhood. 'My dearest Alice,' it began before moving into what he wanted to say.

I am writing this letter to you, not knowing if it will reach you. I am alright, but sometime after our regiment landed in Italy, I got separated from my company. Then I was attacked by a German soldier and knocked unconscious. The next thing I knew I was in some kind of barn, and gradually realised I had been captured by what I think is an Italian family. They are treating me well, I get food and water and clean clothes. No one speaks English so I

can't talk to anyone, but I'm keeping my spirits up. I cheer myself up by thinking about you and about our child. By the time you get this letter and I see you again I imagine he will be born. I say he, because I feel it in my bones that you are carrying a boy. I've been wondering what we might call him. What about Jack, or Tony? I'm longing for this war to be over so I can be released and get back to blighty and see you again. See both of you! I can't wait to take you in my arms and kiss you and our lovely baby.
From your loving husband,
Tom East

He read the letter with amazement. Although it was a photocopy it was obvious the original had deteriorated in the years since it was written, and there were blotches of some kind which he could only assume had come from the original letter. Remembering what it had looked like from the brief sight he'd had of it from the meeting with the ministry officials it was hardly surprising. The father he never knew was coming to life on the page in his hand, giving some kind of reality to the shadowing figure who had only been in his life previously through his mother's memory. It was hard to grasp, and reading about himself as an unborn child felt very strange. At least his father was right about him being a boy, something he could never have known for certain. There was an old fashioned reserve about the letter. He knew it was the style of his father's generation, but the distancing of the feeling was something he would have tried to break down in the counselling room.

It felt surprisingly uncomfortable. How much like his father was he really? He picked up the letter again. He had no one to talk to, but he was keeping his spirits up. What must that have been like? And how long was he in what must in effect have been like solitary confinement? What did that do to him? And then he became conscious of the big question the letter posed. How did he die? Found in a valley, Price Williams had said. He needed to find out, follow up the contact at the Italian embassy they were going to give him, maybe even go to Italy and find the priest. But first he needed to tell Liz.

*

Max picked up the telephone.
"It's Patrick for you, mum."
He handed the telephone to her and immediately disappeared again to the computer. She listened to his story with growing astonishment.
"That must be such a shock. Do you want me to come round?"
She could feel the tension in him, knowing he would say he was alright, but believing in herself that he needed some support. Should she try to insist?
"I'm fine, really I am."
"What did the ministry people say to you?"
"Said I should make sure I had someone to talk it through with."
"Well doesn't that speak for itself?"

"Yes I know, but they have to say that, it's their job."
"What do you think you would say to one of your patients?"
"I know, but you must be busy, and what about Max?"
"He'll be fine for an hour. I'm on my way."
She didn't wait for him to prevaricate, putting the phone down decisively.
"You'll be alright Max, if I go out for an hour? Patrick's got a bit of a problem."
His murmured reply told her he was already back into the game and that he would hardly notice she was gone. She got her coat on and grabbed her car keys.

When he opened the door his embrace was tighter than she'd known before. She'd been right to go round. He let her take her coat off and then straightaway put the letter in her hand.
"That's a copy. They didn't let me keep the original. It's quite fragile."
Who's fragile, she thought taking the letter from his hand and reading it. He stood next to her and let her finish before speaking.

"It makes me feel quite emotional," he said.
"Are you surprised?"
"Well not really, I suppose. Why don't we sit down?"
"Do you want to talk about it?"
"Yes, I think so."

"This is from your father," she said, holding the letter out once they were sitting together on his sofa. "It's a massive shock, surely."
"'Lost in action' is all I've known till now. I've wondered about that every so often in my life. Now I might be able to find out what happened to him."
"Do you wish your mother was able to know this?"
"I don't think so, not really. The shock would have been very big."
"Big enough for you."
"Yes."
He looked pale and withdrawn, more shocked than he was admitting, or even realised perhaps.
"So what do you want to do now?"
"They're going to put me in touch with the Italian Embassy. I have to wait till they contact me."
"When will that be?"
"I don't know. Soon I guess."
She didn't quite know what to say, so she leaned towards him and stretched out a hand. He took it in his and squeezed hers. She looked at him and smiled and as she did so she could see the composure drain out of him. She leaned forward to embrace him again, but he moved back, resisting her.
"You don't have to be strong all the time."
"It feels like I need to be . . . for now."
"Do you want to come back to my place? Stay for the night?"
"What about Max?"
"He'll be alright. He knows we're friends."

There was a moment's pause. She thought he would refuse, but he nodded his agreement. The wall may be coming down, she thought to herself.
"I'll just get some things."

When they arrived, the sound of computerised action told her Max was still involved in his game.
"I worry about him sometimes. Always on that computer."
"Isn't that what most lads of his age are like?"
"Seems so, but it still worries me. Not very sociable."
She went into the kitchen to make him a drink. He turned to look at the bookshelf. A voice behind surprised him.
"Hello."
He looked round to see Max standing in the entrance to the living room, wearing a blue track suit with a white stripe. It looked as if he'd just been to the gym.
"Hello. Your mum has invited me over this evening."
"He's had a bit of a shock. I thought we could cheer him up tonight."
Liz was standing behind him in the doorway. Max turned to look at her.
"Shock? What sort of shock?"
"It's not easy to explain, but it's about his father."
"Oh."
"Would you like me to tell you?" he said.
"Yes, if that's alright with you."
Max's politeness felt surprisingly moving.
"Is it alright if I sit down here?"
"Yes of course."
Max sat himself at one end of the sofa. He sat slightly uneasily at the other end and turned towards him while Liz went back into the kitchen.

"You see, I've never known my father. He died before I was born."

Max sat quite still, looking across the sofa at him with wide open eyes. 'Counsellor' sprang to mind, it's like he's counselling me.

"He died in Italy, during the second world war. Nobody knew where or how. Missing in action it's called. At least that's what I've always thought."

"That's sad."

"But today, I've discovered his body has been found, and it's a bit of a shock really."

Max nodded, but sat quietly without saying anything as his mother came back into the room.

"I've brought you some orange Max, is that OK?"

He nodded again and reached out to take the drink. She handed a cup of tea to Patrick and sat in the chair opposite the sofa on which he sat with Max, who looked like he had drifted into a world of his own.

"I've just got something I need to sort out for school tomorrow," she said, "I'll be back in a few minutes. Can you two talk to each other for a little while?"

Max lifted his arm in a way which resembled a salute. There was a moment of quiet after she left the room before Max broke the silence.

"Did you know my dad died?"

"Yes I did. I'm really sorry."

"It's OK. I've got used to it now."

"Is it three years ago?"

"Eighteenth of January. Almost three years ago." The reply came quickly. "I always remember. You don't know what day your dad died?"

"No. I don't."

"That's sad," he said again.

He smiled at Max. There was another brief silence between them. It felt like they were both coming to terms with the unexpected intimacy of what they were saying to each other. It surprised him that he didn't find Max's openness difficult. He knew that with another adult he would struggle.

"Do you think you've got used to not having a father?" Max said.

It felt like a strange question. The obvious answer was to say he'd never known anything different, but in the pause that followed before he answered it felt like a small window opened inside him onto a more truthful answer.

"No I don't think I ever have."

There was another silence.

"I don't think I really have either."

Sadness. The elephant in the room. Yet only Max had spotted it sitting there between them on the sofa, filling the space. The little elephant eyes seemed to look sadly round at both of them, inhabiting their lives. He was the vast hinterland of loss, and his sharp tusks could attack them at any time whether they acknowledged him or not.

He looked towards Max without smiling.

"Then it's the same for both of us."

"Yes. I try not to think about it too much . . ."

"But it's always there."

Max nodded. "In my class, I'm not the only one who doesn't live with his father. But I think I'm the only one without one."

"Yes, I was too. Long time ago for me. But I remember."

Again there was the nod of understanding. He was sure of that, something quite new.

"Do you think it's good to talk about it?"

"I do, yes. It's what I do for a living."

"Mum said you were a doctor."

"I'm a psychotherapist. Similar, but I try to get people to talk about what's upsetting them."

"Like not having a father."

"Yes."

"And now you're talking to me about it. Like we're sharing it."

"Yes. Do you think that's good? That this is good?"

"I haven't talked about it before. No one at school would understand. But you do."

Max looked across and smiled at him. He could feel a welling up inside himself, which seemed to come from the mutual sharing. He held it back, knowing it wasn't appropriate to cry, burdening Max with his feelings. For a moment he wondered if he was also picking up Max's feelings. And then he knew with absolute certainty that it was both of them. Neither wanted to cry in front of the other. Not yet anyway. But the sharing seemed to have opened up feelings for both of them in a way they hadn't been able to experience before.

Liz came back into the room. The intensity within it struck her immediately, but not as something difficult. She couldn't identify what it was. Patrick spoke first.

"We've had a chat between us. Men's talk."

"Does that mean I shouldn't ask anything about what you've been saying?"

"Men's talk between me and Dr East."

"You can call me Patrick."

"Cool."

Suddenly, almost incongruously, he looked younger, grinning from within his track suit and seeming to nestle into the cushions on the sofa.

"Then I won't ask."

Max grinned at him. It felt conspiratorial .

Afterwards, when Max had gone to bed, she asked him again.

"What were you two talking about?"

"Men's talk!"

"It seemed very intense."

"We just had a brief chat about fathers."

"Really? He's never seemed to want to say anything to me."

She pushed down what felt like an irrationally jealous feeling.

"It's because he's discovered we share something. Or rather we both lack the same thing."

"Fathers that is?"

"Yes."
"You could be very good for him. Take Guy's place."
She could hear his voice in her head from that last Christmas. 'When I'm gone you'll need someone else; for Max as well.'
"He's a great lad you know. He nearly made me cry."
As he said it, the tears he'd held back for so long couldn't be halted any longer, and he found himself sobbing on her shoulder. Something also released in her and as she comforted him, she could feel tears running down her own cheeks. She let them fall, and they shared their feelings together, holding each other tightly until the intensity subsided, and they could separate safely.
"You don't do that too often, do you," she said quietly.
"It doesn't come easy. Lifetime of holding it back."
"It's better for me, much better, if you share your feelings. Max has done you some good."
He blew his nose on an already wet tissue, and she passed him another from the box on the table beside the sofa.
"Were you expecting this?" He indicated the ease with which she found the tissue. "It's like the counselling room." He blew his nose again, managing a laugh. "Max – he's been my counsellor." He wiped his nose and pushed both the wet tissues into his pocket with an air of completion.
"Everything I've done has been around keeping my feelings under control. It's not so easy just to change that."
"Maybe what's happened today can be a turning point. In private anyway. With me and Max."
He nodded and waited for a while before saying anything.
"Tonight I've experienced a sadness that's always been there really. But I've kept it down. Somehow I think Max sensed that, even if he couldn't give it words. Maybe feeling it is the way to healing."
"Isn't that what you do for other people all the time?"
"Physician, heal thyself," he said.
"Who said that? They were certainly right."
"Ye will surely say unto me, do also here in thine own country."

"Is that the bible?"
"Luke chapter four."
"I thought you were a non believer."
"Doesn't mean I don't know about the bible. Anyway, as you've seen, I'm not very good at it."
"Well, you can change."
"Become religious?"
"No! Heal thyself."
He laughed again. The elephant eyes were looking at him.
"Maybe. But it's not easy. Lifetime of bad habits."
"You're never too old to learn."
"That's just an old English proverb. But yes, it is true. In counselling we use an old cliché. We talk about the elephant in the room. Something very big which you haven't admitted, maybe don't know it's there. When I was talking to Max I got a sense of my elephant. Maybe his too."
"And what is your elephant?"
"Max used the word sad. I think for me it's a feeling of loss. It's been there so long I stopped noticing it. That's why it's an elephant."
He stopped for a moment and turned towards her, still sitting beside him on the sofa.
"You must have felt that too."
"Of course. But it's not an invisible elephant."
She moved her arm around the room. He followed its direction and wherever he looked he could see the pictures of Guy, smiley, happy pictures he'd already got used to as part of her house.
"Mine's out in the open. I still talk to him."
"Talk to Guy?"
"Yes. It helps me. I do it less often now, but at first it felt like I had to. I just couldn't believe he wasn't, well, somewhere, that he didn't exist anymore. But enough about me. How are you feeling now?"
"O keep that dog far hence!"
"More quotations? They help you to hide from your feelings you know."

"Maybe. But sometimes they also help me to come to terms with how I'm feeling. Make sense of them. It's been a strange and very emotional day. I just don't want to dig it up again. Not tonight anyway. I need some time to absorb it all."

Later, in bed, she wrapped her arms round him and he allowed her to do it. It felt new and different. There was no resistance.
"How are you feeling now?" she said.
"Better."
The reply didn't feel like denial. It satisfied her and she fell into a deep sleep.

31

Josh sat in the staff room waiting for the briefing. For once he was organised and could sit watching colleagues moving around in various directions finding books and papers for their lessons. Leticia the French student was standing by the pigeon holes talking to another young woman teacher. Her short skirt revealed well shaped legs and his eye was drawn to them. Next to them Len was engaged in some kind of animated discussion with one of the science staff, a severe looking older woman with what seemed like quite long hair held upwards in a bun. Some days he noticed the bun wasn't quite strong enough to hold it all in place and strands gradually released themselves. This morning everything was held in place and to his surprise the teacher was grinning.

He'd already noticed how different a Friday morning felt from a Monday morning. The imminent weekend, just hours away, seemed always to result in a lightening of the overall mood. If there was a gravitational pull at work, it was at its strongest on Monday morning when everyone appeared drawn downwards by the weight of the week ahead, while by Friday the pull was less marked. Perhaps there was some other force lifting people upwards on a Friday he mused fancifully. Maybe it was the winter sunshine easing everyone's mood and revealing the staffroom window hadn't been cleaned since the autumn.

Mrs Broad came in and walked with her usual air of efficiency to the seat she always took for briefing to the left hand side of where he was. Was it his imagination or did she look unusually tired, not really like Friday at all. But when she began there was no hint of tiredness, only her usual efficiency. How did she manage it day in day out? He was sure he would never be able to run a school, not that he would want to. For a moment his mind drifted to the sky diving he would be doing over the weekend with Anna. Maybe this would finally be his chance he wondered, before being sharply drawn back by mention of Wesley Freedom.

"Wesley's mother has telephoned me this morning. His father is apparently back on the scene and he is upset. She wants all staff to be alert in case he seems to be struggling."
A ripple of sympathy ran through the gathered staff and he distinctly heard the word 'bastard' from one of the women near him.
"Let me know if you are worried in any way at all."
He watched as her gaze moved round until she spotted him.
"He might seek you out Josh. Any of you, please make sure you let me know if anything happens."
"I saw him with his mother on Monday," he said. Everything seemed OK then. In fact that's what Mrs Freedom said to me."
"Seems like father is back in the area and called round unexpectedly yesterday. Mrs Freedom has alerted social services, but just wants us to be aware."
There was a murmur of voices as the briefing ended and the staff room chat began again. The bell rang for registration. No immediate movement followed, but within the minute he found himself amongst the last members of staff making their way to their classrooms.

"First week nearly over then."

He was standing with Len in the sunshine at the top of the yard looking down on the scene in the large play area below them. Occasional footballs rose randomly into the air above the endlessly moving crowd of bodies below them. School blazers had been discarded and piled together to create goal posts. Boys ran about with the flaps of their white shirts flailing behind them and blue striped ties at incongruous angles around their necks. Around the edges were girls, still wearing coats and scarves and generally looking tidier than the boys. There was a continuous noise rising up towards them, punctuated every so often by high pitched squeals from the girls when boys ran into them or a football cannoned against someone.
"Like something out of Breughel, except there's no snow."
Josh looked at him, not quite understanding.
"Breughel. Flemish painter. Did lots of scenes of random bodies all over the place. Usually someone pissing against a wall somewhere. Doubt if we'll see that down there, though you never know. Anyway, how are you getting on with that young reporter? Still nothing?"
"Maybe."
"Is that yes or no?"
"Got a date tomorrow. Sky diving."
"Ha! Icarus - Breughel indeed! A boy falling out of the sky."
Connections in his brain from somewhere.
"Is that Auden?"
"Thought you'd know it, being a literary man. So you're planning to fall out of the sky by choice."

He laughed, and as he did so a particularly loud shriek made its way upwards from the yard below them. They both looked down to see a boy chasing after a girl. Len lifted the whistle hanging round his neck and blew it hard. Briefly the noise quietened as most of those in the yard looked up at them. Len gesticulated manically to the offending boy, who stopped in his tracks and grinned at him guiltily.
"Not as subtle as you Greenwell, but he'll learn."

They watched together as the noise quickly rose again to its former level.

“So you’re going to fall out of the sky to win her over.”

He looked at Len laughing.

“I’m not sure I would put it quite like that.”

“What’s the fascination of this woman then? What’s wrong with our new mademoiselle for example? Not thought of making a move there?”

“Well she is good looking. Nice legs.”

“That’s why we’re all here. Propagation of the species in any way we can. No other purpose. We do all this stuff,” he stretched out his arm towards the activity below them, “education and so on, to improve survival chances. But in the end it’s all a biological urge, whatever else we pretend. It’s not love that makes the world go round, it’s sex.”

“A few months ago, before I came into teaching, definitely. But I’ve realised I need something more now.”

“More than sex you mean?”

“If that’s how you want to put it, I suppose so.”

“How else would you put it? I guess you fancy this reporter.”

“Of course. But I’m looking for more of a relationship now.”

Len looked at him quizzically before adopting his Groucho stance.

“Remember, life is what you make it, and as I always say to Mrs Turner, if you don’t like my principles, I have others.”

He mimed taking the usual fat cigar from his mouth and tapped imaginary ash from it onto the ground where they stood. Josh laughed dutifully.

“As for our leader, that may be a different story. But say no more.”

He tapped the side of his nose conspiratorially, and at that moment the warning bell rang for the start of afternoon school. Immediately he was down the steps to the gateway from the yard and ready to patrol the entry to school. Josh followed him in support, but with Len’s presence the progress was quiet and orderly so he made his way into the school amongst the students and back to his own classroom.

Ahead of him in the corridor he could see Wesley talking to another boy. He looked up as he approached.
"Wesley, you alright?"
"I'm OK."
"Can we have a word?"
Wesley didn't answer, but nodded. His friend nodded back to him and walked off.
Walking into his classroom, Josh knew he had just a couple of minutes before his class began to arrive but he signalled for Wesley to sit down, and sat himself in a seat opposite.
"Problems with your dad again?"
"Mm."
"How are you coping?"
"It's me mum more. She's scared he'll do something."
"Has he been round to your house?"
"Last night. Mum rang the social worker and he went away."
"You're not going to do anything this time I hope?"
Outside there was a banging noise and then the sound of feet running away, but he ignored it.
"No sir, I'm alright."
"No jumping out of windows?"
He thought he detected a slight grin, which reassured him.
"No. Social worker said he won't come back."
"Do you believe that?"
"Think so. I'm seeing Dr East again."
Josh nodded as the bell, located just outside his classroom, made them both start, and Wesley laughed out loud, easing the pressure.
"You will come and see me if you need to."
"Thanks sir."
He stood up and walked to the door, then disappeared into the crowd of bodies moving noisily in various directions to their next lessons. Josh sat still, relieved, but still troubled by what Wesley had to carry.
"Can we come in sir?"

The request, more of a shout, from a large girl standing at the door was followed immediately by a squeal as two other girls crashed into her and all three fell into the doorway together. For a brief moment, with his head still involved in the conversation with Wesley, he wanted to shout at them, but suppressed it, contenting himself instead with a disapproving tut. He allowed them to enter noisily and take their seats. They were just kids, doing what kids do.

The classroom began to fill. He drew himself with some effort away from the conversation with Wesley. He knew he was reassured that Wesley was coping and still getting some support, but it was as if the weight of Wesley's father had jumped across the gap between them and settled in his own stomach with a sickly heaviness.

The figure of Mrs Broad walking past the doorway explained why those still coming into the classroom were quiet. A moment or two later she was in the doorway again, her head framed by the bright blue scarf she was wearing. He assumed she had doubled back. She beckoned to him, and he walked across to the doorway.

"I believe you've spoken to Wesley."

Did she have invisible radar?

"Mr Turner said he saw you talking to him."

That was it. Twitter at work.

"I've just seen him. He says he's alright, and seeing Dr East again."

"Good. That's a relief."

She smiled at him warmly before departing the now quiet classroom, and her smile helped to settle the unease in his stomach as he turned back to start the afternoon teaching.

*

"You're seeing Wesley Freedom again?"

"How did you know?"

They were sitting opposite one another at Liz's kitchen table. She'd changed out of what she called her school uniform and was wearing a pair of jeans and a blue sweater. Having just come from his clinic,

Patrick was still in his suit, about to take the first sip from the tea she'd made him.
"Wesley had a chat with the young teacher who rescued him from the Woolworth building."
"His mother rang me last night. Says he's upset and in need of another session, but coping she thinks. I'm seeing him Monday."
"That's what he told my teacher. Worrying though."
"It's hard not to be concerned."
"How do you manage not to bring everything home with you?"
"I don't always."
"Nor me. We have to find ways of taking time out. It's about survival."
"You've helped."
She put her hand across the table and onto his, which was resting by the side of his cup.
"I didn't really think I'd find this again."
She watched him, read his instinctive caution, felt movement in the hand she was still holding. She released her grip and he drew his hand back into himself.
"You don't need to worry. I won't trap you, you know."
"It's not . . . . I am very fond of you."
He stretched out his hand to take hers again. The squeeze made her feel as if she was a life raft. Who's clinging, she thought.
"I'm getting there. It just takes time."
They sat together looking at each other and she noticed he didn't break the gaze.

The shrill ring of his mobile phone disturbed the intense silence. He answered. She watched as his face changed quickly to one of suppressed alarm.
"I'll come now. Yes, straightaway."
He finished the call and stood up. She followed him with her eyes.
"It's the hospital. A turn for the worse. They want me to go there now."
"Do you want me to go with you?"

"No, you stay here for Max. I'll keep in touch."
She wanted to be with him, but it did feel like his vigil. Something he had to see through alone. She nodded reluctantly.
"You will ring me?"
"If there's a change, yes."
She guessed there was only one change likely and hoped he was ready for that.

32

Her head was raised on two pillows when he got there. Her eyes looked more deep set than he remembered and her mouth was half open. She looked impossibly old, emaciated even. Her breathing was harsh and rackety so that he guessed it could only be a matter of time. There was a chair beside the bed so he sat down. In his head the proper thing to do would be to take her hand and talk to her, but he couldn't do that. The body in the bed looked vaguely like his mother, but the filial feelings weren't there and he recoiled from the thought, feeling guilty and inadequate. At least the curtains drawn around them gave him some kind of privacy. It crossed his mind that the space he was in with his mother was almost womblike. Was this some kind of rebirth made possible by her death? It seemed absurd, but the thought lodged itself in his brain.

Suddenly she breathed out more noisily and he waited, wondering if it was the moment, but another inbreath kept the flickering life within her. He watched her like a detached observer, waiting for the end, but still the slow noisy breaths kept her alive. Her hand lay on top of the bedclothes beside where he was sitting. Should he hold it? Outside the noise of ongoing life, human interaction about a bedpan, was taking place. His own suspended existence felt separated from that living world. Could he touch her hand? How would it feel? He hesitated for a moment, then put his own warm living hand on her cold dying one. No response. The breathing continued while he held her.

'The hearing is the last thing to go,' he remembered. It was what nurses usually said. He wasn't sure he believed them. Bedside fantasy, comfort for the living, something that couldn't be disproved. Should he talk to her? What was to lose?
"I'm here mum. It's Patrick."
No response. No change in the breathing, but in his head, the words he'd said, calling her mum after so many years, released a memory.
"I'm here mum, it's Patrick." She is young again, wearing a floral summer dress and he is a boy. Her back is towards him, but she turns around smiling with bare arms stretched out towards him and lifts him from the ground. He can feel the closeness for a moment and the warmth of her skin.

In the bed now there is another sound. A long rackety breath out which then stops. He watched for the next inbreath but it didn't come. For maybe a minute he waited, knowing another breath was still possible, until enough time had elapsed for him to be sure it was the point of no return. He lifted his hand from hers and eased his body back. She was dead. There was no impulse to do anything; just sitting there in the stillness seemed enough for the moment. His own timeless capsule; stepping out would be to move into a new life and for just a while he needed to gather his strength to be sure he was ready. Was he sad? He didn't think so. It felt like a release for both of them. He stood up, looked down on the body that was no longer his mother and smiled. It felt in his head like a gentle smile of acceptance. Life and death.

Suddenly there was someone at the curtain. A nurse coming in to check on things.
"I think she's just died."
A nod, a check. Pulse, breathing, another nod.
"I'm sorry Dr East."
"Thankyou."
"Do you want to stay with her for a while?

"No. It's alright. Do what you have to."
Another nod. They both stepped outside the curtain and the nurse pulled it to behind them, with his late mother inside. He was stepping out of the womb.

Outside the ward he sent Liz a text. *'She's gone. Can I come back? P.'* Only then did it occur to him to look at his watch. It was just before ten. His phone rang again almost immediately, and he answered the almost indecent shrill ring.
"Of course you can. How are you feeling?"
"Not sure. Strange."
"Are you OK to drive back?"
"Yes, I'll be fine. See you soon."

She was standing at the door when he arrived, and she took him in her arms once he was inside.
"Max in bed?"
"Yes. Why?"
"Just didn't want to upset him."
She walked him through to the lounge and sat down next to him on the sofa.
"It felt strangely distant. As if I wasn't part of it. Or it wasn't part of me. I don't quite know how I feel."
"That's normal isn't it."
"Yes, I suppose so. I'm having to learn from the inside now what I've only understood externally before; from a counsellor's point of view."
She looked at him, impressed by his honesty but it felt like too hard a judgement. Then feeling it was time for the usual ritual, she went out into the kitchen to make the tea.
"Unless you want something stronger?"
"No tea's fine."

He looked around the room and his gaze settled on a small figureen of a chimpanzee standing on the mantelshelf. When she came back into the room with the tea he wanted to ask her about it.
"Is that new?"
"Max bought it for me for Christmas. Not expensive I guess, but I quite like it."
"Back in the 1960s a psychologist named Harry Harlow did some experiments on baby monkeys, horrible experiments we wouldn't let him do today, but he discovered something really important about animals, which includes us of course. What he did was take them away from their real mothers. They had fake mothers. Some were a kind of terrycloth and some were just wire. They were fed from the wire mothers but it was the terrycloth mothers they always clung to, even though that wasn't where their food came from. That's how they survived, not without long term harm, but they did survive. And there were monkeys without terrycloth mothers at all. They just died."

He was speaking not particularly to her, but as if to some audience somewhere in the room. His mother has just died she thought. Why is he talking about monkey experiments, is it just another distraction activity? He must have read her surprised look, and began to talk to her more directly.
"Max's monkey present made me think about all that, and it occurred to me that's what psychotherapy is. It's the terrycloth mother. People like me, short term, or sometimes longer, putting the caring back in, so people can get on with their lives again."
She looked at him with increasing amazement.
"So counselling is a terrycloth mother?"
"In a way, yes. It can really be the survival kit that makes the difference."
"But what about all the skills you've developed?"
"Oh yes, they're important of course. There's a century of development behind what I do. But at its heart is the caring. It's what Carl Rogers the counselling guru called absolute positive regard. He

thought that, plus a couple of other key things like empathy and being OK in yourself was enough. 'All you need is love,' as John Lennon put it. I don't really think it's as simple as that. But it's what's at the centre of everything."

As she looked at him, it occurred to her that everything that had happened to him seemed to have animated him, almost given him a new kind of emotional strength which made him seem . . . she wanted in her head to say bigger, as if he had grown, but she didn't mean physically . . . . somehow there was a kind of release, a stepping out. Yes, that felt right, a stepping out into a wider sense of who he was. Not really because of what he was saying, but in his whole manner. She hadn't experienced him like this before. He was more open, like something in him had been freed.

"What you do is similar really," he said.
She smiled, wondering what was coming. She was enjoying the man in front of her, on his mission to solve everything.
"No, I'm serious."
"I'm smiling because I like you like this."
He ignored her comment and carried on with his train of thought.
"You have to educate children, that's what it's all about, but you also have to create an environment in which children can learn. Especially those whose home backgrounds don't make it easy for them. Isn't that what you call pastoral care?"
"So I'm a terrycloth mother too?"
"In a way, yes. Like me, there's a huge amount of skill In what you do of course . . . ."
"Of course."
She smiled at him as she echoed his words and reached out to hold his hand. He let her, but still carried on with what he was saying.
"But once someone like you stops caring, stops seeing each one of your children as having emotional needs too, just becomes a

mechanical teacher of facts, everything is diminished, the children don't thrive."

"No terrycloth."

"W.H. Auden said we must love one another or die. That's in a poem dated 1st September 1939. Just as the war began. How many people died in that?"

"Millions." She knew it was a rhetorical question but still wanted to answer.

"Simplistic message, but a central truth of our existence."

She turned towards him and put her arms around him.

"Enough now. You'll exhaust yourself. You need to accept the shock of everything that's happened."

He looked at her. She could see him trying to assess what she was saying. For a moment there was suspicion before he relaxed and accepted her invitation to let his brain take a rest and allowed himself to be held.

"Terrycloth mother?" he said to her.

"Terrycloth mother. It's also called love."

Suddenly, almost from nowhere, the tears that had up till now been elusive began to flow. She could feel him letting her embrace him again and finally it seemed like he was allowing himself to accept her in a new way. She held him tightly as he cried, not with the intense wrenching tears as before, but more quietly, more like a release of feeling than a harsh outpouring. Over his shoulder she could see the picture of Guy, smiling down at her, approving, she thought. Was it really possible to love another very different man? Yes, it probably was.

*

Salvatore asking to see him was a surprise, even a shock. Hardly a stalwart of the congregation and generally sullen, Leo always got the impression he was seen as a poor substitute for his longstanding predecessor Father Luigi. After all, they did share wartime experience. Salvatore was a problem for him; he struggled with the open contempt he showed for Marco, and knew there had been occasions in the past when he'd deliberately tripped him. Unpleasant teasing still sometimes happened and he suspected Salvatore was still encouraging it. In recent months however he'd heard that he was ill, and in his late eighties, was not expected to live much longer. Such circumstances he knew often made even the least religious become more devout, fearing the afterlife consequences. Terrified himself of dying in sin, he couldn't imagine what it must be like for someone like Salvatore. Seeing him felt like a necessary duty; even if it was one which made him anxious and slightly fearful. So it wasn't a complete surprise when he appeared at the vestry door.

"I have to talk to you father," he said gracelessly, "it's like a confession, I have to get it off my chest."
Moving instinctively into his professional and pastoral mode, he nodded encouragingly and sat him down in the vestry to continue.
"The soldier that's been found; I know what happened."
Immediately he felt excited, but kept calm and waited for him to continue.
"After Marco's mother, it's only me who's left who knows what happened. The others are all dead now. She won't tell you what happened, but I'm not going to die with it all on my conscience, and anyway it wasn't me killed him. Carlo, her brother, did that, after what he did to her."
A cough rose from inside him and into his mouth, preventing him carrying on for some time. Leo waited while he collected himself.
"What he did?"
"Shot him. After she told him the soldier raped her. I don't know exactly what happened, and I don't suppose Carlo did either, but that night I knew there was a great commotion. Lots of running about and shouting. Me and three others, all dead now, 'cause we were young men then, got rounded up by her father to do a job he said. Seems like they had this prisoner in the barn for a while. There were rumours, most of us knew there was something strange, but seeing that lifeless

body covered in blood was a shock. We were made to pick him up, carry him down the valley and bury him that night. It was dark. Not long before Christmas."
He was stopped once more by harsh coughing.
"Should never have smoked. Too late to change now though. The stream was running high 'cause there had been a lot of rain, so we had to bury him above the water line, where you found him. Even with four of us digging with shovels it was hard work. At it well into the night we were. Afterwards I was knackered. We were all sworn to secrecy. Told we'd be done for if the story got out. Far as I know it never did. Till now."

He stopped, overcome by another bout of coughing, and it occurred to Leo that the stress of what he was saying must be contributing to how he was. Eventually, he calmed down again and carried on.
"Can I be forgiven father? I've carried that all these years."
"You're telling me you didn't kill the soldier. Just helped to bury him?"
Salvatore nodded.
"Then your sin is not mortal. You can be forgiven."
He could see that the sense of relief in the old lined face was immediate. He led him through to the church, knelt him down in front of the altar and began to pray with him.
"*Santa Maria, Madre di Dio, prega per noi peccatori, adesso e nell'ora della nostra morte*," he began, and with the repetitive cry for forgiveness he knew that the old sinner's burdens were lifting. He could feel the healing grace of Santa Maria entering the church and filling their hearts. It felt very special, and he wanted it to go on and on but eventually he sensed the old man tiring, so he stopped and traced the sign of the cross in the space between them.
"You will need to go on praying for forgiveness yourself, letting the peace of Jesus Christ enter your heart through the intercession of the holy mother. I will pray for you here too, and your sins will be forgiven."
They stood, Salvatore with the sound of creaking in his aged knees.

"The more you let prayer into your life and your heart, the shorter will be your time in purgatory."
He could see a quizzical look on the old face for a moment, and then suddenly it seemed like he remembered the teachings from some far distant place in his mind.
"Thankyou father."
He watched him slope out of the church, coughing, but looking relieved. In the porch outside, he put a cigarette in his mouth, lit it and drew heavily before stepping out into the darkness.

It was astonishing news, but made sense of how the English soldier came to be found at the bottom of the valley. He sat back on a pew at the front of the church and automatically crossed himself before offering his own prayer to the Blessed Virgin. What should he do with the information? And as that thought went through his brain, another even more shocking thought entered it, and he knew he had to go and talk to Lucia.

33

As soon as he was on the plane the feeling he'd been denying during the detailed briefing and then while he waited to be prepared for the jump came surging up into his consciousness. He was scared stiff. Watching Anna's enthusiasm and excitement he wanted to share in it, but something had seemed to be missing. Now it was too late to go back, the force of it hit him fully in the stomach. He wanted to be sick; the last place in the world he wanted to be was the noisy plane that was shortly going to open up and make him jump out into the air thousands of feet above ground. How could he have been so stupid as to suggest this idea? She was sitting opposite him, grinning in childish excitement. He made a half-hearted effort to smile back before closing his eyes. It was far too noisy to hold any kind of conversation so at least he was spared having to share his thoughts.

Suddenly it was all action. The instructor was beckoning to him to get ready, and the same was happening to Anna. He could see the excitement on her face and wanted to feel the same, but the sickness in his stomach prevented any other feeling. Now he was being attached ready for the jump. He tried to smile and look enthusiastic, but didn't think it was very convincing. He was obviously going, before Anna, which would at least get it over with sooner. Then they were standing at the exit hatch and he could see stretching out beneath him the undulating English landscape. It was terrifying.

They stepped out of the plane into free fall. The whooshing noise of the wind together with the sensation of hurtling downwards was alarming. All his muscles felt tense and he wanted to hold on, but there was nothing to hold onto. All he could do was wait for the feeling of the parachute pulling them back but it seemed forever before there was movement from the instructor and the relief of feeling the jerk upwards like a brake suddenly being applied. Above them like a giant umbrella the parachute swelled outwards into action. The relief was overwhelming.

Now he could appreciate the drift downwards to the ground below and for a short while he began to feel slightly better. Below them was a field. He could see it at first coming gently towards them, but as they got further down he was sure they must be travelling too fast. Once more he was scared. The ground got closer and closer without seeming to slow at all until with a bump his feet touched the ground and he knew at last that he'd survived.

He felt cold. His whole body was shaking. His instructor, already free from the parachute himself, was now detaching him and helping him to his feet. He felt awful.
"You alright?"
"Yes I'm fine. Just a bit cold."
The instructor looked at him disbelieving.

"We need to get you back to the base."
He nodded, rubbed his hands together. He really was cold and struggling with some kind of shock. His teeth were knocking together inside his mouth.

There was no sign yet of Anna. Vaguely he thought he'd seen her come down in the field the other side of a line of trees about a hundred metres from where he had landed. He didn't want her to see him just yet in his shocked state. It felt embarrassing, out of control, like the whole experience of falling through the air. Out of control like when he was struggling with Mac. Losing control was what he hated.
"Sit down mate. You'll feel better in a minute."
He followed the instructor's advice and sat himself down on the dry canvas of the parachute.

Gradually he began to feel calmer. The feeling of rushing towards the earth at great speed was still there inside him, but less powerful now. He allowed himself to sit for a while not quite knowing what to expect, until he saw a range rover driving across the field towards them. He got inside and sat down. The shaking had stopped. He watched the parachute being collected up and put into the back of the vehicle. Then they were moving towards the line of trees, and soon he could see Anna standing with her instructor waiting for them. As soon as she climbed on board he could see she'd really enjoyed it. She gave him a cheery wave as she sat with her instructor chatting excitedly. He stayed quiet on the other side of the vehicle, gradually allowing himself to settle as it made its way across the ground towards the main road. Every bump and jolt reinforced his contact with the ground, reassuring him that he was safe. Then they were driving more smoothly back along the main road towards the small airfield where they'd started. Soon he knew he would be out of the truck and standing safely on his own two feet.

"You didn't enjoy that much did you."

It sounded more like a statement than a question.
"Probably not as much as you, no."
She laughed loudly and looked at him in disbelief.
"Looks to me like it really shook you up."
Why did she have to rub it in? She was sitting in front of him with her coffee, her hair windswept and her face radiantly red. The enjoyment was obvious. Wasn't that enough?
"Well, yes, it did a bit."
"But you got out on that ledge to rescue that young lad. Surely that was much more scary?"
"I didn't think about that. I just did what I had to. But speeding down to the ground like that wasn't me at all."
He could feel it again in his body as he said it and shuddered involuntarily. It was embarrassing admitting it, but as he looked at her, feeling inadequate, as if he'd let himself down somehow, her expression changed and seemed to become less aggressive, softer. She stretched a hand across the table to his and smiled. It felt genuine, as if she'd noticed how uncomfortable he felt.
"You didn't have to enjoy it. It's not a requirement."
He wondered for a moment if she was being patronising, but that wasn't what it felt like. He dismissed the thought and allowed himself to smile in response.
"But I paid good money for that!"
"Use it as a learning experience."
"What am I supposed to learn?"
Now they were laughing together, but already he knew what the learning was. He didn't like being out of control. Long ago he'd decided he never wanted to go ski-ing. Hurtling downhill at top speed, unable to stop was never going to be him. Sky diving was obviously the same.
"But why do you like it?" he said.
"Sense of freedom. Being out of time. It is a bit scary, but that's part of the enjoyment."
"Mmm."
"OK. It's not for everyone."

"Not for me!"
"No problem. There will be other things we can do together."
He smiled and nodded. "What else do you like?" he said, "apart from clay pigeon shooting."
"You were better at that than me."
"I'm not boasting. How about ice skating?"
"Can you do that?"
"Sort of. I can get around the ice."
"Me too. I did ice hockey at school."
"That sounds good!"
"I wasn't all that good. I kept falling over."
"OK let's try it."
All the warmth and energy felt like it was coming back into his body. He felt excited, as if there was a way forward again.

*

He was better than he'd admitted. She watched him in admiration as he sped across the ice away from her. But she knew she was as good as he was. All those hours at school charging around on the ice with a hockey stick being battered by other girls and sometimes getting her own back with a satisfying thwack on another leg hadn't been wasted. She waited, pottering about cautiously, getting used to the ice again, letting him reveal his abilities to her first.

He was across the ice waving back at her. Until the sky diving adventure she'd have thought him arrogant, but now she knew he could be vulnerable. The chill of the ice was rising up around her, but inside she was warming to him, wanting to know him better. She kicked into action with her right foot and made her way across the ice towards him. It was tea time, and apart from a few children round the edge, the ice was clear. As she caught up with him, he obviously decided to skate off in a kind of chase. She followed, and soon they were circling round at some speed. She kept on course for a short while before suddenly shooting across diagonally and then it was he who was following after her. She kept on moving, showing that she

could skate as fast as he could before bringing herself quite quickly to a standstill so he had to brake too. He lifted his arms round her shoulders to steady himself and she let him, before turning round towards him grinning.
"Shall we dance?"
"Why not?"

Then they were off again, not at first completely together and not particularly elegantly, until gradually their movements co-ordinated and it felt to her like they really were ice dancing. It was exhilarating to be synchronising her movements with his and gliding round the ice rink, first backwards then forwards. His face told her he was enjoying it as much as she was, and it was obvious neither of them wanted to stop. Eventually they slowed and she stumbled slightly, falling towards him. He caught her, laughing, and they stood still in the middle of the ice catching their breath together.
"Drink?" he said.
"OK."
She let him put his arm round her shoulder to escort her from the ice.

Near the exit, two boys of about twelve were cautiously stepping round the edge of the ice. One of them looked up and recognised Josh.
"Didn't know you could skate, sir."
"There's lots you don't know about me, Adam."
"One of your students?" she said.
"He's in my Year 7 English group. Not always easy to escape notice as a teacher."
As they were taking their skates off she could hear the boys giggling together. As they walked away the same boy shouted after them.
"That your girlfriend, sir?"
He turned around and waved back non-committally. Well managed she thought to herself.

You couldn't really call it a coffee bar. Plastic tables and chairs in a large square room with two machines, one dispensing hot drinks, the other cold drinks and chocolate bars. They sat down at the opposite end from a couple with two young children. Otherwise it was empty. Anna wanted an orange drink and Josh decided on the same, so he went over to the machine and chose two brightly coloured cans which arrived in the space below with a thump.

They drank from their cans grinning across the table at each other.
"So where do we go from here?" he said suddenly on an impulse without really thinking what he was saying,
"My place?"
It was an offer he couldn't refuse; all that effort and suddenly it was easy.
"OK," he said trying to sound cool.
"I've got a flat a couple of miles from the centre. It will be better than sitting around here. You can follow me in your car."
"OK," he said again, almost in a state of shock.

Sitting at the wheel of his car following her blue Peugeot he tried to stay calm. This wasn't a new experience he told himself. His track record was good. Getting girls had always come easily to him, but the hypnotic beat of the music on his sound system couldn't entirely allay his feeling of anxiety. She was leading him into an area with attractive older houses in one of the more upmarket parts of the town. He was impressed, but not surprised. Soon she was slowing down, turning into a side road and parking her car. There was a space behind, so he stopped there too and waited for her to get out. She seemed to take a while, but eventually he could see her stepping out of the car and locking it with a click from her key. He followed as she walked a few steps along the road and then turned into a passageway leading to a doorway along the side of a large Victorian house.
"It's a ground floor flat, so no climbing."

The doorway led straight into the living room. Along the wall ahead of them was a pale cream sofa covered with pastel coloured cushions. All around the room, most surfaces were covered with potted plants and ornaments. Most of them seemed to be pot cats, but there was no evidence of a real cat. On one wall was a textile design of some kind.
"I used to share this with Ben. I've made it my own now."
"It's really nice."
"You like it?"
"Definitely."
There was a pause.
"Sit down," she said, indicating the sofa, "I'll be right back."
He did as she asked. The unfamiliar anxiety was still in his stomach as he sat there waiting. He didn't want to get it wrong.

"Do you want another drink?" she asked as she came back into the room.
"Not really."
She nodded and sat down beside him on the sofa.
"Do you know, I would never have believed a few weeks ago that you would be sitting here. Not after that first meeting."
"Or the one after that. Strange isn't it?"
She moved her position, tucking her legs underneath her and to one side on the sofa so that she leaned towards him. It was a gesture which seemed to invite physical contact. He leaned towards her and stretched his arm out so that it was round her shoulder. In response she eased herself closer to him. He was aware of her perfume, not strong, but noticeable, stirring his desire. He moved his head towards her and brought his other arm round so that they were very close, and at the same time she lifted her face towards his. Their lips met, gently at first, then more energetically.

After a while he felt her easing him away from her, breaking the contact.
"Come," she said, standing up.

Vaguely he registered an unintended double meaning, but decided not to spoil the moment. Instead he let her take his hand so that he had to stand too, and followed her across the corridor into a large bedroom. At the pillow end what looked like a soft toy elephant was placed. Moving round to one side of the bed she lifted the elephant and placed it on a chair, smiling as she did so.

She began slipping out of her clothes. For a moment he watched her, until it occurred to him that he needed to be doing the same. Undressing with a woman had never been something he'd worried about before, not even in his first fumbling experience. For the first time in his life he felt conscious of taking his clothes off. He didn't doubt that he could make it, but he also wanted to be good enough.

Erect at the sight of her naked body in front of him, he noticed her eyes looking downwards.
"As good as any Jewish boy," she said approvingly.
It took a moment to register that she was referring to his circumcision.
"Not something I've thought much about," he said, lifting his hands to touch her firm breasts, but she moved away from him and bent down to open a small drawer beside the bed. She stood upright again, holding out a small pack of something. He stretched out his hand to take it.
"Left over from Ben's time. Insurance policy."
He looked at the pack of condoms in his hand and smiled slightly, knowing what he had to do.
"Let's get into bed."
He didn't need to be asked twice. Together they slid under the duvet and their lips met once more, dispelling all his anxieties and self consciousness.

Lying in bed afterwards, with Josh sleeping beside her, she found herself smiling. He was a better lover than she expected. Why had it taken so long to get to this? And how strange that after the trip to

Auschwitz she should allow herself to start a relationship with a goy, even if a circumcised one. The thought made her smile again while Josh lying next to her snorted but didn't surface into consciousness. She looked at him lying on his side, inclined towards her, with his eyes still closed. A schoolteacher. A few weeks ago if someone had suggested to her that she'd get in bed with a schoolteacher who wasn't even Jewish she would have laughed. But this one was breaking down stereotypes.

Just as she was wondering how long he would sleep, he stirred again and opened his eyes.

"Why do men always fall asleep after sex?"

"Do they?"

She watched him stifle a yawn then turn to look at her.

"Must be because we work hard."

She nudged him in the ribs with her elbow, causing him to flinch.

"Sorry. That was harder than I intended."

His response was to scare her, turning towards her in mock retaliation, which ended with an extended kiss.

"You're very sexy," he said afterwards.

"Speak for yourself!"

"OK. So am I."

She sat up and flicked him playfully with the back of her hand before getting up and walking across to the bathroom.

Afterwards she made him a coffee and they sat back together, each on one of her sofas, facing each other.

"I didn't think this would happen," she said.

"Nor me. I didn't think you liked me."

"I didn't. Not at first."

"So what changed?"

She sat back and thought for a moment, aware that he was watching her closely.

"I think I always fancied you a bit. You are very good looking."

He grinned boyishly but didn't reply.
"But at first you were arrogant; when you crashed my car, then at Sophie's wedding."
She stared back at him, almost daring him to challenge her, but he merely grinned back.
"I was surprised that we kept bumping into each other," he said after a while. "If I believed in fate, which I don't by the way, I would have thought we were destined to get to this point."

34

The funeral was a simple one. It was late afternoon, not long before dark, which seemed appropriate. Liz said that she would go too, meet him there from school. The only other mourners were two old friends of his mother and a colleague from the hospital who turned out to support him. Five mourners for a lifetime. 'The number of mourners is in inverse proportion to the age of the deceased,' he remembered hearing from somewhere, but it really didn't seem many.

They waited outside the chapel at the crematorium while the funeral in front of them filed out, led by a weeping woman in black supported by two younger women. There were many mourners and the funeral had obviously filled the small space within. Then it was time for his mother and the five of them went inside in silence. The absence of music was his choice. The small coffin containing his mother was at the front and the cadaverous vicar with glasses perched on the end of his nose smiled apologetically as he greeted them and waited for them to settle in the front row. He looks like he feels guilty she's died and that in some way we might think he's responsible, he thought to himself as they all sat waiting for the ceremony to begin. He'd made it clear there was to be no religious message. Maybe that was what the vicar looked apologetic about. Well that was tough, it was his mother and he made the decisions.

They sat through twenty minutes of platitudinous homilies about her life. Things obviously gleaned from the chat with him a few days back in his hospital consulting room. There was no way he was going to let a vicar into his home. He was aware of feeling consciously unmoved as the curtains came round the coffin during the proceedings. They buzzed electrically as they closed, unmasked by any anodyne music. Then, his one musical concession as the five of them came out, the sound system played Duke Ellington's 'Solitude,' his own private commentary on her life. He could have chosen 'Eleanor Rigby,' but the Ellington was more subtle and more to his taste.

He felt uncomfortable as he stood next to Liz outside. Should he be feeling anything? All he really felt was emotionally numb, detached. No sadness. No need of any terrycloth. The funeral staff were offering their condolences and asking if everything was alright. He nodded.
"Everything's fine," he said, "Thankyou."
His mother's friends insisted on telling him what a wonderful lady she had been and wanted to share a couple of anecdotes with him. He listened dutifully until they seemed to read his unresponsiveness, made their excuses and left. His work colleague came to speak to him.
"See you later. Chin up old boy."
He had a strange vision in his head of lifting his chin in the air, but contented himself with an appropriately manly shake of the hand by way of thanks for coming. Then it was the vicar's turn. They shook hands awkwardly and nodded to each other. It was obvious the vicar thought he was cold and unfeeling, but that was fine, he could think what he wanted. He could see Liz looking at him, wondering what was going on. Probably his body language was telling her not to embrace him, and he was glad she didn't.

His eyes took in the view across the grounds of the crematorium. There were white snowdrops everywhere and a few yellow crocuses coming into bloom.
"Beautiful isn't it?"

"It is," she said looking at him.
He knew she was wondering what he was thinking, but he couldn't yet engage. She seemed to read it.
"Let's go. Come back to my place for a cup of tea or something."
He nodded his agreement. He got into his car and followed her out of the crematorium gates.

*

Simon was the first to wake. Behind the curtains, pale sunlight told him it had to be after eight o'clock. Beside him, still sleeping, was Daniel. He looked at his peaceful body and smiled. Was it possible to fall in love within twenty four hours? Or was it just self delusion? It didn't feel like that. He lay still, enjoying the moment. Had he ever felt more at peace with himself? It couldn't last, but he wanted to prolong it, just for a few minutes.

Daniel stirred. He waited. One eye opened, squinted, and then the other eye, till he was looking at him, obviously needing a moment to make sense of where he was. He sat up on one elbow and smiled down at Daniel, ruffling his hair, sort of maternally he thought after he'd done it. Then Daniel was awake and sitting up too, so they were both sitting up in bed with their bare chests out of the bedclothes like an old married couple.

"Can you believe this?"
"You mean us? No, not really."
Daniel stretched out his arm and drew him towards him. The excitement of the night before was still there between them.
"Does this really happen to gay guys?" he said, wanting to voice the thoughts in his head, and at the same time smiling at the clumsiness of his expression.
"Gay guys? That's us is it?"
"Well what else are we?"
"How about lovers?"
"Sounds good to me."

"I didn't think this would be possible, not for me."
"That's how I feel too. Stefan was fun, but I didn't love him. It's different with you."
"Bit scary?"
"Mmm, very," he said, "we've only known each other for a day. Less than that."
Daniel looked at him, leaned towards him and kissed him on the mouth before leaning back to speak.
"Then it's love at first sight, more or less."
The kiss resumed, and It was another hour before they got up.

"Is this just sex?"
He looked at Daniel perched naked on the bed, one knee held in his hands, not really believing what he'd just said but wanting reassurance. The bright January sun was shining right into the window of his flat and a beam of light illuminated the bedroom door on which Daniel's concert suit was hanging. He was sitting equally naked on a chair by the bed. Daniel looked as if he was considering the question.
"What if it is?"
"Then it's good. Very good. But not enough."
"Why?"
"Because I'm not just a predatory gay like Stefan. I need more. If I was straight I might want to be getting married, thinking about children."
"But you're not a straight guy and nor am I. I'd always thought it was different for us. Being gay has always scared me. It's why I've never wanted to be part of the gay scene."
As he spoke, Daniel stood up from the bed and moved towards his clothes as if to indicate that sex was over. From his travelling bag he took out his toilet bag and what looked like a clean pair of underpants, and walked across to the bathroom. Simon could hear the taps running and the sound of teeth being scrubbed. Three or four minutes later Daniel returned to the bedroom with his nakedness covered by a pair of black boxer shorts. Simon couldn't resist a grin.
"No Micky Mouse today?"

Daniel turned himself through three hundred and sixty degrees so he could see that the back of his underpants was as plain as the front.
"Nowhere to be seen."
"That's a relief."
But he knew he needed to return to their earlier conversation.
"Do you want to be loved? And to love?"
"What does that mean?"
"I think it means to develop a closeness with someone, of either sex actually, so that your lives grow together. Make a lasting attachment. Keep the sex of course, as much as possible."
They both laughed, but he needed to know what Daniel would say.
"I think I've always wanted that. But never thought it was possible for me."
"That's what I thought too."
He waited, not sure whether to say what was on his mind, scared of getting it wrong. He looked at Daniel's still largely naked body, and felt powerful desire. He looked away briefly and then back again.
"Until I met you yesterday that is."
"That's scary," he said, "because I think I feel the same. About you."
Suddenly he felt shy, exposed in a different way, and Daniel seemed to read it.
"Now get some bloody clothes on or we'll never get anything done today."

*

The familiar face was waiting for him outside his office, sitting alongside his mother.
"Do you want to come in Wesley?"
Wesley stood up and followed him in while Mrs Freedom acknowledged him with a smile and a friendly wave. He was glad to see Wesley's smiling face, but didn't want to underestimate how he might be feeling underneath.
"How are things then?" he began once Wesley had made himself comfortable in the familiar chair. He looked taller, and he fidgeted less in settling himself down he noticed.

It was his first counselling session since his mother died and he knew he needed to monitor his own feelings. A large spider appeared from nowhere and ran with surprising speed across the floor between them. Both of them followed it with their eyes as it disappeared under Wesley's chair, making him smile broadly.

"Some of my patients would have been out of that chair by now."

"Don't worry me."

"That's good. So . . . dad back on the scene?"

"He came round again Thursday night. Upset mum. He's gone again now. Social worker sorted him out. But she was worried about me."

"About you?"

"About me doing something again."

He waited for Wesley to continue, but he stopped there and looked down.

"Doing something again?" he said into the silence.

"Like what I did before."

"Is she right to worry?"

"Not done anything."

"No cutting?"

He pulled up his sleeves to show him his arms, which were clear of any damage. He nodded his appreciation.

"So how much has he upset you?"

He could feel there was more than was reaching the surface, and waited again for Wesley.

"A bit."

"A bit?"

"I wanted to kill him," he said quietly. "He's really upsetting mum."

"Still? After Thursday?"

"He upsets her every time he comes. I wish he was dead."

The intensity of the feeling echoed somewhere uncomfortably with his own feelings. In the silence he could see the spider re-emerge and scuttle away to the skirting board out of Wesley's line of sight. The words 'black widow' came into his head.

"So you're feeling very angry at him."

That's stating the obvious he realised as soon as he said it, but Wesley's vehement nod seemed to suggest his remark might actually have been helpful however crass it sounded to him.
"No reason why you shouldn't"
"I know he's my dad. But he's never been like one."
His fists were tightly coiled on the arms of the chair; angry. But somewhere on the edge of awareness he could feel something else.
"That's sad."
It took no more than a few moments before Wesley's face changed, his fists loosened and the sadness became apparent on his face. The memory of Max saying the same to him flashed into his mind. He watched as Wesley's eyes fill and he lifted his hand to wipe away the tear that escaped his right eye and ran down his cheek.
"It's OK to feel sad."
A part of him would have liked to take Wesley into his arms and comfort him. Terrycloth father. But he knew the need for comfort was as much his as Wesley's.

The tears were short lived. He gave him time to draw himself together before speaking again.
"The Japanese say only a true warrior cries."
Wesley looked up at him, his eyes wide open again. It was obvious he liked the thought.
"Can my mum be a warrior too?"
"Why not?"
"So how's the warrior?"
"Bit better."
"So scale of one to ten, how likely are you to go jumping out of windows again?"
"I didn't jump!"
"But you nearly did."
Wesley grinned his wide smile and they laughed together.
"OK, come on, one to ten, how high?"
He made an exaggerated play of thinking hard before saying "One."

"Only one. Not nought?"
"You said one to ten."
"True. I did. So what are you telling me?"
"I'm not going to jump out of windows."
"Or anything else like that?"
"No. Got to stick around for me mum."
"Sure. You have. You need her, and she needs you."
There was a pause. Wesley looked calmer. They sat in silence together as the thought sank in.
"Shall we stop there today?"
Wesley nodded and got out of the chair. They walked together to go out of the door to see his mother.

Reassured, he said goodbye to them both and went back to his room. Just being there is sometimes enough; an old lesson he sometimes forgot. Trying too hard can sometimes be counterproductive. The spider was still moving about the floor so he opened the window, bent down with cupped hands, captured it and dropped it out into the flower bed below. He watched with satisfaction as it disappeared into the undergrowth.

*

Lucia's front door opened out onto one of the steep backstreets that looked down onto the sea. As Leo knocked he was aware of it in the distance looking grey and overcast. It will rain soon he thought to himself. When Lucia saw him she looked immediately unsettled, almost as if she might have done something wrong.
"I need to talk to you," he began.
She stepped back behind the door and allowed him to walk into the small parlour room. She turned off the small television and motioned to him to sit down as she sat opposite him.
"Marco?" he said, wondering whether he might be somewhere else in the house.
"Out. Riding on the bus. It keeps him happy. What can I do for you father?"

"I've been talking to Salvatore."
He watched her face as he said it, and thought he detected anxiety.
"About the soldier."
Still she didn't speak, but her distress seemed to increase.
"The English soldier. Salvatore told me he was one of those who buried him."
Her body seemed to stiffen almost imperceptibly before she said anything.
"So you know my secret now. Like Father Luigi before you."
"I suspect I do. Salvatore told me your brother Carlo shot the soldier. After you told him . . ."
He paused for a moment, uncomfortable about continuing, but she didn't help him, just sat there staring at him and waiting for him to continue.
"After you told him the soldier raped you."
"I shouldn't have told him. I didn't want that."
"But he did rape you?"
"I looked after him. Took him food . . . and clean clothes. Tried to talk to him. He told me his name. Tom. Then it all went wrong."
He looked at her face. There was sorrow, a long distant sorrow, tears that had been shed in the past, but were now . . . the lines from an English poet came into his head . . . too deep for tears.
"His name was Tom?"
She nodded and he paused, waiting before asking the question he knew he had to ask.
"And Tom . . . is Marco's father?"
The pause which followed seemed endless and agonising before she lowered her head, indicating the truth of what he had said. He was tempted to put a hand on hers in a gesture of consolation, but he knew she wouldn't welcome it. Marco, the result of that terrible night was both her ever present reminder and God's gift to comfort her sorrow.

They sat in silence. Nothing in his training or in his life had prepared him for what he was experiencing. He felt completely inadequate. He wanted to leave but didn't know how. Then without quite realising he was doing it at first, in his head he began to recite the *padre nostro*. 'Our father,' felt comforting to him. Someway into the prayer he must have started to verbalise it, and she joined him so that they were both saying the words together. '*E non ci indurre in tentazione, ma liberaci dal male*.' They said amen together and crossed themselves.

"Was it evil father?" she said out of nowhere.
He didn't know what to say. Killing was evil, he knew that. So was rape. But the soldier, the long dead soldier, father of Marco; was he evil? He didn't know. Marco was all simple goodness, and he was about to say that when there was a commotion at the door. Marco burst through, and seeing his mother and the priest together grinned broadly. He was always pleased to see Marco, but never more so than at that moment. Neither of them could resist smiling as the plump body attempted a jump of joy and, completely uncoordinated, fell onto the floor, laughing loudly. He stayed a few more minutes before finding the opportunity to make his excuses and leave.

Outside, feelings of inadequacy swamped him and he found himself praying silently again. Was he asking for strength, forgiveness, understanding? He wasn't sure, so confused was his mind, until he remembered that he didn't have to have the answer for everything, and that maybe it hadn't gone too badly after all. He'd avoided being crass, and they had prayed together. God's will had prevailed.

35

It was mild and not quite dark when Patrick left the hospital. Always by mid January he became aware that the days were becoming noticeably longer. There was rustling in the undergrowth, small creatures preparing for the night and fleetingly he wondered about the fate of the spider he'd saved. He felt good. It had been a successful day, but more than that he could feel a sense of wellbeing within, which he knew came from his growing relationship with Liz. He conjured her up in his mind and saw the glistening wetness of her body when she'd stepped out of the shower in the morning. He loved it when she looked round at him, naked and grinning, peering at him from her short sighted eyes and full of the reawakened joy that he saw in her. It was more than just sex. He was falling in love with her.

That evening they slept together again, and the following morning, for the first time since the early days with Laura, he said it.
"Do you know I love you," he said as they sat in bed together. It was early and still dark outside. The room was lit by her bedside lamp and they were contemplating getting up. Her look was serious.
"Do you really mean that?"
"I wouldn't say it if I didn't."
He could see that she was affected by what he'd said. He hadn't expected her to say the same thing back to him. Not exactly. It wasn't her style. But he hoped that she would find her own time to say it. Obscurely, at the back of his mind it felt right that he should say it first.
"At this time of the morning that's quite something!"
He watched her get out of bed, turn back towards him and blow him a kiss. Her breasts looked beautiful and firm in the dim light and he could feel the familiar surge of excitement. Aware of him looking, she briefly adopted a Greek goddess pose before turning towards the shower.

He allowed himself a few more moments in bed and listened first to the sound of the electric pump starting the shower and then the sound of her brushing her teeth. Then came the clunk of the shower door closing and he knew she was inside. He waited until he judged she might be close to finishing before getting out of bed and moving into the bathroom himself. On the radiator was her pale pink bath towel. He picked it up and held it ready. When she stepped out he wrapped

the warm towel round her shoulders. It felt good to do it. A moment of intimacy that was new to him.
"Thankyou," she said, taking the towel in her own hands and wrapping it round herself more securely before picking up a smaller hand towel to wrap round her hair. Redundant now, he stepped back into the bedroom to wait for his turn to take a shower.

Afterwards, when they were dressed, she turned to him again, her face still flushed from the warmth of the shower, and smiled. He didn't think he'd got it wrong.

*

Josh waited with his class in the main hall. It was quiet as the whole year group waited with their form tutors for assembly to begin. He reached forward to tap the shoulder of a small girl gossiping quietly to her neighbour on the chair next to her and put his finger to his lips when she turned to look at him. Then a stifled giggle from another girl two rows ahead drew an angry look from the teacher of the form in front of his, followed by a quiet 'Sorry miss.'

He hoped it would be Len taking the assembly. His brand of humour, his risqué jokes and elements of audience participation kept everyone amused. He'd laughed to himself when one of his Year 7 group told him in all seriousness that when Mr Turner left school he was going to be a comedian. He'd make a good job of it too. But no Len today. It was Mrs Broad herself who stepped forward to take the assembly. She was usually earnest and serious with a strong moral purpose. Good, but not in Len's league. She was smiling as she waited for stillness before beginning. It was different. Must just be in a good mood today he thought. He couldn't help noticing how unusually animated she was talking about spring and nature's new beginnings, and how much she seemed to be affected by what she was saying. The students looked like they were listening to her in the silent hall, although it was impossible to know who was thinking about the football match last night or the shopping trip on Saturday.

The messages followed. One was delivered by Len, who stepped forward and ostentatiously played with his glasses in a kind of pantomime before giving a Ken Dodd like half laugh. It drew a laugh in itself before he'd even spoken. He wondered if he would refer to his tickling stick until the mundane message about detentions brought everyone back to school life. Josh caught the eye of the form teacher in front, who lifted her eyes almost disapprovingly, but to him it was a tiny cameo performance brightening up life for a moment. He remembered the magic formula; 'life is what you make it.'

On the way out of assembly he literally bumped into Wesley, who was chatting to a mate and not looking where he was going.
"Sorry sir!"
"You alright now Wesley?"
"Everything's fine now, sir, thanks."
His face said it obviously was, and he carried on to his classroom for the first lesson feeling pleased with himself.

Back in her office, Liz was met by Len who seemed to want to talk to her about nothing in particular.
"What is it really, Len?" she finally asked, smiling but slightly exasperated.
"Just an attendant lord, deferential, glad to be of use."
He bowed elaborately as he spoke. The words sounded familiar, Shakespearean perhaps, but only added to her exasperation.
"What are you talking about?"
He grinned and tapped his nose before answering.
"Just wondering how you are."
"Absolutely fine! Why?"
"You're looking pleased with yourself. Time for new beginnings?"
She laughed out loud.
"You really don't miss much do you."
"And how's Dr East?" he said ignoring her remark.
"No wonder the staff call you Twitter!"

"Do they?"
"You know they do."
"I like to keep up to date."
"You could call it nosey."
"You could. But you know I'm interested in your happiness."
She knew the remark was likely to have been calculated, but it softened her. She smiled at him.
"Dr East is very well thankyou."
She knew he would read her response as confirmation of their relationship, but she didn't mind. Twitter also had a private area and she knew he delighted in knowing something others didn't as much as he enjoyed passing on gossip.
"Sworn to secrecy m'am." She watched him incredulously as the Groucho mime returned with fake cigar. "Women should be obscene and not heard, as the great man said."
For a moment she felt offended, but remembered from somewhere that it was actually a Groucho quotation. She was conscious Len looked slightly anxious that he might have been tactless as he tried to dissemble.
"If you know what I mean that is." More fake cigar, with fake ash tapped onto her carpet.
"There's nothing obscene about my relationship with Dr East," she said eventually, feigning shock. Then realising she'd given him what he'd asked for, she laughed, and he resumed his normal voice.
"I'm very pleased. You can trust me not to say anything," he said with a sly grin, tapping his nose again as he left.

She sat back in her chair, feeling outmanoeuvred, but not really minding. She did trust him, more than most, despite his reputation. She conjured up Patrick in her head, the smiling, more open Patrick that she now knew. New beginnings; had she really been talking about herself? Probably yes. Well it still made an appropriate assembly for the time of year; and it was the eighteenth. Through the window, the January sun was shining. She looked up and for a brief moment imagined Guy smiling down approvingly as the familiar sound of PE activities floated up to her office. She smiled to herself before getting up for the morning walkabout.

*

It had been an amazing weekend, but Daniel had to get back home. He was singing Noah in Benjamin Britten's biblical piece in a church near where he lived and had to get back for the rehearsal and the performance.

"Doesn't that involve audience participation?" Simon asked, not really knowing the work.

"Yes. And amateurs in the cast. It's great fun, but we have to get it right or it will be a shambles."

"Two by two of all flesh, and they that went in, went in male and female of all flesh."

"I'm impressed with your biblical knowledge," Daniel said.

"Yes, but where does that leave us?"

"I don't get you."

"Male and female of all flesh. They wouldn't have had us on the boat."

He could see that Daniel's first impulse was to laugh, until he realised he was being serious.

"Do you ever wish you were straight, Daniel?"

"Used to. Most of the time, till this weekend."

"Me too. Even with Stefan sometimes. Till this weekend."

They were sitting opposite each other at the table in his kitchen after eating the Sunday lunch he had prepared for them both. He held out his hands to Daniel who took them in his own as he continued with what he was saying.

Before it's always felt like there was a club out there, a straight club which excluded me, didn't accept me."

"Don't you think it was you who didn't accept yourself? That's how it was for me."

"True. Even in our times, when it's easier for us that it must have been for the likes of Britten and Peter Pears. I could have started going to

gay clubs I suppose, but I was too shy. It felt like a shameful secret. It was only this Christmas I told my parents, and my sister."
"And?"
"And what?"
"What did they say?"
"Just acted like nothing was different. Said I was still me."
"My parents don't know. But I'm going to tell them. Everything feels different now."
They were still holding hands across the table. It felt comforting. Healing was the word that came into his head.
"This is very special," he said.
"I know."
"Can two gay men really fall in love with each other?"
"Why not? I guess it happened to Britten and Pears."
"Our own two by two?"
"Feels right doesn't it. Better without the flood though!"
"You will come back, won't you?" he said, suddenly anxious.
"Try and keep me away. And you can come to visit me at my place."
Reassured, he took another risk.
"One day, perhaps . . . . we could set up home together."
Daniel looked across the table at him, still holding onto his hands, but the anxious feeling was there again. Had he spoken too soon? Was it all too soon? It didn't feel like it.
"We could."
His heart was racing with the thought, with the excitement that Daniel seemed to want to be with him as much as he wanted it. He made his way around the table to take Daniel in a firm embrace.

They held each other close for some seconds before Daniel drew himself apart so he could lean forward and kiss him on the lips. It felt warm and exciting with promise.
"But now I have to get my things together and be on my way," he said.
"Need anything else before you go?"
"No, I'm fine, really."

He sat down at the table again in a daze as Daniel went off to gather his things, reappearing in the doorway a few minutes later.
"I'm off now. I'll ring you."
And he was gone.

The silence in his flat felt strange. After being so intense and intimate it was hard to adjust. He hadn't expected something so incredible to flourish between them so quickly, and then just as quickly to be alone. He'd fallen in love with another man. There was no other way to describe what had happened. I felt like a point of no return. There was no going back.

The sun was shining. He walked across and leaned on the window ledge looking out. People were going about their day's business as if nothing special had happened, while he knew it had. His whole sense of himself had shifted. Everything that was tentative and uncertain about who he was, even after his experience with Stefan, had changed. Now he knew he could love and be loved. He searched in his head for what he was really trying to say and at first couldn't find the right words. Then, as he stood watching a young woman using the cash till in the wall of the bank opposite his flat, it came to him. He felt validated. For the first time in his life he really could accept himself for what he was.

He turned and walked back into the room, picked up his violin case, took out his violin and tuned each string. It felt good to do it, not the chore it was sometimes. Then he rosined his bow and felt ready to play. The bite of the bow into the strings felt good. He played a couple of simple arpeggios. Then without quite planning it, he launched into the allegro last movement of Bach's C major sonata, faster than he usually played it. It was an old favourite, but had never sounded so good to him as it did that afternoon. He was sure now that Bach had written an uninhibited song of love. Why had he never realised that before? Next time Daniel came he would play it to him and it would be their love song.

He was so absorbed in his playing that he didn't want the music to end. But the music had transformed the silence that followed and he felt good in himself. He didn't want to spoil the mood so he put his violin away. After a while he felt the need to talk to someone about how he was feeling. There was only one person he thought might understand, so he rang Sophie and asked if he could go round 'for a chat' as he put it. She was in, and was happy for him to go round. He got himself ready to drive over.

36

After everything he'd discovered, it hardly came as a surprise to receive a call from the British Embassy in Rome. The authorities had traced the family of the dead soldier. His wife was no longer able to travel, but he had a son in England who wanted to come across to Italy to see the place where he died. The news was something of a shock. A son? An extra dimension he hadn't anticipated. More difficult conversations. He would need all his pastoral care abilities there he guessed. His mind drifted for a moment until he was drawn back into the conversation by the embassy official.

"Do you speak English Father?"

Speaking in Italian, the caller was also clearly an Italian national from her accent. But everybody wanted to speak English now. It had been a good decision to spend some time at a seminary in Dublin and learn the language.

"Only with an Irish accent." He smiled to himself as he said it.

"The English won't notice the difference. It's all the same language isn't it?"

"To be sure it is," he said in English out of mischievousness, but clearly, unless he hadn't been heard correctly, the Roman official's English was not as good as his and he had to translate himself back into Italian.

"We are asking you father because when the son comes to your town he will need an escort, and a translator. He's an intelligent man, a doctor we believe, but he doesn't speak Italian. We are wondering if you could do that."
Of course he could. It might act as a closure on everything he had discovered.
"When might that be?"
"Quite soon we think. We would like to give the son your telephone number."
He agreed, and the call ended.

He put the phone down, and as he did so the grinning face of Marco appeared at the door of the vestry. Marco, a brother, and a brother who was a doctor. It was an astonishing thought. He would have to tell Lucia. Not an easy conversation he guessed, but not one he needed to do immediately. There was work to do that he could get Marco to help him with, and keep him busy.

*

The solicitude of the Italian Embassy impressed Patrick. Of course they would arrange for him to visit the village where his father had 'disappeared.' The word felt like a polite euphemism, better than passed over, but not really necessary after all this time. Was it some kind of atonement on their part because his father was a victim of warfare in their country? Whatever it was he was grateful. Reggio was the nearest airport he was told. On the map he could see it was pretty well as far south as you could get in Italy, which made sense since he'd always known from his mother that it was some time after the eighth army had crossed over from Sicily that he'd gone missing. He would have to change at Rome and they would arrange for him to be picked up by the town priest whose English was apparently very good. He made it clear he didn't want his father's remains brought back to England. A decent burial in the town where he died was all he wanted and they reassured him that would be arranged by the Italian authorities while he was there in the town. The local priest would be happy to officiate they reassured him.

“You do realise it will be a catholic ceremony,” Liz said when they met. It hadn’t crossed his mind before. And the thought came as something of a shock. But it would be one of those things he had no control over.
“I’ll just have to go along with it,” he said.
She just looked at him, smiling quizzically.
“It’ll be in a foreign language. I won’t know what they’re saying.”
“What if this priest wants to translate it for you, or even conduct it in English if his English is good enough?”
“I’ll tell him I’d rather he does it normally. When in Rome, or at least in Italy.”
“Do you want me to come with you? I might be able to get some leave, or you might even be able to arrange it for the February half term.”
He thought for a moment, not quite sure how to respond. Her presence would help him to manage his feelings, but at the same time it also felt like it was something he needed to see through himself.
“No,” he said eventually, decisively, “thanks for the offer. It would be nice, but it feels like something I need to do myself this time. It would have been great to have you there, but . . .”
“You don’t need to apologise. I think I understand. It’s how I would probably be myself. I’ll miss you though, when you’re away.”
He thought about what she’d said. Strange to miss someone you’ve only really known for a couple of months, but, yes, he knew he would miss her too. He nodded, making it obvious it was how he felt too.

Unusually, she didn’t stay long. Over the past month they’d got used to spending a lot of their time together and sleeping together regularly, usually round her house because she didn’t like the idea of leaving Max. But it was Wednesday and she had to prepare for her governors’ meeting the next day. As she drove the short distance between their houses she knew she would miss him too. He was very much part of her life now. Her mind wandered, and she was driving on autopilot through a back street shortcut she'd discovered when suddenly there was a child in the road in front of her. She pressed her right foot hard down on the brake, skidding the car across the road as it came to a stop, missing the child by maybe a foot or two.

She engaged the handbrake, switched off the engine and jumped out of the car, leaving it slewed across the road with the headlights on. The child was a girl, maybe eight or nine years old. She was back on the pavement looking dazed.
"Are you alright?" she said, feeling the panic in her voice as she spoke.
The girl didn't speak, but nodded, Seeming to be in a kind of stupor. Then as if realising where she was and what might have happened, she suddenly began crying. It was a cry of shock, not of pain, and the outburst was a relief, telling her that the girl was almost certainly not harmed. Instinctively she put her arm out to comfort the child, but she drew back away from her as if fearful of the contact, and then from around the next street a woman appeared. Seeing the girl crying she marched straightaway up to them and pulled the girl roughly towards her. It had the effect of increasing the volume of the girl's cries, which now seemed almost more fearful than shocked.

"She ran in front of my car. I nearly hit her," she began, but before she could say anymore the woman was shouting and gesticulating at her.
The girl, released from her mother's grasp, backed away.
"Fucking motorists, taking short cuts and driving too fast! One of our children will fucking get killed sooner or later. Nearly killed her you did!"
It was obvious there was no point in trying to be reasonable, but she wanted to placate the mother for the girl's sake as much as anything.
"Look, I'm really sorry. I'm just so glad I didn't hit her."
"So am I . . . I'd have killed you with my bare hands, so help me god!"
"I'm sorry," she said again.

With the girl still crying, she backed away to get into her car. By this time there were three other cars unable to get past because of the way she'd stopped in the road. She waved apologetically, started the engine and prepared to drive off, over revving in a way she never normally did because of her anxiety to get away. Desperate to get home now, she drove the last few hundred yards at some speed, expecting at any moment a police car to force her to stop. A feeling of guilt was hanging heavily on her.

Once home she parked the car on the drive and hurried indoors, calling out to Max at the same time. There was no answer. Remembering he'd gone down to Neil's house, she filled the kettle and made herself some tea. As she carried it across to the table she realised she was shaking and couldn't avoid spilling some of it onto the floor. When she got to the table she became overwhelmed by tears, and crying as loudly as she had done in the worst days after Guy's death. It must have been several minutes before the tears subsided, leaving her exhausted.

Inside herself there was a mixture of guilt and fear. At least she hadn't hit the child. She wasn't speeding and the child had stepped out in front of her, but she had been taking a short cut through a residential area like the mother had said, and her mind had been preoccupied in the moments before the incident. Maybe she'd seen the child late. She would never know, but she was aware the child's confused face had affected her more than the tears that followed. She tried to put it out of her mind, and contemplated getting on with the preparation of the governors' meeting, but knew she wouldn't be able to concentrate. Instead she put the television on and sat watching it mindlessly for a few minutes, trying to distract herself without much success.

She sat back feeling exhausted. It was times like these she knew when she missed Guy most. He would have been there to comfort her and talk it through, make a kind of sense of all the confused and distressing feelings. But a few months ago it would probably have been even worse, and the difference was Patrick. She wondered whether to call him and talk it through with him like she would have done with Guy, but didn't want to burden him; he had his own difficulties.

Absorbed in the thoughts inside her own brain, she didn't notice Max coming home. Suddenly he was standing in front of her.
"Where did you come from?" she said in surprise.
"Front door of course. Where else."
"I was just thinking about things in my head. I didn't notice you coming in."
"I know. Were you thinking about Patrick?"
"Well yes, a bit."
It was partly true. He sat down and seemed to be thinking about something.
"I like Patrick. He makes you happy doesn't he."
"Yes. Yes he does. But what about you?"
"Is he going to live with us?"
"Possibly."
"I'd like that," he said.
She smiled again, warmly.
"Mum, I'm hungry."
"I'll get you something."
"Thanks mum."
She went into the kitchen to make him a sandwich feeling altogether better.

37

"We're ruled by sex," Len suddenly announced in the staffroom. Josh looked up surprised. The comment seemed to come from nowhere. Several of those around him looked up. Aware he'd got attention, he added in his most portentous manner, "can't be denied, doesn't matter who you are."
"Does that include you Len?" Johnno couldn't resist asking.

"Of course. I tell Mrs Turner every night, it's sex that makes the world go round. Trouble is, she says to me, OK, you go round, I'm staying right here."
During the laughter that followed he betrayed no flicker of emotion.
"So how did you get your children then?"
"Immaculate conception."
"Children of God then are they?"
"If that's what you want to call me Mr Jones, I'm flattered by your confidence in my almighty powers."
He smiled then, and settled back into his chair with something of a smug look and a wave of the hand like some kind of conjurer completing a well rehearsed trick. Josh couldn't help admiring his quick wit. He was so much faster than anyone else.

"How do you do it?" he asked when the chatter moved on.
"Do what?"
"Keep ahead of everyone. Always have an answer for everything."
"Survival," Len replied straightaway, "I had to keep my wits about me when I was growing up. Wasn't particularly strong, and wearing these," he lifted his glasses from the side with one hand with a quick Eric Morecombe like flick, "I couldn't fight."
"So you fought with words."
Josh felt like a tiny corner of the enigma that was Len Turner lifted for a moment before it shut down again. He was quick to change the focus.
"And my guess is you've finally made it with that young reporter."
"What makes you say that?"
He tapped his nose in mock mystery. The familiar Len was back. Josh knew he'd wait now until he told him more. Twitter the super sleuth.
"Went ice skating together last weekend."
"Doubt if that warmed up the relationship."
"Did afterwards," he said grinning, unable to hold himself back in the face of Len's penetrating gaze. He could imagine the Twitter blog being written.

"I'm very pleased to hear it. Well must be off. Always work to be done." He mimed wiping his brow as if he'd been perspiring from all the effort as he made his way through the door.

*

The governors' meeting finished. She was relieved it hadn't been as challenging as she feared, despite feeling unprepared. It was almost dark when the last governor left the building. Walking past the staffroom to her office, she noticed the light was on and went in to see who was still there. Sitting in the corner between two piles of exercise books was Josh Greenwell.

"Still here at this time of night?"

"I wanted to get these finished before I went home. I need to get them back tomorrow. The class will be asking for them."

"I'm very impressed." She watched him as he looked up and smiled. There was something about his manner this term which suggested he was more settled, happier perhaps.

"You look well this term," she said. It was as much a question as a statement she realised as soon as she'd said it.

"Thankyou. I am."

"Teaching all going well now obviously."

"Life's better too," he said. It felt shyly cryptic, and she wondered if it was an indication that he wanted to say more. She moved across to the kettle amongst the unwashed cups on the draining board and switched it on.

"Can I make you a drink?"

"You don't have to do that."

"Don't worry. Headteachers can sometimes make tea."

His air of slightly self effacing embarrassment was appealing, as was his polite acceptance of her offer. I'm treating him like Max she thought, as she carefully checked how he liked it and carried the tea across to him.

"I won't disturb you for long," she said.

"It's alright. I could do with a break, Mrs Broad. Thankyou for making me tea."

"Life's better you were saying." God, I'm sounding like Len, fishing for information. She hurriedly added a corrective.
"Sorry, I didn't mean to sound as if I was prying into your life."
"No, it's alright. Life is good. I think I've fallen in love."
Was that a throwaway remark or was he serious? His shy smile told her he was in earnest, and fleetingly she wondered what he meant by love.
"The journalist who wrote about me saving Wesley. We're partners now."
"That's good news. Your good deed has brought you something you didn't expect."
She smiled indulgently and a part of her would have liked to embrace him to recognise the good news, but she stayed firmly in control of her feelings; the role had its restrictions. The tea would have to serve retrospectively.
"Well, I mustn't keep you from finalising your marking. You don't want to keep your young lady waiting."
He thanked her with a shy smile again as she placed her own cup amongst all the others on the draining board and wished him good night. As she walked back down the corridor to her office she could feel some regret that she hadn't been able to talk about her own new love, but in her own scale of proprieties, their ages and roles precluded that.

*

'Today is holocaust memorial day,' Anna typed into the computer and stared at it on the screen for a moment before deleting it. 'Too flat,' she said out loud to herself and tried again. After a while she found her way to an opening that satisfied her.
'The ghosts of six million victims hang over Auschwitz.'
She looked at what she had written on the screen supporting her head with her hands. A bit over dramatic maybe, fanciful, they didn't all die at Auschwitz. There was Treblinka and Belsen and Sachsenhausen amongst others, but it was the sort of thing the editor would like, and if she diluted it some of its power would be lost. Certainly it would

draw people into the article and in her head this was the most important ‘Rosie’s Read’ she had yet written. She needed to get it right. Twenty seventh of January; the day Auschwitz was liberated. Too late for her great grandparents. She wanted to get her own Jewish inheritance into the article, and she wanted to widen it to the perspective the old man and his daughter had given her. It was a lot to get into two hundred words, but all part of the *tschuve* with her past.

The telephone rang and the screen of her mobile phone told her it was Josh. She answered quickly.
“Can I come round,” he said.
“Anything wrong?”
“No. Just want to see you.”
It was Saturday morning, and since last weekend they’d only spoken on the telephone. She knew she wanted to see him too.
“I just need to get my column written. And get myself dressed. Still in pyjamas here.”
“Don’t mind that.”
“Well I do!” she said with a scandalised tone, not entirely without meaning it.
“OK. How long do you need?”
Good, she thought, he’s got the message.
“Hour or so.”
“OK. See you about elevenish. That alright?”
“Fine,” she said, nodding as if he could see her.
The call ended. She found herself wondering whether the thought of Josh coming round would help her concentrate or be a distraction as she walked into the kitchen to make some coffee. She really didn’t want him to find her like she was now, whatever he thought, which meant in effect getting the article finished in three quarters of an hour. She hurried back to the computer to carry on working, and to her surprise, words came quickly and the article was finished in half an hour.

'The ghosts of six million victims hang over Auschwitz. I know because last month I was there, and two of those ghosts are my great grandparents. It's an evil place, a permanent monument to man's inhumanity to man. There you can see the faces of the victims, the cases they brought with them, their false limbs and crutches and the great mountain of shoes they wore. It makes for a disturbing experience.

It's a Jewish tragedy. Most of those killed, like my family, were Jewish, and we Jews rightly claim it as an evil holocaust against our race. But it wasn't only Jews. I met an elderly man whose parents were Romany. They died there too, along with many thousands of gypsies. Homosexuals and disabled people died there too. We should remember them all. Auschwitz reminds us that man has the potential to do unspeakable evil. Hitler and the Nazis embody that. But atrocities are still happening in the world, and the human race is far from fully civilised. We have to be on guard against the evil in ourselves. That's what holocaust memorial day is all about.

She read through what she'd written with some satisfaction. Not quite two hundred words. That would please the editor. He always complained if she overran, which she usually did. 'Yes you're definitely good for me, Josh,' she said to herself before dashing into the bedroom to get herself ready for his arrival. As she stepped into the shower she knew the resistance against him was gone now. She wanted to make herself attractive for him, wanted him to want her. It had never really been like that with Ben. He was her partner, yes, and he'd satisfied her sexually. In her head as the force of the water seemed to enliven her brain she revised that to most of the time. His own satisfaction had been more important to him. Her gratification was incidental. There was a flash of anger, but she let it pass, knowing she didn't need it anymore.

As she stepped out of the shower, naked and wet, she knew she was ready to trust Josh. It was what she'd been scared to do before. Letting him in, emotionally, meant she was risking being hurt. Allowing yourself to become attached to someone else couldn't be other than losing some of your own independence. Some women she knew claimed they would never allow themselves to become attached to a man because it meant giving him your power. She understood that. Could it be different with Josh? He hadn't smashed her defences, just gradually liquidised them. The thought made her laugh. Maybe he was freeing her from the self imposed limits she had put around herself. Maybe that was what was happening inside her. The words 'mind forged manacles' flitted into her brain. Why did that suddenly appear? She must have read it somewhere. But it was *meshugene*, a crazy thought. What was she manacling? Why mind forged? Somewhere there was a kind of sense, but she couldn't quite grasp it, and she didn't know where it had come from.

The doorbell rang. He was early and she was still undressed. Quickly she pulled her dressing gown on and rushed through to open the door, still tying the dressing gown cord as the bell rang again. A fat postman with his glasses on the end of his nose stood holding a small box in one hand and a strange kind of technical box in the other, both of which he was handing to her.

"Parcel love. Sign here please."

She took the box and put it on the small table in her hallway and then signed in the window space indicated by the postman. He seemed to be scanning her body in a cursory sort of way as she did so, making her feel uneasy.

"Ta love. Nice morning."

"Mmm," she said as she watched him throw the sack of letters round to his side and set off again, lighter by one parcel. She smiled to herself and was about to close the door when, passing the postman in the outside entrance way, Josh appeared. She let him in and closed the door before embracing him.

"Thought you wanted to get dressed before I came."
"Well you're just a bit early," she said, but it really didn't seem as important as it had when she spoke to him on the phone.
"Get the article done?"
"Mmm. Think it's OK. Want to read it?" That felt new too, nowhere near as exposed as it would have done. She pulled her dressing gown around herself and led him to the computer, where the file with the article was still open. She indicated for him to read it and waited anxiously. He'd better like it. Criticism wasn't on the agenda.
"Fantastic!"
"Really?"
"Of course. You give me an idea of what your experience was like, and you make an important point about why we need to remember. It's very good."
It felt like a teacher commenting in her exercise book, but she let it pass; he was being genuinely complimentary, and she liked it.
"Thanks," she said, putting her arms round him again to give him a kiss. As she did so she could feel her dressing gown loosening. This time she resisted the impulse to draw it tight again, consciously allowing him to know what was beneath. He couldn't mistake the message, and it wasn't long before they made their way into the bedroom.

The excitement inside her felt more intense than she'd known before. She was aware of his desire, and her own rising excitement matched his. Always before she'd been conscious of a holding back, an ultimate controlling of what was happening. This felt scary, almost a betrayal of the principals she'd held in her life before. She didn't want to let go, didn't want to lose control, but felt unable to stop herself, forced not by Josh but by her own desire to go with the rhythm of the activity, hurtling through the air without the safety of the parachute to save her. He was all over her, everywhere, breathing quickly and excitedly, and she knew she was too. The climax seemed to come quickly and somewhere in the room a voice that was hers shouted out with the ecstasy of what was happening, and somewhere too, a deeper voice that was his cried out and there were several excited spasms in the body above hers before it became peaceful, lying above her, and she was conscious of fast heartbeats, hers and his, pumping in the otherwise quiet room.

After a little while he rolled sideways and lay beside her. He was breathing quietly. Opening her eyes she could see that the room was the same room she had slept in the night before and all the other nights, but it felt different. How had it changed? Sex wasn't that big a deal. Except it was, now, with this man she'd resisted for . . . how long? At least three months? Was this what love meant? She dared not think that, it was fantasy. But something had happened which would take some time to work out in her brain. 'Manacles,' she thought again, and as she gradually came to, she turned towards him and asked,
"Mind forged manacles,' have you heard of that before?"
He made a snorting noise suspiciously like he'd fallen asleep.
"What?"
"Did you fall asleep again?"
"No."
"I don't believe you." She paused, wondering if she ought to feel hurt, but the feeling wasn't there, so she said again,
"Mind forged manacles. Who said that?"
She watched him trying to get his brain in gear.
"Manacles? Handcuffs? Is this some kind of fetish?"
"Will you listen!" she said, poking him playfully, but hard enough to jolt him more awake. "It's a quotation. I can't quite place it, and you're an English teacher. Wondered if you'd know."
"What's the quotation?" He was awake now, so she repeated it for a third time, enunciating it as if he was deaf.
"I think it's William Blake, eighteenth century poet. He was a great believer in freeing ourselves from unhelpful conventions. Why?"
"I was just thinking about how we sometimes tie ourselves down with ideas that actually, well, tie us down, and it's unhelpful."

"Yes," he said, not really grasping what she was getting at.
"I think I've done that sometimes."
"Guess we all do it sometimes."
She looked at him lying beside her and felt a warmth towards him which was new.
"This is good isn't it," she said.
"Sex you mean?"
"All of it. How it seems to be working out; after how I really didn't like you for ages."
"The course of true love etc."
"I know that one, it's Shakespeare."
"But do you know which play?"
She nudged him in the ribs quite hard again, and he flinched.
"What was that about?"
"Stop being a bloody schoolteacher. Anyway, what is love?"
"The deputy head at my school says it's all about sex. Propagation of the species. He thinks that's all life is about really."
"Is that what you think?"
"No. There's something in all of us that goes beyond mere survival. Because we're conscious, because we can think, we have the capacity to care about others. When we don't, atrocities like Auschwitz result. As far as I'm concerned, without caring, without compassion life loses its meaning. Maybe that's what love is. Caring that goes beyond ourselves to other people."
She smiled. He still sounded like a schoolteacher, but she had to agree with what he said.
"This morning I wrote an article about Auschwitz and then got into bed to make love with you, if we use the usual euphemism for sex."
"Making love sounds OK. Better than hate."
They were silent for a moment. She wanted to talk more about love and what it meant, but her mind wandered to another strange connection in her head.
"Not much more than sixty years ago my great grandparents, and six million others, died in those camps. Now I'm here in a comfortable bed

in a warm dry home with you. I'm happy, but that thought worries me."

There was a pause, in which he seemed to be wondering how to respond.

"I think you're talking about survivor guilt," he said eventually.

"The Jewish conscience, you mean. My parents talk about that; the need for atonement that sent me to Auschwitz."

"Probably. But *you* don't need to feel guilty. It wasn't your fault."

It didn't feel convincing. You couldn't talk away the feeling that easily. But again she didn't say it, contenting herself with turning towards him and enjoying his presence in her bed.

38

The flight was on time. He settled into his window seat for the journey to Rome. There he knew he had to change for the internal flight to Reggio. He watched the young man in the seat next put what looked like a violin case into the luggage rack above them.

"Not Mafia gun," he said, "most valuable possession," and smiled down at him before sitting and fixing his seat belt. Patrick nodded and smiled without saying anything back. They both sat silently as the flight staff went through the safety routine making their usual mimes while the recorded voice in alternate English and Italian gave the spoken guidance.

"Pointless. If we crash, all die. Pouff!"

"Mmm," he said above the roar of the engines and watched out of the window as they left the ground and tilted sharply upwards. It became quieter.

"So you're a musician then," he said eventually, feeling he ought to say something.

"I am violinist, yes. I go to Rome to play in string orchestra. Is very fine. I am happy to be invited."

"You're Italian?"

"No. From Poland. Very different country. But I live in England. For now."

"Patrick East," he said putting out his hand, which the young man shook vigorously. "I'm a psychotherapist at the local hospital."
"Very good. You sort out heads. I am Stefan. Pleased to meet you."
Suddenly it clicked. The feeling that he'd met the young man before.
"Friend of Simon. In the orchestra. We met after the concert a few days ago. Strange we meet again so quickly."

Incongruously, they shook hands once more, equally vigorously, and then, without warning the smooth progress since take off was suddenly interrupted. The flight became bumpy and the light above told them to fasten their seatbelts. A smooth voice in English said they had entered a brief period of turbulence which was expected to pass soon. He watched Stefan gripping the armrests, obviously uncomfortable, but the turbulence was over almost as soon as they entered it and the lights for seat belts went off again. He watched the young man start to relax.
"Rough flight is not good."
"Let's hope it's alright from now on." He smiled reassuringly.
"Better now. Too soon to die!"
He watched him sit back in his seat and recover his composure until he was obviously ready to talk. He knew already the young man was a communicator. He smiled to himself remembering the discussion after the concert.
"Life is to enjoy. Make the most of it while we have it. I am still young. I play my violin, enjoy people, make love. This is life for me."
He watched Stefan, animated, moving his arms freely, almost miming what he was talking about. The energy flowing from the seat next was obviously going to make for an entertaining journey.
"And you have sadness in your hospital. Much weeping, much sorrow. Is this form of self harm?"
Patrick found himself laughing at the young Pole's joke at his expense and had to admire his willingness to risk him taking offence. The remark certainly put a new perspective on his work and for a moment

he couldn't help wondering if there was actually some truth in the thought.
"No. Not at all. It's a very rewarding job, especially when people make progress with their lives. Maybe like you learning a new piece on your violin."
But he didn't grasp the comparison.
"How make progress?"
"Well, if they're unhappy, like you suggest, I can work with them to help them come to terms with things in their lives. Find new meaning."
"Ah. New meaning. Yes. Life must make meaning. Otherwise . . . pouff! . . . why not die?"
They laughed together, although he didn't quite understand why.
"But, so sorry. I haven't let you say why you travel to Rome. I talk too much. Beautiful city!"
The last comment was accompanied by a flick of his hand as if to offer an imaginary kiss to the city.

He wondered how much to say.
"Actually, I'm on my way to Reggio. Far south. I change at Rome."
"Reggio! Place of beautiful statues, found in harbour, now in museum. You will see them?"
He didn't know what Stefan meant and had to ask him to explain.
"Greek statues. Very famous. Two beautiful young men as Greek Gods. More than two thousand years old. You must see."
The remark was accompanied by gestures which seemed to be creating the contours of what he was describing.
"Not necessary to be gay like me to enjoy male body."
The remark was made in a matter of fact way. He could just as easily have been announcing what music he would be playing in Rome. If only everyone had as much self acceptance.
"In Rome I may enjoy lover . . . maybe more than one. But I admire beautiful women too!"
The remark coincided with the arrival of an attractive flight attendant with blond hair and an airline smile offering them tea or coffee. The

smile widened as she assumed Stefan was referring to her. She thanked him for something he hadn't deserved, which caused him no problem at all.

They both sat back with their drinks for a while without speaking. He felt relieved that Stefan hadn't wanted to pursue why he was going to Reggio. He doubted if he would want to see Greek statues, even if his schedule in Reggio allowed it. His mind wandered back to Stefan's philosophy. Enjoy life, enjoy people, make love. Not much room there for the inner life and the self doubt which made up much of his own existence and the lives of the people he worked with. Strange though that he talked about the importance of meaning in life. How much meaning might there be in life if he lived like that himself? It seemed to beg more questions than it answered.

The pilot announced they were ten minutes from Rome. It was seat fastening time. But above the noise of the engine he wanted briefly to continue the earlier discussion about meaning.
"So you don't think exploring meaning in life through exploring our inner selves, like in psychotherapy, is important?" he began.
"So sorry?"
He'd forgotten that Stefan's mind had not been following the thoughts in his own head.
"No, no, sorry, I should explain more. You said you agreed with me that meaning in life was important,"
"Of course."
"But you also implied that exploring yourself, from the inside, like I do in my work, is self harm."
"You are like artist, musician, looking at dark side. Yes of course, important, otherwise no Mozart, no Beethoven, no Szymanowski. I play these composers. Of course. I am musician. But life must be fun too. I could not be like Beethoven, deaf as pole, working at night making noises he can't hear. I play his music, I love it, but as for composing . . . is not for me."

"Cabin crew, ready for landing," came across the loudspeaker as Stefan reached the end of his speech. He was already clutching the armrests nervously and not really attending to any reply.

"Flying is hard part. I want travel, airplane is curse to be endured."
There was a bump as the wheels touched the tarmac, followed by the sudden rushing feeling as the plane sped across the runway to its stopping place. Stefan's face looked as if he was enduring torture. Only when it became obvious that they had stopped and a Verdi aria suddenly filled the aural space did he begin to relax.

They stood, waited for the doors to open amongst the passengers congregating in the aisle of the plane, moving forward when they could and boarded the waiting coach together. Then, after what seemed like a double circuit around the airport they reached the terminal, shook hands vigorously once more and went their separate ways. Within the airport, he found himself crossing and recrossing the airport on the shuttle rail and got very lost. Eventually he had to ask and was taken to the right boarding place for Reggio. The second journey was shorter and less eventful, enabling him to rest on the flight, and it seemed like no time before he was at his destination.

*

"Father Leonardo. An honour to meet you I'm sure."
It was noticeably warm and bright in the Italian sunlight. He took the proffered hand and shook it warmly, looking into the bright blue eyes of the young priest in front of him with his black suit brightened only by the white collar around his neck.
"Thankyou Father."
The phrase came almost instinctively but the boyish looking man in front of him with his smiling face could only be half his own age.
"I've got the car round the corner. What did you think of our local airport now?"
Could he believe his own ears? Did this young man have an Irish accent?

"It's a small airport isn't it."
With a strip of tarmac and one shop no bigger than a local newsagent, that felt like an understatement.
"It is to be sure, but it keeps us in touch. I can be in Rome to see the father in an hour."
Which father was that he wondered, his own or the holy one.
"Your er . .English is very good, almost . . . ."
"Irish you were going to say. I studied in Dublin. Beautiful city. Almost as good as the eternal one. But with your name Doctor, I did wonder if you would be Irish yourself."
"Born on St Patrick's Day, and my mother couldn't resist the name, but English."
He smiled, and the priest nodded, acknowledging what he was telling him.
But here we are. We will be in my town in good time."
In front of them was a very old Fiat Punto. It was probably black, he thought, but it was covered in dust and grime and clearly hadn't been cleaned for some time. Without thinking, he walked automatically round to the right hand side as if to drive, only to realise in a double take that he hadn't made a mistake. It really was the passenger side. The priest seemed to pick up his uncertainty.
"Do you know Italy?"
"Not at all. First time, I'm afraid to say."
"Well this is the deep south. *Mezzogiorno* we are called by the northerners. They all think we're half baked here. But it's very beautiful, as you can see."
He looked around him at the winter landscape with the view of what looked like a large city in the distance as the engine spluttered into life startling him.

It was noisy, but the car seemed to have no difficulty in pulling up a slight incline and out onto the road. Father Leonardo became silent for a while, seeming to go into himself. The road rose upwards into the hillside and for a short while was quite deserted, and then after no

more than ten minutes they were driving into a town. Ahead of them was what looked like a steep hillside and the sign on the roadside told him they had reached ***Sottomonte***.
"This is our town. It means under the mountain, which is a bit of an exaggeration, but over there," he said, pointing to the hillside ahead of them, "it rises into the Aspromonte. Very wild and remote, with wolves and even eagles."
They were slowing down, and eventually stopped outside a small church. The priest ratcheted the handbrake and switched off the engine. There was a judder, and the car seemed to settle into itself. They got out.
"*La chiesa della Santa Maria*, my beautiful church. And over there is our hotel." He pointed to a small building just below the church. "I will take you in and you can go and sort yourself out. In maybe an hour, we can talk."

It was sensible. He was tired and Father Leonardo seemed to recognise that. He nodded his agreement. The priest got his baggage out of the car and walked in to the hotel with him. He assumed the hotel owner spoke no English, but his gestures were friendly. A solicitous porter took his baggage to his room and waited determinedly for his tip before showing exaggerated gratitude.

True to his word, Father Leonardo was back in an hour, and they walked together across to the church and into the vestry together, where he sat down. It seemed gloomy and cold despite the day outside being more like spring than winter. The priest began the conversation.
"I imagine this is something of a shock to you."
"You could say that, yes."
"And your mother is not well enough to travel?"
"I'm afraid she died just after Christmas."
"Oh, I'm sorry to hear that. May she rest in peace."

The incongruity of what he was experiencing was disturbing. In front of him sat a young Italian man he could only assume was in his thirties, yet he behaved, and sounded like a stereotypical Irish priest in his fifties. The man had to have a very good ear for language. There were hardly any traces of an Italian accent. He almost expected the bottle of whisky to appear in a moment.

"Your father's mortal remains were found buried down by the river bank last autumn. I think you know that."

"I knew they were found here. I didn't know where. In the letter found in his possession it says he was captured by an Italian family. Does anyone know what happened to him after that?"

The priest looked at him as if he was summing him up, wondering what exactly to tell him.

"I think I do." The gaze was intense. There was a pause before he continued.

"For some while he was held in a barn. He seems to have developed some kind of relationship with a young woman whose job it was to look after him."

"Relationship?"

"I think so, yes."

His mind was racing now. This was completely new.

"What happened?"

"The family discovered it. And he was killed. The body was buried where it wouldn't be found. Until now." For a moment it felt as if he had been kicked. It was hard to take in. He felt unable to say anything.

"This is a shock, yes?"

He nodded. It was as much as he could do. The priest waited for a moment before speaking again.

"You would like a drink?"

He stood and moved to an area behind where he was sitting and switched on a kettle. Then he stepped back and reached out to put a comforting arm on his shoulder for a moment. Patrick let him, hardly aware this was something he would normally have resisted. The sound

of the kettle intruded into the room, preventing any further conversation until reaching boiling point and cutting out. Father Leonardo moved away again, returning with two cups. The black coffee smell was strong. They both sipped from the cups.
"And the young woman, what happened to her?"
Once more the penetrating gaze.
"She is alive. Still here, in Sottomonte. An old woman now of course."
"Will she see me?"
"Yes. If you want to see her. I've checked that."
"Thankyou." He smiled for the first time. Overlaying the shock now was the thought that he might discover more about the father he had never known. He could feel excitement at the thought.
"There is more. She has a child. Or rather, he was a child. He is nearly your age now."
It took a moment for the meaning of the priest's words to register. Then, once more his mind was racing.
"My father's child?"
The priest nodded.
"Yes," he said.
"I have a brother? A half brother?"
"Yes."
"Here, in the town?"
"He lives with his mother."
"I can see him too?"
"With his mother, yes. You need to understand . . ."
"Understand?"
Once more the stare. How many more revelations were there?
"He is not normal. I think you would say impaired. He doesn't really speak."
His brain was struggling to grasp everything he'd been told in the last few minutes. More than sixty years an only child, and now a brother who was impaired whatever that meant. He couldn't really make sense of it all at once.
"When would you like to see them?"

"Is there anything else you have to tell me?"
"No. That's everything."
"I need some time. Could we see the place where my father was found? Is it far?"
"Not far. Just down the hill outside."

Father Leonardo got up from where he was sitting. He did likewise, and followed him out of the vestry, through the drab church and out into the Italian afternoon. Between clouds the sun was shining, and he could see the sea below. Even in the stunned state he was in at that moment, he was aware what an amazing view it was. He found himself wondering if his father had seen it every so often in his last months, or however long he had been in captivity. Did he have a view from the barn? Had he sometimes been allowed out with the woman?

They were walking down quite a steep slope, into a valley, and beyond he could see the hill slope rising more steeply on the other side. He guessed there would be a stream running through the bottom, but as he approached there was no sign of it. As if anticipating his thoughts, the priest spoke again.
"It will be damp at the bottom, but only when it rains heavily is there much water here."
They were virtually at the bottom, and he could see the dampness and a trickle of water running through what was more like a ditch than anything else. The priest led him along the shallow embankment for a short distance, and ahead of them there was a patch where fairly recent excavation had obviously taken place.

"Here?" he said.
"Here, yes."
"And how was the body found?"
"Last summer was wetter than usual. It seems to have disturbed the shallow burial place and partly exposed it."
"And someone walking saw it?"

“Yes.” There was a pause before he continued. “Your brother.”
He didn’t know what to say for a moment. They stood together looking down at the spot. It was steep on both sides, and there was no view from where they were standing, except along the shallow ditch.
“That must have been awful for him.”
“He didn’t really understand what he’d found. Still doesn’t thank God.”
“He’s that bad?”
“In understanding yes. But a lovely man. I look after him a bit now. He comes into the vestry to help out. Keeps him occupied.”
It suddenly occurred to Patrick that he didn’t know his name, and he asked apologetically.
“Marco he’s called. Everyone knows him. He’s very popular.”
He smiled. It was a relief for some reason. The priest smiled back.
“Shall we go back up?”
He nodded, and they retraced their steps up the hill to the church which was visible on the skyline, marking the direction for them.

“I think you’d like him buried up here, properly that is?”
The priest indicated in the direction of the church, and once more he nodded his assent.
“I’ve arranged a spot just outside the churchyard. I’m sure you’ll understand.”
Not a catholic, probably not anything if he was anything like him, but chose not to say it.
“Of course.,” Maybe that would mean a shorter service.
“We could do that tomorrow, if that’s alright? Marco’s mother is happy with that.”
He didn’t know her name either, and feeling embarrassed again, he asked.
“She’s called Lucia.”
They continued walking in silence, and at the top he made his excuses and retired back to his hotel to try and come to terms with everything he’d been told.

It was after dark when Father Leonardo took him to the small cottage to meet Lucia and Marco. He felt anxious, completely unsure how he would react and what effect it would all have on him. But her greeting was warm and friendly. Marco beamed, clearly enjoying himself but obviously unaware of any significance in what was taking place. The bear hug he received from him felt good, and to his surprise made him feel suddenly tearful. He held it back. 'This is my brother' was the thought running through his brain, together with something vague about terrycloth, which he couldn't quite place.

"She says you are a good looking man," the priest translated for him once the Italian hubbub had died down. She laughed, realising what must have been communicated, and then she was signalling for them to sit down. He waited for her, and then took the available seat. It was clear she was elderly, but despite her black dress, she didn't look as old as his own mother. Must have been very young when she knew my father, he thought. Marco perched his large body on a cushion on the floor, grinning at everyone.

"I'd like you to tell me about my father," he said.
They both waited for the translation, and then she began speaking at first quite slowly and he noticed that she said the word 'Tom' twice. Then she became more animated and Father Leonardo had to stop her to enable him space to translate.
"She says he was a nice man, that his name was Tom, and that when he was in the barn in captivity she looked after him. They learnt each other's names."
The conversation went on for some time as she gradually explained that a relationship had developed, and how it had ended when her family found out. Then she was silent, and he guessed she was thinking about what happened. He asked Father Leonardo if she minded telling him. He waited as a significant interchange followed backwards and forwards between them. He wished he could understand what they were saying.

"She says he was shot and then buried where you have seen by some of her father's men. All are dead now she says. It was a sad time."
Lucia began speaking again, more animatedly and seemed to brighten as she continued talking. He could hear the word Marco being mentioned and noticed that Marco, who had sat silently just looking at him during what had so far taken place, now became animated himself, clapping with delight.
"She says that it was a happy day when Marco was born. He has been the delight of her life. Although he doesn't understand much, he makes up for it by his loving nature."

He smiled at her, and she smiled back, as did Marco.
"Lucia wants to know something about your life."
He spoke about himself and what he did, and told her about Liz. He noticed disappointment when he told her he didn't have children.
"But now you have a brother," the priest translated, which was a cue for more smiles, and laughter from Marco, followed once more by a stage managed hug with Marco.
Father Leonardo wanted to draw the meeting to a close.
"I'd like to end with a prayer," he said.
It was what he'd feared, but went along with it, staying quiet while the priest intoned in Italian.

*

He knew he'd lied. Or not exactly lied, rather withheld truth. He'd modified what Lucia told him so that the Englishman's father's sins were hidden. That was a sin. He knew it was. Be truthful St Paul told him, and he hadn't, not fully. What should he do? It wasn't too late to make amends. Before the funeral he could go and speak to the doctor and tell him. 'Your father raped Lucia.' Could he say that? Even as he thought it he knew he couldn't. It wasn't his way. Jesus taught the way of compassion. Human kindness. Why shouldn't the man have a good picture of his father? And of his new found brother.

The whole idea of rape was horrible. He must have been sorely tried. Not by Lucia he added quickly in his mind, but by the circumstances of his existence. Homesick, unloved. The uncontrolled side of him came to the fore. To be sure we could all act like that in extremity. How did any of us know we wouldn't? Another thought entered his brain. Was that why Marco was as he was? Some would believe that, but he knew he didn't. Evil didn't always beget evil. Marco was good, the proof of a loving God. Suffer little children to come unto me. Didn't that also apply to very big children?

It was early morning, not quite light and the thoughts had troubled him through a sleepless night. He felt compelled to rise and go into the church to pray. In front of the alter he dropped to his knees. Above him was the image of Jesus on the cross, and beyond, in the stained glass window, was Mary his mother. He prayed for forgiveness, for all his sins, for lying, for distorting the truth, for wanting to sanitise history. He tried to imagine the pain of Jesus on the cross, but knew what he was experiencing was no more than the smallest part of that pain. And he was guilty.

He had no idea how long he was there before he heard footsteps behind him. Someone had come into the church. He drew himself out of his prayer with a start and looked round to see Dr Patrick standing in the doorway.

"I thought I would find you here," he said.

"Morning prayers."

"Yes, I guessed."

"Shall we pray together?"

"No. That's not quite me. I actually wanted to talk to you."

"Of course."

"It's just that... well, I'm surprised that a prisoner of war, my father ... that's what he was, wasn't he? I'm surprised he developed a relationship with his captor. In the barn? I know strange things happen."

"What are you asking me?"
"Do you know anymore about how it happened? Has Lucia told you anything else?"
"I didn't want to distress you anymore. It's a long time ago."
"There is more then?"
"It does seem that Lucia nursed him. He had been injured it seems and recovered in the barn. She looked after him, made sure he had food, that sort of thing."
"Is that what she told you?"
"Yes. And a kind of relationship developed from there."
"A sexual relationship?"
"On his part, yes."
There was a moment of pause and he could see him taking in what he'd said.
"You mean he raped her. That's why they shot him."
"I didn't want to have to say that."
"But it's true."
He could only drop his head in acknowledgement of what he'd said. Birds were singing outside. Inside he felt relief that his dilemma had been answered for him, but also there was great sadness.
"Thankyou for being straight with me. I appreciate your caring too... not wanting to upset me."
He looked up. The doctor was holding out his hand, wanting to shake hands with him. He stretched out his own hand.

Suddenly it was light in the church. He looked round. The sun had reached the window of Santa Maria behind the altar and above her there was a wonderful bright halo. It was a sign, he knew it had to be a sign. Truth, and forgiveness, a new dawn. He dropped to his knees to give thanks to the virgin for her intercession.
"*Maria, Madre di Dio, prega per noi peccatori, adesso e nell'ora della nostra morte,*" he repeated several times, before saying the lord's prayer out loud. Inside himself he could feel the pain and doubt lifting.

He felt liberated. He stood and crossed himself. The window above the altar was filled with light and he was unable to take his eyes from it.

As he left the church, Patrick noticed the sunlight in the window above the altar. It struck him how well it had been designed to maximise the effect. It wasn't for nothing that altars faced east, and he couldn't help admiring the brilliance of the design. But the architecture of Italian churches was not of any great importance to him. He was glad to get outside into the warmth and light. The priest had confirmed his worst suspicions about his father and now he knew that he'd been shot in captivity for violating the girl who had looked after him.

Had it really been rape? Probably yes in the eyes of a court today. But how desperate was his father? Isolated and mostly alone, with no one to talk to. He knew that from the letter. Another terrycloth moment perhaps. But he would never know the truth. Compassion was the only way forward. The father shaped hole inside him was still there; he knew it always would be. But as he looked out across the shallow valley where his father died it felt almost physically as if ballast had filled the hole a little, maybe giving him a softer landing into the future for the sad thoughts Max had identified.

*

The funeral was shorter than he feared. He could sit through the Italian prayers without becoming involved. He simply enjoyed being next to his new found brother, who kept turning towards him and smiling. Afterwards he watched whatever was left of his father's body being placed in the grave outside the churchyard just a short distance from where he'd been buried before. Looking around him amongst the few elderly Italians who had turned up to pay their respects, he wondered if any of them had been involved in his father's end. Again, he knew there was no way of knowing. It felt strange. He didn't know how to accommodate it all. Maybe more ballast, or closure might be a more conventional way of describing it, although it didn't yet feel like closure. He wondered how Lucia might be feeling, but there was no trace of emotion on her face. Maybe all her grieving had been done long ago.

Afterwards he said his goodbyes. Lucia shook his hand quite formally. Marco gave him a bear hug, laughing loudly. Once he had recovered his breath, he laughed too, which Marco enjoyed and followed up with a second bear hug, encouraging him to make a reasonably speedy exit. "He's quite strong to be sure," said Father Leonardo as the old Fiat took off for the airport. He could only agree, and in just a few minutes they were shaking hands and the priest was driving back to Sottomonte.

*

For Father Leo as he sat on the seat outside the church looking down towards the sea it felt like an ending. The visiting Englishman had gone home. The other Englishman, long dead, was now properly buried. He sighed deeply, and as he breathed in again, he became aware of a comforting waft of incense. Life, his life, normal life, was reasserting itself as he knew it had to eventually. But inside, he knew also that things could never be quite the same again. Yesterday the big bird from the mountains came down again, and he and Marco watched it circling round. Can an angel take the form of an eagle? Or a child? Out of great evil had come something good. He looked at Marco sitting next to him on the seat, absorbed in his own world, and absent mindedly he crossed himself, sure in his own mind that he had become aware of something of great significance, maybe a miracle. Truly the lord worked in mysterious ways.

Marco was looking out into the distance at the sea below them. He followed his gaze. The little wavelets in the afternoon sunshine sparkled like lights. There were spring flowers in whites and pale yellows in almost every part of the churchyard, changing the bare appearance of the winter landscape with their gentle colours. A squirrel ran up a tree unexpectedly and caught Marco's attention. He pointed, and they both watched it sitting on the branch with its bushy tail stretched out behind it. Everything around them was alive, and renewing itself after the sleep of winter, part of God's timeless, ever changing scene. It felt good to be alive. He looked round again at Marco, rubbing his hands together, excited by a second squirrel chasing the first along the branches. Unable to prevent himself, he stood and shouted inarticulately, making both squirrels disappear out of sight. He looked round in fleeting disappointment, then grinned and sat down once more beside him. 'Suffer little children' he thought, and smiled back. Marco's smile turned to a raucous laugh.

39

It was one of those late February days he loved. The cold winter was not yet gone, but there was a clear sky and the sun was warming despite the still cold breeze and a temperature not much above freezing. There were unmistakeable signs of spring. He could sense it in the air, he could see it in the greenness that was tempering the browns and greys of winter. There were new shoots on bushes and in the ground waiting. Inside himself, Patrick could feel a deeper sense of joy and happiness than he could ever remember. This spring was for him.

Beside him was Liz. It was Sunday. Walking through the woods with her felt like a culmination of everything he'd wanted out of life. She moved away from him across to a shrub and called him to look, pointing out the bulbous signs of new growth. His enjoyment of nature was generalised, but hers was much more particular, and this spring she was opening his eyes to detail he'd never noticed before.

For some while inside his head a momentous thought had been growing but he wasn't sure how to reveal it to her. Was it too soon, or was a day like today giving him a message to open out to her? They walked on and naturally, without really thinking about it, they joined hands. He wasn't sure if it was his initiative or hers. The path along which they were walking was becoming narrower, leading them deeper into the heart of the wood, and the sunlight was filtered through the branches of the pines and conifers above them. He knew the path was gradually leading them upwards before it levelled out again into a clearing. As they got there he watched her face, knowing she would be delighted with the view that now opened out below them. It was a place he'd come to before, several times, but always previously on his own. Now he was introducing her to his special place.

There were two double seats in the clearing, both facing outwards to the view below. At his suggestion they sat down together on the nearer of the two seats, and looked out at the panoramic view. Strangely he now realised, it reminded him of the view from the town where his father had met his end. Except here there was no view of the sea and it was far more built up than the southern tip of Italy. As they sat there, the vast changes in his life over the past few months flooded through his brain; his mother, his father, the half brother he now knew he had, and Liz. And amongst all of this was the thought that had preoccupied him for the past few weeks.

"You like the view?" he asked.
"Wonderful. I had no idea this was here."
"I've loved it for a long time."
She didn't respond, merely sitting and taking in the view ahead, and they sat quietly for a while before he spoke again.
"Liz."
She turned to look at him, sensing that he wanted to say something important.
"Liz," he said again, "I've been thinking. I'd like us to get married."
For no more than a second she was silent. He wouldn't have believed how long a second could last.
"Yes, I'd like that too."
"Good. Then it's agreed?"
"Yes, why not?"

Why not indeed, he thought. They turned towards each other and kissed.

*

Saying yes was easy. Coming to terms with it was much harder. Patrick moving in with her wasn't difficult, and Max was no problem. The pair had developed an understanding in which she sometimes wondered who was the father figure. In a strange way it seemed to have improved her own relationship with Max. Almost as if Patrick's presence freed him to be closer to her again. It was as if he didn't need to put up boundaries or hide in his computer. She didn't quite understand what made the difference but she was glad of it.

No, Max wasn't the problem, and nor was her relationship with Patrick which made her somehow feel real again instead of just functioning. And marriage wasn't the problem either. She knew she was sufficiently old fashioned to want that degree of formality. Logically after more than three years on her own, it wasn't too soon. Not really. But something worried her.
"The problem is in your head," Patrick reassured her, "everyone will be really pleased for us."
But she wasn't entirely sure, and couldn't quite grasp what it was that disturbed her sleep, and in the middle of the night she found herself waking and worrying. She didn't tell Patrick. If he woke too, she blamed the restlessness on school worries. Usually then he turned towards her and put his arm over her, which helped her get back to sleep, but didn't solve the underlying fear.

And fear she realised eventually was what it was. Irrational fear of making a mistake, fear that after Guy another relationship as good probably wasn't possible. And there was the strange recurrent feeling that she was two timing. Her marriage to Guy hadn't quite finished in her own head. Still occasionally she talked to him. Once she was married to Patrick she didn't think she could do that anymore. That would feel like an infidelity in the same way she couldn't quite escape the feeling that marrying Patrick was being unfaithful to Guy. The thoughts went round and round in her head.

One evening, when Patrick and Max were both out, she found herself talking to Guy once more.
"What should I do, Guy, I'm so confused," she said out loud. The smile in his picture was still there, the Guy she remembered. And almost from nowhere, inside her head, she heard his voice speak to her.
"I am the past," she heard distinctly, "you have to let me go."
She didn't believe in ghosts, not really, despite her poem. She knew immediately that in her imagination she was answering her own question, giving herself the answer she knew had to be the truth, but which she'd been afraid to face. Guy was the past. She had to move on. Patrick was now and the future.

Something like that was after all what Guy had said he wanted for her in those awful last days. Back then she'd never believed she'd get over him. She realised that even when she'd written the poem she was only part of the way through. She really had to let him go now if she wanted to move forward. On an impulse she reached up and lifted the picture from the wall. Then she went up to the bedroom and collected the two pictures of him there, and took them downstairs. She added the picture on her work desk to those three and found a large piece of brown paper to wrap all four pictures inside together. Then she placed the picture parcel in the large bottom drawer of the desk, underneath her other special memories of Guy and closed the drawer, expecting to feel sad, even to shed a few tears, but to her surprise that wasn't how she felt. More a sense of relief spread itself through her body, like she was suddenly free. For a moment she felt guilty that she felt like that, but the feeling of release was too strong to be suppressed. Inside her she knew it was what Guy would have wanted. It was what she would have wanted him to do if she'd died; after a decent interval anyway. And three years was a decent interval. It was moving on time.

*

It was something and nothing. Maybe nothing. Just a slight tingling in the nipples. Something that was new to her. She put it down to her new sex life after the gap between Ben and Josh. And how much more satisfied she now felt, spending so much of her life now with Josh. There was no comparison between the two men. How could she ever have thought she could be happy with Ben? Jewish boys aren't necessarily the best lovers. She was happy now in a way she never had been before. The strange feeling would probably pass.

But it didn't. Her body felt slightly different, almost heavier, which didn't make any sense because the scales didn't say anything different. Was she imagining it, or was something happening to her? She drove to work as usual, but feeling somehow tired, and not quite so enthusiastic, which was surprising. Spring had always been her favourite time of year, and this spring was especially beautiful. There was a cherry tree outside her flat with lovely pink blossoms, and in the gentle breeze some of the blossom floated down to the pavement below. The colours of yellow and pink and purple and red were everywhere so that the drabness of winter browns and greens was entirely banished in the spring sunlight. It wasn't that she didn't feel good. She actually did, in a different way she couldn't quite describe.

It wasn't that she was offhand or more angry with people. Quite the reverse. The old sparky anger wasn't there. She surprised herself by accepting things she would normally have complained about. An article she'd written about female shop assistants who discovered they had been underpaid and were considering legal action had really pleased her, one of her best she thought. In its own way it was a bit of an exclusive, potentially an article that could run in the national press. Quite a few interviews were involved and a fair bit of digging around for details, then careful editing to get the article exactly right. But when it appeared a bit of sloppy sub editing produced it under the headline **READY FOR SUE**. There was the initial flash of the old anger.

“What bloody buffoon did that?” she said as soon as she saw it, but within five minutes she could see the funny side of it and laughed.

She told Josh how she felt.
“Are you making me soft or something?” she said.
“You’re not pregnant are you?”
“Of course not. How could I be? We’ve always been careful.”
As soon as she said it somewhere inside her she knew he might be right. But she wasn’t yet ready to admit it, even to herself. It had always been part of her thinking to have children one day, and yes, she was nearly twenty eight. But it wasn’t planned. They’d used precautions, pregnancy wasn’t yet part of the scheme of things.

Then she was late. That was unusual. The ratty premenstrual feeling didn’t arrive. There was no show for more than a week, confirming everything. It scared her and she knew she couldn’t deny it any longer.
“Oh, my God!” she said out loud knowing as she said it she was acting like someone in an American sitcom, but still said it again for good measure. “Oh my God, I really must be pregnant!” A rush of excitement ran through her. Could she really be pleased? If it was true it would be such a disruption to her life.

Josh had to know. She sent him a text. *‘Come straight to my place tonight. Need to talk to you.’*
He was there by four thirty.
“Are you alright?” he said as soon as he got in the door, “I’ve been worrying about you.”
“I need to tell you something.”
He didn’t say anything. Just walked through to the living room where they sat down beside each other.
“You know what you suggested, about how I was feeling.”
There was no hesitation in his response.
“You really are pregnant?”

"Haven't done a test yet, but I'm a week late, and I just feel different." She waited for a reaction but there wasn't one. "You don't seem surprised."
"Not really. It's just how you seemed the other day, and how you've been."
"But how could it have happened?"
"Life force. Very powerful."
"What shall we do?"
"Well you need to get a test. And if you are pregnant, we'll be mum and dad."
"You don't mind?"
"It's been on my mind for a couple of days now. I think I would quite like you to have my child."
"Your child!"
Anger suddenly welled in her. It was her child too, she would be carrying it! How was it his child?
"You know what I mean. You being pregnant with a child I've helped you create. Our child."
How could he be calm? The teacherly patronism that first made her mad with him was there again. And then just as quickly the anger subsided and an impulse to laugh run through her.
"Are we arguing over this child already?" she said, more gently, seeing laughter in his face too. "Must mean we both want it."

Later, after he'd gone back to get some work done, she stood at the back window of her flat. It was an unusually clear night and she could see stars in the sky. How many years back in time was she looking? Hundreds? Thousands? The enormity of it was mind blowing. Millions of years of evolution that had led to the development of the life all around her, and now to the life embryonically growing inside her. Her child's ancestry stretched all the way back to those distant stars. The thought excited her and she felt more connected to the universe all around her than she ever had before.

What she was seeing now could have been seen by prisoners in Auschwitz by her own ancestors who had suffered and died there. Yet her grandparents had survived and now the baby she was sure was inside her would keep the spark of human survival alive. It felt like a vindication. Her survivor guilt could be atoned with the new child. Her personal *tschuve*, linking her with all that human suffering. Bearing a child justified being alive. Whoever saves a single soul. She was creating a new soul for the future.

How small and transient each of our lives was in the context of the enormity she was seeing on this clear night. And yet, how vast too was human life in all its potential to grow and develop. It felt to her as if her one single soul was linked to all the souls around it in the one life she knew, Jew and Gentile. And her baby would be both. In the stars, her connection to the past and to the future beyond her own life seemed visible, like she was staring into the whole of existence in all its enormity. Life was now and life was forever.

*

Josh knocked at the half open door, remembering that if it was open it was OK to knock and enter. He put his head round to see Mrs Broad turning away from the window.

"Is it OK?"

"Yes, do come in."

She ushered him to a seat, and at the same time moved to the seat opposite and sat down herself, which felt embarrassing as he knew he only wanted a moment.

"It's very quick. I just wanted to say how pleased I am about your news. Marriage I mean."

He watched her face develop quickly into a smile and it crossed his mind that even someone as old as she was could still be attractive. Not just as a mother figure, and she didn't look like a mother figure anyway.

"Thankyou. That's kind of you to come and say that."

"I wasn't sure whether to. But you've been good to me, you and Mr Turner, and I'm very pleased."
Once more she smiled, and for a fleeting moment he wondered whether to tell her about Anna, but he felt shy and didn't really feel it was appropriate.
"That's all really."
"Well thankyou. I appreciate it."
He got up from the seat and walked across to the door, aware that she was watching him go.

40

They decided to drive together to the registry office in the centre of the town. Both of them wanted a small affair, nothing too ostentatious at their ages they decided. It didn't help to calm her nerves when the morning arrived. They both got up and showered, then she put on the pale pink dress she'd bought for the occasion and which he'd helped her choose. How different from her first marriage she reflected, but not worse, just older.
"How do I look?"
"Perfect, of course."
"Are you sure I look alright in this?"
She accepted his reassurances, but some of the self doubt remained. It was easier for men. A dark suit did for most occasions.
Max looked very smart in the modern suit they'd bought him. He was excited and looking forward to the whole event, almost certainly more than she was.

Eventually they were ready for the drive. It felt oddly unreal. Beyond the car window, ordinary people were getting on with their ordinary lives, while she was doing something very special which they knew nothing about. She remembered it had felt like that in the funeral car on the way to burying Guy. How strange that overwhelmingly sad occasion should resemble this very happy one. She looked across to Patrick, and smiled.

Patrick parked the car and the three of them walked together into the building, already filling with their guests. Her sister was there which felt good. They embraced warmly, and her husband came up and did likewise, and that was strange as he'd always seemed so remote to her. She watched as he shook Patrick's hand too, and enjoyed Max's smile as he got the same treatment. They both seemed genuinely pleased.

Inside there was formality. 'East, Broad?' It was matter of fact. There was a rigmarole of checking details and signing official forms which only helped to make her feel more nervous. She was aware of Patrick putting his hand on her arm and of Max saying 'You'll be alright mum,' which helped by making her smile at his old fashioned ways. Where did he get that from she wondered?
Then her sister took Max off to sit in the marriage room while she and Patrick waited outside. She could feel the tension rising inside as they walked through the assembled guests to where they had to make the formal vows. It was at this point she knew she would have to repeat things said to her. It sounded simple. How many assemblies had she conducted in her time? But she was more nervous than she would ever have believed possible.

When the moment came, she was so emotional she couldn't get the words right. Confronted with the registrar's request to 'repeat after me,' she stumbled twice. Everyone laughed and Patrick joked about her having second thoughts, but that couldn't be further from the truth. She had no doubts. It was just an overwhelming experience. Getting married again wasn't something she'd expected or wanted while Guy was alive, and she knew this moment was the final goodbye as well as a new beginning. It felt vast, but the laughter helped her to feel better. She had support behind her and she got through the rest of the ceremony without further problems.

The tears didn't come till they were pronounced man and wife. Then her make-up was seriously threatened until Sophie came to the rescue with a tissue.

"Why are you crying, you're supposed to be happy," she said.

"I am happy. It's just . . . well, it means a lot."

"I know. You're doing fine."

Through the tears she could see Max looking up at her proudly.

"Well done mum!"

God, he sounds like a bloody teacher she thought to herself, which made her laugh. He was more like a teacher than she was at that moment. She smiled at him, proud of him too, and Patrick, standing next to her, shook his hand, which obviously pleased Max. They stood him with them while guests began taking their photographs.

Jamie, smart in a dark blue suit came across to shake hands with Patrick, and Sophie gave them both a kiss. Behind them she could see Simon, and with him a young man she vaguely remembered seeing before, but couldn't place. His new partner she guessed. Was it Steven, or David? She couldn't quite remember. When they came across to offer their congratulations Simon introduced Daniel, but afterwards she still had to ask Patrick what his name was.

Then they were ushered out. There was no wind to speak of. When she'd married Guy it was a blustery day and her traditional white dress had blown about everywhere. How different it now was as she stood with Patrick and waited together as many more people than she had expected took their photographs. She recognised a few of her staff, and there was Len and his wife with their three children waving to her. Others she didn't recognise, and guessed they might be colleagues of Patrick's.

He kept wanting to look at her, proud of her. He could hardly believe how it had all worked out. There was a fleeting moment of sadness that his mother wasn't there but she wouldn't have been able to

understand, and she would have been a liability too. Better as it was. He looked around him at all the wellwishers with their cameras taking pictures and at the back of the group spotted an unexpected face. Grinning broadly was Wesley, standing there with his mother, who had a small handheld digital camera. Somehow they'd discovered the marriage was taking place and come along too. He beckoned Wesley across, and his mother followed.
"I didn't know you was marrying Mrs Broad," he said.
"Congratulations Dr East, and you Mrs Broad. A big day for you both," his mother added.
"Thankyou. Thankyou both for coming. It's really nice of you."
Liz smiled and added her thanks.
"You look real nice Mrs Broad. Not like headteacher at all. Can I take a photo with Wesley?"
They rearranged themselves and stood Wesley in his jeans and baseball cap between them while Mrs Freedom took their picture. Then with thanks and smiles all round they were gone.

"How many schoolboys have pictures taken with their headmistress and their counsellor?" he said.
"How did they know?" she said, and at that moment her gaze fell on Len. "Twitter," she added immediately, "that must be it."
"Twitter?"
"Yes, Len, my deputy, I've told you what he's like. He'll have spread the word round."
He looked up, recognising Len from having seen him at case conferences and around the school. He was waving to them as if he knew something and there was a certain look about him which seemed to confirm her suspicions. She waved back and he walked across to them followed by his family.

"May we offer our congratulations to you both."
Patrick noticed something of an affectation in the way he spoke, almost as if it was difficult for him to speak directly. Liz thanked him,

and then Len turned towards him and spoke in a conspiratorial way to him, but clearly wanting Liz to hear him as well. He spoke theatrically with a kind of American accent.
"Never try to impress a woman. If you do, she'll expect you to keep up that standard for the rest of your life."
He lifted his finger as if speaking some kind of universal truth, but there was an obvious hint of humour in his tone.
"Pay no attention to him, Dr East, he thinks he's Groucho Marx." His wife, a rather large woman in a dark blue dress smiled but looked embarrassed. Len turned towards her and bowed elaborately.
"My good woman, those are the immortal words of W.C. Fields."
He spluttered a laugh, offered his congratulations again and said he hoped they would be very happy in a voice close to his west country normal before walking off smiling.
"Is he always like that?"
"Quite often, I'm afraid, but he means well. Just can't help acting the comic. He really is pleased for us."
He looked at her standing in the sunlight under the cherry blossom and leaned over to give her a kiss. When she responded there was a wave of applause and cheering. They both turned smiling and feeling almost regal.

Simon enjoyed the moment, aware how strange it was for him that his aunt, the serious teacher he'd known all his life, was marrying the counsellor who'd helped him come out. Now, standing beside him, applauding with him as they kissed on their wedding day, was the partner he'd wanted but never thought would ever materialise. His own Prince Charming. He looked at Daniel feeling an urge to kiss him, but resisted. It still felt good to be standing there openly with Daniel and for people to know and accept him. It was a new kind of freedom.

"Look good don't they," he said to Daniel.
"Yes. Must be strange for you."

"It is. But good too. They're both great people. Thanks for coming to share it with me. I wish I could give you a big kiss."
Daniel's look of surprise amused him.
"Not here, surely?"
"Why not?"
"You're not serious?"
He couldn't help laughing then, and Daniel's nervous laugh was part of the enjoyment.
"No, course not. But they are." He indicated towards Patrick and Liz, who were kissing again.
"Show's we've still got some way to go though doesn't it."
"I can live with it as it is, thanks."
"You're just shy."
"What would you do, if I tried to kiss you now?"
"OK. Fair enough, but you know what I mean."
They stood together and watched Liz and Patrick moving away towards the car which would take them to the reception. The sun was shining in their eyes from that direction, making it difficult to see clearly, but he didn't need to be told that they were happy.

He walked with Daniel back to his car. They'd left Daniel's parked by his flat. As they did so, it seemed an appropriate moment to suggest the idea that had been forming in his mind for several days. They got in and he started the engine. There was a ten minute journey in which to talk. He put the car into gear and pulled away.
"Dan, I've been thinking."
He knew Daniel was likely to stay quiet while he talked. That was his way. Easier in some ways; he could say what he wanted without interruption. More difficult because it didn't give him a chance to know what reception he was getting, especially as he had to watch the road.
"You did say you didn't have to live where you do." He paused for a moment at a traffic light and looked at Daniel, who looked back at him

expectantly, without saying anything. The lights changed and he pulled away.
"You're a freelance. You can live where you like. More chance of work too on the edge of the city." He paused again and glanced at Daniel, who as he expected was still waiting quietly for him to get to the point.
"We don't have to live apart, only seeing each other when both of us are off at the same time. My flat's big enough for two. You could move in with me."
He glanced again at Daniel who was now looking at him, before turning his eyes back to the road. They were within a couple of minutes of the reception hotel. Daniel waited for what seemed ages.
"Well . . . . I'd like that. Yes. Good idea."
He wanted to shout out 'yes!' but held himself back until he'd parked the car in a quiet corner spot at the edge of the hotel car park. He turned the engine off, turned to Daniel and couldn't resist a quick kiss.
"More later!" he said flirtatiously. They laughed together in anticipation and excitement before getting out of the car and walking briskly into the hotel.

*

Anna learnt from Josh who got it from Twitter that her psychotherapist was marrying his headteacher.
"Are you sure about that?"
"Well he does say things like 'never let the truth get in the way of a good story,' but I don't think he'd make that up. He seems to like her and he always supports her."
"Can you check it out. It's a story for my column if it's true. Local doctor marries local head. But I'm sure the sub editor could improve on that if he gets his brain in gear this time. We're far enough away from the capital to be properly provincial here."

Next day he came back convinced it was true. Everybody was talking about it around the school. So she rang Patrick to ask if she could come to the big day and do a short interview.

"Won't take much of your time. Won't be intrusive," she reassured him, but it wasn't so much the time as the picture and article in the newspaper he didn't like. But she was an unscrupulous enough journalist to suggest that if she didn't cover it 'tactfully of course,' maybe someone else would. He said he had to consult Liz. She put the phone down confident that he would ring back his agreement, which half an hour later he did.

So she was waiting for them as they drew up at the hotel for the reception with Josh close by, and a cameraman in tow. The photo was quick, which just left her enough time to ask a few simple questions.
Josh came up to her from his discreet vantage point a few yards away and they linked arms.
"That go well?"
"Fine. She seems nice."
"She is. Good at what she does. Caring, but not soft."
"That's how she came across, even in that short interview. Did you know her previous husband died three years ago?"
"I think Twitter mentioned it. Life can't have been easy."
"Life isn't. It's how we cope, how we survive that matters."

As she spoke, it seemed to her that something moved inside her. Was that the baby? She put her hands to her womb, waiting for any further movement.
"You OK?"
"Yes, fine."
She rubbed both hands over her womb, but still there was no further sensation. Had she imagined it?
"Just thought I felt the baby move. But I might have imagined it."
"That's exciting! How many weeks is it now?"
"Probably fourteen. Bit early yet perhaps."
"Sign of things to come though."
He put his arm across her shoulder and they walked back to the car. Their closeness felt reassuring, and the movement of the baby inside

her, real or imagined, excited her. A real life, separate from hers, was growing inside her, making its presence felt.

The sun was shining directly on them, and they had to look down to protect their eyes. In her hand she carried the notes from the interview. It occurred to her that while she had been working with Patrick as her psychotherapist, helping her through her own difficulties, he had been living his own life. She knew enough about psychotherapy to know it was something clients rarely saw. She felt quite privileged really. Insight into his personal love story. Now with Josh beside her she was living her own growing love story. With the earth beneath them and the sun in the sky above she felt connected to everything around her. Life was overwhelmingly good at that moment as they reached the car, got into it and drove back to the home they would create between them.

Inside the hotel it had grown more noisy. A few bottles of wine had loosened tongues and contributed to the good will and bonhomie. Patrick found himself watching Max for a few moments. He seemed to be enjoying himself, taking in the whole experience. More than anything it seemed like his mother's newfound happiness enabled him to relax. It was an added bonus for him that he had been able to develop a relationship with Max almost as a surrogate father. Briefly, like a stray cloud in an otherwise clear blue sky, he felt a wistfulness that his own mother had never achieved that, and how strange that Lucia in Italy had also been the same. Two long term widows as a result of the death of one man had then lived through their sons.

Liz seemed to notice his abstraction and wanted to know if he was alright. The cloud passed as quickly as it had arrived. He knew he needed to stand soon and make his short speech of thanks. 'You will keep it short won't you,' she had asked him and he'd been more than happy with that. Long rambling speeches weren't his style he reassured her. He'd almost rather not say anything, but that didn't seem to be an option. So he'd made a few scribbled notes to organise his thoughts, and now he stood to say what he had to. Twenty or so assembled guests became more or less quiet, and he began.

Simon sat with Daniel beside him. It felt like Patrick's words were reflecting his own happiness. His growing relationship with Daniel, soon now to enter a new phase when they lived together, was no longer secret. He looked around him, at his mother and father opposite them and Jamie and Sophie at the next table, and felt proud. He'd come out. He was openly who he was, and he'd found his man. Just for a moment, he found Daniel's hand beneath the table and gave it a squeeze.

Patrick was becoming more serious, and Liz wondered what he was going to say.
"Happiness is a human need," he was saying, "not just as an end in itself, but because it helps our survival, and for that we need relationships. We must love one another or die, W.H. Auden said, or as my late mother used to say, love makes the world go round. I think they both got it right. And now we have each other, and that makes us both very happy. I wish you all as much happiness as we have found. Thankyou for coming."
He sat down to polite applause and a little discreet cheering.
"Was that OK?" he whispered.
"Fine," she said, "not too long," and grinned at him.
He grinned back and they kissed, which was a cue for more cheering.

After it was all over, they took Max back home with them and settled down for the rest of the evening. It felt surprisingly ordinary.
"I suppose you're my dad now," Max said, suddenly.
"I suppose I am, in a way, yes. Is that alright with you?"
"Yes. It's great. What do I call you though?"
"What do you want to call me?"
"Is it still alright to call you Patrick?"

“Of course. What matters is that we get on well.”
“Good relationships. Like you said in your talk.”
“Good relationships of all sorts, yes.”
Max came over to him and lifted the palm of his right hand. She watched as it took Patrick a moment or two to grasp that he was being offered a ‘high five,’ but once he did, they managed it three times, and each time the force seemed to be greater. It felt very much like Max’s way of communicating affection.

She smiled and went into the kitchen. Yes, she thought to herself, this is something I never imagined could happen again. Bit of a repair job really, healing all the broken strands. Recovery, and a new start. Quite incredible how life has that capacity for renewal. She picked up the kettle and ran the water into it from the tap. From the lounge behind her came the sound of laughter. She stretched out her hand to turn the tap off and smiled quietly to herself.

THE END